PRAISE FOR

Now That We Don't Talk

"Hilarious, tender, cozy, and hot! *Now That We Don't Talk* should be on everyone's holiday TBR. Filled with all the best tropes, Norah and Henry's story is what snowed-in, one-bed, second-chance-romance dreams are made of. A total delight from start to finish."

—Victoria Lavine, international bestselling author of *Any Trope but You*

"*Now That We Don't Talk* is a charming, heartfelt childhood friends-to-lovers romance about family, the bittersweet joy of yearning, and what it means to forgive the person who knows you better than anyone else in the world. Rachel Pologe's debut is dazzling, and a perfect romance for the holidays—or any time of year."

—Jenna Levine, *USA Today* bestselling author of *Road Trip with a Vampire*

"*Now That We Don't Talk* perfectly captures the swirl of magic, nostalgia, and grief that is being back in your hometown with all of your memories at the holidays. Pologe's debut is a sufganiyot-sweet love story about the people who've known every version of us, and who help us hold onto memories of what we've loved and lost. This rom-com hits the genre's most beloved tropes just right and thoughtfully explores one of the truest expressions of love: owning up to our mistakes. This is pure childhood-friends-to-enemies-to-lovers joy."

—Ellen O'Clover, author of *The Heartbreak Hotel*

"*Now That We Don't Talk* is charming, heartfelt, and hot! The childhood-best-friends to enemies-to-lovers yearning hits so hard. Rachel Pologe perfectly taps into the unique mixture of comfort and bittersweetness that comes from returning home for the holidays as an adult and realizing exactly how much has changed—and how much hasn't. Highly recommended for anyone looking for a holiday romance from a fun, fresh voice."

—Rosie Danan, *USA Today* bestselling author of *Fan Service*

"This novel made me laugh from the very first page and I just knew I'd adore it the whole way through. *Now That We Don't Talk* is funny and cozy and filled with yearning. What I enjoyed most about it is how true to life Norah feels as our main character. I found the balance of humor and sexual tension while Norah and Henry were working through a complicated history so refreshing. This is an emotionally rich, sexy story, and Rachel Pologe is a writer to watch."

—Riss M. Neilson, *USA Today* bestselling author of *The Bridge Back to You*

"Warm, heartfelt, and perfectly steamy, *Now That We Don't Talk* is chock-full of childhood friends-to-lovers goodness, with all the tense glances and only-one-bed moments this trope deserves. An effervescent debut about second chances, grief, and the people we'd wait forever for—I can't wait for more from Rachel Pologe!"

—Katie Naymon, author of *You Between the Lines*

"*Now That We Don't Talk* has everything I love in a romance book—relatable characters, tension-filled forced proximity, and enough steam to have me blushing. This story beautifully tackles real, complex emotions amidst a cozy, festive setting, and readers will be rooting for Norah and Henry on every page! Rachel Pologe's debut is a knockout!"

—Jillian Meadows, *USA Today* bestselling author of *Give Me Butterflies*

"I fell hard for Rachel Pologe's utterly charming debut, which is a perfect blend of all my favorite tropes. *Now That We Don't Talk* glows with tenderness, yearning, and an emotional payoff that's well worth the heartbreak along the way."

—Lindsay Hameroff, author of *Rewrite the Stars*

Now That We Don't Talk

RACHEL POLOGE

Berkley Romance
New York

BERKLEY ROMANCE
Published by Berkley
An imprint of Penguin Random House LLC
1745 Broadway, New York, NY 10019
penguinrandomhouse.com

Book design by Daniel Brount

Library of Congress Cataloging-in-Publication Data

Names: Pologe, Rachel author
Title: Now that we don't talk / Rachel Pologe.
Other titles: Now that we do not talk
Description: First edition. | New York : Berkley Romance, 2026
Identifiers: LCCN 2025050677 (print) | LCCN 2025050678 (ebook) |
ISBN 9798217189472 trade paperback | ISBN 9798217189489 ebook
Subjects: LCGFT: Romance fiction | Fiction | Novels
Classification: LCC PS3616.O56969 N69 2026 (print) | LCC PS3616.O56969 (ebook)
LC record available at https://lccn.loc.gov/2025050677
LC ebook record available at https://lccn.loc.gov/2025050678

First Edition: October 2026

Printed in the United States of America
1st Printing

The authorized representative in the EU for product safety and compliance is Penguin Random House Ireland, Morrison Chambers, 32 Nassau Street, Dublin D02 YH68, Ireland, https://eu-contact.penguin.ie.

For Anthony—

I only write love stories and kissing books because you love me so hard and kiss me so well. I'm sorry you accidentally read the first spicy chapter while you were in the office. That's on me!

Now That We Don't Talk

Chapter 1

WHEN SOMEONE MAKES a grand declaration, you're supposed to feel ooey gooey, right? When you're lying next to a perfectly attractive guy after he's given you two earth-shattering orgasms, and he's telling you he wants to make it official, that's supposed to be a good thing. I should be looking into his eyes and nodding along, but I can't. All I want in this moment is to get up and go pee because the last thing I need is to travel tomorrow with a burgeoning UTI.

I sit up and look at Rob. I try to really, really look at him. The slope of his collarbone, giving way to a sprinkling of freckles that must be present year-round because they're definitely not being coaxed out by a frigid December in New York. Hazel eyes, flitting between green and gold, depending on the light. A mess of sandy hair, thick and wild on the top, but buzzed close at the sides. He has a real bed—a mattress *and* a frame, which actually does say a lot, considering, even if it is an IKEA Malm.

I guess he shut up for a moment.

Shit.

He's staring back at me now. Prompting me to say something with his all-too-manicured eyebrows. It wasn't supposed to be like this. Rob was just supposed to be a hookup. I must be doing something wrong if my fuckbuddy, who I've exclusively spent time with horizontally (and perpendicularly), is asking me to DTR.

When Rob said it the first time tonight, that he wanted to be my boyfriend, it was at the height of foreplay, while he teased my entrance. I thought it was a weird direction to go for dirty talk, but figured it was just the hormones and he'd shake himself out of it after he came. But he's lying next to me, his now-shriveled cock still inside the mess of the condom, and he's saying it again.

"I want to be with you, Norah. I'm serious. Don't you think there's something here?"

There is nothing particularly wrong with this man. I just don't quite know how we got to this point. I can count the non-physical and sexual things I know about Rob on one hand. He's from the Bay Area. He likes IPAs and Monster energy drinks. I think he has a job? He's in a band, because of course he is, but he has a day job. I know he does. I just can't for the life of me recall what it is in this moment. Because that's not what we do. We have a good laugh and then get down to business. I can tell you so much more about his deliciously curved cock than his greatest hopes and dreams.

"You're a . . . great . . . guy?" I say, every word out of my mouth sounding like a question I don't have the answer to. "I just need some time to think about it. Plus, I'm flying home super early tomorrow, so I should probably get going."

Rob's face falls. I take a deep breath, hoping we can put this all past us. But then I almost see the wheels in his head start to turn. I watch the idea travel from his brain down to his lips, and I jump in before he can even suggest it.

"My mom has such a hard time around the holidays ever since my dad died. This family time is so important."

He nods, understanding. He doesn't know my dad's been gone for nine years. And isn't that the point? How did we go from hooking up to *I think we should be together*? When did that shift for him? I'm usually so good at cutting things off before we even need to reach this awkward conversation. I thought I was sending the right message by explicitly not inviting him home with me, but I guess the signals got crossed. How did I miss it?

I've been distracted with this trip home, sure, but I should have seen the signs. I shouldn't have had to play the Dead Dad card. Though, to be fair, my dad would have honestly loved to be the excuse for me to not force this asshat upon my poor mother. *You never brought anyone home while I was alive. Why start now?* He would have gotten a real kick out of it.

Sometimes, on the rare occasion when I catch myself actually starting to fall for someone, I feel a little hitch in my heart, realizing my dad will never know the person I end up with. It's dumb, but sometimes that's enough to snap me out of whatever love haze I've been in.

I roll off Rob's bed, gathering my clothes, and silently head into the bathroom, making a mental note to pick up some cranberry pills on my way home, just in case.

AFTER STOPPING AT Duane Reade, I walk home, the cold December air biting my lips more raw than Rob had. I never should have made the detour to Rob's house on my last night in town. I should have known better. Now I've got this terribly inconvenient *be my girlfriend* situation hanging over my head. I should have just stayed in and packed for the trip. Stupid hormones.

I reach my building, making one last stop at the Middle Eastern pastry shop next door, and blessing this city that they're still open after eleven p.m. Talha, who runs the shop, looks up and smiles at me.

"I did not know if I would see you before the New Year," he says, his graying hair frizzed out from a long day.

"Come on, I had to do one last pick up."

Talha nods, folding together a white cardboard box. He begins loading pistachio baklava inside.

"Can I get some kunefe too?" I ask, smiling angelically. "One hard, one soft?"

Talha closes up the box. I leave the cash on top of the counter, already knowing the familiar total, and wanting to leave before he tries to give me any change. When his sons are working, he lets them take tips, but he always refuses mine.

"See you soon!" I call out behind me as I leave, stopping ten feet later to fiddle with the glass door to my sad, yellowing building, barely renovated since it was built in 1926. I see one of my roommates, Aya, smoking a joint up on the fire escape. No one has ever looked as glamorous and as New York as Aya in this moment, her long black hair cascading over one shoulder as she leans an arm on the wrought-iron railing. We share a wave as I jiggle the handle with my key upside down, and then I burst inside the building.

I trudge up the five flights of steep stairs to my apartment, thighs already sore from the night's earlier activities. I open the door to my other roommate, Luisa, and her boyfriend, Michael, cooking a stir-fry in the kitchen.

"You hungry?" Luisa asks, adding a hefty flick of soy sauce into the pan. "I made too much."

"Always," I reply, giving Michael a wave as I put the box of pastries on the counter. "I brought treats."

"Oh, thank God." Luisa quickly hands Michael the wooden spoon to stir while she goes to inspect my haul. She pulls her dark, thick hair up into a short ponytail, brushing her knuckles over her widow's peak twice, an unconscious habit.

"I even got the hard kunefe, just for you."

"What am I going to do without you?" Luisa asks, giving my arm a squeeze.

"It's only a few days. And the kitchen will be so much cleaner."

Luisa sighs. I'm the messy one in our apartment, but at least I'm self-aware.

I fill a tall glass of water, then dig through the Duane Reade bag, pulling out the box of cranberry pills.

"Oh no," Michael says as I push two red pills out of the foil packet.

Luisa rolls her eyes. "Oh, Rob."

I shrug as I toss the pills back, chugging the entire glass. "Can't take any chances. No one wants another UTI debacle."

"No one wants to hear about your *urinary tract*, Nor," Luisa replies as she takes a forkful of kunefe.

"I'm going to hop in the shower, but save me a plate," I say, taking the opportunity while the bathroom is free to wash all of Rob right off me.

Luisa and I became friends at my first job out of college. We were both working as assistants at a digital marketing company and bonded quickly over the low pay and generally terrible environment. While Luisa found her way to a design agency, I suffered through years of stagnancy and half steps in the right direction, only getting promoted to a copywriter position this fall, four years later. But Luisa and I stayed friends, and we've lived together for the last two years.

I'm sure Luisa has many complaints about me as a roommate, but my only qualm with her is her and Michael's excessive shower use, so I jump at the opportunity to get in there before they take it over as they do every morning and night for an hour. I don't mind too much, especially when they feed me at all odd hours of the night, but I've also learned to be strategic about my bathroom time.

I take a long shower, knowing that it's already almost midnight and there's no chance I will get to shower again in the morning before my flight. Afterward, I collect my toiletries, tossing them on my bed next to the empty purple suitcase. I really did not plan this right at all. I emerge briefly in sweats to collect the bowl of food Luisa left. Aya has joined them at the tiny dining room table we found by the subway when we first moved in.

We met Aya through an online post when our last roommate decided the city wasn't for her and moved back to Jersey. Aya's lived here for almost a year and we still barely know anything about her. She's very fun to be around, but Luisa and I have an ongoing game of who can get even the tiniest bit of personal information from her. One time, she mentioned her brother was in a K-pop group and I had a fucking field day, but that's the most we've ever learned.

I take the bowl into my room (another pet peeve of Luisa's) and shove a huge piece of broccoli into my mouth as I start to pull sweaters out of my closet and ram them into the suitcase. I no longer have time to be discerning. I'd put off packing this long with the hopes that work or something else would come up, and I'd have an excuse to cancel another trip home like I did at Thanksgiving.

My phone pings with an email, and I swipe open the notification. It's a reminder to respond to the annual class reunion bar night e-vite. I sigh. I truly have no interest in going, but I click on the link and scroll down to the attendees.

I would be so very happy to never be in the same room, or building, or frankly, zip code as most of my former classmates ever again, for the rest of my life. I scroll past the sea of exclamations claiming Absolutely cannot wait!!! and I am SO there!!! My eyes roll so hard that it feels like I really should have had an audience for that.

I scan through the rest of the Yes, No, and Maybe columns, searching for his name. *Give me this one win*, I think, as I reach the Not Replied column. There he is.

Henry Cole.

Maybe I'll have garnered enough goodwill from finally going home that I'll at least be spared from seeing him. I click Maybe, and am about to go back to packing when the phone buzzes again in my hand.

It's Frankie Carlisle, FaceTiming me. I answer to her screaming, "You're going!" Frankie's platinum blonde hair pops into frame, grazing her collarbones, as she cackles at me over the phone. Her usual perma-frown is nowhere in sight.

"That was fast," I laugh, relishing the sight of my best friend's face.

"I get the notification emails when people respond," she explains, and I see her collapse onto her charcoal-colored comforter.

"That's what happens when you organize the whole damn thing." Frankie is an event planner and may or may not have been being taken advantage of by our alumni committee. I think she's getting paid at least?

I sigh, settling onto the corner of my own bed, the only spot that hasn't been taken over by stuff.

"You're going to make me go, aren't you?" I ask, already knowing the answer.

"Nor, I'm completely slammed with holiday parties for the next two days. Then it's the reunion, and then I leave on the cruise with my parents. This is the only chance we'll have to see each other. It's been two years. It's getting ridiculous."

"You're the only person in the world I would suffer through this night for," I say.

"I really am," my forever best friend replies. "Who knows, it might even be fun. I've put a lot of work into making sure it'll be the best time possible. And you know I hate almost everything, so I mean it."

"Fine," I say, leaning back on my pillow. "But I'm not changing my RSVP. I need to maintain the air of mystery."

"For whom?" Frankie snorts, her orange tabby cat, Monsieur, crawling briefly into frame.

"I don't know! For my own dignity! I have such little dignity when it comes to high school, Frankie. You know this."

"Norah, you've had the biggest glow-up I've ever seen IRL. Show it off a little."

I roll my eyes, but she's gotten me to smile.

"I suggest you pack that teal sweater you sent me pics of from your thrifting haul."

That's actually not a bad idea. I stand up and pull the oversized teal sweater off its hanger, tossing it into the suitcase.

"Wait, are you only packing now? It's after midnight your time."

"Frankie, it's me."

"I guess some things don't change. Have a safe flight. I'll *see you at the reunion*," Frankie says, emphasizing those last few words with her dark brows.

I blow her a kiss and hang up.

Off Frankie's encouragement, I add my favorite going-out jeans that are not meant for sitting. If I have to see a bunch of people who ruined my life, I can at least look hot and confident while doing so.

Chapter 2

AS I SIT squished into the middle seat on this completely full flight, I'm regretting every decision that brought me to this moment as the men on either side of me stake claim to their respective armrests. Every delay in purchasing tickets home for the holidays. Every time I thought *Oh, it'd be nice to be back with Mom and Hannah.* Every nagging text from Frankie, begging me to come to the reunion bar night she'd so meticulously planned.

The anxiety is only mildly quelled when our flight attendant returns with a tiny bottle of wine and a plastic cup to accompany it. I pour the bottle into the cup without a moment of hesitation, and clock a side-eye from the dude to my right. I glare at him and almost spill as the bottle empties and the deep purple liquid reaches the brim. He looks away, and I turn back to my cup.

Before I can even take a sip, the seat in front of me slams back, knocking at least half the wine onto my light gray sweater and jeans. Great.

I peer over the edge of the seat in front of me, trying to get the attention of its incredibly rude occupant. He's reclined as far back as the seat allows, in a navy suit and a crisp white shirt. He's got a sleep mask on over his eyes and earbuds in. He doesn't respond to the few pokes I give him. I briefly consider pouring the rest of the cup's contents onto his starchy shirt to try to get his attention, but I decide I need it more.

I settle back into my seat and look around for a napkin beyond the drenched one in my hand, but both men in my row have turned away from me.

I down the rest of my wine in one gulp, but not before "accidentally" kicking the seat of this rude man in front of me in the process.

I sit, boxed in on all sides and stewing, for the remainder of the flight.

AS SOON AS we land, I'm beyond antsy to get off the plane. I keep trying, but I'm not able to get a look at the asshole in front of me. I spent the remaining two hours of the flight plotting out exactly what to say to him, how to lecture him on proper plane etiquette. I think I've got it down to a tight two minutes. It's only when the man in the window seat clears his throat that I realize we can exit, and that I've completely missed my demon in well-tailored armor.

I scurry off the plane and look around for his navy suit at the terminal, but he's nowhere to be found. I hurry into the bathroom to try to salvage my clothes, though the stain has already clearly set. I sigh. Maybe I can scold him at baggage claim, I reason.

Baggage claim itself is a nightmare, as it always is around

the holidays. It's been so long since I flew home at this time of year, I'd almost forgotten. I finally find the carousel for our flight, but I don't see him. I position myself near a family with three kids under five, who are all screaming because they want to help get the bags off the conveyor belt, and their dad keeps saying they're too small.

I have this memory of being here at O'Hare, probably about the same age as these kids, maybe even before Hannah was born. Dad lifting me up and putting me on top of the suitcases, placed haphazardly on the luggage cart. Mom yelling about how wildly unsafe it was, but laughing all the same. I'm giggling with pure glee as he slowly starts pushing the cart. I yell for him to go faster, but Mom says that's enough. Dad winks at me, scooping me up into his arms. I think he'd forgotten his razor that trip, and he had more scruff than usual. I remember it scratching my forehead as I leaned my face on his cheek, but I didn't even care.

I'm snapped back into reality by the buzz of the conveyor belt starting. I look around, and that's when I see him. Fitted navy slacks. What I now can tell is a perfectly pressed white shirt. How did he manage that after sleeping on the plane? Navy suit jacket. No tie. My gaze rolls up until I realize he's staring right at me. Maybe he has been this whole time.

Henry Cole.

He doesn't even pretend to look away when we lock eyes. His are still that striking blue I could never get out of my head, only now they're searing right through me. His thick dark hair is well coiffed.

I haven't willingly spoken to him since the fall of our senior year of high school. The day my dad died, when it was unavoidable. Henry came to the house every day that we sat shiva after that. Even though he was missing school, just like I was, he was still there. Seven days, and we didn't exchange a single word. I couldn't. Not after everything that happened. I wouldn't let myself.

This is worse than I thought.

Before my brain has connected with my feet, they're already moving me into his space. He still doesn't look away until I'm right in front of him, when he glances down to my stained sweater, then back up to meet my eyes.

"I know people like to travel comfortably, but Norah, come on."

His voice runs like ice through my veins. I don't like my name on his tongue.

"This is your fault. Your basic disregard for airplane etiquette sent my pinot flying all over me. If you're going to lean your seat all the way back, next time give the unlucky person behind you a little heads-up. It's selfish and rude, and bad enough to be bombarded by men who don't allow you to take up the space you deserve on all ends, but—"

I stop because his eyes are narrowing into a look I can't decipher.

"You're judging me." I fold my arms over my poor wine-soaked sweater, and turn to the conveyor belt to start searching for my suitcase.

"Why ever would I judge you?" he asks with only a hint of sarcasm.

"I don't know, I'm drinking wine in the afternoon, and I'm clearly a mess, and—"

I glance over to catch his lips barely flicking up into a smile as he interrupts me.

"You're going to your mom's, right?"

I nod.

"We should split a cab."

I eye him skeptically.

"For efficiency," he continues.

I look at him, a little dumbfounded, honestly. Yes, our moms still live next door to each other. Yes, sharing a cab would, in fact, be efficient. But there is absolutely zero chance I want to spend any more of my day with Henry Cole, unless I can enact revenge, specifically involving a dark beverage and his pristine white shirt, which I'm now close enough to see is tailored to perfection, his frame no longer that of a lanky teenage boy. Now he has the body of a man. Which I don't want to be thinking about, at this moment in time or ever.

I turn back to Henry and see him lifting his bag off the belt. He returns to me and waits for a response to his offer.

"I'm good. It was . . . fine? Seeing you?" I pause. Neither of us is buying that. "No, that's a lie, it was truly terrible and exactly what I would have expected."

Henry nods but doesn't walk away. I keep an eye out for my suitcase.

We wait in silence as the bags on the belt dwindle down. I tell him he can go, but he just stands there next to me.

Perfect.

When it becomes clear that my bag is not in Chicago with me, I brace myself for all the paperwork.

Henry finally turns to head out. "Too bad you don't want to ride together. I would've even taken pity on you and covered the cost. Anyway, I'll give your mother your regards."

He smirks as he walks out the doors to get a cab, and I'm left wondering what the hell that's supposed to mean.

Chapter 3

I FINALLY MAKE it home, suitcase-less, after hours of waiting and then a grueling cab ride into the suburbs. I was informed that the airline would try to locate my bag and deliver it to me within twenty-four hours, but with the holiday season, there were no guarantees.

The house I grew up in looks mostly the same as it did two years ago on my last visit. The white wraparound porch could still use a refresh, but the curtains are open on the bay window that faces out toward the street, and before I even step inside, I'm hit with the feeling of home. The familiar rust-colored reading chair in the window. The needlepoint garden my grandmother stitched hanging on the wall. Inside smells like it always has—roast chicken and lemon and my mother's tiny indoor herb garden, but there's a strange feeling amid the comfort. I'm no longer nose-blind to the scents of home.

Without any of the clothes I'd packed for the trip, I'm forced to go through my childhood bedroom, where I find jeans that went out of style years before I gave up wearing them, and a worn pink pullover from high school. It was my favorite sweatshirt, a souvenir from a class trip to Michigan, endlessly soft even after a hundred times through the laundry. I thought I'd lost it when I went to college, but here it was, this whole time. With my hair up in an unkempt bun and no makeup, I really do look like the ghost of my teenage self.

I don't want to be this person, the person who only just lost her dad. I don't like being the version of me that he knew. Grief does funny things to you. All Hannah ever wants is to reminisce. But I have to keep it all locked away, in a sacred place no one else can access.

This room is a still photograph of my former life. Eighteen-year-old Norah. Pink walls that don't feel like they reflect any iteration of the person I've been.

I need to get out of my head. I notice a photo album from my bat mitzvah on my nightstand. Mom said she found it while emptying the basement.

I flip it open, running my fingers over the pearly matte of the photos, still perfectly crisp thirteen years later, and start to page through. The purple satin dress I'd absolutely begged my mom for. The purple bands on my braces, which I thought would match but ended up looking like I had gum caught in my teeth. But even that couldn't stop my cheesy grin. Little preteen Hannah and the fluffy pink dress that she'd somehow aged out of by the big day, that Dad talked her into wearing anyway, just to keep Mom from having a breakdown.

Posed photos of my parents and me on the bimah.

Frankie and I at the reception, with oversized sunglasses, thinking we were the coolest.

Henry and I. Slow dancing, probably two feet between us,

my hands on each of his shoulders, his gangly arms a little high on my waist. I think Henry's mom, Kristine, had told him he had to dance with me. We both look completely mortified, like we couldn't get away from each other fast enough.

Before he grew into his long limbs and those broad shoulders that are now seared into my brain, he was always beautiful. It was those soft blue eyes, the slight curl of his dark hair. I hate this memory of him. I want to exorcise it from my brain, or go back in time and warn my younger self about all the irreversible harm he would one day do to her.

I hear a knock on my door and slam the book shut.

Mom enters slowly and hands me a mug full of chamomile tea. It's ceramic, something I painted at my eighth birthday party. Everything here is a constant reminder.

Being here, in this house, in these clothes, in this life, it's all too much.

This is why I come home as rarely as Mom will allow.

I know that's not fair. To Mom, to Hannah, even to Dad.

In New York, I can pretend I'm a normal, well-adjusted person, but here, I can't hide from anything.

Mom is looking at me like she's on the precipice of a speech. She sits down with me on the bed, but I can tell she's barely able to hold it in. She runs her thumb and pointer finger over a face-framing curl. After years of blowouts and straightening her hair, it's nice to see Mom's natural curls out in full force in a layered bob.

"Lay it on me," I say, knowing she's about to burst.

"I know you're only supposed to stay for a couple days," she begins slowly.

My eyes narrow. I know where this is going.

Mom pushes her thick-rimmed burgundy glasses up her

nose. "But I want you to extend your trip. At least through all eight nights of Hanukkah." She starts to dig in about how long it's been since I really spent time at home, how we need this. As a family.

I can't even think of a time growing up where we remembered to light the menorah beyond the second night.

Mom tells me it's important, but holding this mug, surrounded by too many painful memories, I can't. I know I can't.

"I'm sorry. I have to get back for work," I lie. "I can only stay through the weekend."

I can tell she's hurt, and it immediately makes me regret the words that came out of my mouth. I don't know why I can't be normal, can't be here. I don't know why I can't tell her any of that. Mom just seems so chipper, and I haven't seen her like that in so long. I don't want to dredge up more of the past and burst this Hanukkah-shaped bubble.

I WAKE UP too early, still on New York time. I've got a barrage of drunk texts from Rob, but knowing him, they're more likely fake-drunk texts with a slew of carefully thought-through "typos" to try to suss out the info he's desperate for. He likes me sooooo much. He misses me. He wants to know if I have an answer yet. I obviously do, but I'm just not ready to deal with him.

The house is still quiet, so I layer up with what I can find in my room and downstairs on the coat rack, and slip out.

Sure, it gets cold in New York, but it's not quite like this. I've gotten spoiled, soft, in my years away from the Midwest. As I start to run, the only way I've ever found to quiet my brain, I can feel the chill deep in my lungs. It starts to burn as I press on. But I focus on the bitter inhale and the harsh exhale and that's the only thing getting me through.

As I approach the house, cheeks numb, eyelashes frozen open, I see Henry pull into his driveway. He gets out of the car with a to-go cup of coffee, earbuds in, clearly on a call that isn't going well based on the distressed, tense nature of his body, his ramrod-straight spine. I can't hear what he's saying, but as I reach our driveway, a mirror image of his, he looks over at me, like maybe he wants to say something. I sprint to the door, not giving him an opportunity.

I spend half the morning trying to track down my suitcase, and after the fifth person I'm transferred to, I learn that the bag is still en route, and likely won't arrive until tomorrow morning. Rob continues to blow up my phone with apologies for the drunken texts, and I continue to ignore them all.

Hannah emerges from her room at some point, while I'm on hold again, shoving her phone in my face. "Why is Rob the Slob DMing *me*?" she demands, the stream of messages having woken her.

When Rob and I first started hooking up, I discovered there was no hand soap at all in his bathroom. There was a bar in the shower that I had on good authority he stuck directly into his ass, but that was it. I ended up buying a soap dispenser from Duane Reade for his bathroom on my way over once because I couldn't take it anymore. I made the mistake of telling Hannah this fact, and he's been Rob the Slob to her ever since.

I sigh deeply and go back to my string of unanswered texts. I slowly type, **I had to extend my trip. Sorry! Going off the grid!!!**

Hannah peers over my shoulder and then squeals. "Mom, she's staying!" my sister exclaims as she runs down the hall.

I follow Hannah back into the kitchen, where Mom is putting

on another pot of coffee. "Oh, honey, this is my gift for the first night. You don't even need to give me anything else."

I look at Hannah and mouth, *Gifts for every night?* when Mom turns back to counting out scoops of coffee grounds. "She didn't even do that when we were kids. What's going on?" Hannah shrugs.

"I'm over the moon you'll be here the whole holiday. I have big news, and I've been trying to figure out a way to tell you." Mom barely waits a beat. "Do you remember Ms. Cole? Kristine?"

"Henry's mom?" I ask.

"Yes, honey, Henry's mom. Well . . ."

"Mom's dating Kristine!" Hannah interrupts. "What? You were taking too long to spit it out."

Mom shoots her a look but clearly can't stay mad for more than a moment. I don't know how I didn't see it last night. My mother is fully swooning.

"She was the girl next door," Mom says wistfully.

I'm happy for my mom. All my own hangups about Dad aside, I want her to be happy and in love. He would want that too.

"They're coming over for dinner tonight," Mom says as she turns the coffeemaker on. "For the first night of Hanukkah. To celebrate."

"They?" I ask, knowing exactly who *they* entails.

"Kristine and Henry, of course."

Of course.

"HOW LONG HAVE you known? Why didn't you tell me?" I bombard Hannah with questions, flopping dramatically onto her princess bed.

"I figured it out when I came home for Thanksgiving. They're not subtle. It'd be too much if they weren't so stinking cute all the time."

"Thanksgiving?" It's been a whole month of this ginormous secret.

"You were stuck working," Hannah reminds me, repeating the excuse I made in November. "They've actually been dating for like, a year. Mom swore me to secrecy. She wanted to tell you herself. She thought you'd make a big thing about it." My sister gives me a very pointed look, warning me to not start.

"I knew she was dating again, but . . ." Mom had always been open with us about her bisexuality, ever since she first gave us talks about our own bodies. She never wanted Hannah or me to think it was something she was hiding, or feel we ever had to do the same with anything of our own.

"But?" Hannah challenges.

"But Kristine? Henry's mom? Really?"

"Yeah, that's the part Mom was talking about. I always thought Kristine was really nice. She had the best Halloween candy."

"Yeah, she's great. But she's Henry's mom. *My* Henry."

It slips out before I can even realize what I've said.

Hannah's eyes grow wide with amusement. "Oh, he's your Henry now, is he?"

She knows that's not what I meant. She knows what went down back then.

She knows he was never mine.

I roll my eyes at her. "Of all the people in the greater Chicagoland area, she has to pick the one who birthed the boy who ruined my life."

"Love is wild."

I look at my sister, more serious than I've been with her in years. "Hannah Arielle Gold. I am begging you. If you ever loved me, ever had any sisterly goodwill toward me, you will let me borrow something tonight since Henry ruined the one piece of clothing I have left in this time zone that's not, at minimum, eight years old."

Hannah leans forward, eyes brimming with pity. "The way you treat your clothes? Not a chance."

Chapter 4

THE DOORBELL RINGS while Mom is basting the brisket and Hannah is nowhere to be found, so I drag myself to the door, take a deep breath, and welcome in our guests.

Kristine immediately pulls me into a hug, her blue eyes warm with affection. Her honey-brown hair is now streaked with gray, but she's more or less the same as I remember. "Oh, Norah, look at you. I'm so happy we're family!"

Over her shoulder, I see Henry, lingering on the top step of our porch. He laughs a bit at his mother's gushing, but honestly he doesn't look like he wants to be here any more than I do. He holds up the bottle of Manischewitz he's carrying.

As Kristine breaks away, she giggles, taking the bottle and handing it over to me. "Happy Hanukkah, sweetie."

I take the bottle from her as politely as I can and usher them inside.

I walk to the built-in bar on one side of the living room and quickly shove the Manischewitz in a cabinet where it won't be discovered. It's a cute gesture on Kristine's part, but there is no way in hell I am going to sit through this dinner with Henry fucking Cole drinking some syrupy sweet nonsense. I covertly grab the first red wine I see, uncork it with ease, and pour it into a decanter. I know, without question, that my mother exclusively stocks her house with good wine, though truly anything would be better than the Manischewitz I was handed. I carry the decanter and some glasses back over to the couch, desperate to dive in.

I'm pouring myself a glass after passing one over to each of our guests when my mother calls out, "Not before we do the blessing!" and I almost drop the glass in my hand.

I think she's expecting me to hold off, but I have never in my life seen Mom insist on blessing the copious amounts of wine this household has consumed over the years. So I hold up my glass, and loudly say, for Mom's benefit alone, "*Baruch ata Adonai, eloheinu melech ha'olom boray peri ha-gafen*," the words coming back as muscle memory on my tongue. I raise my glass in cheers to Kristine and Henry and take a large sip. They look confused, but do the same.

"Wow, this is much better than I thought it would be," Kristine exclaims, going back for a second sip.

Hannah comes downstairs finally, and Kristine rushes over to her. I watch my sister and the bane of my existence exchange a wave, and the smile on Hannah's face makes me nauseated.

I stand to go check on Mom in the kitchen, but I feel Henry's large shadow looming over me.

"You switched the wine, didn't you?" he asks quietly enough that only I can hear.

I turn to him but do not respond.

"This is from Sara's collection?"

I keep my face stoic, not wanting to give him anything, but he tips his glass toward mine with a simple "Well, thank you."

It's almost . . . affable, the way he says it, and it catches me off guard.

Henry Cole and I are not friends.

We haven't been in a long time.

I feel a strong urge to send the clearest message I can that we are not *in this together.* We're not anything at all.

"If I did switch the wine, which I'm not saying I did, it would have only been because I knew I would never get through tonight, having to share a meal with you, without something I could easily chug." It comes out with perhaps more hostility than I'd planned, so I take another long sip from my glass.

Henry's eyes shift over me, turning icy. I'm frozen in front of him as his gaze swoops past my messy hair, the too-high-waisted jeans I found in a drawer that barely still fit, the sweater I've definitely had since I was fourteen.

"I take it your suitcase is still lost," he says, raising an eyebrow, all of the warmth drained from his voice.

Good. That's exactly what I wanted—to know what to expect from him. Without another word, I turn on my heels and finish my mission to the kitchen.

AS THE LAST sliver of sunlight fades, we gather by the bay window in the living room. Most other families on our street, the Coles included, display their Christmas trees in this space, but we have an end table we use to prop up the Tree of Life menorah my parents received as a wedding gift. I always loved the way the eight silver branches wove around each other, the gold cups that hugged the candles in place, the rooted base that held the shamash after lighting its cousins.

Hannah retrieves the box from our freezer, nudging me affectionately with her shoulder as she opens it and hands two candles over to Mom. Mom twists one dip-dyed blue candle into the far right branch of the menorah, and then Kristine strikes a match, holding it up to the candle in Mom's hand.

The brief look that Mom and Kristine share in the glow of the shamash makes my heart swell. It's been a tough couple of years for all of us, but the last few, since Hannah went to college and left the house especially, have been hard on Mom. I should come home more. But I'm glad that, in our absence, there was a wonderful person here to take care of my mother, look at her so adoringly, laugh with her. They are so blatantly and obviously in love.

Mom starts the first of three blessings as she lights the other candle, placing the shamash down in its home at the base. I mouth along with her. I probably haven't said these prayers in almost a decade, but they come back like second nature, words rooted in my core, in who I am.

We finish reciting the third blessing, the Shehecheyanu, and I can only hear my dad's uproarious laugh. "The blessing of firsts!" he'd always exclaim, the first day of school every year, the first time Hannah lost a tooth, the time he caught me scrubbing off my lip gloss after my first Spin the Bottle party. Whether a rabbi would deem the ancient blessing situationally appropriate or not, my dad would chant *Shehecheyanu v'ky'manu v'higiyanu lazman hazeh.*

Hannah takes my hand and gives it a squeeze. "The blessing of firsts!" she belts softly in my ear, and knowing she's also thinking about him helps.

We sit down for dinner, Mom only insisting on one more prayer before we can finally eat.

"Norah, sweetie, tell me all about your life in New York," Kristine says, mouth full of brisket. "You know, Henry lives there too now," she adds, pointing her fork at him.

"I gathered. We were on the same flight here."

Kristine swats a hand at her son next to her. "You didn't tell me that."

"It was uneventful. Hardly worth mentioning," he replies with a shrug.

"Oh, I wouldn't go that far," I say quickly. "What with spilling wine all over me and the general lack of regard for other—"

"You spilled that wine all by yourself," he interjects.

"It was his fault," I say to Kristine, who looks horrified.

"Henry," she reprimands, and I can't help but smile.

Kristine asks more about the marketing firm I work for, my recent promotion to copywriter. She asks about Hannah's MFA application for Northwestern. It's so clear how much she cares about my mom, and how much she wants to know us. I always liked Kristine, but tonight makes me love her.

Unfortunately, I can't say the same for Henry.

He starts talking about the brokerage firm he recently started working for in the city, Karlin Stein. I'm only barely making rent with two roommates in a fifth-floor walk-up, even with my new promotion. He just moved into his own place because he's that successful and wants me to know how much better in life he's doing than I am. He's really raking it in, in commercial real estate.

I stand to clear the table and barely make it to the kitchen before I realize Henry is steps behind me, once again, carrying more dishes than seems feasible for one man. I notice the definition in his biceps as they twitch through his fitted sweater, and I hate that we're in close enough proximity that I can see that. I hate that I want to reach out and see if the emerald fabric is as soft as it looks.

"A real estate agent? Don't you have to be likable for that?" I ask, because I'm several glasses of wine in and can't believe I have to spend my holiday with Henry Cole.

"Don't you remember how charming I can be?" he retorts, handing me a plate, which I rinse.

I let out a snort as I put the plate into the dishwasher, and I see his hand tense in my periphery.

"I remember *you* finding me charming enough to agree to a kiss once upon a time."

The audacity of this awful man. How dare he bring that up. In my house. Where he is a guest.

I turn to lay into him, a soapy fork precariously close to his strong jaw, but Mom shuffles into the kitchen at that exact moment.

"Oh, you two. It's so nice to see you catching up. When you're back in New York, you'll have to get together. We are family now!"

My mom begins to hum, pulling out Tupperware containers for leftovers. Henry hands me another plate, which I silently rinse. We continue like this until all that's left is the stuff to wash by hand, at which point he grabs a towel and starts drying pots and dishes instead. We don't exchange a word, but every time his fingers brush against mine, I silently fume. And every time, I see him smirk. That damn smirk. As if he's trying to get under my skin.

It's a cruel fucking joke given everything that went down almost a decade ago.

I finish scrubbing the last Pyrex and shove it into his hands. I rinse my own quickly, and instead of drying them, I shake them in his general direction. It catches him off guard. *Good.* I pat my hands the rest of the way dry on my jeans as I head upstairs to my room.

As soon as I slam the door, I regret not bringing some wine or dessert up here with me. Henry really does ruin everything. If nothing else, a decade later, at least he's still consistent in that regard.

There's a small knock on my door, which can only be Hannah. "I'm coming in," my sister says. The knob turns, and she slips inside.

"So . . ." Hannah starts, overly chipper, clearly here to test the waters. "How's it going in here?"

I fall back on the bed and sigh. "I can't do it. I can't be around him. He's a terrible, miserable human. I don't understand how someone as lovely as Kristine could have spawned *that*."

Hannah lies down on the bed beside me, snuggling into my ribs as we've always done. We stay that way for a minute, and I brush some of my sweet little sister's reckless curls off her face.

"Can't we just put it all behind us?" she asks finally. It's soft, hopeful.

I hate disappointing Hannah. I'm the big sister. I'm supposed to be the example.

"Henry Cole has made it his mission to humiliate me every chance he gets," I say slowly. "It's the same after all this time, and clearly nothing is going to change that goal. So it's easy for you to say the words *Let's move on*, but I genuinely don't know how to do that."

Hannah rolls onto her side, propping herself up with an elbow to face me. She looks at me, her light eyebrows furrowed. "Mom is the happiest I've seen her in years," she says. "Since . . . you know."

I do know, and I can't dispute Hannah's statement.

"Henry is Henry. But you have to pull it together. For Mom."

I know she's right, but I hate admitting it. I sigh, dragging my body upright, against all instincts I have toward self-preservation.

"Fine," I tell her. "I will go back down there. I will smile, and laugh, and emanate warmth toward Mom and Kristine."

Hannah smiles, victorious. She stands up and heads to the door with me.

"But I won't, under any circumstances, engage with him for the rest of the trip. Okay? I can't."

"Understood." Hannah nods, opening my bedroom door, and gesturing for me to lead the way.

Downstairs, the candles have died out. Henry barely looks up as we make our way down. He has made himself entirely too comfortable on the couch. He's completely absorbed by something on his phone, typing away with such focus that I almost don't notice the old photo album open on his lap.

He was there for all of the awkward moments, everything cheesy that my parents felt inclined to capture. I don't know why in the world he'd want to relive it, but at least there's nothing new he could blackmail me with or lord over me.

Henry only puts down his phone and closes the album when my mom claps her hands together upon seeing us.

"Oh good, there you girls are," she says.

Kristine comes up and puts her arm around Mom. "We have news! Sara and I booked a cabin at Great Blue Lodge for the rest of the week. So pack your bags! We leave bright and early tomorrow."

"Tomorrow?" I ask, hesitation ringing through that one word. "I have to stay for the reunion. It's the only time I can see Frankie while I'm home. She made me promise."

It's true, and I desperately need to see my best friend, the only person who knows everything I'm juggling with this man who's spread across my couch. Plus, the last thing I want to do is spend more time with him. I need a break. Or for him to be at a cabin hours and hours away, and me to be right here, not sharing any of his toxic air.

Mom and Kristine exchange a look. "You know," Kristine begins slowly, "Henry has some business to tie up, and he was going to drive up a day late anyway."

I can already see where this is heading and I hate it.

"Sweetie," Kristine continues, turning to Henry, "you'll drive Norah, right?" She smiles, eager.

I look everywhere in this room but Henry's general direction. *Absolutely not*, I want to scream.

But I hear Hannah's voice. *For Mom.*

Frankie would never forgive me if I didn't see her.

And it's only then that I hear his gruff response. "It would be my greatest displeasure."

Well, at least that's one thing we can agree on.

The first in nine years.

Chapter 5

THE NEXT MORNING, after much convincing on my part, far more than should be necessary when leaving your twenty-six-year-old adult daughter home alone, I finally got my mother to agree that I am, in fact, a grown woman who can handle one night as a townie.

"Don't forget, the second night of Hanukkah is two prayers! Candles are in the freezer for you!" Mom says before kissing me goodbye.

"Breathe." Hannah gives me a squeeze. "And don't murder Henry. No one trusts you to drive to Great Blue Lodge yourself."

I open my mouth to argue with her, but Hannah just taps my chin closed. "See you tomorrow."

Not long after I finally have the house to myself, Frankie calls.

"Oh my God, I have had the wildest few days—" I start to say, but she cuts me off.

"No time. No time for any of that. Today is fully dedicated to setup for tonight."

"Oh-kay. So what do you need?" I ask, immediately cutting to the chase.

Frankie puts on her most angelic voice. "Your mom's famous latkes?"

I sigh, and before I can reply, she shouts, "Threedozenthankyouloveyabyeeee," and hangs up.

There goes my day.

A few hours later, I've already destroyed the kitchen, trying to fulfill Frankie's request. Mom swore off homemade latkes this year, claiming they were more trouble than they were worth. While I disagree, since latkes are a perfect food, I'm beginning to see where she was coming from. I think I've shredded more potatoes into my hair than the bowl itself. I've broken two nails in the process and just barely still have the knuckle of my thumb in one piece. My once-black student leadership hoodie is now bordering charcoal with the amount of flour covering my entire torso.

But we're almost there.

I look at the bowl of mush and grab a small measuring cup from the drawer.

Almost there.

I turn the heat up on a burner and wait for the pan to get hot. I grab the vegetable oil from the cabinet and frown. It's barely enough to fry three latkes, let alone the three dozen I promised Frankie I'd bring tonight.

I turn off the burner and sigh. I could go to the store, but I don't have a car, and the airline promised that my suitcase should be delivered within the hour. I check Postmates, but the estimated delivery time is way too long to be convenient or worth the exorbitant upcharge for a four-dollar bottle of oil. The frying is going to take a while, and I really need to get started.

I look out the window, and I see lights on next door.

Henry.

I sigh, ready to give up all my dignity, and head over.

He answers the door, a bemused smirk spreading across his lips as he looks me up and down. "Norah Gold, really swinging strong for the holidays, huh?"

"I wouldn't be here if I didn't have to be," I tell him.

He leans on the frame of the front door, crossing one foot in front of the other. "So, to what do I owe—"

"I need oil," I say, cutting him off because that lean is doing something to me that I don't like. "Do you have any vegetable or canola oil?"

"There are stores for that, you know."

I tell him that I'm waiting for my suitcase to finally arrive, and how I couldn't risk missing it.

"You certainly couldn't," he says, giving me another once-over.

"Surely you can spare some oil," I say. "I mean, we're practically family now, right?"

The look on his face is completely unreadable, but he steps aside, allowing me to plow into the house.

I head for the kitchen, muscle memory leading me there, but quickly get overwhelmed by the familiarity. The smell of patchouli that always lingered here. The wooden cabinets I used to love. The one weird hot plate tile attached to the kitchen counter, a quirk of the house.

When we were maybe six years old, Henry and I made it our mission to get rid of the tile, whatever it took. We tried prying it up with sticks and a metal nail file. Bashing it with the end of a large serving spoon. When Kristine found us, she was furious. It's honestly shocking we didn't get hurt. We weren't allowed to play together for a few days as punishment, but our parents quickly gave in, and then I was back at the Cole house like I always was.

I haven't been in here since the day everything went wrong.

Henry emerges from the pantry with an unopened bottle of vegetable oil. "I was raised firmly *nothing*, so correct me if I'm wrong here, but isn't there a joke to be made about running out of oil? Wasn't the whole point that it lasted eight nights?"

He says it so innocently that I almost want to laugh, but I can't give him the satisfaction. Yes, that's absolutely the Cliffs-Notes version of Hanukkah, and yes, I am royally screwing up my people's history here.

"Look," I tell him, taking the bottle, careful to not let our fingers come within four inches of each other, "I promised Frankie I would bring my mom's famous latkes to the reunion, but Mom is gone, so I'm figuring it out. She refused to make them this year because of how labor-intensive they are, and honestly?" I pull some shredded potato I can see in my periphery out of my hair. "She's not wrong. So thank you for the oil. You did your mitzvah."

I start to head out of the house and realize that, on my mission to the kitchen, I failed to notice the cardboard boxes lining one wall in the living room.

"What's with all these?"

Henry whips around to stare at the Tetris of boxes, then turns back to me. "I'm shipping stuff back to New York." He gives a single shake of his head, then tilts his chin toward me. "The latkes are for the reunion?"

I nod.

"In that case, I might have to go after all."

I roll my eyes, saluting him with the bottle of oil. "Hope I don't see you there."

As I stomp out of Henry's house, I see a man next door, wheeling my beloved purple suitcase back to his car. I chase after him. I can barely believe that Henry made me so distracted I almost missed this delivery. I thank the driver profusely and head back inside, ecstatic to finally be reunited with a piece of myself and my real life.

I remain focused and only burn myself twice while frying the latkes.

Then I take a long shower and prepare myself for the night.

I would have been completely fine never seeing the bulk of my classmates ever again. If not for Frankie, I would probably be able to accomplish that. I'd been doing a great job of avoiding them for this long, with my rare trips home and refusal to follow through on the occasional "OMG let's get drinks!" from someone who never said two words to me back then. I'm doing this entirely for Frankie, and she knows it.

After spending the last two days feeling gross and inferior, I can't wait to feel like myself. I put on makeup, which I absolutely never wore in high school but have since figured out. Learning how to steadily apply liquid eyeliner on the train has been an accomplishment that made me feel like a true New Yorker. I select the oversized teal sweater that Frankie told me to bring, the jeans I know hug all the right places, and, double-checking that I won't be encountering ice, black heeled boots. I confirm in the mirror that my curls are bouncy and defined now that I've finally learned what to do with them, instead of the frizzy halo of my youth. I'm not always confident, but I know I look great tonight.

As I lock up the house, juggling the tray of latkes in my arms, Henry appears on his own porch. "Look who's out of her fourth-grade gym shorts," he calls.

I roll my eyes. He's pulling a scarf around his neck, looking like a poster for J.Crew.

"No thanks to you. I almost missed the drop-off while you were quizzing me on the history of my people."

He doesn't apologize. He doesn't say anything. I can't believe that for once, he's actually quiet. He almost looks lost in thought.

"Do you want to share a car?" he suggests for the second time this week. "We're going to the same place."

I shake my head. It's the last thing I want.

He runs a hand through his hair. "Right," he says, some of the animosity gone from his tone.

I almost feel bad, but the sentiment is fleeting. "Frankie is picking me up. There's no space for you in her car. Sorry!"

As if she heard my siren call to hurry the fuck up and get me out of this awkward conversation, Frankie pulls up in her red convertible.

I'm almost relieved that Henry can see I wasn't lying—that there really was no space for him. As I open the passenger seat and slip in, I swear I hear him muttering, "Who has a fucking convertible in Illinois?"

"Wow. Twenty-six really agrees with Henry Cole, huh" are the first words out of my best friend's crimson-stained lips when I get in the car. Thank God I slammed the door closed quickly behind me so he didn't hear that.

I disregard her statement and throw my arms around her. "I missed you, Frankie Marie, but kindly shut the fuck up," I tell her lovingly.

"Oh my God," Frankie says, nudging the tray of latkes, then throwing the car into drive, "my mouth is already watering. I am ready."

Chapter 6

FRANKIE AND I have been best friends since fourth grade, when she arrived at Laketon and I was assigned to be her new student buddy. We haven't seen each other in person in about two years, which is why it was all the more necessary for me to see her tonight, before she ships off to spend Christmas on a cruise to Alaska with her parents and brother.

"They said the cruise is all-inclusive—and all you can drink," she informs me. "So I figured I'd pace myself tonight. You know I don't usually drink much anyway, but if I'm trapped on a ship with my family, I'm going to need it. Plus, I'm on the clock."

Technically true. Frankie is, in fact, being paid by the alumni committee for her event planning services. I think they are gunning for more alcohol-fueled donations so they can build a new science center. Otherwise, there's no way they would be putting any effort into gouging our pockets when it's not even a reunion year for us. We're far enough out from eighteen that we might be mildly successful, but most of us don't have families yet. We are perfect targets. These wintertime reunion drinks happen every year, but as far as I've heard, they've never gone all out like this. Not that I would know from personal experience, having managed to avoid the last eight of these nostalgia-filled shit shows. Before I agreed to attend, I'd asked Frankie why they even do these reunions every year. Shouldn't they space them out, give us time to miss each other at least? But she just laughed and replied, "You've never been, so how would you know?"

"I missed you so much," I say, squeezing my best friend's hand. We text constantly, and we try to do long phone catch-up sessions or FaceTimes at least once a month, but it's nothing compared to the feeling of sitting next to her as we pass through our hometown. Frankie is driving the exact route I used to take every day to school. It's almost eerie how things still look the same, until we pull up to a stoplight at the strip mall where we used to walk for off-campus lunches, which has been entirely redone, leaving no remnants of the tiny Chinese restaurant with the $7.99 lunch specials we loved so very much.

"Capitalism," Frankie mutters.

We drive a little farther, and as we pass Laketon Academy, it takes me a moment to realize that we're not actually stopping at our alma mater.

I've spent such little time here as an adult that it barely even occurred to me that we were going to a *bar* in town. Any time I come home, I usually just sleep over at Frankie's apartment in the city, and we stay up all night talking and reminiscing.

This is something I have never done before.

I don't know what it is about being home that makes me feel

like a teenager who's about to get caught, get in trouble. I am twenty-six years old. I am perfectly welcome at an establishment that serves alcohol. I don't know why I fumble with my ID.

As we walk into the dimly lit bar that Frankie has rented out for our former classmates, I immediately want to turn around and get the fuck out of there. We weren't exactly cool in high school. Didn't have a huge group of friends.

Frankie can read everything I'm thinking right off of my face.

"Nope. Uh-uh. I see you wanting to slink right back out those double doors and I simply won't allow it." Frankie takes the tray of latkes from my arms, and I follow her over to a table on the side of the room, where there are warming pans set up.

"Now listen to me, Norah Abigail Gold," Frankie says, pulling back the foil and using tongs to transport my latkes onto the proper serving tray. "This is our one night together. Plus," she says, pointing at me with the tongs, "we look fucking hot. Let's make all the boys who didn't like us in high school regret their entire lives. Starting with Henry Cole, who was absolutely eye-fucking you back at your house."

"Oh my God, Frankie, shut up. I promise you he was not. If the last few days have reminded me of anything, it's that that boy absolutely despises me."

"Yeah, okay," my best friend snorts.

"It's bad enough that our moms are so flipping cute together that they're probably going to get married and we'll be forced to spend every holiday together for the rest of eternity. But now I'm going to be stuck in a car with him for like, four hours tomorrow."

"Great Blue Lodge?" Frankie asks, mouth already full of latke.

I nod.

"It'll probably be more like six."

"*Six hours?*" I screech. I thought it would be bad, but I did not anticipate six hours trapped in a car with Henry. "He's done nothing but make me feel like an absolute idiot ever since we got on the same plane, and I . . ." I trail off when I feel a warm hand lightly touch my back.

"Norah Gold? Back in the 847?" I hear, and I spin around. Trevor Hayes, a sea of strawberry blonde waves that graze muscular shoulders, stands behind me.

"Trevor!" I exclaim, and he wraps me up in a huge hug, lifting me a foot into the air. I swat at him a little, and he puts me down.

"Never thought I'd see the day." He smiles, his perfect teeth gleaming, even in the dim light of the bar.

"Trevor Hayes! All those years of braces finally paid off. Look at you!" I touch his cheek, and his eyes dip for half a second.

"Thirty-eight months," he says, almost unconsciously running his tongue along his teeth. "Francesca," he adds, nodding to acknowledge Frankie.

She somehow manages to frown at him with her mouth still full, and keeps her priorities—namely, devouring her latke—in order.

"How *are* you?" I ask, trying to think if I've seen Trevor since we graduated. He was the class treasurer to my class secretary for all four years of high school, so we spent a lot of time together, and it's honestly really nice to see his face after all this time.

"Well, I'm working with my dad, running the business side

of his construction company. Bought a house about a year ago, been fixing that up slowly. But who cares how I am? Nothing too interesting to report. How are *you*, Miss Big Apple?"

I would roll my eyes if literally any other person said that to me, but Trevor is so genuine and cheery that I have to let it slide and not fall prey to the jaded New Yorker I've become.

I start to open my mouth when I see two hands clasp Trevor's shoulders. Trevor looks at me apologetically, but my eyes are fixated on the face behind his.

"Henry motherfucking Cole!" Trevor exclaims.

He grabs Henry and wraps him into a hug. None of that handshake/shoulder-bump/one-pat nonsense. This is a full, sincere, arms-wrapped-diagonally-around-each-other hug that reeks of familiarity and fondness.

Of course they're hugging. Trevor is Henry's Frankie. His best friend. Has been since Trevor moved to Laketon in eighth grade.

A best friendship that long outlasted ours.

The only updates I've seen of Henry since high school are from Trevor's Instagram. They seem to hang out a few times a year, presumably whenever Henry is in town. I've seen them cheersing at a distillery in the city, dressed up at a fundraiser for our high school's baseball team, faces pressed together in the close way you only have with people from your youth.

In a few moments of weakness, I've clicked on his tagged name—careful to never like the photos, but just to see Henry's own page, which I do not follow. Last I checked, he hadn't posted anything since college, and even then, his profile was sparse. His tagged pictures aren't much more revealing. The most recent one was a black-and-white shot in profile with the Hollywood sign out of focus in the background (which I will begrudgingly admit was a gorgeous photograph) from two years ago.

I forcibly shake the memory of his sharp gaze captured on film out of my head.

When the two men separate, Henry's eyes fall to me, narrowing.

"Norah," he says, his voice laced with disdain, but Trevor does not take note of his friend's demeanor.

"I didn't think you were gonna deign to come tonight, man!" Trevor pats Henry on the back. "It's good to see you."

"I was promised some world-famous latkes," Henry replies, looking right at me.

"I made no such promises." I shake my head, wanting to make that exceedingly clear. "I simply told you where the latkes would be."

"Nor, they're so fucking good," Frankie says, finishing her last bite.

I feel a sense of pride, this being the first time I attempted them myself. Despite the oil setback and the infuriating neighbor who won't leave me be, I did it.

"Come find me later," I say, squeezing Trevor's arm and averting Henry's gaze. The last thing I want is to be stuck in another conversation with Henry. "I know you're not drinking but I could certainly use something strong." I take Frankie's hand and drag her over to the bar.

"Can I get a whiskey ginger, please?" I ask the bartender. She nods, looking to Frankie as she starts to pour my drink.

"I'll have a club soda with lime. But freshly cut. Not one of the ones that have been sitting out, touching everything, for hours." The bartender gives her a look. "I know you have plenty, I approved the budget."

My drink appears in front of me, and as I start to back away from the bar, I smack right into a classmate I can't even place anymore.

Why does everyone I encounter from this town insist on spilling my drinks?

Luckily, the golden mixture splashes onto the floor instead of my person, though I wouldn't have been mad if it had landed on the woman's pale pink sweaterdress, if I'm being honest. When she just shrugs, I briefly consider not-so-accidentally pouring the remaining half of my drink on her shoes, but as soon as the thought enters my mind, I yell at myself because *hello, I'm an adult.*

This town really brings out the worst in me.

Frankie looks between me and our former classmate who I still can't remember, her gray-green eyes wide.

"Bathroom. Now." I grab her wrist and pull her toward the restroom.

"You gotta stop dragging me around, Nor. You're gonna leave marks," she says once we're inside, rubbing her wrist.

"I'm sorry, it's all just too much. I don't think I can do this."

Frankie places her drink on the sink and faces me, putting her hands on my shoulders. "You don't have to talk to Henry. You don't have to talk to anyone you don't want to. You got out, *Miss Big Apple.* That's going to be fascinating enough for most of our classmates who've never even left our zip code. Plus, Trevor was definitely checking you out."

"Why do you keep thinking everyone is hitting on me tonight?"

"Because you look fucking hot! And it's obvious. Look, I love you, and I think any boy would have been lucky to have you back then, but I mean, come on." Frankie takes my hand

and twirls me around. "Back then, you looked angry all the time and were all frizzy. You figured it out. Enjoy it."

I sigh, giving my friend a look, knowing she's won.

"I'll go distract Henry because I'm the best fucking friend on the planet, and you keep talking to Trevor."

"Fine, but don't act like hanging out with Henry is this great sacrifice for you," I say, giving Frankie a once-over. "I know you can't stand Trevor. Maybe I'm the one helping you out here."

Frankie rolls her eyes, leaning her elbows back on the edge of the sink. "He's just so much. Like a ray of fucking sunshine's bursting out of his ass at all times. He still won't call me Frankie either, even after all this time. You know I can't stand being full-named. He's a ridiculous excuse for a person. No one is that cheery. But by all means, if it's working for you." My best friend wiggles her dark, borderline severe eyebrows at me.

When we emerge from the bathroom, I see Trevor and Henry at the bar. Trevor turns around with fingers full of shot glasses. He gives me a head nod and we walk over to join them.

"I was just looking for you ladies," Trevor says, genuinely happy to see us. "Fancy a shot of Jameson?"

I eye the brown liquid in those tiny monogrammed glasses. I'm not a girl who does shots. I like mixers, and too much ice, and sipping slowly through a straw. I don't like the reminder of throwing back cough medicine when I was a kid. But Frankie raises her eyebrow at me, a clear challenge, so I extract one of the glasses from between Trevor's fingers. His hands are large and rough, like he could toss me around.

Is that half a whiskey ginger already getting to me?

He raises the glasses for us all to cheers. I see Henry, eyes boring through me, as I toss back the shot. It burns my throat, and I can't help but cough as it goes down. A very cool-girl look, I'm sure. I blink open my watering eyes, and Frankie hands me her shot as well.

"Bottoms up, Nor. It's party time."

I down the second shot and my whole body shivers in response. Trevor's eyes twinkle as he smiles down at me. Henry gives me a look like he's never been more appalled by anything in his life.

Who fucking cares what he thinks about me?

And that's when I hear the infamous electric guitar opening of "Mr. Brightside." People start to gather, singing along to the riff. I grab Trevor by the sleeve. "Come dance with me," I say as I lead him into the crowd of our classmates, leaving Henry's obvious sneer far behind me.

Chapter 7

I WAS SUCH an innocent teenager. My friends and I were nowhere near cool enough to drink, save for that one night on our New York trip senior year that we don't talk about. After we graduated, while the rest of our classmates rented houses on the waterfront and spent a week being blackout drunk, my friends and I had a wholesome camping trip.

Blinking awake, parched, a dull pounding in my head the next morning is the first time I wake up hungover in my childhood bedroom. The bright pink walls feel like they've been waiting years to mock me like this. I fumble around for my phone to check the time, shocked to see it's nearly eleven a.m., and notice five missed calls from Hannah with no accompanying texts.

Shit.

She knows the effect this many missed calls has on me. She knows the panic it will cause, so it must be something serious.

I chug a glass of water that I discover next to my bed as I dial her back.

"Have you guys left yet?" Hannah asks, answering on the first ring.

"Just about!" I lie, gulping down the rest of the glass. I look out the window toward Henry's house. It's completely dark. I grab a bag and start indiscriminately throwing things inside. For having received my suitcase less than twenty-four hours ago, this room somehow looks more lived in now than my parents would have ever allowed while I was still a resident.

"You have to hurry up and get here," Hannah says, her voice dropping slightly. "Something big is happening."

I stop, clutching a pair of long underwear. "Big how?"

"Look, I'm not supposed to know, but—" She pauses for dramatic effect. She's enjoying this. "I found a ring in Mom's bag! I was looking for some Tylenol, and it was right there!" No way was it *right there*. I know that much. Hannah knows she's not fooling anyone. "She's going to ask Kristine to marry her!" Hannah's whisper cannot contain her excitement.

I hear shuffling in the background as Mom comes to the phone.

"I wanted to tell you once you were here. Your sister wasn't supposed to know yet either." Mom pauses, testing the waters. "And before you say it's too fast, I want you to remember that I've known Kristine Cole for over twenty years. And when it's right, it's right."

Hearing the love in my mom's voice seems to melt away my hangover. "I'm so happy for you, Mom. Dad would have been too. He always thought Kristine was the coolest."

I feel Mom beaming on the other end of the phone.

"Now get in the car and join us! There's a storm coming in tonight. I don't want you kids getting stuck in that."

I promise Mom that we'll be there soon, and then hang up.

As I scoop up last night's outfit from the floor and put it in the hamper, a hazy memory returns from the evening. I open my phone back up and see a slew of messages I barely remember between me and Rob, culminating in my final text: We're not gonna be together!! That's not what this was. I'm sorry!!!

Not my most tactful or gentle severing of ties, but the lack of response from him tells me he finally got the message, literally and figuratively.

I take a quick but necessary shower, trying to rid myself of the guilt about how poorly I handled things with Rob. I pile my dark curls into a haphazard bun on the top of my head, get dressed as fast as I can, and reluctantly go next door.

I knock, almost knowing that the attempt will be futile. I peek into the window and can see Henry, still dressed from last night, passed the fuck out on the couch. *At least Drunk Norah got herself into pajamas and her bed,* I think, feeling a small sense of superiority. I rap on the window loudly and see Henry spring up in a panic, then immediately regret his decisions from last night. He blinks a few times at me through the window, looking disoriented, then gestures for me to meet him at the door.

"What?" he grumbles, throwing the door open.

"We have to go," I reply.

"What?" He runs a hand through his disheveled hair. He's always so well put together, but seeing him in this unfamiliar way brings me a bit of glee.

"Oh, you are hungover!"

Henry rolls his eyes at me but steps aside and lets me into the house. I go to the kitchen and start setting up a pot of coffee to brew. Henry slowly follows me.

"Go shower." I turn around to fill up the water basin, and feel his eyes on me. "You smell like a distillery rotted," I say without even turning around.

I hear him sigh, and that one step that Kristine always refused to fix creaks as he concedes and heads upstairs. I don't turn around until I know he's gone.

Once the coffee is brewed, I find two mugs and fill them to the brim. I carefully go up the stairs, pausing when I reach his room, the door still halfway open. Panic washes over me as the memory of the last time I was up here assaults my brain and my heart. But there's no time for that. I take a deep breath, then knock on the frame with my elbow.

"Hey, Henry? Are you decent? I brought you some coffee." The shower is running in the adjoining bathroom. I peer around and see that luckily, that door is shut. I place his coffee mug on the nightstand and take a sip of my own, mostly as an excuse to drink in this space that was once so familiar.

Out of the corner of my eye, I see an old bulletin board full of pictures. I remember this. I start to move toward it, drawn to a photo in the corner, partially obscured by others placed on top of it. That unmistakable purple satin. One hand too high on my waist.

It's us.

The same photo I saw in my bat mitzvah album.

Before I can look any closer, I hear the shower turn off and quickly announce myself again. "I'm in here. I brought coffee. I can step out if you need a minute."

"It's fine," he mutters through the door.

"You really need to pack," I call back, spotting his suitcase. I put down my mug and heave the suitcase onto the bed with a thud.

"Don't go through my stuff," he orders from the bathroom, but I disregard it.

"I'm helping," I say. "I'm the queen of a quick turnaround." I unzip the suitcase and throw it open. It's already packed in a perfectly Type A fashion, soft clothing rolled up and organized in even columns. This shouldn't surprise me but somehow it does.

"I told you not to go through my stuff," he says, coming up behind me, and the gruffness in his voice makes me jump.

I spin around and feel my whole body flush, not just from the steam coming out of the now open bathroom, but because Henry Cole is standing inches away from me in nothing but a towel wrapped low around his waist. And he looks better than I even assumed from that fitted white button-down on the plane, all lean muscle and olive skin.

"Eyes up here," he says, and my gaze flits up to meet his, gold flecks dancing almost playfully in a sea of blue. He cocks an eyebrow at me, and I swivel back to the suitcase, unable to stand to look at him for another second.

"Looks like you're good to go!" *Shit.* "I mean, as far as packing is concerned."

"Sure, Gold." I detect a hint of a smile as he says my last name, though I don't dare look back to see.

"Ugh, just get dressed already. Coffee's on the nightstand. I'll grab my bag and meet you back here in ten." I shuffle out, continuing to avoid eye contact.

The bite of cold air is a welcome relief as I rush out of Henry's house and back to my own. *What the hell was that?*

AS IF I hadn't had a difficult enough time so far escaping the nostalgia of home, Kristine still has the same old CR-V from when we were teenagers, and that's what Henry is currently driving. When I first got into the car, I had to physically fight the urge to kick off my shoes and put my feet up on the dash like I used to do. Before. When we had that kind of familiarity and I knew I was well within my rights because this was my seat. Permanent shotgun.

The last time I was in this car was the worst day of my entire life.

We spend the first two hours of the drive mostly in silence. He keeps glancing over at me, so I throw all of my focus into the liner notes of an old Ed Sheeran CD that I remember he bought in high school because he couldn't connect his phone to the CR-V's speakers.

"We can play the album if you want," he says finally. "You can stop pretending to read the whole damn thing."

My eyes meet his, just briefly, and I tense. Whether it's from being called out or from the way he's looking at me, I'm not sure.

When I don't respond, he shakes his head and slaps on the radio, scrolling with a dial until he hears music. Anything to end the silence, I guess. We come into the middle of the bridge of "Drops of Jupiter."

I can't help but laugh. "Oh my God. I can't hear this song without thinking about junior year homecoming."

This song played at every school dance, despite being basically as old as we were, until the student government finally voted to ban it after homecoming our junior year. The vote made the local paper.

"Those dances were always a nightmare," Henry agrees.

Caught up in the nostalgia of the song, and perhaps forgetting who I'm sitting next to, I say, "That night, Ashley Majors told me she wanted to dance with you. So I walked up and tapped you on the shoulder and told you that."

Henry is quiet, so I continue.

"And you looked at me and were like, *Are you being sarcastic or serious?*"

"I remember," he says quietly.

"I guess maybe you had a crush on her or something."

It's not a question, but he replies anyway. "I did not have a crush on Ashley Majors," he says, and it feels almost pointed.

He's giving me that look again, the one that makes me feel like surely he must think I'm an idiot.

"Why are you looking at me like that?" I ask, the forced proximity making me feel bolder somehow.

"I'm not looking at you."

"You were."

"My eyes are on the road."

Liar.

"You were looking at me weird."

"It's nothing," he says, the word feeling loaded on his lips. He sighs. "I just thought . . ." Henry stops himself. Now he's definitely looking at me. "I thought we could use this time to talk."

"And what would you like to talk about?" I ask, but as soon as the words leave my mouth, I already know.

When he says, "The New York trip, senior year," my stomach sinks in confirmation.

I jump in with a quick "Oh, I don't want to talk about that."

"We've got hours in this car, just us. It's as good a time as any. We have to talk about it at some point."

"We really, really don't," I reply.

"We're going to be in each other's lives now, whether you

like it or not. This thing between my mom and yours is serious."

He doesn't even know how serious. But he's right. The issue isn't going away. This is no longer some faded memory from when we were seventeen. We'll see each other at holidays, family gatherings. Going forward, his presence will be the new normal.

But under no circumstances do I want to relive that period in time. I can't. I feel cornered, panicked, stuck.

"Can't we pretend it never happened? Just breeze right on past all of that?"

"Is that what you think you've been doing for the last few days?"

No, it's absolutely not. As much as I'd like to have let go of everything, I haven't. But I can't give him that satisfaction. I can't even look at him, so I stare at his hands on the steering wheel, knuckles turning white as his grip tightens the more silence I let linger in the car.

I see brake lights from the car in front of us, and Henry eases to a stop. Some cars honk around us, but all the lanes have skidded to a halt.

"Forget it." It's a whisper I might not have even been meant to hear amid the honking.

I tuck my knees under my body, hugging my arms close into my chest. I turn away from him to face out of my window, eyes burning hot, but I can't let him see that I'm upset.

At first, I think it's just my vision blurred from the tears I'm trying to suck back up into my eyes.

But then it starts to pick up, and I think about the call with my mom.

The storm.

Snowflakes fall at an alarming rate as freezing rain starts to beat against the roof of the car. Since we're not moving, Henry hasn't hit the windshield wipers yet, allowing the flakes to smear the red reflection of the brake lights in front of us.

We both sigh almost in unison, and I would make a joke but neither of us is in a place for that.

Shit.

ANOTHER HOUR OF silence, and we've hardly inched along at all. The snow sticks to the road, collecting on the hood of the barely moving car. None of this is good.

Henry takes another deep breath and lets out a haggard sigh. "If we'd gotten an earlier start, we wouldn't be in this mess."

It catches me off guard. I'd gotten used to the quiet hum of the car.

He looks at me pointedly, as if this is my fault, his brows furrowed.

"Who's the one who slept in?" I counter, because the truth of why we left late is so blatantly clear to me.

"Who's the one who insisted we go to the stupid reunion and get so intoxicated we slept through an alarm? I haven't missed an alarm since . . ." He trails off. The memory of one crucial alarm that never sounded hangs heavy between us. "I usually wake up three minutes before it goes off. My internal clock was impeccable before you came along."

I stare at him for a moment. He looks nervously at me, then quickly glances back to the road, as if suddenly we'll be moving again at a normal speed, getting the fuck out of here.

"I didn't insist you go last night," I say slowly, softly. "I didn't even invite you. I went. With Frankie. I just mentioned latkes and you were drawn to them. Look, my family latke recipe is perfect. I get it. I can't blame you for thinking the same." I pause, quietly fuming that he thinks this is all somehow my fault. "But that's on you. Not on me. Or my latkes."

"Norah, we—" he starts, but I cut him off, that one word after my name blistering through me.

"There is no *we* in this scenario. There was never a *we* in any past, present, or future scenario." I don't know why I say *future*, but I'm carried away by the heat of my fury at this man.

He stares straight ahead. "I didn't have to stay the extra night."

"You were working," I point out, repeating what Mom and Kristine told me.

"Did it look like I was working when you barged into my house, covered in flour, looking so goddamn—" He stops himself, even though I'm desperate to hear him finish that sentence. Messy? Disgusting? Anything to further fuel this anger I'm feeling toward him right now. But he refocuses. "I could have gone with them yesterday, but I was instructed to wait. For you. Because Sara was worried about you driving since you don't have a car in New York."

My sister's goodbye rings in my ears. *No one trusts you to drive to Great Blue Lodge yourself.* A validation of his statement that I didn't want to hear, so I deflect.

"What, and you do?"

"Of course I do."

Somehow this admission doesn't surprise me, but it does make me angrier. True, I haven't had a car in years—because who has a car in the city? But I still have my license. I rent cars when I need to. I don't like the implication of any of this, that I am beholden to Henry Cole for some gentlemanly duty I didn't even realize was happening.

So I decide not to address any of that.

"I know how to drive. I definitely drove you to school plenty of times before—" I catch myself. *Before everything went to shit. Before it became unbearable to be in a confined space with you. Before you hurt me.* "I can prove it," I say instead. I unbuckle my seat belt and gesture for us to switch seats.

Henry looks so pained right now that it's almost comical. He clearly doesn't have the energy to fight me on this. The traffic is at a standstill anyway, so he throws the car into park and opens the driver's-side door. I follow his lead, running around the front of the car to the driver's seat.

I slam the door closed and pat down the snowflakes that fell into my mess of curls. In the seconds it takes to switch seats, we're somehow both soaked. I adjust the seat all the way up, silently marveling at how a human could possibly take up so much more space in this car than I do, and adjust the mirrors. I'm shivering so much I can't tell if he is too, or if it's all just my own shaking. He reaches a long arm into the backseat and offers me a blanket, but I tell him I'm fine. The idea of him wrapping me in a blanket, of him helping me in any way at this point, makes me want to slam his mother's poor old CR-V into the Benz in front of us.

As I'm picturing this, the Benz eases off its brakes and starts to move. I gasp, as if the sheer magic of me now being in control of this car has forced the universe to get us out of this mess. As we start to move, I see what's happening. Workers in reflective vests are gesturing. The road is closed, and we're being put on a detour.

"This is the only way to get to Great Blue Lodge," Henry

states flatly as we exit the interstate. He pulls out his phone and starts trying to map another option.

I follow the hundreds of other cars, all along the same unhelpful route, for a while as Henry frantically looks for another way. In the time that he's been looking down at his phone, the snow has really picked up. I'd forgotten how New York snow and Illinois snow are two entirely different beasts, and I definitely haven't driven in a storm like this since I left the Midwest. It's getting hard for me to see anything but taillights, but I don't want to give him the satisfaction of having been right about me.

"You didn't have to prove anything," he says finally.

I feel his eyes on me and wonder what gave it away. Was it that my knuckles were the same color as the falling snow? The grimace I could feel even in my neck?

"It's fine," I say, though it's clearly not.

"Maybe we should pull over," he suggests.

"I'm fine," I repeat, needing to get out of this car, out of this situation, away from him.

It's only then that I realize how dark the sky has gotten. I should have known, since I'm pretty sure today is the winter solstice, but somehow the early sunset caught me off guard. I suck in a shallow breath, trying to stay calm.

"You're doing great," he says, which is such a lie I can't even hold in the scoff that forms low in my chest. "But next time you can, maybe we should pull over."

I don't say anything, and I certainly don't dare to look at him, so I just continue on. I don't know how long it is, or how far I've gotten, when I see the lights. A bed-and-breakfast.

"Pull over." This time, the command in his voice forces

something in my body to comply, because when I can, I flip on my blinker. "We'll switch in the parking lot, where it's safe."

I nod and turn into the lot.

Relief washes over me when I finally put the car in park. My hands flex off the wheel, regaining blood flow.

"You're okay," he says gently. "You did great."

I still know it's a lie but something in me softens. Instead of brushing it off, I just look over at him, my head pressed into the headrest. He gives me a smile that feels almost apologetic, but we don't dare say anything more.

When I feel like I can move, I say, "Okay," and he nods. I get out of the car and am almost immediately smacked into the door. The wind has picked up, and the swirls of white now make it nearly impossible to see more than a foot ahead.

"Henry?" I call out. I hear him trudging toward me but can only see his face once it's in arm's reach.

"We can't keep going in this. It's not safe. Who knows if we'll even be able to reach the lodge with all the road closures."

"So what are we supposed to do?" I ask, the wind whipping my cheeks raw.

He points up ahead, where I can just barely make out some of the letters of a neon *VACANCY* sign flickering nearby.

He must be kidding. I give him a look, but he just shrugs. "What else can we do?"

Chapter 8

WE SPEND TOO long debating outside in the storm, so when we finally trudge into the bed-and-breakfast, we are both soaked all over again. I immediately feel guilty when I look around. It's rustic and warm but trying to pass itself off as Victorian, with large red parlor chairs set up around a lit fireplace, and shelves of books covering the length of the two walls I can see. There's a staircase of dark wood at the center of the room, and a long hallway off to the side, covered in fresh patterned wallpaper.

Henry takes charge. He plasters on a smile I have yet to see directed toward me and walks right up to the older woman sitting behind what looks like a large converted bar. She smiles back at him.

"Hi there, good evening," he says warmly. "We don't have a reservation, as I'm sure you could guess, but I was wondering if you had any rooms available?"

"Two rooms?" I pipe in.

The woman, who we learn is named Alice and has lived

here with her husband (before he passed) for over forty years, looks through a large leather book, flipping through pages with handwritten notes.

Of course this is all low-tech. Of course there's no computer system.

Of course there's only one room.

I knew this was the answer before she even announced it. This must be my punishment for something I've done to someone who wielded a lot of pull with a higher power.

"The storm brought in a lot of stragglers," Alice explains.

We're lucky to have gotten the last room.

Lucky.

To spend a night in a room with Henry Cole.

I briefly consider sleeping in the CR-V.

As if Henry can sense what I'm thinking somehow, his head swoops down so his lips are close to my ear. "You'll either freeze to death, or the car battery will die, or both. Let's go."

"You kids must be starving," Alice says as Henry silently takes my hefty duffel bag out of my hands and places it on top of his suitcase. "There's plenty in the kitchen and pantry. Feel free to help yourself. We only ask that you clean up afterward. No dirty pans in the sink, please."

"Of course," Henry says, nodding solemnly before heading down the hall with our bags.

I trail behind him, taking everything in.

Alice told us each room was named for a plant that was indigenous to the area, and as we pass Coneflower, Wild Bergamot, and Elderberry, I am beginning to see how the Swamp Milkweed room was the only vacant one.

Henry seems so confident as he leads us up the grand staircase, and then down the hall to our room, easily turning the brass key and swinging the door open. He stops suddenly at the entryway, and I collide into his back.

"Dude, come on," I say, sliding past him, until I see what caught him so off guard, and suddenly I'm frozen too.

In the center of the room, one queen bed, with a gothic wooden headboard and deep purple quilts. Or maybe it's a full-size. Fuck, that's even worse.

I knew sharing a small space would be a nightmare, but with this new issue quite literally right in front of me, the walls feel like they're closing in. We had sleepovers when we were little, sure, but this one bed taunts me with the intimacy of the situation.

"We should call our moms and let them know what happened," I think I hear Henry say, but I still can't stop staring at the bed. My eyes roam around the small room, desperate for an alternative. They land on a Victorian chair in the corner. That will have to do. I grab a pillow off the bed and place it on the chair. Henry's gaze follows me, a question he doesn't verbalize lingering.

I need to get out of this room.

"I'm going to take a shower and try to get the chill out of my bones," I say to him, turning to my bag so he doesn't see me mouth *What the fuck?* to myself over my word choices. Immediately overwhelmed, I wind up taking my entire duffel into the adjoining bathroom with me, throwing it on the floor and making sure to lock the door behind me.

I strip layers of damp clothing off my body, the clammy chill still latched onto my skin. The shower takes forever to heat up, and I keep looking to the door handle, turned to its locked position. The idea that Henry is on the other side of this wall, knowing I'm naked, is absolutely too much for me to process. I can hear his muffled voice, probably on the phone with Kristine now. I can't hear what he's saying, but I can tell it's the same soft tone he used to tell me I was doing great when I nearly got us killed driving in the snow not even thirty minutes ago. I shudder and finally step into the shower, letting all of these confusing thoughts run out of my head and out of my body.

WHEN I EMERGE from the bathroom, wearing leggings and a cozy gray sweater, I see that Henry has also changed out of his wet clothes and is rummaging through his suitcase.

"All yours," I say, and he nods, only half acknowledging me as his search through his suitcase becomes more frantic.

"Shit, I forgot my steamer," he says, finally looking at me with dismay. He walks over to the closet, where I now notice he's hung a garment bag. He unzips it and begins smoothing out the contents—a full deep blue suit, different from the navy one I saw him traveling in. Brighter. He's running his hands over the fabric in such a frenzied manner, he must know that he's making it worse.

Is Henry . . . in a tizzy?

"What do you need a suit for?" I ask tentatively. "We're on vacation. Lighten up."

"I haven't seen my mom this happy in over a decade," Henry says, still turned toward the suit.

"Me neither," I admit. "Not since before Dad died."

I see Henry's shoulders loosen up a bit, the muscles in his back retracting.

"And look, she told me to bring a suit for the, uh . . ." He pauses. Runs a hand through his hair, then grips the back of his neck.

"The what? Do I need something nice to wear? I don't have

anything fancy with me. Mom didn't say anything about needing—"

He spins around to face me. "No, I . . . uh. Shit. Never mind."

"Henry, what's the deal with the suit?"

He doesn't respond, his face growing red. He won't meet my eyes.

"We're stuck together at this inn for the next"—I glance at the clock on the wall—"sixteen hours minimum. I'll get it out of you eventually, so it would be great to save us both the anguish and just tell me now."

He sighs. "I need a suit because my mom is going to ask Sara to marry her."

I can't hide my smile, whereas he looks absolutely tortured.

"She made me promise not to tell anyone. Please don't ruin the surprise. I know I'm the last person you'd want to help, but please, Norah."

"As long as you don't tell Kristine that my mom has the same plan," I counter, and I swear his knees nearly buckle with relief.

"I thought I was fucked," he says with a carefree smile.

"I mean, you are, but not about that," I reply as sincerely as I can. "You still don't have a steamer."

He rolls his eyes at me, but then something else flashes across his face. "Look, I know you and I . . ."

"Can't stand each other?" I fill in.

"Sure. That. But maybe we can play nice for the holidays. For our moms."

I don't hate this idea. "A temporary truce wouldn't be a bad idea considering this . . . new development."

"I just want to make this trip as perfect for them as possible."

I nod. "The most romantic double proposal. We can call it"—I pause, racking my brain—"Operation Latke."

"Why the hell would we call it that?"

"Because latkes are the only thing we can agree on without drawing suspicion."

He looks at me intently, his blue eyes searching my face like I'm a mystery he can't crack.

"Are you starving?" he asks. "All of a sudden, I'm starving."

"Alice did say we can use the kitchen."

Henry nods, almost as if he's telling himself yes, and then I follow him out of our room and down the stairs.

Even though Alice told us the B&B was fully booked, we don't see or hear any other humans. It's almost like this whole place magically appeared just for us.

We enter the kitchen, which looks like it got stuck in the 1970s, in contrast with the more Victorian design of the rest of the B&B. Aging yellow appliances. Nearly orange wood—out of style in any era. Henry starts to survey the fridge, and I find my way into the pantry. I spot a giant container of pretzel rods and stand on my very tiptoes to try to grab it. My fingers just miss a solid grip, and the canister comes crashing down. I yelp as I try to grab for it.

"Everything okay in there?" Henry asks.

"Just grabbing some pretzels," I say, collecting myself.

I twist off the lid and begin to chomp on a pretzel rod. Henry opens a cabinet, pulling down a ceramic mug. He pours something in, back still turned to me, obstructing my view, then places the mug in front of me on the kitchen island. I finish chewing slowly and sniff the contents, suspicious.

The sugary bite of apple juice hits, and I'm immediately six years old again.

"I remember how you liked to dip your pretzels," he says quietly, turning back to the fridge so I can't see his face.

"When I was a kid," I reply, not sure where either of us is going with this.

"Weirdo," he says, back still to me, but I can almost see the smirk on his face.

I take another pretzel rod out and swirl it around in the juice-filled mug. I can't believe he remembered that when I barely even did. Not until the sense memory hit me like a ton of bricks.

Sitting up in the tree house my dad built one summer, and one summer only. "Never again," he said with determination, even though Hannah and I knew we could probably wear him down fairly easily. Spending hours up there with Henry, sprawled out on our stomachs, knees bent, feet crossed in the air. I had gotten a Shel Silverstein book of poems. Maybe *Where the Sidewalk Ends*? I read every single one aloud to Henry, our only sustenance being pretzels and apple juice. I tried desperately to convince him that this was a winning combo, but he just crinkled up his nose at me, refusing to take my word for it. Refusing to even taste it and see for himself. In Henry's mind, pretzels were for eating and juice was for drinking, separately, always. Stubborn boy.

I take the pretzel out of the mug, deeming it sufficiently intermingled, and hold the rod up to him. "You never did try it," I say in my most angelic voice.

He turns back to me, nose crinkling up in the same way I remembered. His eyes stutter between my hand and my face, and for a second, I feel him lean into me. I'm so distracted by the thought that he might eat this pretzel out of my hand, the impending, and seemingly unprompted, flirtation of it all, that I jump when he grabs the dry end of the rod from me. His fingers brush lightly against mine for the briefest moment before he takes a bite, and somehow, that touch feels even more intimate.

He mulls it over, chewing slowly. "Not terrible," he finally concedes, two decades too late.

I cannot hide my glee at this win, which is good because it masks how fast my heart is still racing from the proximity of his mouth to my hand.

"So what are you making me?" I ask, gesturing to the fridge he's been exploring so thoroughly.

"Check the pantry for tortilla chips."

I follow the order, emerging with an unopened bag of blue corn chips. "Got 'em," I say to his shape behind the refrigerator door.

"Nachos it is," he replies, turning on the oven.

"Who uses an oven for nachos?" I ask. "Isn't that what microwaves were made for?"

"If you want soggy chips, go right ahead." He gestures to a microwave built into the wall that's definitely older than we are.

I must make a face.

"That's what I thought," he says confidently, and turns to the sink to rinse the bell pepper in his hand. A bell pepper!

"This is not what I was envisioning when you said nachos," I admit, eyes falling to the counter where, in addition to the bell pepper, he's pulled out an onion, cilantro, a jalapeño, a block of cheese, and a couple eggs.

"Don't worry, I would never put beans in this. I know you."

I know you.

The words burn in the air. Does he? Sure, he once knew me better than almost anyone else.

When we were little, he knew that the one surefire way to make me laugh when I was having a bad day was to let me knock him down from the swings, so he would stand in front of me as I pushed higher and higher, until my legs flew out, hitting his little body with my feet. He would fall to the ground with such a big smile as I howled with laughter.

I wonder if he remembers that too.

Henry dries off the bell pepper and begins to chop it.

I need to take a walk, but I don't want him to know the way he's affecting me, so I wander back into the pantry, looking for any excuse to put more distance between us.

Is Henry fucking with me? Trying to get under my skin? What is his game here?

Once I get my breathing back to a normal pace, my eyes fall on a rack of magnum-sized bottles of wine, surely a bulk buy from Costco for happy hour or the like.

But tonight, it's for me. I need to calm my nerves, quell whatever is brewing inside me. I grab a giant bottle by the neck, and reemerge from the pantry.

I must have been hiding in there longer than I thought because somehow the tray is already in the oven, and I can smell scrambled eggs on the stovetop.

I watch him stir the eggs in a pan, a dish towel over his shoulder, looking so . . . domestic. A Henry Cole who cooks is so far from the image I had of that buttoned-up man in the city, ordering Postmates every night.

He glances up at me, then sees the wine I've also commandeered, and raises an eyebrow.

"What? Alice said to make ourselves feel at home."

He looks at me like he wants to say something. I know that look. It's the one he gave me at baggage claim, in the car, and a million other times. Before. Whenever I did something stupid.

"Stop looking at me," I tell him.

"I'm not looking at you."

"I remember that face. It's the same one you used to give me when we were partnered up for chem lab. I know you're judging me."

"This is not my judgment face," he says, turning off the heat on the stovetop.

"Yeah, then what kind of face is it?" I ask.

He moves the pan filled with the fluffiest scrambled eggs I've ever seen to a wooden trivet, and then he stares straight into me. His pale blue eyes have turned almost oceanic. Maybe it's just the lighting. I feel my body flush at this prolonged eye contact. I'm too close to the oven, I assure myself, as his long dark lashes flutter ever so slightly.

"Wanna grab two glasses for all that wine, or is your plan to just drink the entire thing yourself, straight from the bottle?" he asks, breaking the silence.

"See, you *were* judging me!" I exclaim, practically grateful to be arguing with him again. The silence was . . . charged?

"I can wholeheartedly confirm that I am not judging you." The timer on his phone goes off and Henry uses a towel to remove the baking sheet from the oven. The competent gleam in his eyes makes my stomach flip, and I reason that I must be hungrier than I thought if my mind is playing tricks on me like this.

WE TAKE THE breakfast nachos and the wine back to our room, sitting on the floor as we dive in. I rip open two Lactaid pills, and I feel instantly better once I'm eating. Everything in the kitchen was just a fluke. Hangriness is definitely a thing, and clearly hunger makes you feel things that aren't real.

That's all that was.

"David, uh," Henry says, slowly testing the waters.

It's so weird to hear him say my dad's name. Mom and Hannah are the only people I really ever talk about him with, and with them, he's always just *Dad*. I look up at Henry, taking a sip of wine, desperate to hear what he has to say.

"David," he starts again, "taught me how to make scrambled eggs."

My eyes search his face for further explanation.

"I was maybe eleven or twelve," he continues. "David came back from a run and saw me sitting on the porch, waiting for you to come back from dance class, I think. He invited me inside, said he was gonna cook some food. Asked if I knew how to make eggs."

Henry is looking down at his plate, but I can tell he's smiling.

"Of course I didn't know how to make eggs, I didn't know anything. He took out the whole carton and cracked an egg one-handed. I couldn't believe it. He tried to show me, but I dropped the first one right on the floor. *No problem, Hen*, he said to me. He wasn't mad. He just wiped it up and we tried again. *Let's start with the basics. One simple crack, and then two thumbs open it up.* When that one actually made it into the bowl with his perfectly cracked one, he showed me how to whisk them together, how much to season them. Then he made sure I watched carefully as he moved the spatula around, handing it over to me to finish up. *Now you've got yourself a true staple in the kitchen*, he said to me when we were finished."

Henry finally looks up at me.

"He was the best," he says simply. "I think about him every time I make breakfast." There's a twinge of regret, of deep hurt in his voice as he clears his throat.

Henry and Kristine were a complete family unit. She picked

out the sperm donor from a giant binder, and that was that. She wanted a kid, and after she broke up with a serious girlfriend, she decided she would make her dreams of a family happen with or without a partner. Kristine and Henry were always a team, and I knew he never felt anything lacking. But hearing him talk about my dad in such a warm and loving way makes me feel a pull in my sternum.

Our friendship ended the day my dad died. I avoided Henry at the funeral and shiva for my own sake. I'm the one who lost her dad; I never thought about how it might have affected Henry. But now the pain is so clearly etched on his face. Another person who misses him like I do.

"I didn't know that," I say quietly, because it's all I can muster. My dad's been gone for nine years. I never thought I was going to get a new story about him this far down the road. A new thing to know about him. Henry's given me a gift. I feel a swell, too much all at once. I can't crack myself open and be vulnerable with him like this. I can't handle it.

"About that day—" Henry starts, but he must see the panic on my face.

It's dangerous to be this familiar with Henry. I know that.

So I deflect.

"The eggs could use a touch more salt."

I hold my breath, waiting for his reaction, hoping he's giving me permission to change topics. A heavy sigh of relief escapes from me when a huge smile spreads across Henry's face. He shakes his head, and I take another big sip of wine.

"You're impossible," he tells me. But he's still smiling. Over the last few days, I've gotten plenty of smirks from him, but I haven't seen this smile in so long. A faded imprint on my heart. I want to memorize it.

"So tell me what your life is like," I ask, my mind chanting *deflect deflect deflect*.

"My life? I work in commercial real estate. I just moved out of an apartment I lived in with three other guys and into my own place."

"I've already heard all that."

Henry rakes a hand through his hair and stretches his legs out on the floor, his feet almost meeting mine.

"What do you want to know?"

"Do you like living in New York?" It's a surface-level question, but if we're stuck together, I can at least make small talk with him.

"It was always the dream, right?" There's none of the malice I would have assumed from this statement, given our history. "Not too much like the *You've Got Mail* or *When Harry Met Sally* life that we envisioned, though, huh?"

I press my lips into a thin line. It feels risky to dance around our past like this. "Not too much," I echo.

"I like how you can be surrounded by people at any moment and at the same time, no one looks at you twice."

Loneliness drips from his words. Or maybe I'm just reading into it. After that story about my dad, I'm suddenly greedy for every new insight he willingly hands over to me, even though I should know better.

"You like that?"

"I don't know, it's so different from home. It feels exciting, like you could dip into someone's movie moment just by passing them on the street, as an observer, and then you'll never see them again."

So it isn't loneliness after all. Of course Henry isn't lonely. Look at him. He's just doe-eyed about this place where he always wanted to live. "You haven't been there that long, then," I surmise.

"Only a year and a half," he admits.

"It's nice that you can still see the city in such a romantic light."

"You've been out there since college, right?"

I nod, the novelty of what he finds so enchanting having worn off after eight years there. "It's my home now. I don't see myself ever leaving. I guess there is something oddly comforting about being able to weep openly on the subway with no one bothering you."

"Is that a frequent occurrence in your life?" Henry asks, cocking an eyebrow.

I clutch my chest, feigning shock. "You don't cry on the subway?"

"Why do you think I have a car? I'm saving those tears for a parking garage, obviously." The corner of his mouth flicks up, sending a shiver down my spine.

Are Henry and I joking around? Is our temporary truce actually kind of . . . nice?

"Favorite spot in the city?" I ask.

"Look, I know it's cliché, but nothing beats wandering around Central Park. My new place is close, and that's at least nineteen percent of why I moved there."

"One of my favorite places to run if I can find a reason to be in Manhattan," I admit.

He smiles. "Where do you live?"

I break off a stack of chips, playing with a strand of cheese that's starting to congeal. "Oh, just a fun little five-story walk-up in Astoria."

"Is it a shoebox? My last place was a shoebox."

"I prefer to think of it as more of a banker's box, but yes, it's tiny. I've got two roommates but our apartment is rent-controlled, so I can never move."

"Living alone is great, though," Henry tells me, taking another bite of his own. "You don't have to worry about anyone else's dishes. Walk around as clothed or unclothed as you see fit. I can finally be at peace."

"One of my roommates has her boyfriend over constantly," I say, trying not to think about how *unclothed* sends me right back to this morning, a towel wrapped low around his waist. "They take two hour-long showers every day. One in the morning, and one at night. It's impossible."

"They've gotta just be having sex in there, right?"

I feel myself flush as the word *sex* leaves Henry Cole's mouth. Probably from the wine. And the oddity of this boy I've known since I was three years old talking about *sex* of all things. And maybe because the image from hours earlier, his strong chest defined by droplets of water, hasn't successfully left my brain. I blink twice, getting the thoughts out of my head.

"You would think," I exclaim, trying to recover, perhaps a bit overenthusiastic. "But a lot of times one of them is in there alone and they just leave the water on and swap out. I cannot for the life of me find a consistent time to shower. I'm in a constant battle with them over the damn bathroom."

Henry's brow furrows. "That sounds very wasteful."

"Worst part is that her boyfriend only lives like, two blocks away. He has a perfectly good shower so close by. With one of those rainfall showerheads too! Like, hello, I will trade you, sir!"

"My old roommate when I lived in LA—don't get me wrong, he's still a close buddy of mine—but he was always bringing girls home and hooking up in the living room. On my leather sofa."

"At least leather is harder to stain?"

Henry just shakes his head like he's recalling a memory from war. "There are some things that just make you say, *No, Nick, you keep the sofa*."

"That bad?"

He nods, a slight shudder running across his back. "Nowhere near worth the cross-country trek."

"What about you and girls? Or people. I don't want to assume." It slips out the way things tend to around him, or maybe it's the wine I drank too fast.

"Girls," he repeats. "Norah Gold, are you asking about my love life?"

"Love life? Oh God," I laugh, when I really want to say *Tell me about a girl so I can lock whatever nonsense I'm feeling back away for another decade.*

"Do you really want to talk about this?" Henry asks, his words heavy with trepidation.

No, yes, tell me everything.

"I'm about to be your sister," I say, and I swear I see him flinch. "I should know things about you."

"I'm a busy guy. I work long hours. And sure, there have been some women, but . . ."

"Anyone important?"

"Not for a long time."

It hangs in the air for a moment, maybe longer, the wine coursing through our bloodstreams making it impossible to tell.

"And you?" Henry asks eventually.

I shrug. I should have expected it. Never pose a question

you're not prepared to answer yourself. I should have known better.

"There have been some guys. But I'm not great at relationships," I blurt out, the wine acting as a truth serum.

"I don't believe that," he says, looking at me earnestly.

I panic when it gets serious, I could say. Or *I have a hard time trusting*. Or *I bolt before they get the chance to hurt me*.

I could say *I don't need a therapist to tell me that this stems from you*.

Instead, I try to keep it simple. "I'm a runner." And then, for some reason, I add, "I only extended my trip beyond the weekend to avoid a guy I was hooking up with in New York who tried to Girlfriend me."

"You don't like this guy?"

"No," I admit. "He was just . . . there."

Henry looks like he's taking that in. "I was seeing someone back home too," he says finally.

Somehow, I know that *home* means New York to us both, and the realization of our shared childhood dream fulfilled sends a tingle up my spine.

"Didn't work out. It wasn't that serious anyway."

"Smart," I say, trying to shake off the refrain of *home home home* beating along with my heart. "Better to end things now so you don't get stuck in the holiday relationship cycle. You'd be saddled together past Valentine's Day, and no one wants that."

He nods, his face completely unreadable.

"Are you happy?" I ask, trying to change the subject when the silence feels too intimate.

He answers after a beat. "I'd like to be. I'm working on it."

I smile at the honesty.

He taps my foot with his. "What about you?"

"I'm working on it too. Sometimes I feel like I don't know how." I try to offer up another smile, but I know I just look helpless. I know Henry can see through it. I watch his mind churn and before it even happens, I sense that he's decided to move toward me, to comfort me. I stand up abruptly, allowing him the cover to think I didn't clock exactly what he was about to do.

"I should clean these before the cheese gets any more caked on," I say, scooping up the tray and plates, and hurrying off to the kitchen to wash them. "It's a one-woman job since you did all the cooking," I call over my shoulder when he starts to follow.

Always a runner.

I SCRUB THE dishes until they're clean twice over, letting the soap and the hot water prune my fingers, a welcome distraction from everything brewing in that guest room that suddenly feels far too small for both Henry and me to exist in.

When I come back to the room, Henry is lying back across the foot of the bed, staring up at the ceiling, feet firmly planted on the floor.

"I think we should talk about the elephant in the room," he says, sitting up.

"What, how I'm going so hard against traditional gender norms and letting you have the bed?"

His fingers graze the side of the quilt so gently I'm not even sure he knows he did it.

"I meant how you hate me," he says, something behind his icy blue eyes that I can't read.

"I thought we called a truce, Henry. Operation Latke? Plus, you're no fan of mine either," I remind him.

"I never said that." He's not even being defensive, he's just stating a fact, plain as day.

"It's been nine years. You don't have to say it for me to know it's true."

"Norah," he starts, standing up abruptly, but then stopping short. "I never wanted things to be like this. Not now. Not . . ." He trails off.

I look at him, waiting for him to meet my eyes, but he doesn't.

He runs his hand through his hair and down his neck, as if he needs the extra support to look at me. "Not then."

"Then," I repeat.

I can barely process that word, *then*. Before we wrecked each other. There's no other *then* to speak of in our sordid history.

He must feel bad for how it all went down. He's trying to smooth things over now that we're being forced back into each other's lives.

Maybe he missed my friendship. We were such good friends. For so long. Kristine and Henry moved next door when we were three, before Hannah was even born. I can't remember a time when they weren't our neighbors. Dad used to say that I was Hannah's first friend, but that Henry was mine.

It's been so long. The last thing I want is to reopen old wounds.

"Look, we don't have to talk about that," I tell him. I will power through the hurt and be his friend, for Mom's sake, hoping my decision shows on my face, and Henry just drops it.

"I knew there was a *we*," he says, pushing us in the exact opposite direction from what I wanted.

"There's no *we*, Henry. Not now and definitely not then." *Lies lies lies*, my heart beats out.

He meets my eyes with equal determination. "Maybe there should have been."

Why is he doing this to me? My head feels like it's spinning out of control. He can't be saying what I think he's saying. He just can't. That would go against every understanding I have formed about the world over the last decade. That can't be what he means. I think back to all the nights before the New York trip, when I lay awake, so sure of what the future held for us. What we could be.

We.

Goddammit.

"You've had too much wine, Henry," I say, because I can't respond to the words that actually just came out of his perfect mouth.

"I haven't," he insists. He takes a few steps toward me.

"Then maybe the frostbite got to your brain or something . . ." I trail off as he closes the distance between us in two long strides. He smells like cilantro.

"You're telling me," he starts, his eyes falling to a curl that's come loose from my bun, "you're not even a little bit curious about how things could have been?"

I feel one firm hand on the small of my back. I don't know when or how it made its way there, but suddenly it's the only thing keeping me upright.

There's no longer any meandering around what Henry means.

Friendship is not what he was missing.

And if I didn't know it from the words, the look in his eyes, melting my flesh until I feel it pool between my thighs, makes it unmistakably clear.

Henry Cole is going to kiss me.

His lips part slightly, and his tongue slips out to wet them. Almost an involuntary action of need.

Henry. Cole. Is going. To kiss. Me.

I've spent so long feeling so much pain over this man, who was once the boy who ripped apart my entire life.

Is this really happening?

My whole body burns, feeling betrayed by my brain, as I slip away from him. I can barely breathe. I cross my arms over my chest, knowing my taut nipples are revealing a different story than the sudden distance I've placed between us.

Henry turns magenta immediately, from the tips of his ears, all the way down his neck, as far as I can see before all his dumb clothes get in the way. His eyes are huge, panicked saucers.

"Shit. Fuck. I'm so sorry. I—" He paces back to the bed, slumping down and burying his head in his hands. "Fuck."

I can tell he's completely mortified. There's a piece of me, the part that still aches over everything that went down, that takes a small amount of pleasure in seeing him in this state. Over me.

And then it hits me.

Henry and I almost kissed.

In all this time, all that he meant to me, for all those years, we never came this close to kissing. I would steal glances at him, spend hours hoping, wishing on every 11:11 clock that Henry Cole would kiss me, but nothing ever happened. In fact, when given the chance, he actively chose *not* to kiss me.

It feels like a cosmic joke from some other dimension that this near-kiss happened now, nearly a decade later, when we are quite literally trapped in a hotel room with one bed.

I glance back at him—still on the bed, head in hands, elbows on thighs, hunched. His knee is bouncing as if it could pop right off his body.

"Of course I was curious," I say quietly.

His whole body stills.

"Of course," I continue. "Are you kidding me?"

He looks up, and it feels almost hopeful? It's a fleeting look, a split second, and then it's gone.

"You're the one who was so repulsed by me that you—"

His face falls and it throws me.

"I had to smother that piece down. Because it hurt too much to leave that wound open."

He drops his hands beside him, almost like he's restraining himself from reaching for me. "The last thing I ever wanted to do was hurt you. It was all so much more complicated than you know, Norah, than I can even get into."

"Yeah?" I ask, eyes pressing him further for an explanation he doesn't provide.

"Yeah," he repeats, sounding so weary I almost feel bad for him, but he doesn't say anything else for a while, and it just hangs in the air.

Without knowing where to go from here, I grab some things from my bag and shut myself up in the bathroom.

I splash cold water on my face, hoping to bring down my body temperature, which is blazing. It doesn't help. I go through the motions of brushing my teeth, moisturizing, my whole multi-step routine, but I can barely keep track of what I've done in the last ten seconds. I sink down onto the cold tile floor, hugging my knees into my chest. How can we survive the rest of the night after that?

When I finally go back into the room, Henry is still frozen at the edge of the bed. I slide onto the Victorian chair I placed a pillow and blanket on.

"I have to go to sleep," I say.

He nods and silently makes his way into the bathroom.

I wait until he comes back, then pull a string switch on the lamp next to the chair, killing the only remaining light in the room.

I try to get comfortable, swiveling from side to side, hoping there's a sliver of cushioning I can force out of this awful piece of furniture. I drag over a small ottoman, which squeaks miserably upon being moved. I hoped that stretching out on it would help, but it's just as stiff as the chair, which rustles every time I shift.

"You okay over there?" Henry asks.

"It's just this upright back. It's not the most conducive to sleep."

I look over, and in the shadows of the now-dark room, I can see that he's lying down, hands folded at his sternum.

"You can sleep in the bed, you know." It comes out as a low grumble caught in his throat. "You can't possibly be warm enough over there."

He's right. The blanket I grabbed is doing practically nothing to cut the bite of the cold that is seeping into this room.

"We can make a pillow wall," he continues when I don't answer. "There's plenty of space."

I don't say anything. I can't.

"Nothing will happen, Scout's honor," he adds.

"You were never a Boy Scout."

"I hate that you know that," he says, and even though I can't see it, I know I've gotten at least a quarter smirk out of him.

"I thought you didn't hate me."

He's quiet for a moment. I hear him shift on the bed. I don't dare move.

"Stop being ridiculous and come lie down," he says finally, in the same stern tone he used to tell me to pull the car over.

"Fine."

"Fine."

I drag my pillow back to the empty side of the bed, which happens to be the one I sleep on normally, and slip under the covers. Without a word, I turn onto my side, so my back is to him.

There is decidedly no pillow wall.

I don't move to change that, and neither does he.

This bed is definitely not a queen. I feel breathless all over again from the heat coming off him, just inches away from me. Suddenly, I'm deliriously warm.

I know his eyes are on me. I can feel them, icy blue, searching for a read on this whole mess.

I don't have a fucking clue.

The mattress shifts, and he rolls away from me.

I exhale a little too loudly, knowing how little sleep I'm going to get tonight.

Chapter 9

I DON'T DARE turn to lie on my back until I hear his breaths deepen and I know he's asleep. I feel like I'm back in high school, insomnia paving the way for intrusive thoughts and romantic delusions.

Only this time, instead of replaying the perfect little moments we shared that made me so certain he felt the same way I did, my brain won't stop showing me flashes of *then*.

Henry was always my friend. Always, always. But there was also a part of me that longed for it to be something more, even before I had the words for that.

It all came to a head at the beginning of our senior year, when our school announced a trip for students to tour colleges in New York City. Laketon Academy had done this before based on where students were applying—there had been past trips to Boston, Philadelphia, Los Angeles—but Henry and I were thrilled that this one would land us in the place we'd always dreamed of ending up. I think I probably made him watch *You've Got Mail* and *When Harry Met Sally* a thousand and twelve times growing up, and we were both in love with the idea of New York City. We had this plan to go to NYU together, and the more we talked about it that summer between junior and senior year, the more real it felt. I kept thinking, *If we can just get out of Laketon together, maybe we'll finally get our chance for more.*

We sat next to each other on the flight to New York, and that recurring wish of mine started to feel more tangible. We argued, as we always did, but it felt . . . more. Charged, somehow. When his arm brushed mine on our shared armrest, every hair on my body stood up against my will. I felt a swoop low in my stomach. He didn't move, and neither did I, and we stayed like that, arms pressed, for the remainder of the flight. It was such an innocent gesture in retrospect, but I felt like he was watching my hand the whole time, just as I was watching his. Waiting to see which of us would lock our fingers together first as we made the descent into what could be our new home.

We made so much sense, in my head at least, and in that moment especially, I felt so certain that I couldn't be imagining this. That he must've felt it too. Henry was always gangly and awkward, but as soon as hormones hit, I could no longer read what he was feeling at all times.

Of course, neither of us ever made a real move, but that was the dance we always did with each other. Instead, we distracted ourselves with talk about how "adult" we were for being unleashed upon NYC in this way, basically left to our own devices.

That night, after the teachers did a half-hearted curfew check at the hotel, the majority of our twenty or so classmates on the trip reconvened in Henry and Trevor's room—per Trevor's request, of course. I was surprised Trevor had even come on this trip—the likelihood of him ever leaving the Midwest, or even our town, seemed slim, but maybe he just wanted to have a good time. He'd procured a surprising amount of beer from his older sister's friend who was in college nearby, and the logical next move was for him to throw a party. I remember Henry being stressed at first because he and I had our NYU interviews the following morning, but Trevor's easy nature always had a way of wearing Henry down.

Soon, Henry had a red Solo cup in hand just like the rest of us, careful to mask any bottles or cans in case there was photographic evidence. I'd never had beer before, and I was pretty sure Henry hadn't either. Our friend group was not usually the partying type, and the only alcohol I'd tried up until this point was a little bit of wine during the Jewish holidays, under my mother's supervision. If I close my eyes, sometimes I can still taste the room-temperature piss-liquid on my tongue. Maybe this is why, to this day, I still don't care for beer.

As the night wore on, someone started a game of Truth or Dare, and things quickly devolved from there. During a dare that involved some sort of clothed lap dance on the bed, someone knocked an entire beer onto Henry's phone, which was plugged in on his nightstand. The phone went dead almost immediately, and Henry completely flipped out.

"The interviews are tomorrow," he said to me, his hand gripping the back of his neck so tightly that I could see the strain on his forearm. "I can't miss it, Norah. I can't."

I assured him that I would act as his replacement cell phone, both serving as a personal alarm system to make sure that he was awake and to navigate us to the NYU campus. Because our names were early in the alphabet, we were the only two students slated for our meetings there the following morning.

I sat next to Henry at the foot of his bed as classmates whose names I can't even remember admitted crushes and revenge plots. As make-out dares became more and more unprompted. Frankie, the only person who knew about my all-consuming crush on Henry, kept eyeing us, giving me a look that clearly said *Now is the time*. I remember a silent conversation between us through raised eyebrows and glares across the room, and my slow resignation that my best friend was definitely about to stir the pot for my own good. She leaned over to her new boyfriend, Kevin Chen, who was oddly enough my accidental first kiss during an ill-fated middle school Spin the Bottle game (an unfortunate side effect of Laketon Academy being fairly small). When it was Kevin's turn to pick the next victim of the game, he turned his attention to Henry.

"Truth or dare?" Kevin asked, and I swear I didn't imagine the sideways glance Henry gave me before reluctantly deciding on a dare. "I dare you to kiss Norah."

In the moments that immediately followed the dare, I felt relief. It was my Spin the Bottle ploy all over again, only this time, I was sure that I would finally get some answers. Back in middle school, I had plotted to make Henry my first kiss at that sixth-grade party, but he opted not to play. A low-stakes kiss would finally tell me how Henry really felt about me. My seventeen-year-old self was convinced that this was a genius idea on Frankie's part, especially for enlisting Kevin as the darer so it didn't come from my best friend directly. She was helping me get exactly what I'd needed to know for so long. If he didn't share my feelings, we could laugh it off as part of the game, but I felt pretty certain it wouldn't go that way. I was sure that this would be the moment that changed everything.

In a way, it was.

Henry stood, the bed shifting under the abrupt change in weight. He took a giant step away from me, looking at me with disgust in his eyes that had never been directed at me before in the fourteen years that I'd known him.

"No. Nope. I'm not—pick something else."

Confusion washed over me from Henry's sheer panic at the thought of kissing me.

"Come on, man, it's just a game," Kevin started, but Henry began pacing the room.

"I don't want to play some meaningless game. I'm not kissing *her.*"

The last word launched itself out of Henry's mouth like a grenade. I was the target.

"Actually," Henry continued, "we should call it. Everyone out. This is over."

All eyes were trained on us, the previously noisy room suddenly filled with stark silence and the occasional snicker that scorched my ears as I took a tentative step toward him. I tried to push down the embarrassment of being so exposed like this.

"We don't have to kiss. It's not a big deal," I lied. "We don't have to end the party."

"Get out, Norah. I mean it."

I could hear my pulse flying. My cheeks burned hot as I fought back tears. I refused to let them fall. I couldn't let him see how much this was affecting me.

"Okay, you really don't want to kiss me. Fine. Everyone gets it."

In the second before I turned to storm out of there, I saw a look I couldn't place flash across his cruel face. I didn't let myself linger in it. I booked it right out of that room, with Frankie close at my heels. Not only did Henry reject me without an ounce of kindness, but he did so in the presence of twenty of our classmates. Soon our entire grade would know about my rejection, my humiliation. The way he spat out *her* at me like I meant nothing.

Sure enough, the wave of texts from people who weren't even on this trip started before Frankie and I got to our own room two floors up. It hurt that he didn't want me and that I finally had an answer to the question I'd wondered my whole life, but the public nature of it all was really what irked me. This was what other people would remember about this trip. This was what we'd come back to when we returned to Laketon. I'd never done anything significant enough to warrant being at the center of gossip, and I instantly hated it.

I didn't sleep at all that night, even once my phone stopped blowing up. I was hurt and my head felt fuzzy from the one gross beer I'd sipped for hours, but pretty quickly that pain shifted into anger. How could Henry do something like that to me, in this way, after claiming to be my friend? After we spent the entire flight dreaming up our combined future. He didn't have to kiss me, but the way he handled that all made me feel like he didn't even want to be in my life anymore.

I could make that happen.

In the morning, I got ready for my interview. I did not knock on Henry's door and make sure he was awake. I did not help him navigate the city. I went all by myself, figured it out alone, and honestly? I knocked it out of the park. I knew when I shook hands goodbye with the admissions officer that I'd done it. I was going to get into NYU. I was going to move here in less than a year and start my new life. I only had to make it through a few more months of high school, and then I could forget that any of this happened.

I managed to avoid Henry for the next day and a half, using Frankie as a human shield when necessary. I felt him glaring daggers at me the entire flight back to Chicago, as well as the bus ride from the airport back to school, but I didn't let myself care. I couldn't allow myself to slip back into feeling my actual emotions about any of this.

I was successful at this until we arrived back at Laketon Academy, and I remembered that Henry was my ride home. I honestly would have rather walked than get in his CR-V, but it was raining, and without a word, he yanked my duffel bag out of my hands, threw it in his trunk, and scowled at me while both of us got completely drenched.

"We have things to discuss," he shouted at me as the rain pummeled his car. "We can do this now, or we can do this in half an hour when I show up at your house after you've walked home just to prove some fucking point."

I'd never heard Henry curse before. It felt unnatural coming out of his mouth. Maybe that's why I relented, shrugging into the passenger seat without a word.

We maintained a brutal silence on the ride home, both stewing, until he pulled into his driveway. He clocked me eyeing my porch and said, "Don't even think about it," before leading me into his house.

We barely made it through the front door before he started in on me.

"How could you do that to me? You know how important this trip was for me," Henry said, stripping off his soaked coat and boots.

I shrugged, removing my own coat and heel-toeing off my boots at the door. "Oops."

"Are you fucking kidding me right now?" Again with the cursing. This was not my Henry. This was some alien double. A body swap was the only explanation. "I can't believe you would be this petty. This is my life, my future! It's not some game for your amusement."

"Oh, it's not some meaningless game, Henry? Sure had me fooled. But you probably weren't getting texts all night about how embarrassed you must be, how completely humiliated."

"I wouldn't know if I was getting texts," Henry shouted, "because my phone is broken. You know that."

My own phone started to ring but before I could reach into my pocket, Henry shot me a death glare.

"Do. Not. Answer. That phone. Norah, I am so serious right now." He looked at me with such fury that I put my hands up like he was keeping me at gunpoint. It was the hold he'd always had on my heart, only suddenly, it felt sour.

He began trudging up the stairs and I followed, furious. When we got to his bedroom, he ducked into the bathroom and launched a towel at me, drying his wet hair and clothes off with his own as well.

"I needed you," he continued. "I needed you, and I needed that interview, and I can't believe you would be such a selfish asshole after everything we've been through together. It's like our friendship means nothing to you."

"That feels really genuine given how much you clearly valued our friendship the other night," I said.

Henry dragged a hand over his face in frustration. "You know that's not—"

"As for the interview," I interrupted, "I'm sure there are other opportunities, so you don't have to make such a thing about it. Julia missed the trip for her cousin's wedding but she said there are still alumni interviews in the city, so—"

"No." Henry's tone was firm. "That was my only shot. It just was, Norah, and you ruined that for me."

We argued in circles like teenagers do, carefully avoiding the issue of the non-kiss while throwing as many cheap shots at each other as we could think of. This was the part of knowing someone your whole life that I hadn't accounted for—we had a lot of ammunition and knew how to fight dirty. Years later, I don't even remember what was actually said at that point, but I remember the slew of calls that followed, my phone blaring repeatedly from my pocket until Henry finally shouted, "Just answer the goddamn phone, Norah," as he stormed out of the room. I heard that one creaky step groan under the weight of his stomping feet.

The first missed call was from Dad almost an hour ago. I couldn't believe Henry and I had been fighting for that long. Then, a text from him saying that my voicemail was full, but to call him back because he was at Jewel-Osco and had a question about the grocery list. The other nine missed calls were from my mom.

When I called her back, she was crying hysterically. She told me that my dad had an "episode." I'll never forget that word—*episode*. He was at the supermarket and they didn't know what happened. We'd later learn that it was his heart. Dad was gone before he even got to the hospital. My mind went silent in that moment. I don't remember where she was, all I know is that she was asking if I was somewhere safe, and if I could find someone to pick up Hannah from dance practice.

"I can get her," I remember Henry saying.

I guess the call had been put on speaker at some point. I guess he had sat me down on the edge of his bed. I guess he had brought me some water. I tried to take a sip but my hand was shaking so much that I spilled all over the carpet. Henry just shook his head, telling me it didn't matter.

He took the glass from my hands, and I think he tried to embrace me, comfort me, but I didn't want that. I stood up and flew down the stairs, shoving my feet back into my wet boots and not even bothering with my coat. I burst outside, needing more air. The rain had stopped, and I remember thinking that it was a cruel joke that there was a rainbow in the sky at a time like this. Henry unlocked the car and we both got in.

As Henry began to drive the familiar route to the dance studio to pick Hannah up from her tap class, he must have started and stopped fifteen different sentences. I stared out the window, unable to process whatever he was trying to say. What if I'd answered my dad's call? What if my voicemail hadn't been full? I didn't even know the last thing I said to him. It must have been days ago, when we were leaving for the trip. Was it *I love you?* Why couldn't I remember?

"Norah," Henry said finally, when we were at a red light. His voice was softer than I'd ever heard it. "I know there's nothing I can say right now to make it hurt less, but I hope you know that I'm here for you. Let's just forget everything from this afternoon and—"

"No." I heard the ice in my own voice. "If I'd answered his call, I would have gotten to talk to him one last time. I would have had that."

Henry let out a slow exhale. "Nor."

"You took that from me," I said quietly. "I don't know if I can ever forgive you for that."

I couldn't look at him directly, but I saw him nod out of the corner of my eye. I felt him shut down entirely.

This became our new normal for the remainder of our senior year. We could only cause each other hurt, so soon enough, we avoided each other altogether. In one afternoon, I lost my dad and the person I thought knew me best for the last fourteen years. My first friend. My first crush. My first heartbreak.

Henry could never want me. I don't know what I'd been thinking. Then, or truly, now. This was all a fluke. Just snow, and proximity, and wine, and hormones. That was the only explanation.

I WAKE UP with a start, not sure when or how I had possibly dozed off. In the night, we'd both turned in toward each other. Henry stirs next to me, his dark hair tousled in the most infuriating way. His eyes blink open at me, and his face floods with what I can only describe as . . . soft affection? He blinks a few more times and it settles into a smirk. I think he hopes I didn't see that first emotion before he put his walls back up.

Or maybe I'm wrong because then he says, "Norah," and I feel it all the way down to my toes.

"You were in my dream last night," he tells me fondly. "Only it wasn't you-you, it was teenage us."

I don't give him the satisfaction of admitting that my subconscious took me to the same time and place, albeit decidedly less tender versions of him and me.

"Why do we have to dredge up the past?" I ask softly. "Haven't we put each other through enough?"

He shifts slightly, an arm under his head to prop himself up a little.

"Norah—"

"Please, can't you just let it be?" I roll onto my back, not able to say this part to his face because I don't even know if it's true. I just want this conversation to be over. "Fine, I forgive you for the missed call or whatever. Happy?"

"Norah."

I get up out of the bed. Everything about this moment is far too intimate to be lying next to each other for a second longer.

"Norah," he repeats with urgency. "Say you mean that. Say it."

I hear the bed creak. He comes toward me, standing so close, but hesitant to touch me again. It makes sense given what happened last night, but the way he's looking at me, with regret, with understanding, with need, I almost wish he would.

"Do you really forgive me? Please. Say yes." It's a whisper right next to my ear, his warm breath on the nape of my neck, waking up every particle of my body.

I turn my head to look up at Henry, his face lingering for an extra moment near mine.

"Please." There's stern desperation in his voice that tilts my heart into something raw, and maybe even a little healed.

I nod because in that moment, it's true. I do forgive him. He sucks in a harsh breath, and I can tell he's watching my pulse flutter under his stare.

His hand rises like he needs to feel me, but he stops himself. "I won't try to kiss you again, but goddammit, Norah, you have no idea, do you?" It's so quiet, I don't even know if he meant for me to hear. His light eyes are almost stormy, pleading for permission to be closer.

I feel in the pit of my stomach like I've misjudged every moment since Henry reentered my orbit. Like if I don't kiss him now, we'll never have this time back. We'll never know.

I lean up on my tiptoes, tilt my chin toward him, and gently brush my lips against his, a featherlight prelude. I feel his entire body come alive with that brief contact. He catches me as I start to lower on my toes, a firm hand on my hip, anchoring me close to him. His other hand is in my wild morning hair, twisting through as his mouth crashes hungrily into mine, biting my lower lip in a way that makes heat pool low in my stomach. I'm gripping his shirt with both my fists, trying to draw him closer, or yank the stupid cotton right off his body, I'm not sure.

Henry pulls away so abruptly that I let out an involuntary whimper, and I can feel a muscle in his jaw flex at the sound. He presses his forehead to mine, both of us gasping for air. I can't tell what he's thinking, but I'm desperate for his mouth to be back on mine.

"Henry," I start, pulling away to try to get a look at him, to see if I can read what he's thinking on his face, but he draws me back close to him.

"I just need a moment to convince myself this is really happening," he says, his voice unsteady.

Before I can respond, his hands are on my face, cupping my cheeks. He's gazing at me like I'm something precious. Delicate. Perfect.

This time, when he kisses me, it's slow, purposeful. As if his tongue is trying to map my mouth, as if he needs to commit every tiny movement to memory.

The first kiss was all hunger, need.

This kiss is intentional. Inevitable.

I wrap my arms around his neck, and he pulls me flush against him.

We stand there, intertwined, for what feels like a decade of lost time. Tongue on throat, fingers in hair, every grunt, every gasp electric, until I desperately need to be closer. To feel more of him.

I lift his shirt over his head, exposing his chest. I saw him shirtless yesterday, but that was a million feelings ago. My sigh is shaky as I take in the sight of him. There's something intoxicating about seeing this gangly, awkward boy, who I loved before I even knew what that word meant or how it could hurt, as a man in his truest form. He has no right to be this beautiful.

He fumbles with the hem of the sweatshirt I slept in, lifting it slowly to expose my stomach, higher, higher.

"Fuck, Norah," he says, revealing my bare breasts, peaks already at perfect attention for him.

"You can't sleep in underwire," I explain as his eyes feast on my chest. He raises two fingers and rolls my nipple between them.

A hiss escapes from somewhere deep inside me and he snaps to reality with a look of worry. "Too much? Did I hurt you?" he asks.

I lift my gaze to meet his. For the briefest moment, the concern on his face cracks my whole chest open. Suddenly, this isn't enough. I need to feel the weight of him on me. I shake my head slowly, lips pulling into a devilish grin, and I watch his pupils dilate with knowledge of the true meaning of that hiss.

I give his chest a gentle push and, catching on, he grabs me and pulls me down onto the bed on top of him. He lies back, my knees folded on either side of his hips. He shifts, and I become increasingly aware of how hard he is through these drawstring pants that leave little to the imagination. We are aligned dangerously. I tilt my hips down slightly, and the delicious friction is almost too much.

We are in over our heads.

We are done for.

He groans and pulls my torso back down to meet his, the

bare skin of our chests growing sticky with heat. He runs his tongue along the underside of my jaw and I wonder where else he might be skilled with that muscle.

I kiss him, hard, and we roll over. I let out a sigh at the glorious feeling of his weight on me. His hips grind into mine, and I match the rhythm, as close as we can get with our lower halves still clothed. Breathless.

Henry steadies, propping himself up on his forearms over me.

"Norah," he says, my name on his tongue like a prayer. "Can I touch you?" Henry burrows his head into my neck, kissing my pulse point softly. "I need to feel you. Please."

His simple *please* unravels me. It's all I can say back to him. "Please." Heady, breathy *please*.

Henry's teeth scrape my bottom lip, biting down with the perfect amount of pressure as he shifts us onto our sides, his hand gliding between us. My pajama pants are thin enough that when his finger lightly grazes the place I need him most, my whole body hums.

I feel the knowing smile spread across his face, his mouth still pressed against my own.

He knows that I'm drenched for him.

"Please." I've been reduced to that one word, one syllable, my whole brain clouded by years of want, and the fact that Henry Cole is slipping his hand into my panties, which have been rendered useless since I first felt his hot breath on my neck.

"*Fuck*, Norah," he says as he makes contact with the place he's made me impossibly wet, and it's only then that I feel him shaking ever so slightly.

We lock eyes, and his brows rise with a helpless laugh.

He's nervous.

He's looking at me like he would fall into the center of the earth for me.

I've been in love with him my whole life.

I can't believe I ever thought this was just hormones.

And then he moves.

A slow circle with the pad of his middle finger, magnetically drawn to the exact spot that will undo me.

"Henry, this is—"

"—I know," he says softly.

Another slow circle, maintaining deep eye contact. This is the most intimate moment I've ever shared with another person.

As I'm starting to get lost in him, a buzzing noise jolts us back to this plane of existence. My cell phone is ringing incessantly on the nightstand.

"Ignore it," he whispers, kissing me like I'm something to be cherished, and instead of the panic I usually feel when my phone rings, stemming from the worst day of my life, I trust him and listen. My phone quiets, and I sigh into his mouth. But a moment later, the buzzing moves to his phone, on the other nightstand.

I slip his hand out from where I want to hold it forever. "You should answer."

He takes an unsteady breath, and with one more look at me, he turns to grab his phone.

"Hello?" he says, winded, adjusting himself in his pants.

I can tell immediately that it's Kristine.

"Oh, uh—Norah didn't pick up? Uh, shower. She's in the shower," he lies poorly. A pause, then, "No, we're, uh, still at the inn. We had to wait for them to dig out the driveway." I look at him and gesture *WTF?* but he just gives me a nervous shrug.

I glance at my phone and realize it's already after ten. Shit. That explains the missed call from my mom too. We should have been at the lodge by now, or at least close.

I was the only thing that was close. And goddamn, I was so close.

Henry says a few more reassuring things to his mom, and then he hangs up quickly. I already know what he's going to say—we have to go. The moment has passed, and like two little kids, we're in trouble with our mommies.

"I wish we could stay here all day and finish what we started," he murmurs into my hair.

"We can't," I say, longing for any other way. "I have to shower."

Henry raises an eyebrow at me.

"If you come into that bathroom with me, we will be decidedly more behind schedule than we already are."

He concedes, kissing me once more so deeply I nearly go limp, then patting my ass to usher me into the bathroom.

As I let the water run over me, my whole body is still humming.

If it felt that way with just the touch of his hand, without even reaching climax, him being inside me will surely ruin us both.

Goddamn, Henry Cole.

How did we even get here?

Questions begin running through my head in rapid succession. *What does this mean? Is this real? Is this a fluke? Is this* it? I feel my racing heart switch from being fueled by arousal to panic.

He stands as I enter the room, wrapped in a towel, having

forgotten to grab clothes as I floated into the shower minutes earlier. He lets out a shaky breath. "You're so beautiful. It physically pains me that I've never told you that."

I melt. What else am I supposed to do? Every concern jumps right out of my head as I kiss him softly. "Go shower before I jump your bones," I say into his lips.

"Is that really an option?" he asks, and I roll my eyes, pushing him toward the bathroom.

Once the door is closed, I get dressed, feeling positively high. My phone buzzes with a text from Hannah.

Hannah

Hurry up and get here already!

WTF is taking you so long??

Mom needs our support to get it together and make this happen!

Shit.

This is not the time to figure out what this means. This is the time to make everything perfect for our moms so they can live happily ever after. Operation Latke. That has to be the priority.

He reemerges from the bathroom, wrapped in a towel, and I cannot believe everything that's happened since he stood in front of me the same way twenty-four hours earlier. "Eyes up here," he jokes, and I smile half-heartedly.

He sees right through it. "No no no, what happened?" he asks, stepping toward me. "What could have possibly happened in the last five minutes?"

"Just get dressed. We have to get back on the road. We've got plenty of time to talk in the car, Hen."

He softens. "I can't remember the last time you called me that."

"Yeah, well . . . just hurry up. I'll grab something easy for us to eat on the way out."

Before he can say anything else, I slip out the door and scurry down to the kitchen to grab some breakfast. I settle on bananas, coffee, and DIY sufganiyot, one of my favorite Hanukkah treats. While a normal sufganiyot is a jelly-filled powdered donut, another deep-fried reminder of the miracle oil that lasted eight nights, I had to work with what I could find—a box of ultra-processed powdered donuts and individual packets of raspberry jam. When I return, he's packed up the room and is ready to go, and we eat quickly and silently, trying not to make any more of a mess than we already have.

I take one more look around the room, the purple bedding that's in complete disarray, the awful Victorian chair, and everything in between, and hope this wasn't just the site of some perfect anomaly.

Chapter 10

BEING BACK IN the CR-V feels like a hard punch of reality. I'm quiet as Henry finishes scraping the snow and ice off the windshield and gets in the driver's seat. He drops the plastic tool in the backseat behind me, and his fingers brush against my arm as he turns back around. Even through the layers of my sweater and jacket, I feel the light touch like it's just been tattooed on my skin.

I am twenty-six years old. I am a grown woman. I have had sex and been intimate with a moderate number of men, and yet the simple act of fingers fluttering past my arm has reduced me to my near melting point. Teenagers feel everything so much bigger, rawer, more consuming, and I guess it's always like high school with Henry. Every touch, every look, every feeling is amplified to a ten. Or a fifteen, if I'm being honest. But I can't let myself be distracted.

"Henry," I say. It's a complete sentence, and he turns in his seat to face me, the buzz of the idling car lingering underneath us.

"Okay," he sighs, resigned. "Out with it. Tell me how you've already convinced yourself that this is a mistake."

I take a deep breath. Being this vulnerable doesn't come easily to me. "This was unexpected and inevitable, and I have never wanted anyone the way I want you right now. Including Past Henry."

The exposed part of his neck flushes pink. "But," he says, because he knows there's a *but*.

"But this week is not about us," I add gently. "I know you know that. We have to focus on our moms and on Operation Latke."

"You're making excuses." It's not exactly an accusation, but it hangs heavy between us.

Even though we had free rein of each other's bodies less than an hour ago, my heart suddenly races when I reach over to take his hand and lace my fingers through his.

"I promise I'm not," I say, and he lifts the hand that holds mine to place a kiss on my wrist. I want to stop talking and climb over the glove compartment into his lap, make out with his stupid face until our lips are raw, but I can't. *Focus, Norah, focus.*

"Think about it. Are you ready to explain this to Kristine? To my mom and Hannah? Because I'm sure not. If we arrive at Great Blue Lodge holding hands, we're going to get pummeled with a million questions we don't have answers to yet. We need to figure this out for ourselves first. Preferably when we're not staying in one cabin with our families. It's just a few days."

He looks at me with understanding, but the hold he has on my hand tells another story. "I don't know if I can go a few days without touching you," he says, his normally gruff voice thick like honey. "It's like we cracked open a dam or something."

"Hen," I start.

He cuts me off with a quiet intensity, his voice low. "Baby, I don't know if I can go a few days without finally making you come."

I let out a haggard breath, feeling the low pull between my thighs, a somersault of need. I squeeze his hand, then extract my fingers from his. "You managed for long enough. What's a few more days in the grand scheme of things?"

He moves his hands to grip the steering wheel and leans his head back on the headrest, trying to pull himself together. After a moment, he nods to himself, then shifts the idling car into reverse and backs out of the parking lot.

It's quiet for a few minutes as I wait for the look of anguish to fade from his face.

"'Baby'?" I finally say, suppressing a giggle, because I absolutely have to address that.

Henry hangs his head in embarrassment. "I got swept up in it all. I mean, come on, look at you."

I glance down at myself, bundled and frazzled. He said it so earnestly, but he must be out of his mind. There is no way that *this* necessitated a "baby," the world's least creative pet name.

"You're a mess, dude. You gotta get it together before we see our moms," I joke.

He smiles at me, giving me that look that I still can't decipher, only now I'm pretty sure it's filled with something much softer than judgment.

"DO YOU WANT to play a game?" Henry asks once we're on the road.

"Like the license plate game?" I slip off my shoes and press my feet onto the dash like I used to, the gesture feeling natural again. "I'm pretty much only seeing Illinois plates."

"No, a questions game. A getting-to-know-you game, no holds barred." He glances sidelong at me for a beat, his gaze dancing over my propped-up legs, the moment laced with longing. "For half my life, you were the person I knew better than anyone, but there's so much we missed out on over the last nine years. I want to know everything about the woman you are now."

I had done my ten thousand hours of a previous version of Henry Cole. At one point in my life, I could have been a sworn expert.

I want to earn back that title.

"Okay." The idea of having this kind of familiarity with him now, erasing all the years of separation, just Henry in the present tense, is almost as intoxicating as his touch. "What's your go-to karaoke song?"

Henry gives me a once-over. "My karaoke song." It's not a question, but his tone is curious.

"Yeah, the more embarrassing the better."

"I tell you I'm an open book and that's the first thing you want to know about me?" he asks, a smile breaking out across his face.

"Yes," I tell him, knocking my knee into his forearm, his hand hovering over the gearshift. "It's the barometer for me to judge the rest of your existence."

"I'm really going to disappoint you, then," he says, shaking his head. "I'm not much for karaoke."

"Henry!" I gasp. "Don't make me call off whatever this is between us now over motherfucking karaoke."

"I'm not opposed to it; it just hasn't come up that often. Plus, I have a terrible voice."

"Oh, I remember," I snort. "But the worse you are, the more fun it is."

"Well, what's your go-to?" he asks.

"'Like a Prayer' by our queen, Madonna. Obviously."

Henry laughs, a full-body, shoulders-shaking laugh. "Seriously?"

"Wait till you see the interpretive dance I do alongside it," I say with a goofy smile. He's so rarely dropped this buttoned-up side of himself over the last few days that each time I get to chip away at it a little more feels like an enormous victory.

"I'll have to keep that in mind. Okay, worst date you've ever been on?"

"Oh, we're just really cutting right in there, huh? Right to the juicy stuff?"

He shrugs. I mull over what to tell him. It's definitely going against my intention to pump the brakes on this until we get our moms engaged. But we're stuck alone in this car for the next few hours anyway. We can't do anything for Operation Latke yet. This drive is our interlude from reality until we arrive at the lodge and *then* we'll shut it down.

"Okay, so I met this guy from the apps for drinks. He'd gotten there before me and was on his second beer, even though I was on time. I was barely twenty-three and he was definitely in his thirties but dressed like a teenager. Dirty T-shirt, hoodie with thumb holes in the sleeves. I asked how his day had been going, and he told me he'd gotten stoned in his living room and watched *Elysium* twice."

"That Matt Damon movie?" Henry asks, glancing over at me.

"Yeah, I guess. Anyway, we had zero chemistry, and he kept trying to grope my ass while I was still sitting on this barstool, and I kept looking at him like, *Do you think you're being successful here?*

"So then after one drink, I know I have to get out of there because this dude is insufferable. I hadn't realized he'd opened a tab before I got there, and I really did not want to feel like I owed this guy anything, but the bartender wouldn't put my drink on my card instead. At first, the guy was super offended that I wanted to pay for my own drink, but he finally conceded that I could give him cash. I was one dollar shy and then he got unreasonably angry about it, and I'm thinking, *Thirty seconds ago you didn't want to let me pay* anything *toward my drink*. But whatever. So we settle up and he says he has to go to the restroom before we head out.

"Henry, I knew there was not a chance in hell I was letting this thin-lipped little creep kiss me. And this was my golden opportunity. I could just leave while he was in the bathroom and avoid the situation completely. He didn't even know my last name. I could block him on the app and be done with it forever. But then I got in my head about it. Was that too mean? Too harsh? And I didn't factor in how much quicker it is for men than women in the bathroom, so before I'd even made a decision, he was back."

"He totally kissed you, didn't he?"

I sigh. "It was a sneak-attack kiss. The worst. And then we were both walking to the subway stop. I had to dip into a CVS just to get away from him. But then, sure enough, he messaged me at two a.m. with a classic *u up* since I'd been so thrown by the kiss that I forgot to block him. I did not respond to that."

"Gross."

"Right? What about you?"

"Well, Gold, I hate to say it, but I've got you beat. Back when

I was living in Los Angeles, I met up with a girl at this bar—I think she used to work there. And the whole time, servers kept coming up to her and asking how her brother was, and finally, after the third person, I asked what was going on. Apparently, her brother had been in a bad motorcycle accident and was in a coma. I asked her if she wanted to leave, said we could reschedule, but she said no, and we kept getting free drinks from her old coworkers. In the middle of our second round, her phone rings, and she takes it. I mean sure, you're having a family emergency, of course you should answer the call. And her whole face lights up—her brother had woken up from the coma."

"You can't be serious," I say, shaking my head.

"I swear! So I told her to go to him, and she left. I finished my drink, and never heard from her again."

"And you're sure that wasn't a fake call to get her out of a terrible date with you?" I ask playfully.

"It'd involve a helluva lot of setup—the coworkers asking about him, the free drinks . . ."

"Hen, that's not fair, that's a wild story but it's not necessarily a bad date."

"It's not until I got home and realized someone stole my wallet."

"No!"

He sighs. "Whoever it was went buck wild at the Brothers department store, maxed out everything. I had to cancel all my credit cards. It was a nightmare."

"The *Brothers* department store! And it was her *brother* in this alleged coma?" I'm laughing so hard I can barely catch my breath. It doesn't surprise me terribly that this sweet man had been a sucker. I feel confident that he was so genuinely excited for his date to go see her brother, he never would have batted an eye.

Henry leans his head back. “Somehow I never put that part together.” He looks at me, his smile so wide I can see his molars. “Your turn.”

“Tell me something important that happened to you this year.”

Henry’s eyes rake over me briefly before turning back to the road. His hands flex on the steering wheel. I watch him suck in a slow, deep breath.

“This doesn’t count,” I add quickly, sensing where this is heading. “I already know I’m amazing.”

“The best I ever had.”

“I barely even touched you,” I say, heat rising to my cheeks.

“I know,” he replies, the corner of his mouth tugging up ever so slightly.

“Something important that happened to you this year,” I repeat, emphasizing each word, needing to get back on track before my inclination to pull the CR-V over in the emergency lane and ride him senseless wins out.

“Well,” he starts, “I found my, uh . . . the sperm donor.”

I had heard many stories from Kristine when we were old enough about the “sperm binder” she used to pick the other half of Henry’s DNA. He looked so much like Kristine, fierce blue eyes and olive skin, that I wondered what pieces had come from this mysterious sperm donor. Maybe his dark hair, the slant of his nose, his long limbs?

“What?” I ask. “How was that? Did you meet him?”

He looks immediately uncomfortable, like he maybe regrets bringing it up. His eyes are fixed back on the road.

“We don’t have to talk about it if you don’t want to,” I add gently, hoping never to cause that uncertainty in his icy eyes again.

"No, I want to. I want you to know." He looks more sure than he sounds. "We sent a couple emails back and forth. His name is Edgar. He's a mechanical engineer. I actually flew to Indiana to see him back in March." His Adam's apple bobs as he swallows hard. "We were supposed to meet at this coffee shop. He never showed. Three hours later, he sent one last message saying he was sorry, then stopped responding to me. Just like that."

Henry glances over at me, eyebrows tented, his face twisted into a sad little smile. My entire chest cracks open for him. In this moment, I can see the little boy who, in kindergarten when he was asked where his dad was, replied, "I don't have one! I was made by science!" Fully confident in the family he had.

"Want me to find his address and we can go egg his house?"

He lets out a sad little chuckle. "Nah. It's not worth the energy."

We sit in silence for a minute, or maybe ten. I can't take my eyes off him. I think about Henry, sitting alone at that coffee shop, in a strange city, full of hope and curiosity. I wonder what he ordered to drink. Did he get a blueberry muffin too? He used to love those whenever we'd walk to Brew, Laketon's local coffee shop, after school. He would split apart the muffin horizontally, giving me the sugar-coated top that he deemed "too sweet and crunchy" for his liking, settling for the soft base of the muffin instead. I never knew if that was really how he felt or if he was just indulging my sweet tooth.

I wonder who he called when he realized he'd been stood up. Or did he carry this burden, this pain, this disappointment on his own? For some reason, the hazy look on his face makes me think it's the latter.

Henry clears his throat finally, and as if he was reading my thoughts, he says, "I never told my mom that he and I were in contact. Or about Indiana. So . . ."

"I won't," I promise.

"I know," he says quietly. "You're the only person I've told."

He's been sitting in this alone for the better part of a year. It feels big, him telling me this. Like I'm someone he trusts to hold it with him.

Suddenly, I don't care about the rules I've imposed on us. We can worry about that when we get to the lodge. I reach for him. His fingers weave between mine, as if drawn together by some magnetic force. He's holding on to me like this intertwined mess of bones and skin is the only thing keeping him afloat. He draws us up to his lips, placing a long kiss on the back of my hand.

"Well, that got heavy fast, huh?" Henry says with a slight smile.

"I don't mind," I assure him.

I want to stop the car, climb into our own private bubble, and hear all of his most intimate thoughts from the last nine years. Every time he cried, the things that hurt the most, what he did to celebrate the wins. Whatever he'll give me. But he's done for now. I can see it on his face, the vulnerability too overwhelming to continue.

"So, what's your take on Chicago versus New York pizza?" he asks, changing the subject.

"Honestly? Do you really want the answer to this? Because you can walk down the street with a slice in New York. You can't dismiss the convenience of that. Plus, it cooks so much faster. You don't have to pre-order at a restaurant before you're even seated like you do back home."

"Traitor," Henry says, but he still hasn't let go of my hand, resting it on his thigh like it's his now.

WE PULL INTO Great Blue Lodge and I feel complete. We knew so much about each other, so deeply, for so long, and then everything shattered to pieces in an instant. But now he's here, and he's real, and my heart is very nearly bursting. I'm confident that we're doing the right thing, hitting pause until we get our moms engaged, but a part of me is vibrating with the need to kiss him once more.

As if he's inside my brain, and I honestly wouldn't be surprised if that was the case, he parks the car, kills the engine, and unbuckles his seat belt. He reaches across to unbuckle mine as well.

"Norah," he says tenderly, like my name is a precious gift on his tongue. He looks at me with the same nervous intensity as he did in that bed, before he touched the most sensitive part of me.

I've been in love with you my whole life.

It rings in my ears, the memory, the understanding of myself.

"Norah," he says again, like he's working up to something. Like he's trying to be brave.

Is it really possible that he feels the same way?

I'm hanging on the air of his exhale, immune to everything except his cool blue eyes, long lashes fluttering.

He sucks in a sharp breath, breaking my gaze, his whole body going rigid. I look around, and there is a barrage of women surrounding the parked car. Mom, Hannah, Kristine. And a blonde woman I've never seen before, who's wearing a tan beanie and an oversized knit sweater. She's absolutely fucking gorgeous.

I turn away from Henry and open the car door because they're all waiting for us.

He takes a breath and plasters on a smile I've never seen before, getting out of the vehicle almost robotically. I'm hugging Hannah as I watch him go straight to the beautiful woman and exclaim, "Gen! What are you doing here?"

Who is this person beaming at Henry like he's the center of her world? Shouldn't that be my thing?

"Surprise!" She practically jumps into his arms, but he catches her, two hands planted firmly on her biceps, her heels rocking back onto the ground.

"What are you doing here?" he repeats, this time softer, as if it's just for her.

She reaches up to touch his face, looking into his eyes. Now that I know what it's like to be the subject of his full attention, I can't look away. My whole body tenses in Hannah's arms, and when we pull apart, my sister raises her eyebrows.

"I knew you didn't mean it," the blonde woman says as her thumb runs across his cheek. Henry's eyes flutter closed, but mine are fixed on the two of them as she continues. "I knew you just needed . . . what are those things called from the rom-coms you love? A grand gesture! Sorry, I've been traveling all day and you know airplanes turn my brain to mush. Well, ta-da, here I am!"

The whiplash is almost unbearable enough to distract from the betrayal.

Henry has this beautiful woman here, touching him, making it seem like they're together. Or *were* together, if she's pulling out a grand gesture. But those rom-coms? The fact that this is an intimate detail she knows about him? That hurts almost as much. That was our thing. We dreamed of ending up in New York because of the movies we grew up learning by heart. If he still loves them now, that's because of me. I know that with complete certainty.

"Genevieve," Henry says, wrapping the strong fingers that were inside me mere hours ago around her hand and dragging it off his face.

Genevieve blinks twice and then turns toward me, smiling warmly. No one should look so effortlessly put together after a day of travel. I've been in Central Time for days and I'm still a disaster.

"Hi, I'm Genevieve Karlin," she says. "Henry's girlfriend."

Girlfriend.

I guarantee my face is not hiding either the shock or the gut punch of that last word, but I try to slap on my most convincing smile. My disloyal eyes find his automatically behind her. He shakes his head once, a subtle but clear *no*, but I'm at a loss to discern what's real anymore.

"Henry's girlfriend!" I exclaim, forcing out some false positivity. "It is so nice to meet you! I'm Norah!"

Henry tugs on Genevieve's arm, which is extended toward me in an unfulfilled hug. "Can we go grab a cup of coffee?"

She swivels back to face him, placing a hand on his chest, over his heart. "You know you can't have caffeine past noon, baby."

I'd be able to see the strain in his neck, the tension in his jaw, from all the way back at our B&B. He leans into her, whispering something I can't hear, and tucks a piece of sandy blonde hair back into place under her beanie.

Our moms exchange a look as Genevieve waggles her fingers and heads toward the main lodge.

"Norah, can you help me with the bags?" Henry asks, even

though he's extremely capable of handling his one suitcase and my duffel on his own. He did so as we went to and from the car last night and this morning. He shoots me a pleading look, and even though I don't know what I could have to say to him at this point, I shuffle around the CR-V, toward the trunk.

As soon as we're out of sight of our family, his face grows panicked. "I swear we broke up," he murmurs, his voice low and urgent. He reaches for me but I jolt away.

"Why doesn't she seem to know that, then?" I bite back.

"I don't know, maybe because in all those movies you and I spent a thousand hours watching together, the grand gestures always just work out," he volleys back, and then immediately seems to realize his mistake, referencing our history. "Norah, please."

That one word that nearly unraveled me completely hours earlier.

Please tell me what's going on. Please tell me this was a joke. Please tell me I didn't let you in, just for you to break me apart again.

"We are broken up," he continues. "Have been for—"

"Come on, Nor." My sister's voice rings out from the other side of the car. "Mom said we had to wait for you for lunch, and I'm starving. What's the holdup?"

"One sec!" I reply, grabbing my duffel bag, unconcerned when it knocks into his elbow as I swing it over my shoulder.

"Norah," he pleads as I start to walk away. "I'll explain everything. You just have to trust me."

I don't respond. I can't. I feel like I'm underwater, suffocating. I round the corner toward my sister, leaving Henry to deal with whatever the fuck Genevieve is to him.

Trust him.

Doesn't Henry know that that's the hardest thing he could ask of me?

AS OUR FAMILY, sans Henry, heads to lunch at one of the onsite restaurants, Hannah pulls me by the arm so we can hang back.

"What's going on?" she asks immediately.

"I don't know. Nothing. I'm fine."

"Norah, what the fuck happened while you were snowed in?"

"It was . . . confusing. That's all," I say, not wanting to make any of this about me. Because if I tell Hannah the truth right now, she will absolutely punch Henry in the face, and it will become so much bigger than it should be. This is about Mom and Kristine. It has to be.

"Is there something going on between you two?" Hannah asks, like I'm a wild animal she's carefully approaching.

"No! No. Of course not. We just called a temporary truce. That's it."

Hannah gives me a look; she's not buying any of it.

"Plus, Genevieve is here," I say a little too enthusiastically.

"Yeah, she showed up maybe an hour ago? Kristine had no idea how she got here. It was really fucking weird."

"I bet," I say, a million questions running at full speed through my brain. "Did you know he had a girlfriend?"

Hannah shakes her head, and we keep walking.

Chapter 11

GREAT BLUE LODGE is huge. The resort is more expansive than I could have imagined. There are several levels of slopes for skiing and snowboarding, hiking trails, an ice-skating rink, two restaurants and a bar onsite, tons of nightlife activities. I've always heard about the lodge from a number of our classmates over the years. This was the thing to do. The epitome of woodsy-chic.

The perfect place to propose.

There's a central lodge with individual rooms, and then tons of small cabins surrounding it on the property, which was where we were staying.

The cabin is adorable. High ceilings with long beams and tall windows. Gorgeous stained wood paneling. A stone fireplace from my dreams. I'm able to drop all my complicated feelings and revel in this moment for my mom and her soon-to-be fiancée.

When we return from lunch, per Mom's request, Hannah begins to move her stuff out of the second bedroom. Presumably because of the looming question of our new visitor, who

Kristine didn't even seem to know existed until she arrived at the lodge two hours ago.

I should feel relieved that Kristine doesn't know Genevieve. Surely his mom would know about a serious girlfriend, so there must be an explanation, just as Henry promised. But the sinking pit in my stomach persists.

Hannah shimmies her overflowing suitcase past the bedroom doorframe and out into the common area. The thought of Henry and Genevieve sharing a bed behind a closed door twenty feet from this sofa, the one it appears I'll be sleeping on, makes me want to bolt.

I sit down on our new bed, still folded up. I feel nearly absorbed by it. I wish I could just sink all the way in and let it transport me far, far away from here.

"So," I say loudly, "what's on the agenda for today?"

"We were just talking about hitting the slopes." My mom does a swooshing motion as if she's holding ski poles, and Kristine cracks up like it's the funniest thing she's ever seen. These two really were made for each other.

"Is it okay if I go for a run? I can catch up with you for dinner. Just—" I glance toward the door. *I can't bear to be here when the two of them return.* "Between the drive and getting snowed in, I feel like I need to get out for a little while."

Kristine gives me a map of the resort and trails. I change and try to leave as quickly as I can.

Henry told me he never wanted to hurt me. How did I let it happen twice now? How could I have been so stupid? I feel humiliated, betrayed, confused.

This perfect moment in my life, that I thought I would treasure, that felt transcendent. It's tainted now.

The emotional upheaval of this day is exhausting.

Just as I'm getting my shoes on, Henry sweeps into the cabin, Genevieve close behind. He looks like he's aged about ten years in the last hour.

"Can I talk to you outside?" he asks, catching my arm as I put in my earbuds.

I'm both desperate to talk and absolutely not ready to speak to him right now. The fact that Genevieve is still here, in our family's cabin, only solidifies to me how fucked the situation is. It makes his plea for trust even harder to buy.

"Oh, there you are," Mom says to Henry, emerging in her ski gear. "I just had the girls move their things out here to the pullout sofa. You two can take the second bedroom. For some privacy."

Mere hours ago, Henry and I were starting to learn each other's bodies, but it's a reminder of what he's already had with Genevieve. The fact that she has this knowledge, this intimacy with him that now I don't know if I'll ever fully get, aches in a whole new way.

For once, my mother's chattiness comes in handy, and before I have to hear anything more about sleeping arrangements, I slip out the door. I don't warm up like I know I should. I just *go*.

My dad loved to run. I inherited this habit from him. At this point, though, it feels more like a vice. A way to avoid, to disengage, to hide.

My dad's passion was pure. He ran track all the way through college. He was supposed to participate in the U.S. Olympic trials when he was twenty-two, but then my grandfather had a heart attack and he had to go home to help my grandmother. My grandfather was in a coma for a few weeks, but ultimately had lost too much oxygen. My dad was the same age as his father when he dropped dead at the Jewel-Osco deli counter while trying to order some slices of Muenster cheese. He was in great shape, healthy. There were no signs of heart disease. They don't know why it happened.

I look down at my hands as I move through the dirt trails, covered in crunchy snow. My thumbs rest loosely on my middle fingers, hands as relaxed as possible. Just like he showed me when I joined cross-country my freshman year of high school. I know Dad's morning jogs didn't save him. I don't think they'll save me either. Sometimes I wonder if I'll make it to fifty, a milestone lost on the last two generations of my family. My pulse rams against my eardrums, the most quieting I can seem to do for my brain right now.

I'm so frustrated. With Henry for what he's putting me through, for tearing me open all over again. With myself for letting my guard down, for giving him the power to do this to me. How could I let his pheromones drug me into stupidity and uncertainty?

This is why I don't do intimacy. This is why I don't get vulnerable with men. I don't know what made me think it would be different this time.

I guess Henry was always a big *what if* in my head, and I let the curiosity get the best of me.

Now I can answer that question at least.

What if? Seems like I'd be just as lost and confused as I was at seventeen.

I run as long as my lungs can take it, but it doesn't alleviate anything I'm feeling. As I walk to cool down, I try to call Frankie, desperate for the comfort of my best friend, the person who knows all of my baggage with Henry. Whose mind would be completely blown by the last thirty-six hours. The person who would understand what it meant that I let those walls down, only for Henry Cole to torpedo them once again.

Frankie's phone goes straight to voicemail, and I don't have the energy to leave that message, so I fire off a few broad-stroke texts instead. They don't immediately register as delivered, so I guess she's not in service. Frustrated, I delay my return by taking an extra winding path, praying that the cabin will be empty. Of course, in keeping with the theme of the day, no such luck.

I don't see Henry, but Hannah and Genevieve sit on the couch together, silently scrolling on their phones. Genevieve's hair is wet, darker like this, twisted into a long braid over her shoulder.

I duck into the bathroom, hoping to splash some water on my face and compose myself before I have to engage with Genevieve while grabbing my shower items from the living room. I take a deep breath and am immediately hit by the floral smell of a shampoo that must be hers. I feel like I'm going to be sick. I inhale slowly, trying to let my nose adjust to the sweet, rosy notes, and when that doesn't work, when it just makes things hurt more, I rummage around and find a pack of matches with the Great Blue Lodge logo. I strike the matchstick against the box, and let it burn a few seconds too long, then shake the flame out. Genevieve's smell is replaced by the memory of birthday cake and too-sugary frosting.

I can't escape thoughts of Henry even when I'm desperate to.

Instead, I'm transported to the time we found a tub of vanilla frosting when we were eight, and devoured the whole thing in one sitting, until we felt the sugar pulsing through our veins, until we both got stupidly sick.

I wash my face and brace myself to see the other inhabitants of this cabin. As I open the bathroom door, I'm almost immediately swiveled back inside, a firm hand on my back like we're in a tango.

"Hey," Henry says, looking down at me with so much affection that I feel even more nauseated than I did from the floral shampoo.

"Don't touch me," I reply, wriggling out of his grasp. "We can't be in here together."

"Let me explain."

He looks sincere, yet his girlfriend (*ex-girlfriend? Grand-gesture-maker?*) is still sitting out on that couch in the cabin where my mom is planning to propose, with her perfect hair and her ability to smell like a goddamn botanic garden despite a day of travel.

"You said there was no one important," I start, letting out the words that have been whirring through my brain. "That girl flew halfway across the country during a snowstorm to fight for you. Sounds pretty serious to me."

"If you knew I'd just called something off," he says quietly, his voice a reminder that we shouldn't get caught like this under any circumstance, "you would've run. Tell me I'm wrong."

I can't. He's right. But none of this adds up.

"When?" I ask. "Exactly when did you break up?"

Henry rubs the back of his neck, a slight grimace across his face. "Three days ago."

I try to do some quick math. Three days ago was our first full day in Laketon.

"Nor?" I hear my sister's muffled voice on the other side of the bathroom door.

Henry and I both freeze. There is no good way to explain why we're whispering in a bathroom together.

"Uh, just a minute," I call out.

"No rush," she says, her voice louder as she moves closer. "Just letting you know your bag's in the bedroom."

I look at Henry, confused, as Hannah's footsteps pad back down the hall.

"I should go," he says quietly, reaching for the handle.

"Why is my stuff in the bedroom?" I ask. "Aren't you two—"

"She's leaving tonight," he jumps in quickly. "Red-eye."

I nod slowly. "Okay."

"We'll talk more later?"

I shrug as his lips pull into a thin line of defeat.

"Should we find a swing set or something so you can kick me?" he suggests with a self-deprecating smile. "I'm sure there's one somewhere on the premises."

I almost want to say *Maybe* because the sheer fact that he remembers the way he used to cheer me up when we were kids warms a small piece of my frozen heart. But I can't give him that. I try to keep my expression as neutral as possible as I watch his eyes scan my flushed face.

"I will explain everything," Henry promises before cracking the bathroom door and quietly slipping out.

I count to ten before I head to the second bedroom, grab my shower supplies and a change of clothes, and then let the water burn my skin until it's pink.

I'VE SAT THROUGH my share of strange dinners. The night Luisa and Michael tried to initiate a double date that neither Michael's friend nor I were aware was happening until we were neck deep in the spiciest Thai food I've ever had in my life, eyes, mouth, and later, asshole on fire. The time a bone-numbingly boring former coworker invited himself along to our girls' post-work tapas. Yet sitting here, at this large oval booth, covered in emerald upholstery that squeaks when anyone moves, with Henry, our families, and Genevieve, takes the cake. We have a perfect view of the ice-skating rink next to the restaurant, lights twinkling outside, reflecting perfectly on the snow-covered trees, but things are significantly frostier here.

I've pieced together some of her plan since I got back from my run, but the logic evades me all the same. Apparently, flights were hard to come by given the proximity to Christmas and the sheer number of cancellations the day before from the snowstorm. It sounds like she maybe comes from money, hence the travel here and back appearing out of thin air, but even so, she couldn't get anything earlier than the red-eye Henry mentioned when he was crowded up against me in that bathroom.

Despite knowing that Genevieve will be flying back to New York in only a few hours, her choice to stay here boggles my mind. If it were me, I would have booked it off this mountain before Henry even finished the coffee he allegedly shouldn't have been having past noon. Instead, she's chosen to spend the last (and next) several hours with us. Her demeanor has changed significantly. To Henry's credit, she definitely knows they're broken up now.

But she sure is chatty.

I think we're all too uncomfortable to really process this interruption of our supposed family vacation.

Genevieve asks to hear our parents' love story, and as my mom starts to share how she fell in love with the girl next door, I realize that I'm an asshole for not having asked this myself. She has Hannah text her a link to the murder podcast they must have been discussing when they were alone on the couch earlier. She wants to know all about my favorite spots in New

York to see if we have any overlap. She's familiar with Talha's pastry shop next to my apartment, and after realizing that we were both at the Sick Hypnotic End of Summer party, she tells me I would *love* her roommate's older brother, and asks if I want her to set us up. My sister snorts in what I think is more of a statement on my dire relationship track record than any indication that she knows what happened with Henry, but it allows me to dodge the question.

Genevieve ignores Henry entirely, but honestly, fair.

I too am attempting to ignore the way his arm is draped loosely around the back of the booth behind his mother. How he quietly keeps everyone's water glasses filled. The movement of his throat as he swallows some of his salmon fillet.

And I certainly ignore the way his eyes try to find and hold mine throughout the entire meal.

WHEN WE GET back to the room, Genevieve still in tow, Mom insists on lighting the menorah she brought with her, a classic bronze piece that's far less fragile or sentimental than our Tree of Life one that's back at the house.

"Sara, I love you, but we absolutely cannot set a bunch of open flames loose here."

"What's the big deal?" Mom asks Kristine. "They're not going anywhere."

"We're in a giant cabin made of wood," Kristine says slowly. I have to agree with her. This seems like a precarious idea at best, a liability at worst.

But Mom sinks her teeth in. "This is the one thing that's vitally important to me and my family's traditions. My girls are both here now, and I want to light the fucking menorah with them, okay?!"

Hannah and I exchange looks. We've never remembered to light the menorah past the second night. Why is this becoming a thing?

"I need to talk to you. In there," Mom says, all of the warmth gone from her voice. She walks into their bedroom without a second look. Kristine nods, following her in and shutting the door behind them.

It's quiet for a moment. We all stand around, unsure of what to do. Finally, Hannah gets up and retrieves a handful of dreidels and a large bag of gelt from her suitcase, placing them on the dining table.

"You brought these?" I ask.

"I figured it was going to be a long couple days." My sister shrugs, sliding onto the dining chair closest to her.

"What's all of that?" Genevieve asks with genuine curiosity.

"You've never played dreidel?" I try to cut any judgment out of my voice.

She shakes her head no.

I sigh, sitting down at the table, then pull open the yellow mesh bag of gold-wrapped chocolate coins and start divvying them up into four piles on the table.

"Okay," I say, picking up a neon pink plastic dreidel from Hannah's stash.

Henry and Genevieve fill in the remaining seats next to, not across from, each other. I'm not sure that she's looked in his direction since they returned from their coffee, but if this is the way to keep the peace for the rest of her time here, I'll do it.

"We all start by putting one piece of gelt in. Then it becomes kind of like UNO, you follow the direction of the side you land on. So give it a spin," I say, dropping the dreidel from the air, and watching as it lands on the table and twirls around on the dark wood. It lands on the shin. "This one is *shin*, which means I have to put one piece into the pot." I spin the dreidel around, explaining the other sides to Genevieve. She's the only one who's new to this.

Henry mindlessly twists a dark blue plastic dreidel in his palm, the same one he always favored as a kid.

We start to play, and Henry lands on gimel, giving him the full pot, three rounds in a row.

"Unfair!" my sister exclaims. She always gets very competitive.

"You're working at an advantage!" I say. "It's those big hands! You've got more velocity!"

"My big hands are to blame?" he asks innocently, and I detect the smallest hint of devilishness in his tone. "It's a twenty-five percent chance. Completely random."

Suddenly, the arguing from my mom's bedroom cuts through the closed door. I can't make out everything, but I hear their mix of indiscernible voices: "blatant disregard" and "irrational behavior" and "shouldn't be this hard."

We all look to the door, waiting for something. Someone to emerge? The fight to escalate? But the room goes silent, or maybe they just realized we could hear them.

"I'm sure it'll blow over by the morning," Henry says, and I nod.

Mom and Kristine have been nothing but absolutely enamored with each other. He's probably right, as much as I hate to give him any credit at this moment in time.

"At least our breakup involved less yelling," Genevieve mutters, the first (albeit indirect) thing I've clocked her saying to Henry since we first arrived at the lodge.

"Sorry, are you sure you don't need me to drive you to the airport?" he asks sharply.

"Don't worry about it," she says as if he should, in fact, be deeply worried. "Daddy is sending a car, but he is *not* happy about any of this."

"I really am sorry, Gen." His voice is earnest as he twists a chocolate coin between his fingers, eyes on her. "I hope this won't affect things at work."

Genevieve pushes back in her chair, disbelief on her face. "Oh my God, grow up, Henry. I'm not a supervillain. You're the one who made us DTR. That's on you. If you weren't into this, you could have just said so, or breadcrumbed me like a normal person. I'm not going to fuck up your job. I can't believe you would even say that. You may not want to be with me, but surely you know me better than that at this point. Gonna be really easy to get over you if that's what you think of me."

Hannah and I exchange uncomfortable looks. Dreidel can get heated, but not usually like this. There's clearly a lot more to their story than we know, and we're stuck as unwilling audience members watching it all play out.

"Did you want to take a look at that . . . thing . . . ?" I lie poorly to Hannah, who jumps in with an eager "In the bedroom, yes! Let's—"

"No, no, it's fine." Genevieve waves us off, forcing a look that makes us both sink down into our chairs. "I'd like witnesses to what a little bitch Henry is being about all of this. Everyone thinks he's like, some sort of golden child. Daddy called him a wunderkind the first time he came to my parents' for dinner. You're twenty-six. It's not that impressive. And you're spineless as fuck, that's for sure."

I chance a glance in Henry's direction, his head hung slightly down, resigned to take it all.

"Now Daddy knows you're an asshole," Genevieve continues, "but he's not going to fire you. He's an asshole too. He'll probably like you even more after this."

Genevieve Karlin, I realize. I was so swept up in the *girlfriend* of it all that somehow I missed it. Henry works at Karlin Stein. Her father must be the aforementioned Karlin.

That's messy, even for Henry.

Eventually, after an epic dreidel loss, Hannah retreats to bed, and not wanting to be stuck with just the two of them, I say goodbye to Genevieve and follow suit. Henry catches my eye before I disappear into the bedroom, a pleading look on his face, which I don't have an answer to.

I slip inside to find Hannah in bed, scrolling on her phone. "Well, that was fucking weird."

I nod, unsure of what to say. Soon, Hannah is conked out, curled up next to me, emanating an intense amount of heat for such a small person, and all I can do is pretend like I'm ever going to sleep.

Chapter 12

UNSURPRISINGLY, SLEEP EVADES me. Eventually, I hear Henry's and Genevieve's voices fade, and the front door open and shut, then open and shut once more, several excruciating minutes later. There's a loud sigh as footsteps pad toward the other side of this wall, and I wonder if Henry will knock. Slide a note under the door. *Something.* I shouldn't have to be the one to initiate this conversation.

But my curiosity, my pain, and the realization that twenty-four hours ago we hadn't even kissed yet prevail, and I slip out of the room to see him.

He sits on the pullout sofa, still in its couch form, elbows bent on his knees, head in his hands. This must be the longest day of Henry Cole's life, and it shows.

"Never mind, we can do this later," I say quietly, and his eyes shoot up to meet mine.

"Please stay."

I rarely remember him looking so helpless in all the years I've known him. Maybe that's why I sit down. Two cushions over, but with him all the same. There's a low buzz of sharp voices coming from our moms' room and I glance toward their door before giving him my attention.

"I'm so sorry, Norah. I never meant for any of it to happen this way. This morning." He pauses. "Jesus, was that only this morning?"

I nod, my mouth twisting against my will at the memory. I know he clocks it.

"That was one of the best mornings of my entire life. Everything that came after aside, I need you to know that. I need you to not give up on this just because today got complicated."

"*Complicated* is the word you're going with?" I ask, and he flinches. "You can talk. I'm not going to ream you out. Seems like you got plenty of that already."

Henry runs his hand through his hair. "I deserved it." He takes a long slow breath. "Genevieve works reception at Karlin Stein, her father's company. We officially met at my interview, but turns out we'd chatted a few times before on a dating app without ever going out. Gen and I weren't right for each other. It was very obvious that we should've never been together. It sounds shitty to say out loud, but it's true. I had just started this new job, one I'd worked my ass off for, and she was . . . very persistent.

"I wasn't going to enter into anything with my boss's daughter that wasn't completely aboveboard. But then, going through HR and everything, it added this whole other layer. It made it seem more serious than it was before we even went out to dinner. It put a label on this *thing* before I knew how I felt about her. Or didn't feel. I thought I was doing the right thing by not bringing her home for Christmas, that it would send the signal that I wasn't as . . . invested as she was."

His words are familiar. It's exactly what I did with Rob.

Henry pauses. His eyes are soft and I want to cry, or maybe make a home there. "And then I saw you at O'Hare and knew I was done for."

This time, when he reaches for me, I let him. His fingers dance with mine over the cushion between us.

"I tried to let you go," he continues. "I feel like I've spent my whole life trying. But if just seeing you glaring at me across baggage claim caused every old feeling I had to come roaring back into my heart, regardless of what, or if anything, happened between us, I had no right to be in a relationship with anyone." His thumb traces circles across the inside of my palm. "I broke up with her the next morning. I knew doing it over the phone wasn't ideal, but I never expected her to show up here. I didn't end things with some master plan to make this"—he gestures between us—"happen either. It just felt unfair. To me and to her."

Despite his proclamation to the contrary, *to you* hangs in the air between us.

"Do you have any idea how hard it is for me to let people in?" I ask slowly. "To be vulnerable enough to give someone a way to break my trust, to hurt me? This is why, Henry. I don't do this. I'm terrible at it. Maybe this is a sign."

"It's not," he says quickly. "It's only a sign if you're looking for a way out, and I really hope you aren't. You can trust me, Norah. I'll be gentle with your heart."

It's hard to face him when I feel this much, but I need to see him when I ask, "No more secrets?"

He's looking at me like he can see all my fears and insecurities, and he's ready to hold them. "No more secrets. No lies. I promise. Can we just get back to where we were this morning? This could be so good, Norah. I know it."

A particularly harsh whisper cuts through from the other side of our moms' door, a bucket of ice water on the moment. I want to say yes. I want to fling myself into his arms and kiss his dumb face until our lips are raw. But today was a nightmare. It can't be like this if we want to put our moms first. I fold my hand back into my lap.

"I think we should stick to our original plan."

His brow furrows. "As in?"

"This is a distraction. We need to stay focused on getting them engaged."

Henry looks like he's about to challenge this idea, but before he can start, I add, "Look at all the drama from today. It was a mess, and now they've been fighting for hours. We have to temper whatever is happening between us until the proposal. Just friends until Operation Latke is complete."

Henry opens his mouth, then abruptly shuts it. With a tight-lipped smile, he nods. "Right. That makes sense."

I'm halfway back to my room when he asks, "Can friends watch a movie together?"

That's how we did friendship for a million years before. We'd put on a rom-com and I'd think about all the ways I could touch him if we were just a little closer.

I return to the sofa, this time to the cushion next to him, as he flips on the TV, and I let myself sink into the nostalgia of being friends with Henry Cole.

I WAKE WITH a start, shooting up from the couch and nearly elbowing Henry in the throat in the process of detaching myself from his strong hold. The cabin is still dark, save for the glow of the TV, *Serendipity* having long since ended. Now there's some low hum of a nineties sitcom I wasn't allowed to watch growing up. Henry remains extended on the too-short couch, where our bodies were cocooned moments earlier.

"We fell asleep," I whisper, and Henry lets out a soft grunt, only half awake, and tousled in a way that makes me regret the rules I set earlier.

He stretches his legs, the slacks he never changed out of now wrinkled, and there's a small satisfaction in finally seeing him rumpled like this. Knowing it's because of me, even if it's not in the way we both might want.

"I should"—Henry stands, adjusting himself—"make this into an actual bed, huh?"

I nod, and we quietly remove the cushions, unfolding the springs and setting up the blanket our moms laid out for him hours ago.

"Do you think Hannah noticed you were gone?" he asks as I linger in the living room, a pillow clutched to me.

"She could sleep through the end of the world," I tell him. "But I should go back."

Henry nods once, his fingers brushing mine in what could be played off as accidental when he takes the pillow from my hands. "Sleep well."

"You too," I say before I quietly turn the knob and sneak back into the bedroom.

Hannah stirs as the mattress sinks under my weight, but settles back in almost immediately, her eyes never even fluttering open.

I'm wide awake, wired. We probably only slept for two or three hours, but I feel fully rested. As a general rule, I don't do sleepovers with men. Waking up together is far too intimate an act. But the last two nights with Henry, even as anxious as I was, or as suboptimal the sleeping conditions—I should be running on fumes. I should be barely functioning. Instead, I feel energized.

I lie there, restless, until around six, when I hear coffee brewing. I double-check that the bed looks sufficiently slept in before creeping back out.

I shuffle into the kitchen, where Henry grasps a mug with two hands. He looks drained, but the sleep clears off his face when he sees me. He places his own mug on the counter and grabs one for me from the cabinet. It's on the third shelf, which I wouldn't have been able to reach without him. I give him a smile of gratitude and pour the dark liquid into the mug.

We stand there in easy silence, taking sips of coffee, when I hear the voices again. Kristine and Mom, back at it.

"Did this start up again after I went in?" I ask softly, tilting my chin toward their door. "Have they been going all morning?"

He nods. "More or less."

We heard them on and off during our movie, an ever-present reminder of why I couldn't let my arm cross the barricade, why our thighs needed to maintain a healthy distance. Why the way we awoke was such a problem.

"Do you think they'll be okay?" I ask. "You seem more familiar with their relationship than I am."

"I don't know. They're both stubborn. I've never seen them like this," he admits.

While my mom kept this huge secret from me and my sister for basically a year, Kristine was open with Henry from the start. It seems like he spent a lot of time going back and forth between Chicago and New York, so he got to see their love grow. Something in my chest feels funny about having missed out on that.

"We have to fix this," I say, and he nods, draining his mug. My mind is churning through what we could do. Without the full context of what's really going on between them, all I can focus on are the facts we have.

"Mom's love languages are acts of service and gifts," I explain, trying to see if that will get us anywhere.

A memory hits me. The sound of Velcro ripping and being replaced. Felt material under my fingers. *Baruch ata Adonai . . .*

"Where did you go?" Henry asks, blinking at me.

I look up at him, breezing past the genuine curiosity on his face, like he's studying me with great care.

"When Hannah and I were little, we had our own wall-hanging menorah. It was silver and crinkly, with felt candles and detachable fabric flames so we could light it ourselves."

"Without it being a fire hazard," Henry says, finishing my thought. "I remember that. It was in the hallway between your rooms, right?"

"We always fought about who got to have custody over it, so that was the compromise. Dad measured the wall so it was exactly equidistant."

"Sounds like David," Henry says, and I push down the overwhelming feeling of our shared history.

"Maybe there's something along those lines we could find," I reply so I don't do something stupid like reach out and touch the bit of scruff that formed on his jaw in the last few hours. "As a gesture. We could even give it to Kristine to give to Mom, so it comes from her."

"I like the way your mind works, Gold." He's staring at me intensely, and even with five feet of space between us, I feel his gaze running over me like one of his strong fingers along my spine.

"Why don't you see if there's a toy store or something in town and find out when it opens?" I suggest. "I'm gonna go for a run."

"You sure go on a lot of runs," he comments. There's no judgment behind it. Just an observation.

"Yeah, well . . ." I trail off, not sure what to say to that.

I have too much going on in my brain.

If I stay in this room whispering with you any longer, I'm going to give in and kiss you.

"Thanks for the coffee," I say finally, taking one more sip. I place the mug in the sink, and this time, there's no mistaking the way his fingers graze mine on my way out.

ONCE I'M BACK from my run, everyone is awake. Henry informs me that my mom went for her own walk, and Kristine didn't seem pleased, opting to head to the slopes early. He found a few stores, but they don't open until ten, so we take our time, sitting quietly around the lodge.

Henry is all right angles, seated upright on the sofa we fell asleep on, perpendicular to Hannah, who's sprawled out on the love seat. He's reading some nonfiction book that I want to say is about the economy, and she has her earbuds in, probably absorbed in the latest episode of her new favorite murder podcast, which dropped this morning. I pick up my sister's legs and sit down next to her, even though there's more space on Henry's couch. I don't trust myself there.

When my phone reads 9:45, I leap up. "Let's go!" I say a little too enthusiastically.

Henry closes his book and goes to grab his keys.

"Come with us?" I ask my sister, jiggling her knee to get her attention. The idea of being back in the CR-V, sitting shotgun, the place where I felt like I got to know him again, shared secrets with him, where it felt real on a whole other level, is too risky a task for our newly minted status as *friends*.

My sister briefly takes out an earbud so I can repeat the question, but crinkles up her nose and puts her podcast back on.

"Shall we?" Henry asks, holding out my coat for me.

"It doesn't have to be weird," he insists once we're outside. "I heard what you said. We can be friends for now. Believe it or not, I have some modicum of control over myself."

But I don't, I think, opening the passenger-side door.

Henry places his hand on the headrest behind my seat as he backs out of the parking spot in an annoyingly thrilling display of competency porn, and something snaps in me.

Maybe getting my friend back is the key to making whatever is happening between us work down the line.

THE FIRST TWO stores we go to are a bust, and I start to question why I expected there to be any Jewish memorabilia in the middle of this nowhere town. But the third shop on Henry's list is called Friedmann's Toys, so if ever there was a Hail Mary equivalent for my people (a Hail Maccabees, perhaps?), this is it.

A bell rings as we walk inside, and I look up, seeing an actual bell, not just a sensor. It's the day before Christmas Eve, and the store is understandably packed with anxious parents. We move through the narrow aisles, tan laminate reflecting the overly bright fluorescent ceiling lights, past rows of stuffed animals, books, puzzles, the store a maze in and of itself.

"How'm I doing as your friend so far?" Henry uses his height to our advantage, scanning over the tops of the short shelves between aisles.

"If you really need to ask," I tell him, plucking a finger toy shaped like a duck off a hook, slipping it onto my pointer, and bopping him with it. "It's already a losing battle."

Henry looks down at me, his lips twisted to the side in amusement as he reaches for the duck. "Do you want to play another game?"

"Like our car game? Didn't that get a little heavy? And uh . . ." I fix my eyes on the other finger toys in the row. A pig, a panda, a cow. I want to say *intimate* because that's how it felt, but instead I opt for the safer term. "Personal?"

"This is the third store we've been to and everything's blending together at this point for me, so I was thinking, what if we split up, and each pick out a toy that we think encompasses the other person? It'll help us cover more ground to separate anyway and see if we can find something for Sara." His lips are folded between his teeth, but the ask feels vulnerable somehow. He's opening himself up to be playful if I just say yes.

"Ten minutes and then we meet back here," I say, extending my right hand. He shakes it, then dodges left, disappearing down the aisle in two long strides.

I scramble away, turning in the opposite direction. I move quickly past Barbies and Bluey and Batman action figures. I spend a few minutes perusing the stuffed animals, until I see Henry's dark hair over the shelf, approaching the aisle next to me, and flee.

In an effort to get as far away from him as possible so he won't see what I'm doing, I head to the opposite end of the store. It's there that I find a rich midnight blue train set. The box touts that although the design appears complex, there is only one path through.

There's an elegance to it that reminds me of our sophomore-year biology teacher. *Elegant can mean the simplest solution.* Not that Henry is simple, but he's concise.

And I have a memory of him and Kristine going to visit his Great-Aunt Jean one Christmas when we were small. He came home raving about how the fire station in her neighborhood had a toy train display he was obsessed with.

I grab the box with seconds to spare, and hope he's been more successful with the other part of our quest.

We meet back up, and Henry has a large orange turtle about the size of my head pressed to his chest. Its plush, squishy body is a soft velour, with a shell made harder by the sparkly fabric covering it. Part of me wonders why anyone would decide that a turtle should be orange, but its little beaded eyes are comforting somehow.

"Me first," I say, shoving the box in his direction.

He tucks the stuffed turtle into the crook of his elbow.

"The fire station trains," he says immediately, his eyes full of affection. "That's cheating. You can't dip into our history."

"I believe per the bylaws set—"

He cuts me off with a simple "Norah, I love it."

"It wasn't just that," I huff, causing Henry to smirk. "You bring order to chaos. This week aside, I mean. A grounding presence. That's how you always felt to me. When we were in the car the other day and I was driving . . . it's how you still feel to me," I admit.

Henry smiles warmly at that, then turns his attention to the turtle in his arms.

"Tough exterior, but soft underneath," he starts, holding the stuffed animal up to me as an offering. "Playing the long game. Both cute," he adds with a wink.

I hug the turtle to my chest.

"Any luck with a menorah?" he asks as we stand there, a little too close for *just friends*.

I shake my head and we both turn toward the front registers in defeat. The checkout line has grown threefold since we got here, the one employee, a man in his sixties with a full head of luxurious white hair, looking remarkably calm under the circumstances. We weave around, finding the end of the line right next to the clearance section.

"Hey." He nudges me with his elbow. "Think that'll work?"

Henry gestures to a box in the clearance bin. A menorah made of sky blue plastic on the cover, with little orange bulbs. I shove the turtle into Henry's arms, then reach down to grab the box, flipping it around in my hands. It's got LED lights and tiny switches for each individual candle. The side of the box advertises that the lights flicker like real flames too.

"Seems like a good option to me."

There's a little girl parallel to us in the curve of the long line, maybe two and a half years old, with jet-black pigtails that stick straight up in the air. She's sitting on her mother's hip, having an absolute meltdown, while her mom tries to stop her twin brothers, who must be five or six, from poking each other's eyes out. The little girl leans her head on her mom's shoulder, screaming as she looks back toward us with despair.

I haven't really been around kids since I stopped babysitting when I was fourteen, and I panic. I stare back at her with alarm, which doesn't make things worse but definitely doesn't help the situation. I watch her little eyes shift away from me, and up to Henry. I glance over at him, and he's contorted his face so he resembles a monkey with startling accuracy. Lips curled inward, but cheeks puffed out, his eyes like saucers. The little girl quiets, assessing him. Suddenly, Henry pops his cheeks, making a fart sound with his mouth, and the skepticism on this little girl's face shifts to immediate glee. She sits up in her mother's arms, giggling, and demanding, "Again! Again!"

Henry resumes his position, and I let my eyes linger on him a little longer as he breaks the next time, laughing right along with the little girl. Her mom turns over her shoulder and mouths *Thank you* to Henry.

"Please, she's doing *me* a favor. Lines are boring, huh?" he says, and the girl nods enthusiastically, gripping her mom's shoulders as she swings her whole body back in agreement.

How does he do this? Be so seamlessly helpful and kind. I can't loiter in these warm feelings that keep bubbling up for long. They make me think about waiting in lines with him at the grocery store, the movie theater, a host stand at a restaurant. All the mundane things we could do together if this were real. If this *is* real.

We move apart from the mom and her gaggle of children as she gets called up to the register, and Henry waves goodbye to his new little friend.

"You're good with kids." The underlying question is *how*, but he doesn't need me to ask.

"I've been thinking a lot lately about how I grew up," he says, shifting his feet so they're parallel to mine. "It's not that I didn't appreciate how much my mom did as a single parent, I just had no idea. I'm sure I won't even grasp the full extent of it until I become a dad myself, and even then, I'm not the birthing parent. I'm not the food source if—" He pauses. "If my partner decides and is able to nurse. There's so much I can never understand, but if I see a parent struggling, I think about my mom, and how I hope people treated her. How I know a lot of times they didn't."

"You're the guy bringing the stroller up and down the subway stairs, aren't you?" I tease, but his sheepish smile tells me he's done exactly that on more than one occasion.

"You know how her parents were," Henry says, looking down at the floor.

When Kristine came out to her parents in college, they stopped paying her tuition. She moved to Milwaukee for a while to live with her aunt, the only remaining family member who stayed in contact with her, and later followed a girlfriend to Chicago, where she stayed until she and Henry transitioned to the suburbs, next door to us.

"She says it as a throwaway comment sometimes, how grateful she was when we arrived in Laketon, but she didn't have a community as a mom until we moved there. I was probably older than that little girl," he says, gesturing to his pigtailed friend who has kept eyes on him even still. "A tiny bit of kindness takes nothing from me. Why wouldn't I try to help in any way I can?"

Henry is so serious in this moment, and I feel my heart swoop. *Soon soon soon.*

"You want the whole wife-and-kids shebang, then, huh?" I ask, immediately regretting the fact that we're blazing right past friendship boundaries.

"I want a partner," he says, his blue eyes so clear. "I want a family, but how that looks is up to her. I think I could be a good dad, even though I never really—" He stops, shifting the boxes in his arms as if he needs something to do. "I think I have a lot of love I could give to a child, whether they're biologically mine, or we adopt."

My hackles go up at that loaded *we*, but before I can spiral too much about it, Henry adds, "I saw how David was with you, with Hannah. With me. I love my mom so much. She's everything. But the world could use more dads like yours."

A throat clears behind us as the man at the register waves us forward, in what must not be the first time. I try to covertly wipe my eyes with the heel of my hand as we approach the counter.

I rummage through my bag for my credit card, but Henry is already returning a signed receipt. He takes the nondescript brown paper bag in one hand and reaches for me with the other. Our fingers weave together as if on instinct.

"Is this really what you do with your friends?" I ask, but he just grips me tighter. "Trevor? Or your LA buddy who has all the couch sex?"

"It's what I always wanted to do with you," he replies, eyes forward as we approach the car. "I'm sorry. I didn't intend to talk about all of that." He's still not looking at me. "I'm not trying to freak you out or anything. I don't want those things now, or even soon. Just . . . one day."

"One day," I echo quietly, slicing off a piece of my own vulnerability.

He squeezes my hand once before opening the passenger-side door and ushering me inside.

Chapter 13

I DON'T SEE Mom for the rest of the afternoon.

Hannah and I go for a walk, exploring some of the grounds, but I can't focus. I'm so nervous that I'm going to spill something about Henry that I basically clam up entirely, letting Hannah tell me about the nine-part murder podcast she's been listening to in excruciating detail. I know she knows something is up because I normally have a very low tolerance for people going into too much detail about books, movies, or podcasts. Just tell me it's good and let me see for myself. But I'm relieved when she carries on about how the dead girl's second ex-boyfriend would have done *anything* for his new girlfriend, and her theory that he's protecting this other woman who totally murdered his ex.

Kristine comes back at some point, her cheeks pink from the cold, or maybe the reflections of the sun on the snow. She plasters on a fake smile before going back into the room, and Henry shakes his head, a clear indicator that things aren't any better.

When Kristine emerges an hour later, Henry and I exchange a look and a nod. It's time.

"Look, Mom, I don't know what's going on with you and Sara," he says, Kristine's eyes narrowing at my mom's name, "but we want you to know that we all love you both. I'm sure it's a larger debacle than just the menorah, and that you're both responsible for your own happiness or lack thereof, but we'd hate to see this all go to waste over something so small. I know she's the love you've been searching for all this time," he says, glancing sidelong at me so briefly that I might have imagined it, "so we thought this might be a small gesture to smooth things over."

He reaches down, grabbing the plain brown paper bag and passing it to his mom. She reaches inside, pulling out the box, trying to muffle a smile.

"We thought maybe you could give this to Mom," I say, jumping in. "It would mean a lot to her. For it to come from you."

Kristine puts down the box, stretching out her arms and gesturing with her hands for us to come hug her. I let Henry approach first, and wait until he's pulled away to hug Kristine myself. I can still feel his hand in mine, but I can't afford to lose any more of my body to his touch. We've already close to bulldozed the line of friendship in mere hours.

"You kids are so sweet. This is a lovely idea. You two were always such a good team."

"I'll go see if they have any wrapping paper at the front desk," I offer, taking the box from Kristine before grabbing my coat and booking it out of there.

I briskly make the now-familiar walk to the main building, throwing open the door with abandon as I enter the lobby. There's a huge Christmas tree set up in the center, too picturesque to be real, with families and couples bustling around, taking photos and clutching to-go cups and ski gear.

I'm greeted warmly by a pretty girl about my age in a lodge uniform.

"Hi there! I hope you're having a wonderful stay at Great Blue Lodge. My name's Pauline. How can I help you?"

"This might be a weird ask," I say. "Or maybe it's not? It is the holidays. Do you happen to have any wrapping paper? Or know where I could get some . . . quickly?" I shake the box, as if providing further explanation.

Pauline gives me a knowing smile and holds up one finger as she ducks away behind the desk. While she's gone, I take another look around. There's a fireplace across from the Christmas tree with a number of cozy armchairs set up in a semicircle. It really is straight out of a Hallmark movie here.

Pauline pops back up. "Here you go!" She pushes a tape dispenser and scissors my way, and then holds up two rolls of wrapping paper. One is red, with polar bears in Santa hats sledding down a snowy mountain. The other is white, with metallic snowflakes of different sizes. I point at the nondenominational one, and she nods. "I thought that might be preferred," she says, glancing down at the LED-light menorah.

"You're a lifesaver, Pauline," I reply as she slides the snowy roll my way. I gather the supplies and scoot over to the end of the desk so she can help the impatient man behind me who keeps sighing loudly.

I carefully unroll the paper, measuring out how much I'll need. The even *riiiip* as the scissors slice through the sparkling snowscape is honestly therapeutic.

Operation Latke is working.

We're fixing this.

Henry and I are fixing this.

Kristine's right. We have always been a good team.

My hands are decidedly less steady as I fold the edges of the paper in to tape them together. I shrug it off as good enough, and slide the supplies back across to Pauline.

When I return to the cabin, Kristine waves me in, raising a finger to her lips for me to be quiet.

"Your mom is still mad," she says softly, "but she's in the shower. So this is perfect timing. Thank you again, sweetie." Kristine gives me another hug, and I pass her the box before she slips back into their bedroom.

A few minutes later, I hear the paper tear open and the squeal escape from my mother's throat, and I know we did good.

Henry puts his book down and comes over to me, his hand extended in a high five. My palm meets his, and even that one small touch sends an unwanted wave of goose bumps over my skin.

"Great idea, Gold," Henry whispers, his breath warm against my ear.

Our parents come bursting out of their room. My mom is beaming, having unboxed the menorah. The sun is close to setting, and Mom decides it's good enough, so we gather around, saying the prayer as she flicks the switches on each fake candle, watching with glee as the lights dance around like real flames.

"I think I was trying to hold on to the traditions that were important to your dad," Mom says quietly to me at one point, while the rest of the group is trying to decide on dinner. "He always took celebrations fully to heart. That's why you staying for all of Hanukkah has meant so much to me this year, honey.

I wanted his memory to be a blessing in this new chapter, for all of us."

I nod along, understanding. I feel Dad's presence every time I participate in Jewish activities, from attending a Passover seder at a friend's house in New York where we sang "Dayenu" until the end of time, to the simple act of buying challah at the deli. Even though none of us would ever think that my mom was trying to replace him with Kristine, I see where she's coming from. Even if her menorah meltdown was a little misguided.

They decide to bring in pizza for dinner, and I try not to listen as Henry gives Hannah advice about some issue with a coworker, imagining what else our future could potentially bring.

HENRY AND I repeat our pattern from the night before: We watch a movie we used to love, this time with the couch bed fully extended. For comfort. We fall asleep together, again, and don't even wake up intertwined.

This time, when I sneak back into the bed with Hannah, she rolls over immediately, scaring the shit out of me. This is the same girl who once slept through a smoke detector going off in our house.

"Interesting," she hums as I get settled.

"What?" I ask, trying to play dumb.

"It's three a.m., Nor."

Thank God it's dark enough in here that she can't see my face. "I got up to use the bathroom."

"Well, if you just took a six-hour shit, we should probably

take you to the ER." My sister wiggles around, trying to get comfortable. "I forgot to turn on DND and TJ sent me like, seventeen texts about a guy they went out with. When I looked over, you clearly hadn't been here."

"It's nothing," I say, grateful she hadn't gone out in the living room and seen us for herself, even though yesterday was much more damning.

"Right," she snorts.

"You're the one who told me to try and get along with him. We were just watching a movie. That's how our friendship worked back then. You can't blame me for falling asleep, it's been a wild few days. Smoothing over things with Mom and Kristine was quite an undertaking. Which you'd know if you'd bothered to come with us."

I can feel Hannah roll her eyes as she shifts onto her back.

"Fine. It is nice to have you guys not at each other's throats anymore, I guess," she mumbles, then promptly passes back out.

I wish I could sleep like she does, but instead, I lie awake, thinking about what might have happened if my bigmouth sister had caught us wrapped up in each other the night before.

LATER THAT DAY, still feeling a little spooked, I find myself in the lobby of the main lodge, needing to get some space beyond the walls of the cabin. I find a cozy armchair near the fireplace and sink into it, sliding off my snow-soaked boots so I can pull my knees into my chest.

"Well, if it isn't Miss Big Apple herself," I hear.

I look up, and Trevor Hayes stands before me, smiling widely, his long golden hair tied up into a messy bun.

I blink twice. "What are you doing here?"

What *is* Trevor doing at Great Blue Lodge?

"Oh, we've been coming here for years," he says, crouching down in front of me to chat. "My family has a time-share. You're here with Henry and your moms, right?"

I nod.

"Oh good, yeah, I'm the one who hooked you guys up, told him all about it."

That does make sense. The Hayes family would have a time-share here. They seem like the outdoorsy types.

"How did you get here in the storm?" I ask.

"That was pretty brutal, huh? I left right after the reunion and drove through the night. Slept half the next day, but it was worth it. Henry mentioned you guys got caught in it. We were supposed to hang out up here that night you got stuck."

"How did you . . . drive?" I trail off, thinking about how drunk I'd been at the reunion.

"Oh, I just had that one shot at the beginning of the night. I was fine. You know, you're very cute when you're tipsy," Trevor chuckles.

I roll my eyes, giving him half a smile.

"There she is," he says, touching my calf and giving it a little shake. He sits back on the fluffy rug in front of my armchair, relieving his knees of the crouch I can't believe he held for so long. He folds his hands loosely around his shins. "Well, I don't have too much to do before I drive back tomorrow morning, so if you'd like company, I'm your guy."

"You're driving back tomorrow? On Christmas Day?"

"Yeah, my sister, Bea, I don't know if you remember her, she's four years older than us. She had a baby last month, so they obviously weren't going to come, but we wanted to spend Christmas Day as a whole family. Gotta see that little smush of a niece of mine dressed as an elf. Classic."

"Are you here by yourself?" I ask slowly.

"Nah, my buddy lives in Minneapolis, so he came and met me so we could do some snowboarding. He's staying a few extra days. If we don't use the time-share, it just expires anyway. Though I think he's been spending some time with one of the locals."

Trevor nods at the check-in desk, where there's a man whose back is to us leaning over the desk while Pauline, the same pretty employee who helped me with the wrapping paper yesterday, laughs a little too loudly.

"Wow, he must be hilarious," I deadpan with a hint of another smile.

"I can assure you he's not."

My phone buzzes with a text from Hannah telling me to come back to the cabin so we can discuss dinner.

"Back into the front lines, then?" Trevor asks, looking at me like a sad puppy.

I stand up. "How could you tell?"

He stands too, activating some intense core strength I definitely don't have. He extends his arms and I smile, pulling him into a hug.

"If you and Henry want to hang out later, give me a call. He still owes me a drink for missing the other night. I know he got sidetracked with his surprise visitor, but tell that guy I better see him again before he goes back to New York."

"I'll mention it," I promise, trying not to cringe internally at the mention of Gen. I'm honestly surprised that Trevor seems to know about her but not whatever's been going on between me and Henry, though I guess I'm the one who insisted we keep it all under wraps. "It was good to see you."

He doesn't say anything more, but I feel his gaze on me as I head out to the cabin.

Chapter 14

AFTER LIGHTING THE little LED menorah, Kristine ducks into the bedroom and returns with a stack of lumpy, wrapped gifts.

"We've loved learning all of your Hanukkah traditions," Kristine starts as she hands out the presents. "Here's one from our family that I wanted to share."

Mom beams at Kristine, clearly knowing what's coming next. And suddenly I do too. I tear open the paper to find cozy black-and-white plaid fleece. When I unfold the fabric, it's exactly what I'd figured—a set of handmade pajamas that matches what everyone else is opening.

As far back as I can remember, Kristine made Henry and herself matching pajamas to wear on Christmas Eve. Then they would take their holiday card photos—always delayed, and usually mailed out (or hand-delivered to us by Henry) in late January.

As Kristine explains, Henry's eyes are fixed on mine so clearly that I can't imagine it isn't telegraphing to everyone standing here. For years when we were growing up, I used to picture a future where I was on the Coles' card, Henry's arms wrapped around me. Another way I dreamed of being his. This isn't how I envisioned myself getting onto the card, but it still feels like a step closer.

We all change into the matching pajamas to head to our dinner reservations at the Drop, the trendier of the two restaurants onsite. While we'd spent our first night here at the more casual eatery, today is, after all, Christmas Eve. Not my holiday, but it means something to the Coles. After the meal, we have a time slot with the lodge's photographer at the giant tree in the lobby, hence the inherently cringe dinner attire. But it seems to make our moms (and Henry) so happy that I can't even be too embarrassed about it all.

As we walk over to the lift that will take us to the Drop, I realize that, given my insider knowledge about Henry's bright blue proposal suit, Kristine must be waiting until tomorrow, our last night at the lodge. We're in the home stretch, and then Henry and I can figure out what all of this means for us.

Mom and Kristine get on the chairlift first, and I can hear Mom's giggle as she starts up the incline. I get in next with Hannah, snuggled together for warmth, the pajamas not providing enough on their own, even with our coats on, but it's a cute gesture all the same. As we ascend the mountain of snow, watching the ballsier night skiers still at it, zooming past floodlights, I glance behind me at Henry. His eyes are unabashedly locked on me, and I feel my entire body flush. I whip back around so abruptly that my dangling knees feel tingly and weak, and Hannah tells me that if I go catapulting out of the chairlift, she is not equipped to rescue me.

When we finally reach the top of the slope, we head into the Drop, which has floor-to-ceiling windows, looking out on the full scope of Great Blue Lodge's property. I get the same fantastical sense of looking out an airplane window close to the descent as I do peering through the glass here as we're led to our table. The restaurant has sleek, minimalist decor, the view itself being the real showstopper.

We sit down and order wintery cocktails. Henry and I both opt for the bourbon mulled cider, and it makes me think about him biting into that apple-juice-soaked pretzel rod back at that inn, the way his fingers brushed mine as he took it from me. The moment that started unspooling the nine years we didn't talk into something made of hope and promise.

That must be why I down that first cocktail so quickly.

"We actually have some news," Mom says as I pick at my Brussels sprout appetizer. "Girls," she starts, turning to Hannah and me and taking Kristine's hand. "Kristine and I are moving in together."

"That's great!" I say, mouth full. They're about to be engaged. Living together makes sense.

"I'm so glad you feel that way," Mom continues. "With all you kids out of the house, both of our homes feel so big and empty. Henry's been helping us run the numbers and figure out what's feasible so—" She takes a dramatic pause. "We're selling the houses and moving to a condo downtown!"

"City living! Sounds fun," Hannah says, and I shoot her a death glare.

My fork drops onto the plate with a clatter. "You're selling our house?"

"Well, yes, honey," Mom says, fiddling with the stem of her wineglass. "It's too much for even the two of us."

I hear the words, but I can't process them. "But that's our home. That's where we grew up. Where all our memories are."

"To be fair, Norah, you haven't been home in two years. We think it's time for a fresh start." Mom says it kindly, but her eyes narrow, telling me to stay calm.

I don't know why I'm melting down. Mom is right. I hate going back to that house. But flashes of Dad run through my mind—him in the kitchen with his favorite cheesy apron that read *Penne for your thoughts*. Him lying on the floor of my bedroom when I'd wake him up in the night, crying from a bad dream. Him setting up flags in our backyard so we could run sprints together, zigzagging through the dying grass. It takes everything for me to not throw back Mom's words from the night before about honoring Dad's memory. Selling our house feels in complete conflict with that truth.

I glance at Henry across the table. His brow is furrowed but he's taken a sudden interest in the grilled artichoke on the plate in front of him.

For the first time in days, he can't be bothered to meet my stare.

"Is this decided?" I ask, hot tears prickling behind my eyes, ready to make an escape at any second.

"We're in escrow on the condo now, and putting the houses on the market next week."

"You knew about this?" I ask, spitting out the words. Only this time, they're directed at Henry. I don't care about subtlety anymore.

"He's been a huge help," Mom says. "He put us in touch with one of your old classmates to list them."

My head starts spinning, the impact of all this news more to blame than the bourbon cocktail.

Henry places his utensils down slowly. "Norah, I didn't think—"

The pity in his eyes is almost too much for me to bear.

"I can't be here right now," I say, taking my napkin out of my lap and placing it on the table. I scoot my chair out and stand, but I'm flooded with voices.

"Norah, you're an adult. Sit your butt back down right now," Mom says sternly.

"I can't believe you would do this to Mom," Hannah says in a harsh whisper.

"I'm sorry. I can't. I have to go."

I grab my coat off the back of my chair and quickly make my way through the restaurant.

"Wait."

I hear his low voice cut through all the chatter from the tables as I pass, but I don't turn back around.

"Can you just wait? I really need to talk to you." He catches up to me as I reach the doors of the restaurant. "*Norah.*"

"You said no more secrets," I bite out. "You knew about this, and you didn't tell me."

"I'm just as surprised as you are that they chose tonight to share," Henry starts, but then I'm hit with a wave of understanding from our time in Laketon.

"Oh my God. This is what the boxes at your house were for. I'm such an idiot."

Henry runs a hand through his hair. We must look ridiculous, arguing in this fancy restaurant at the top of a picturesque mountain in these stupid matching pajamas. "For what it's worth, I am shipping some of my stuff back to New York."

I scoff. "That's what you want to say to me? You want to try to ride this out on a technicality? God, we can't even go two days without something going wrong." I pause, but Henry looks like he's at a complete loss. "You know what? This is too much. You keep asking me to trust you, and every time, I'm the one who gets hurt."

I turn away from him so he can't see how wrecked I feel.

"Norah, please don't leave. I know it's hard to understand right now, but this isn't my fault. Let's just talk."

"If you ever cared about me at all," I tell him, "you won't follow me out of here."

And then I head out into the cold.

I HAVE TO wait several minutes for the chairlift down the slope, but Henry stays put. I see him at the door, his eyes never leaving me, until I board the lift. It's colder now, either because I'm alone or because the temperature has dropped even further in the time we had our appetizers. I don't have much of a plan, but I know I can't spend another night at the cabin now that I know everyone has been keeping secrets from me.

My hands shake as I pull out my phone, trying to clutch it as tightly as possible so I don't lose it forever to the mountain. I start to pull up Frankie's number, then remember her stupid family cruise. What an inconvenient time for my best friend to be completely out of cell service. I pause, then scroll through my contacts, landing on *Trevor Hayes*. I'm not sure if this is still his number. I probably haven't used it since our freshman year of college. But he did tell me to do this. I take a deep breath and press *Call*.

Trevor answers after the second ring. "Hey there, Miss Big Apple," he says, and I feel immediate relief.

"Thank God this is still your number," I mumble.

"It's really hard to hear you, Norah. Where are you?"

"On the chairlift," I say, a little louder this time, sniffling.

"You okay?"

"No" is all I can muster.

"Do you need me to meet you somewhere?" he asks, his voice laced with concern.

I nod into the phone, realizing a moment too late that he can't hear the gesture.

"I'll be at the bottom of the platform," he adds, and I hang up, clutching my phone to my chest for the rest of the ride.

Trevor meets me at the lift, sweeping me into a tender hug. "Let's get you warmed up," he says, leading me into the main lobby.

He parks me in the same chair he found me in earlier, disappearing for a moment. Hannah is texting me incessantly with questions.

Hannah

Are you serious??
Did you really just go down the mountain, you absolute bitch????

I put my phone face down in my lap as Trevor comes back with two to-go cups, steam pouring out of the lids.

"I thought you might need some tea."

I accept the heavy plastic cup, letting it warm my fingers.

"What's going on?" he asks finally.

I let out a helpless sniffle. "Did I ruin your Christmas Eve?"

"Not at all," he laughs. "Cooper went ice-skating with that Pauline girl, so I was just hanging out."

"Okay, good," I say.

"Is there anything else I can do?" Trevor asks, his puppy-dog eyes wide and hopeful.

"Can I go back to Laketon with you?" This wasn't my plan when I pulled up his number, but suddenly it seems so clear—this is my way out.

"Of course," he says.

I nod, finally lifting the tea up to take a sip. The peppermint hits my sinuses as I bring the cup to my lips, scorching the tip of my tongue as the liquid hits me. I don't really like anything minty, but the warmth is the only thing bringing my whirring thoughts back down to this planet.

"Is there any chance I could convince you to leave tonight?"

Chapter 15

HALF AN HOUR later, after I've gathered my stuff from the cabin and changed out of those ridiculous pajamas, Trevor and I are loaded up in his truck. Convincing him to leave now and drive through the night was almost too easy. He didn't even hesitate. He just said goodbye to his friend, and then we were on our way.

I wait until we're on the road to text Hannah back, telling her that Trevor Hayes is taking me home, and then refusing to respond to the immediate call that pops up.

After declining a second call from my sister, Trevor's phone lights up in its holster attached to the air vents. Of course it's Henry. Trevor's hand moves toward the phone.

"If you answer that, I swear to God I will cannonball myself right out of this moving vehicle."

Trevor doesn't ask me too many questions after that. He just gives me that hundred-watt grin of his, and we drive into the night. He plays the radio softly, tuned to some country station

I don't really care for, but it's easier than unpacking how I'm feeling.

I don't know how it happens, but I must have drifted off to sleep, because when I jolt up in the seat, nearly three hours have gone by.

"I'm so sorry," I say, rubbing my eyes with the backs of my hands. "Worst road trip buddy ever."

"It's okay." He shrugs. Everything that comes out of his mouth has a hint of easygoing cheer. "Seemed like you needed it."

"I haven't been sleeping much," I explain.

He says, "Hate when that happens," and then we drive a little longer in silence, until we see a sign signaling food at the next exit, and my stomach growls so loudly that I can't even pretend to play it off as anything else. Without saying a word, he turns off of the interstate and makes his way to the drive-thru of those golden arches.

"Thank you," I murmur, grateful. I order chicken nuggets and fries, and he gets a cheeseburger. I insist on paying but tell him he'd better order his own fries because I'm not sharing, and his laugh booms so loudly that I can't help but smile along with him.

Trevor parks the truck in the lot as we eat, and even though he didn't order his own fries, I concede, tilting the large red box in his direction. He pulls out three fries, munching softly on them.

"You know," he says, his smile only faltering for a moment, "I had the biggest crush on you in high school."

I squint at him. Impossible. Sweet Trevor Hayes? Not a chance.

"Shut up, no you did not."

"I would swoon every time you came into the cafeteria."

"You're just saying that 'cause I'm a sad mess," I laugh. That must be it.

"I'm really not. Why do you think I was always pestering you for those sliced green peppers you had packed for lunch? You can ask Henry. I was crazy about you." Trevor nods at my look of confusion, like he's explaining simple arithmetic to me.

"You don't like green bell peppers?" I ask, trying to recover from my shock. I shove a handful of fries in my mouth.

Trevor shrugs. "Just an excuse to sit near you, I guess."

"Really?"

"Norah, I didn't give a flying fuck about being class treasurer. I just wanted to spend every other Wednesday hanging out with you after school."

"But you ran all four years," I say, as if there clearly must be another explanation.

"I did."

Trevor Hayes had liked me? *Like*-liked me all that time? I try to process this idea. My complete obliviousness. Would things have turned out differently if I'd known? Could I have put aside my forever-festering feelings for the boy next door and fallen for my student government buddy instead? Would Henry and I have avoided our whole mess because I was dating this sweet puppy dog who went through hell with our student budget just to spend two hours twice a month near me? Would Henry and I have been able to stay friends?

God, even with this admission from Trevor, my mind can't tear itself away from Henry. Why does this keep happening?

Trevor looks at me for a moment. Like I'm fuzzy, a shape he can't quite make out. I guess I was supposed to say something more instead of letting his words hang in the air like I did.

Trevor drops his gaze. He crumples up his trash and throws it back into the brown bag. He brushes his hands off on the sides of his jeans, then puts the car back into drive, heading for the interstate.

I'M WIDE AWAKE for the rest of the ride, making conversation that doesn't scratch a deeper surface than work, people we knew in high school, and the Bulls' season. The roads are empty for the second leg of the trip, which I suppose makes sense for the middle of the night on Christmas, and the drive only takes four and a half hours total. As we pull into town, I start to give him directions to my house, but Trevor gives me a funny smile, and I realize of course he knows where he's going. He's Henry's best friend. He knows I lived next door to the Coles.

As we turn down the street I grew up on, I dig through my purse for my house keys. I start emptying my bag, knowing that this is the only place they could be. We pull up in front of the house that will soon enough no longer be mine, and it hits me.

Getting into Henry's CR-V to go to the lodge. Being annoyed with how bulky the keys I wouldn't need for the next few days were in my purse. Dropping them into the glove compartment of Henry's car.

I brace myself and turn in my seat toward Trevor. "I'm an idiot. I left my keys back at the lodge." My mind flickers to Frankie, but then I remember she's on the cruise. "I can call a Lyft from here, and get a hotel or something."

Trevor looks at me like I've lost my mind. "You're going to find a hotel at one a.m. on Christmas?" he asks, raising an eyebrow. "Don't be silly. I have a guest room. You can stay there tonight."

"You've already done so much for me. It's really okay. I don't want to put you out."

He throws the car back into drive, not even giving me a chance to get out if I wanted.

"It's a nice room. Bea got throw pillows and everything. At the end of her pregnancy, she got deep into nesting and when their house was all in order and she ran out of things to do there, she moved on to my place."

I can see that arguing against this will be futile, and I'm honestly so drained at this point that an easy path to a place to sleep wins out.

Fifteen minutes later, Trevor's truck comes to a stop in front of a 1950s ranch house with gray and white siding. The large front yard is still covered in remnants of the storm, with two winter-barren crab apple trees that frame the home. I bet those would be idyllic in the spring. I can picture blooms of pink and tiny apples falling onto the grass. This is a grown-up's house. This is a home for a family.

Trevor said at the reunion that he'd been fixing the house up over the last year, and the space tells that story. A completely redone kitchen, with quartz countertops and modern white cabinets. A bathroom that still has fading blush tiles on the wall, and a dingy bathtub that looks like it hasn't been used in this millennium.

"Guest room awaits, m'lady," Trevor says, leading me down a carpeted hallway and into a small but adorable bedroom, with a fluffy ivory comforter and modern wallpaper with fruit trees on it. The throw pillows match the oranges from the wallpaper.

"Thank you so much, Trevor," I say, placing my bag by the foot of the bed. "You really saved the day. You have no idea. My knight in shining armor."

"Anytime, Miss Big Apple," he replies, pulling me into a long hug.

It's reassuring, comfortable, to have my arms around his waist, cheek pressed into his chest, shoulders enveloped by his hands.

I take a deep breath. "You never said anything. Back in high school." The words are muffled by our embrace.

"I was pretty sure you didn't feel the same way," Trevor says simply, his arms dropping down to his sides as he steps back, away from me. "That's why Henry wouldn't kiss you at the Truth or Dare game on the New York trip. Think our buddy was protecting my feelings." He nods once before adding, "Sleep well, Norah," and closes the door behind him as he goes.

Everything comes back to Henry, no matter what I do. He was protecting Trevor's feelings? He was trying to be a good friend? That goes against everything I've held as fact about this scenario for so long. Maybe if I'd known this then, Henry and I could have remained in each other's lives for the past nine years.

But is that even what I want? Henry Cole has found so many ways to hurt me and betray my trust over the last few days. That morning between us, Genevieve, the house. I don't think this is supposed to be so hard.

I lie back on the bed, the mattress firm under my back, as if it hasn't really been broken in yet. I don't have a plan for tomorrow, or *today*, I guess, seeing as it is one thirty in the morning. It's Christmas Day. Trevor will be with his family. I'll still be locked out of the house.

I start looking at flights. Maybe that's the answer. To get out of this place, away from these people who are suffocating me, as soon as possible. Mom will be better off if I'm not there for the proposal. I'm just ruining everything. I can get the rest of my things from the house whenever I come back next. Another two years, or three. Or whenever the wedding is. That might be sooner.

But by then, it won't be our house anymore anyway.

My mind drifts as the sleep debt of the last two nights catches up with me, and I fall asleep in my clothes from the drive, with the airline app still open on my phone.

Chapter 16

I WAKE UP with a start, unsure where I am, freezing on top of a thick comforter. I turn my head and see a digital clock. *11:10* glows in fluorescent red. Holy shit, I slept late.

I sit up and check my phone, and that's when the panic really sets in. Between Hannah and Mom, I have about thirty texts and missed calls, stemming back to the wee hours of the morning. It appears that they decided to all drive back early this morning, and then discovered that I was not at home, causing everyone alarm. I tap out a text to Mom and Hannah that I didn't mean to worry anyone—I'd just been locked out and will be home soon.

I have a missed FaceTime from Frankie too, along with a smattering of texts. First, pure smugness that she'd been right about Henry, and then the hard left to wanting to skin him alive for all his nonsense, and then a note about when she thinks she'll next be in service. I no longer have the energy to relay all the new terrible, confusing developments to my best friend. I know she won't be thrilled that Trevor was the one who rescued me either, even if I could not be more grateful to our golden-haired former classmate.

I splash some water on my face before grabbing my bag. Trevor is wrapping gifts on his dining room table. When he hears me, he looks up and smiles.

"Sleeping Beauty lives!" Trevor says with a grin, putting down a roll of tape and abandoning the box he was wrapping, the paper slowly unfolding without the anchor of his finger or the adhesive.

"I'm so sorry," I say, covering my face with my hands. "I don't think I've crashed that hard in ages. I hope I wasn't keeping you from your family."

"Not at all," he replies. "Don't meet them till noon."

"Great," I say, taking in the cheesy sweater Trevor is wearing, a reindeer with a pom-pom red nose. "That's cute."

He does a spin, and it makes me laugh, the pom-pom nose bobbing in the air. "Want breakfast?" he asks.

"I really should get going."

"I can drive you," he offers, but I shake my head.

"Thank you for everything," I start, "but I have a Lyft on the way. I've already put you out so much."

We hug goodbye, but this time I keep my distance. I don't want to give him the wrong idea, even if I don't think his feelings are present-tense.

My phone pings that my driver, Forman, is here, and I slip out before either of us can say anything more.

FORMAN TELLS ME he's an opera singer, and then he proceeds to spend the rest of the drive proving it. I firmly believe it would have been too much for me under any circumstance, but having not had any coffee yet this morning, it is brutal. I've never been so thankful to see the roads this empty.

When I get out of the Lyft, I see lights on at our house. Or what's temporarily still our house. I drag my duffel out of the white Prius and head up the steps of our porch. I take a deep breath, brace myself, and open the door.

"Oh, sweetie, there you are!" Kristine says, running over to me. "You had us really worried!"

"Sorry, I didn't mean to scare anyone."

Mom walks up and joins Kristine. "We didn't want the family to be apart for the holiday. Merry Christmas!"

The family. It's singular now, this joint thing forged by my mom and Kristine.

"Merry Christmas," I reply, reading between the lines and understanding immediately. Neither of them was going to propose without me there. They may have independently made that decision, but I know the full picture. I instantly feel terrible.

"Where were you, bitch?" Hannah calls from the kitchen.

"Oh, I was at Frankie's," I lie. It slips out before I even think about it. I'm not sure why I don't just say where I really was, but then I notice the sound of sizzling oil. I look past Mom and Kristine into the kitchen. He's got his back to me, but I can see an apron around Henry's neck, tied at his waist. He's got a spatula in his hand, and jumps back just slightly when the oil hisses.

Henry Cole is cooking latkes in my house. I see him confer with Hannah, and she nods encouragingly. I think she's saying the color is decent.

My heart breaks right in half.

"I'm sorry again," I say, giving my mom a kiss on the cheek.

I do the same for Kristine and she smiles warmly. "I'll be up-stairs."

I'm sitting on my bed, scrolling through my phone and looking at nothing when there's a knock I would recognize anywhere. It's thick, heavy. I sigh.

"What," I say flatly, knowing it's him.

Henry enters slowly, like he's waiting for a booby trap to hit. I just stare up at him, waiting, until I notice the small blue plate in his hand, filled with latkes that look almost picturesque. Perfectly round, golden brown, crispy around the edges. Better than the ones I made for the reunion by a long shot.

"Olive branch?" He extends the plate toward me, and I reluctantly accept. He backs up as I take the plate off his hands.

"Mom?" I ask, using the side of the fork to break off a piece.

"Sara supervised but . . ." He hovers awkwardly in my room.

I wonder if it's as trippy for him to be in here as it was for me to be in his room just a few mornings ago. For it to look exactly the same as before, but be so clearly and permanently changed because of who we now are. And soon it will be nothing at all. Not mine, at least.

"But?" I repeat.

He's trailed off, looking at the ground with intense interest. I stab the potato pancake and put it in my mouth.

"I wanted to learn," Henry says softly.

I can't help the sound that comes out of my mouth when the latke hits my tongue. It's crisp on the outside, soft and salty in the best way on the inside. A muscle in his cheek twitches. He knows it's good, but I won't give him the satisfaction.

"We were all really worried when we got back and you

weren't here," Henry says tentatively. He takes a few steps deeper into my room, looking from the edge of the bed back up to me.

I shrug, gesturing with one hand that he can sit.

"I mean, I was fine. I was just at Frankie's." I double down on my previous lie, mouth too full and happy from the latke to think too hard about it.

"Frankie's on a cruise to Alaska. She told me all about it at the reunion."

Shit. "Oh."

"So where were you all night?" he asks, his shoulders tensing.

"I left my keys in your car," I tell him. "So I . . ." I trail off as I watch the pieces come together in his head.

"You spent the night at Trevor's."

I look at him, sitting at the foot of my bed, one knee perpendicular to the edge, just inches from my outstretched legs. His other foot is on the floor, as if he needs the grounding of my old tan carpet to get through this conversation.

I nod, just once.

"Trevor's," he repeats, standing. "Did something happen?"

I can't help the laugh that escapes. It's guttural. Olive-branch latke be damned.

"Why, because he had a crush on me a decade ago? You've done nothing but hurt me since I got home. At least Trevor is kind."

"It wasn't my intention, Norah, I swear. The house wasn't my news to share, and I certainly didn't think Sara was going to tell you last night, after they'd only just made up." He rubs the back of his neck, looking up at the ceiling. "I could tell it was something you would need to be eased into, and your mother had to know that too. Sara could have handled it way better," he grumbles.

"My mom could have handled it better for your sake? Gosh, between this and Genevieve, you just really can't catch a break, huh? Poor Henry," I spit out, folding my legs underneath me, wanting to curl up in a ball and disappear.

But it's not just the house, or Genevieve. It's not even really the rejection nine years ago that I still don't understand, and feel a little salty about, if I'm being completely honest.

It's the years of betrayed trust and hurt I thought we were finally mending, all gone to shit.

The color drains from his face. "It's your first holiday back home in years. Why would I want to ruin that? For you, for your mom, for us?"

The heavy silence hangs there, thick and ugly between us. I feel his eyes on me, but I can't meet his stare.

"You don't have anything to say to that?" He turns away from me like he's going to leave, but he can't bring himself to cross the threshold back into the rest of the house.

"What do you want me to say? That it's all okay? Again?" I push myself off the bed, hands on my hips. "What do you want from me?"

"Nothing, Norah," he says, still facing the door. "Nothing. Just like you and me. You were right the first time. We've never been a *we*."

Suddenly he turns around and walks briskly toward me. His hands reach out, wrapping around my hips. My breath catches. But then he just moves me aside, grabbing the now-empty plate from behind me on the nightstand.

He leans down so I feel his hot breath on my neck. "You and I just can't get it right, huh?"

I pull back and see the hurt on his face, the vibrancy of his blue eyes dulled somehow.

As if me seeing him has exposed too much, Henry swiftly turns and leaves, closing my door behind him.

Chapter 17

WHEN I FINALLY come back downstairs, having showered and changed into the worn pink sweatshirt I'd found here on my first night back because I needed to feel soft, the house is quiet.

Mom and Hannah are painting their nails, no Coles present. Hannah's got on nice jeans and a baby blue long-sleeve square-neck bodysuit.

"Where'd everybody go?" I ask.

"Oh, Henry wasn't feeling well, so they went back home," Mom explains.

My nose crinkles, knowing that his ailment is probably not physical.

Knowing that it's all my fault.

"He's not so bad, you know," Hannah says when Mom leaves to clean up her cuticles in the bathroom.

"Yeah" is all I can muster.

"I drove back in his car this morning. He was so insistent that he could do it alone, and if we're being honest, Mom forced me to offer to ride with him. But it was nice. Norah, he's good. At his core, he's good."

I bury my face in my hands, unable to look at my sister.

She scoots closer to me on the couch, nudging her elbow into me until I give her enough space to wrap her arm around mine.

"You're an asshole, you know that?" she says with affection, but the words bite all the same.

"I can't talk about this right now," I tell her.

"Mom was going to propose last night. Did you know that? Not everything is about you, as much as you make it out to be."

I look up. "She was?"

"Um, yeah," Hannah says, as if it was obvious. "I caught her putting the ring box away when we got back to the cabin after dinner. She was really weird about skipping the family picture at the tree and going straight back, so I knew something was up. Her plan was to do it when everyone was posing for the photos since the whole PJs thing means so much to Kristine. But someone had to go and ruin it."

That makes me feel even more like a jerk than I did with Henry. I destroyed something monumental that my mother had planned, had centered the trip on. If it weren't for me, they would already be engaged. They'd be in an even deeper love bubble than they have been, dreaming about the future that they both clearly want so much.

I'm still frustrated with my mom for the way she dropped that bomb, but I'm the real asshole here.

"I'm sorry, okay? I'll apologize to Mom. I won't fuck up like this again."

Hannah nods, like it's settled.

Tentatively, I ask, "You really don't have any feelings about her selling the house?"

My sister shrugs. "We're not the ones who live here."

She's right. I know that. My wise little sister, a million times smarter and more compassionate than I am.

"I feel like since I got home, everything I touch turns to shit. I should just never come back again so I stop ruining people's lives."

Hannah waits a while, her head cocked toward me. I know she's giving me a moment to spill more, but I don't have it in me.

Eventually, she says, "The whole car ride, Henry was practically buzzing. He didn't want to let me in, but I could tell. He was desperate to get back to you. And when he came downstairs after you got home, he looked like you'd broken him."

"It's complicated, Hanns."

"Yeah, everyone's shit is complicated. But that doesn't mean it has to be."

Hannah gives me a hard look, like she's debating if she should keep going or not, but she finally gives a light sigh and turns toward me. "He visits Dad, you know."

A jolt of panic runs through me. "What are you talking about?"

"At the cemetery. Henry goes there, and he talks to Dad. He's been doing it for years. Mom mentioned it to me once in passing, and then I saw him there at Thanksgiving. I think he was eating breakfast or something."

I think back to Henry's story about the scrambled eggs and feel sick to my stomach. He's been going to see my dad all this time, even though we weren't speaking. But it wasn't about me. Henry has been part of my family for longer than I can remember, whether I wanted it or not. Whether I still want it or not, assuming I didn't wreck everything for our moms too.

Henry's been sitting with Dad, talking to him, all this time. I can't even bring myself to do that.

Mom shuffles back into the living room, the box of candles in hand. "Well, it looks like the sun is down already. Should we light the menorah?"

I push aside my whirring thoughts, and Mom, Hannah, and I gather by the window. I light the shamash in Hannah's hand, and she lights the remaining seven candles while we all recite the blessing. Mom kisses each of us on the cheek, whispering, "Happy Hanukkah."

I sigh, knowing how much I fucked everything up.

"I'm sorry I ruined the trip. This week has been a lot, but that's not an excuse. It was selfish and childish. I know I'm better than that. And you deserve the world, Mom. You deserve to give the perfect proposal, wherever it is that you want to do that, and not have it blown up by my dumb ass. Kristine is the best. I really am so happy for you both."

Mom pulls me into a hug. "That's something great about Hanukkah lasting eight nights. There's always tomorrow. I know change can be hard, and you girls have been through a lot. But this is a new start for us all. That's why it was so important to me to celebrate each night this year." Mom pauses and side-eyes me with a slight smile. "Or as much of it as we could. I wanted to share the whole holiday with Kristine so it could be part of our tradition going forward. It's what your dad would have wanted. This is our family rebuilding. It's going to be wonderful."

I feel Hannah's arms wrap around us too, and we stay like that for a while, as if years of weight are floating off us.

"For what it's worth," Mom says, sniffling a little as she breaks away. "Dad always hated this house."

"No, he didn't."

"He would always point at the stairs and say, *How are we supposed to grow old here? With your knees and my back? My darling, we need a different plan.*"

"I think he'd love your new plan," I tell her.

"He would," she says with certainty.

There's a knock at the door, and Mom goes to answer it.

"What are you doing here?" Mom asks. She pushes the door open wider, and I see Kristine, dressed in a gorgeous emerald suit that looks like it was made for her.

"The first time I saw you was twenty-three years ago," Kristine starts, and Hannah gives my hand a knowing squeeze. "We had just moved in next door."

"You came to borrow some eggs," Mom says, finishing Kristine's thought.

"I was partway through making pancakes when I realized I was out. It was snowing, Henry was crying, and I thought, *I guess now's as good a time as ever to show our new neighbors exactly how together we are!* David answered the door, and brought us into the kitchen, to you."

Hannah squeezes my hand once more, then quietly slips out of the room. But I'm frozen in place, my heart so full of love for this woman who's made my mom so happy.

"You had that magenta apron on," Kristine continues, "covered with flour handprints. Yours, and a tiny set of little Norah's. You were making what I would come to know as your world-famous latkes. I didn't fall in love with you that day, but I thought, *Thank God for these wonderful neighbors.*"

"For the record, I wasn't crying." His gruff voice barely mutters the phrase, but it's like my ears are tuned to his exact frequency.

I take a few steps around the door, and of course Henry is standing on the porch, several paces behind Kristine. In his deep blue suit, now impeccably steamed.

This is happening. Right now. I can't tell if it's hit Mom yet—she just looks adorably confused. But Kristine takes Mom's hand and leads her outside.

"I fell in love with you here, watching you stand on your porch, realizing how strong you could be on your own." Kristine leads Mom down our driveway. "I fell in love with you here, shoveling snow, seeing the team we could be." They make their way toward Kristine's house, and I step out to follow, lingering with Henry by our mailbox. Hannah joins, tapping my hip with a small velvet box, rounded at the edges. "I fell in love with you in my kitchen, drinking hot toddies and laughing our asses off."

I see the exact moment that my mom finally figures out what's happening. Her whole face lights up. I can't believe it took her this long, to be honest, but the two of them just always seem so absorbed by their love for each other.

"Wait right here!" Mom says. She starts making a mad dash for our house.

"Mom!" I stage-whisper, and Hannah presents the ring box.

"Love you kids," she says, giving each of us a quick kiss on the cheek, then standing on her tiptoes to give Henry a kiss too. Then she confidently walks back to Kristine, who looks a little surprised herself at the shift. Mom takes a deep breath. "I fell in love with my best friend. I couldn't help it."

"I love you," Kristine says, "but you're kind of hijacking my proposal."

"To be fair, the kids hijacked mine first, what with Norah running off, and Henry insisting we go after her."

I look sideways at Henry. His cheeks are definitely flushed, but I can't tell if he's blushing or if it's just the fact that we're all underdressed to be standing out in the Chicago cold for this long.

"Considering what you're holding, and what I'm holding, I'm assuming the answer is yes, but will you marry me?" Kristine asks.

"Only if you'll marry me," Mom says, throwing her arms around Kristine and planting a huge kiss on her lips.

Hannah squeals in my ear. I smile at her. I even smile at Henry.

"Now, let's go inside so I can get changed into something more celebratory. I can't have this story involve you looking like a knockout and me in my pajamas," Mom says, dragging Kristine into our house.

"Don't wait up, kids!" Kristine calls behind her as they go inside, the door slamming closed.

"They're definitely not putting on more clothes, are they?" Hannah asks, and Henry and I exchange an uncomfortable shrug. "Well, can't say I'm bummed I won't have to hear that. I'm late for a Bumble date."

"On Christmas?" I ask.

"He's a Nice Jewish Boy. We're going for Chinese." She shrugs as the Lyft pulls up in front of our house.

And then it's just Henry and me, standing in the cold, impossible to tell if there are new flakes falling from the sky or if the wind is just picking up what was on the ground and spinning it through our awkward silence.

"Well, lucky you. You've now got not one, but two, lovely sisters." I try to be as breezy as possible, but he looks at me so intensely that a whole new shiver runs down my spine that was definitely not brought on by the outside temperature. The blue of his suit makes his eyes even more oceanic, despite the last remaining minutes of dusk. "I'm trying to make a light sisterly joke here. You're an only child. You'll catch on eventually."

"Norah, stop. I don't want to be your sibling, for chrissakes."

"Taking the name of Christ on Hanukkah? That's a weird multicultural thing I'll have to get used to."

Henry just shakes his head and quickly retreats to the house without another look at me. I blew it. He came to me, ready to uncomplicate everything, and I threw it right back in his face.

My feet are moving before I even know what I'm doing. I have to run to catch up with him, to beat him to his door, that *what if* slipping away from me, maybe forever. I hop up to the top step of his porch, and he stays one stair below me, leveling our eyes as he leans on the railing.

"Nothing happened with Trevor," I admit. "It wasn't like that. It couldn't have been."

Henry doesn't say a word. He just slips past me, into the house, his sleeve accidentally brushing my hand as he goes.

It couldn't have been because he's not you.

I curse myself for not forcing the second part of that sentence out while he was still standing here. I ruined it. I ruined this like I ruined the original proposal, like I always ruin everything. I start to sink onto the stairs, the railing the only thing keeping me from tumbling down.

That's when I see the door cracked open ever so slightly. Enough to cut the wind from entering the house, but not enough to keep me out entirely. It seems like as much of a metaphor as I could ask for, so I will myself back up to a standing position and make my way inside.

A KETTLE WHISTLES, and I follow the sound into the kitchen.

"Do you know why I called off the Truth or Dare game a million lifetimes ago?" he asks, his back to me as he pours the boiling water into two mugs that were already laid out on the counter. He's removed his suit jacket in the time it took me to come inside.

Trevor's admission in that McDonald's parking lot rings in my ears. *You can ask Henry. I was crazy about you.*

"Because you were protecting Trevor's feelings," I say simply, trying not to gloat about being one step ahead of him. Now is not the time.

A flicker of confusion crosses his face as he turns toward me. "What? I mean, yes, Trevor was always very vocal about his crush on you, and that was brutal in its own right because it meant I could never say anything to him about how I felt about you. But you're giving me too much credit. I'm not that good a friend. Trevor isn't what kept me from kissing you when it was all I wanted in the world."

My head feels like it's spinning, but Henry has surprised me in so many ways, both beautiful and painful, that I can't trust what's true anymore. Henry finally turns to look at me, placing a mug of steeping tea in front of me. Chamomile. My favorite. I lean my elbows on the kitchen island, rubbing my temples with my fingers.

"But Trevor said—" I try to unscramble my thoughts. "Then why—"

Henry moves around the island, taking my hands and forcing me upright. "Let me say what I need to say. You keep interrupting and misinterpreting, and I want to make it exceedingly clear to you."

I nod because no words are coming.

"I always had feelings for you. Of course I had feelings for you. How could I not? Don't you remember the way we used to talk about the future?" Henry loosens his tie, as if saying these things is constricting his breath. "The reason I stopped the game wasn't because I didn't want to kiss you. I wanted it too much, Norah. I just couldn't have it happen like that. Not in front of our classmates. Not because of a dare. It would have been my first kiss, and I wanted to be sure that it would mean as much to you as it did to me."

My brain is breaking into a thousand pieces. The narrative of everything I thought, every wall I'd built up, every sleepless night before and after moves around like puzzle pieces. *What the fuck?*

"It would have meant everything," I say quietly, gnawing on my lip. "All this time, you let me believe you didn't want me. You never said anything."

"I think I made my feelings pretty clear this week."

"No. Then."

"I tried."

My eyes narrow at him, trying to understand what he means. I'm pretty sure if Henry Cole had come back and professed his love for me when we were seventeen, I would have remembered.

Henry takes a measured breath before picking up our mugs, removing the tea bags, and placing them back down in front of us on the island. He's now standing even closer.

"I knew I fucked up the moment I let you walk out of that hotel room. Even if I still kicked everyone else out, I shouldn't have let you go. We should have talked about it that night. Trevor passed out almost immediately, and it wasn't like I could text you with my phone in the shape it was in, but I couldn't stop thinking about you. I reasoned that you wouldn't have looked so wounded if you didn't like me too, and it all felt so monumentally wrong, knowing that we might feel the same way about each other and not being able to finally, finally kiss you. Not in front of an audience like the game promised, but just you and me. The way it always should have been.

"So I wrote you a letter, used the entire pad of hotel stationery, to tell you everything. How I'd had a crush on you for as long as I could identify that feeling. How I wanted to be with you."

"I never got a letter" is all I can say, placing my hands around the warm mug because I feel them shaking. I can't tell if it's residual cold from the weather or if it's the sudden tilt of my whole worldview.

"I know. After I woke up and realized I was missing the interview, everything changed." His fingers brush against mine, still gripped tightly around my mug. "Norah, why did you ruin NYU for me?" His eyes are desperate, pleading, and I feel it. This is the question that's haunted him for the last nine years in the same way that him not kissing me has for me.

"I was humiliated. People who weren't even on the trip were texting me all night about your rejection. Was it petty? Sure. But in that moment, I didn't want to envision a future where we spent the next four years at college together. Why would I willingly subject myself to that when you'd made yourself abundantly clear, or so I thought. I still don't think it was as big a deal as you made it out to be. Julia Schmidt interviewed at a Chicago alumni event and she got in."

Henry's head drops, his entire focus on the mug in front of him. "I needed that specific interview for my scholarship application. It was the only way I could even think about Mom being able to afford to send me there. It was my one shot."

"I didn't know." I instantly hate seventeen-year-old me for making such a selfish decision. Kristine always shopped at Whole Foods. I never would have expected this.

"How could you have? I was embarrassed. I didn't want anyone to know. Especially you."

I feel the need to reassure him. "It wouldn't have changed anything for me."

"I didn't trust that back then. Missing that interview, losing out on NYU, it changed the entire trajectory of my life."

"I'm not trying to be dismissive here, but you ended up at UCLA. It worked out okay."

Henry grips the bridge of his nose. "Norah, I cannot begin to describe how much I hate Los Angeles. I don't even want to go there to visit unless I'm desperate. My buddy Nick can come to New York. I'm never going back to LA unless there's a true crisis."

I give him a small smile. "What did Kristine say about NYU? If it was such a big deal, I feel like our moms would have conspired and I would have been grounded for the rest of my life."

Henry runs his hand up and down the back of his neck, an almost grimace on his face. "I never told her. She was in Milwaukee when we were on the trip, helping my great-aunt recover from hip surgery, and by the time she got home—" He lets out a huff of air. He doesn't want to finish that sentence. "By the time she got home, it didn't matter anymore."

By the time Kristine got home, we'd already lost my dad.

I feel sick. I've spent the last nine years holding on to so much anger and hurt about everything and I had no idea the pain he was carrying too. I reach for him, my fingers drawn like magnets to his cheek. He leans into my hand, letting out a slow exhale through his nose.

"You must have hated me," I say finally.

"I can assure you I have never hated you. I've come close. I've been furious with you, resented you, felt hurt and betrayed by you, but then David died and none of that mattered. That day, you told me you could never forgive me. When I dropped you and Hannah off with your mom, you told me you never wanted to talk to me or think about me ever again. So I thought, if you need me to be the bad guy, I'll do that for you. If you need someone to blame, you can blame me. You need me to be an asshole to you so you can feel justified in doing it right back? I'm your guy. I already felt half responsible for your feelings, so I just embraced it."

Henry softens immediately, making it clear that I'm not hiding my emotions well. The confusion, the ache on his behalf must have been painted right across my face.

"Hey," he says gently, running the pad of his thumb across my cheek, "don't look at me that way. I get it. This was the only thing I could think of at the time after all the damage I'd already caused. There was nothing I wouldn't do for you, Norah. You asked me to get out of your life. I had to oblige."

His hand falls from my face and I immediately want it back, but he runs all ten fingers through his hair. "When you asked me about relationships back at the B&B, I meant what I said. There hadn't been anyone important in a long time, Norah, I swear. I've only been in love twice in my life, and both times were with you."

I look at him, and he holds my gaze, his eyes the clearest blue.

Henry loved me then, and he loves me now. My head is buzzing. *He loves you. He loves you. He's* in *love with you.* It circles through my head on a loop.

I've been in love with you my whole life. I know that to be true in my core. I open my mouth to say it, but the words constrict in my throat.

"So are there any more loose ends or existential questions you need resolved, or can I kiss you?"

"I dare you," I say with a smirk.

His hands cup my face, thumbs grazing my jaw, the rest of his fingers dancing in my messy curls. "Finally."

Chapter 18

THE SECOND HIS lips meet mine, every particle of my body instantly warms, and I sink into the kiss. We move slowly against each other, like we have all the time in the world. His hands drop to my waist, my hip, allowing my fingers to roam up his body and twist through his hair. A low groan escapes from the back of his throat when I tug ever so slightly, heat pooling at my center at just the sound of him. He breaks away from the kiss, pulling my hips as close to his as possible. His eyes are hazy as he gazes at me.

It's the look he's always given me. The one that appeared when I did something silly or dumb. This whole time, it's been something else entirely. The look I mistook for judgment is Henry tempering his desire. I can see it now, millimeters from his face. This whole damn time.

I pull him back down to meet my lips, kissing him more deeply. Henry's hands grip my waist firmly, and the next thing I know, I'm sitting on the kitchen island, the marble cold through my leggings. How he does this with our mouths still fused together, while also managing to avoid knocking over the mugs of hot, untouched chamomile tea, is beyond me.

Seated on the island, my eyes and chest are level with his. He gently pushes my knees open and steps between them. I let out a choppy breath, feeling how hard he already is through his perfectly pleated blue slacks. His mouth roams around the curve of my neck, the hollow of my throat. His teeth scrape my ear. I wrap my legs around his waist, needing him closer. My hips roll against him and he stops abruptly, sucking in a harsh breath through his teeth. Henry straightens, and I let my legs fall back, dangling in the air.

Henry's head dips down, his forehead resting on my sternum. His palms skim my thighs, up and down, slick along the spandex of my leggings. I breathe him in, all sandalwood and nerves, and place a featherlight kiss on his temple. Henry raises his head, his eyes filled with want, disbelief, tenderness. My heart somersaults in my chest, and I feel my breath stop.

Henry's hands move from my thighs to my back, drawing tightly around me. He buries his face in my neck, gently pressing a kiss into my pulse point before resting his head there. His hands circle lightly up and down my spine as I wrap my arms around his shoulders. Our movements slow until all that's left is the rise and fall of our chests in this embrace that somehow feels more intimate than any kiss.

I have hugged Henry Cole hundreds of times in my life. Every hello and goodbye, every happy or sad feeling, from ages three to seventeen. But this is the first time in nine years. Even back at the B&B, in all the ways we touched each other there, we never hugged.

There is nothing casual or temporary about the way he's

holding me. The heaviness of it all is cement in my lungs, and when he pulls back, I feel drunk under his gaze.

"I love you," he says in a whisper, just for me, even though we're the only ones here. "You don't have to say it back."

I wasn't sure if he realized before, if he knew that I hadn't used that word. Even though he feels so sincere, heat rises to my cheeks at being too seen, too understood.

I've been in love with you my whole life, my heart screams, but when the words rise in my throat, I feel them crumble up and disappear before they can reach my tongue.

Henry's fingers lightly brush against my jaw, tracing the shape like it deserves to be studied by scholars. "I'm scared too, Norah. It's okay. We can be scared together."

"I do," I say, so quietly that he leans in even closer to me, to feel my words on his lips. *Love you*, my heart completes, even if I can't force the sounds. "Always have. Even when I hated you."

Henry cradles the back of my head and pulls me into another kiss I feel with my whole body. I open my mouth to him, needing more of him, all of him. My hand runs along his chest, down, down, until I hover above his belt, feeling the heat of him just a few inches below.

"Is this okay?" I ask, and feel him smile into my lips.

"You don't have to," he tells me, his words in conflict with the way his hips roll toward my palm, an almost involuntary response. It sends a shiver down my spine, watching this put-together man start to unravel at my touch.

"I know," I say. "I'll stop if you want me to."

His hands press firmly into the sides of my hips, thumbs circling at the crease of my thighs. "Give me your phone," he says, his voice breathy, unsteady.

"What?"

"Put it on silent, lock it up, throw it away, I don't care. I'm not letting anything interrupt this again." Henry places his phone on the kitchen island.

"And what do you think is going to happen here?" I ask, arching an eyebrow playfully. He looks down at my hand against the fabric of his slacks.

"As much or as little as you want, Norah. I'd be content just standing here kissing you all night."

The hungry look between us says we both know so much more is bound to happen.

I pull out my phone and place it next to his on the kitchen island, where we used to make Popsicle-stick houses and decorate cookies when we were snowed in and school was canceled. Where we did our math homework in middle school.

Where I'm sitting with an intoxicatingly hard and frustratingly clothed Henry Cole standing between my legs.

"I want you," I say, pressing against him in a way that makes both of us groan. "All of you. As much as you'll give me."

He lets out a sigh, and it sounds like relief.

"Take me upstairs, Henry."

He puts out his hand to help me hop down from the island. My legs barely work, and he has to grasp my hips to steady me.

"That is *not* how I'm bringing you to your knees," I think I hear him say, and my eyes go wide.

"Henry Aaron Cole!"

"Don't you full-name me, Norah Abigail Gold. I didn't say a thing." A devilish grin spreads across his lips.

I weave my fingers through his and tug his arm, leading him through the familiar path of his house, up the creaking stairs, and into his bedroom.

Once we're both inside, I push the door closed with my foot, leaning against it. I suck in a breath of the space I once knew so well. The grayish-brown nightstands I helped assemble when we were fourteen, though Henry would say I just bossed him around while holding the useless instruction packet. The hidden picture of us from my bat mitzvah that I haven't forgotten, that had maybe been telling me everything I needed to know, but was too scared to understand, this whole time.

Henry walks toward me with intention, placing his palm on the door above my head. "Hey," he says softly. His other hand tilts my chin up, and his mouth descends on mine for one slow, deadly kiss. He takes another step into me, until my back is flat against the door. His teeth scrape against my bottom lip, and a soft whimper escapes from my throat.

I'm immediately embarrassed by the desperate sound and pull back.

Henry rests his cheek on his arm, palm still flush against the door, and turns down to look at me. "You have no idea what you do to me."

His voice, filled with want, tells me that I have no reason to be self-conscious about anything. I feel the low throb between my legs. *More*, my brain chants, and I reach for his loosened tie, separating the thin silk fabric until it comes free in my hands. I want to toss it like it doesn't matter and move right on to his shirt's buttons, but the tie feels expensive, so after a beat of consideration, I politely hand it back to him.

Henry laughs. "Thank you," he says, placing it on the dresser, and I can tell by the way he quickly smooths the silk that I made the right call.

"So, uh, you bring a lot of girls back here?" I ask, immediately cursing myself. Being around Henry removes every filter

I have. Or almost all of them, I think, that one four-letter word still stuck in my throat.

What is happening to me? I've had plenty of sex—good, great, satisfying, mind-numbing. I know how to be sexy, enticing, alluring. I normally know what I'm doing and feel confident in it. But here I am, my heart ramming into my rib cage, causing me to ramble like an idiot with the one person who matters most.

"Here?" Henry laughs, running his hand along the front of his throat. "No, Norah, I've definitely never had a girl in here before."

"Really?"

"The whole time I lived under this roof, I was hopelessly in love with my weird next-door neighbor," he says pointedly.

"And after?" I pry, grabbing his arm and spinning him back around to me so I can start to work on the buttons of his crisp white shirt.

"I've never brought a girl home to this house. Now, New York is another story, but—"

"But we're not in New York right now, Hen." I finish the last button and slide the shirt down his shoulders.

He lets it fall to the ground, all of his focus turned to me.

"We certainly are not. Norah Gold is undressing me in my childhood bedroom. I've had dreams about this, you know."

"Yeah?"

I wait for him to respond, telling me every sordid detail of this fantasy, but his eyes are distracted, floating over me.

"I remember this." He reaches down and slowly pulls the worn pink sweatshirt over my head. "You got this on that trip to Michigan in eighth grade."

I nod as he holds it in one hand, the other running up and down my side.

"It's still so soft."

"It was my favorite. I thought I'd lost it." I trail off as his hand traces my skin.

"I could say the same about you."

His statement hangs heavy in the air, loaded. My heart cracks open a little more for the man standing against me. I momentarily curse myself for the undergarments I put on today. A nude T-shirt bra and some cheap underwear from Target. I pray it doesn't have holes in it, but I'm honestly not sure. I was so frazzled after Henry and I fought this morning that I barely registered dressing myself.

"I'm sorry I don't have anything sexier on underneath," I say. "If I'd known this was going to happen, I would have—"

"I don't care." Henry's eyes are fully locked into me.

We're nearly back to where we were in that bed-and-breakfast—basically bare-chested, and fully fucking clothed below. I reach for his belt, his taut stomach sucking in deeper as I slide the metal clasp open, revealing a button, which I immediately undo. I let my knuckles graze his length as I unzip him. Henry seems to relax into me, having been freed from the constriction of those well-fitting slacks. I tug at the pants, wanting them off, and Henry slides them down, stepping out of them with ease. My hand moves to the band of his boxer briefs, but he grabs my wrist, stopping me.

"One for one. Only fair," Henry says, kneeling down in front of me.

"Who's on their knees now?" I say playfully.

He looks up at me, so loaded, and slides my leggings down,

gently helping each of my legs out of the slim fabric, dropping kisses on my knees as he places one down, and then the other.

I glance below my stomach. Blue hipster panties. Could be worse. I feel grateful knowing for a fact that these don't have any holes in them at least. Henry's eyes are laser focused on them too, his pupils overtaking the soft blue of his eyes.

"Fuck, Norah," he says, running a single finger over the cotton covering my seam.

I flush, realizing what he now knows—exactly how wet I am for him. He presses gently at the exact point I need him most, as if his hand had memorized me back at that inn, and I shudder, my palms falling to grasp his shoulders. His fingers run along the elastic of my panties, a moment of hesitation, as if he's debating what to do. I catch his fingers and lace them through my own. He stands, still holding my hands and eyes.

I think it dawns on us in the same moment. We're about to be fully naked together. As intimate as it had been at the B&B, even with his fingers inside me, our pants had stayed on. This is a whole other level of intimacy, to stand bare in front of this man I've known my whole life. There is no hiding in it. I unhook my bra and let it slide to the floor. His hand reaches out, almost instinctively, thumbs circling the peaks of my breasts. Henry's index finger curls up, rolling my nipple between it and his thumb, the man keenly aware of what that did to me before.

"Same time? One for one?" I ask, fiddling with the blue elastic around my hips, trying to be cute, but it just comes out breathy.

He shakes his head, a smirk spreading over his face. "I'll go first," he says, thumbing his own elastic band. "I want to take my time getting you out of those drenched panties."

He slides his boxer briefs down, his erection springing out, as if grateful to be freed. I can't look away from the perfect, hard length of him. My eyes glide over his body, and with one finger, I gesture for him to spin around for me. Henry shakes his head, laughing at how completely ridiculous I'm being, but he complies, and every inch of him is better than I could have dreamed.

"Is this weird?" he asks.

My brow furrows. "Why? Do you feel weird?"

He shakes his head. "I feel whole."

"You're fucking flawless" is all I can mutter, my brain devolving into the millions of things I want to do to this man.

Henry closes the distance between us, lifting me up and placing me down on his bed. He climbs on top of me, lowering himself to his forearms. I reach for him, but he moves my hand away, kissing my wrist as he places it over my head on his pillow, which smells just like him. I want to breathe in all of it.

"Not yet," he says gently. He kisses my neck, my shoulder, the center of my chest. His mouth closes around my nipple, teeth biting down with the perfect amount of pressure, and I squirm under him, my hips rising to try to make contact. His torso moves down my body, a trail of lips down my stomach, my hip bone, my thigh, until he repositions himself between my legs, his last kiss hovering over the blue cotton of my panties.

"Can I taste you? Please, Norah?" There is zero hesitation in his voice.

"Please," I breathe out, and his tongue descends on me, the thin layer of cotton instantly frustrating. He must sense it too, because he props himself up, looking me deeply in the eye.

"I'm going to get rid of these, okay?"

I nod, all my insecurities about being naked in front of

Henry Cole dissipating as his fingers hook the elastic and pull the cotton off me.

He lets out a low hum, his nostrils flaring out as his eyes rake over my whole body.

"Perfect," he whispers, placing a soft kiss on my inner thigh.

He settles in on his stomach, between my legs, as his tongue begins to explore my center. I can hardly believe when he moans into me, the sound vibrating against my clit in a way that makes my back arch, craving more. His tongue begins slow, intentional circles around me, heat building low in my body. Breathing is suddenly a more difficult task as he continues, adjusting himself to slip one, and then two, fingers inside me. His fingers curve up as he adds slightly more pressure with his tongue, and my brain short-circuits.

I'm desperately chasing that release, but every time it comes close, I'm suddenly in my head. All I can think about is that moment at the B&B, the intimacy of his eyes locked on mine while he began to unravel me.

"Henry, Henry," I gasp, pushing at his head lightly with my outstretched palms.

"Hmm?" he asks, pulling away, looking dazed. "Are you okay? It felt like you were close."

Just him being in tune enough with my body to recognize that floods my brain with endorphins.

"I was. I am. But I want you up here."

He plants one more kiss on my inner thigh, then shifts back up to the pillow next to me. I kiss him deeply, tasting myself on his tongue.

"Are you sure you're okay?" Henry asks finally. "We can stop if you—"

"I'm okay," I say definitively, feeling emboldened with every touch. "The first time you make me come, I want you to be able to watch."

Henry's eyes slam closed as his whole body shudders, his cock twitching against my thigh.

"*Fuck*, Norah," he says, and then he kisses me with such ferocity that I feel the precipice of my orgasm building without him even touching any of my trigger points.

And then his hand slides between us, the same two fingers gliding easily back inside me, the heel of his hand pressed exactly where I need him, eliciting a breathy sigh. I'm honestly not sure if it's from me or him. But he's gazing into my eyes with so much raw emotion, it may as well have been the both of us.

"Henry," I gasp as the pressure starts to build in my center with his rhythm.

"I've got you," he tells me, kissing me softly as I run my fingers through his hair, arching deeper into his hand. "I promise I've got you, Norah." His breath is shaky too. "Always."

One more indescribable twist of his dexterous hand, and my body gives in to him completely, waves erupting from my center, warmth spreading across my whole body, up my back and down my shoulders.

"Hen" is all I can get out, my breath completely ragged.

He hasn't taken his eyes off me. His beautiful blue eyes, absorbed mostly by pupils at this point.

"Sometimes I can't believe you're real," he says softly, finally removing his fingers from me and pressing his lips to my jaw.

I laugh shakily. "Is that a good thing?"

"Yes, Norah." Henry slides the fingers that were inside me into his mouth briefly. He shuts his eyes and sucks in a long breath through his nose.

Seeing him in this state is absolutely thrilling. I want more of him. I want to undo him the way he did to me.

I reach for him, my thumb circling around the glistening head of his length before wrapping my hand around him, and with one long stroke, Henry lets out a sharp groan, eyes looking at me with almost panic. His fingers close around my wrist.

"It's okay. We don't have to do anything else. Watching you was enough for me."

He looks earnest, but his cock pulses in my hand, heat gathering between my thighs all over again.

"But what if it wasn't enough for me?" I ask.

His eyes narrow, a question forming between his brows.

"Don't get me wrong, I feel fucking incredible right now. But Henry," I say, "I need you inside me. I need to feel you. Please?"

A muscle in his jaw twitches, then a wicked grin spreads across his face. He rolls us over so he's on top of me, the weight of him alone making me feel heady. He kisses me once, forearms framing my head.

"I want you so badly, Norah. I just didn't want you to feel . . ." He pauses, searching for the word. "Obligated."

"I definitely do not feel obligated." The words roll off my tongue so quickly that they elicit a chuckle from him.

"Good." Henry sighs into my neck, kissing my shoulder. "Good. But just give me a minute, okay? That was the sexiest thing I've ever seen, and I need a sec or I'll come before I even get the condom on. And no one wants that."

"But you have one?" I ask. "A condom?"

"I do," Henry says, sitting back on his heels. "I went to the front desk while you were showering that morning at the inn, after we almost . . ."

I clutch my chest. "Sweet old Alice knew we were going to have sex before I did?"

He hops off the bed, laughing.

"You should have seen the look she gave me. Like she knew all along."

"I didn't even know that night, when we were checking in," I say.

He nods, and swoops into the bathroom. I can hear him rummaging through his bag.

"For whatever it's worth," Henry says, emerging from the bathroom with the blessed foil packet. "I'd been avoiding Genevieve before I left the city."

"I had sex the night before I flew out here," I blurt out, covering my face with my hands. "The guy I mentioned. Who I was running away from."

Henry sits down on the edge of the bed. "Okay. Thank you for telling me."

"I don't know, I just thought you should know. I was safe with him too, but for . . . transparency."

He nods. "None of this bothers me. Does it bother you?"

I shake my head no. "Did I do enough to kill your boner?" I can see it still in evidence, but I ask all the same.

Henry laughs, scooting back up toward me on the bed. His hand caresses my face. "So beautiful," he says to me. "Rude, stubborn, perfect."

My heart swoops, overwhelmed by this moment. Naked with Henry, in his bed, with him looking at me like I'm the most precious thing he's ever touched. I feel the word bubbling inside me, desperate to get out.

"I latke you." I immediately scrunch up my nose, hating myself for not being able to say that damn word.

"What?" he asks sweetly, tucking a loose curl behind my ear.

"I latke you. I want to say the real thing, Henry. I don't know why I can't. I don't understand what's wrong with me. But I need you to know that I do. So, for now, I'm just going to tell you I *latke* you, but you'll know what it means."

Henry looks at me, his eyebrows tented up with emotion. "I latke you too, Norah. So much. It's okay, I promise. I know this is a lot, and all I want is for you to feel comfortable and safe."

I kiss him, hard, pushing him flat on his back and climbing over him, my knees framing his hips. He moans as I drag my wetness up and down the length of him, feeling him grow even harder underneath me. Henry grabs for the foil packet, fumbling to tear it open. He takes out the condom, sliding it on in one glorious stroke, and then flips me over onto my back.

Henry kisses me again, long and deep, until I feel my hips arching, aching for contact.

"Are you sure?" he asks.

I'm certain if I don't feel him soon I'll die. "Yes. Please. I need you."

He nods, and I see a brief flicker of nervousness cross his face.

"It's okay," I say, looking up at him, "I've got you too."

When he pushes into me, my whole world shifts. The gasp I let out is completely involuntary, the fullness of him, perfectly crafted just for me. Henry's breath catches as his heavy-lidded eyes lift to meet mine, saying more than any of the words I can't put together right now, too absorbed by the feeling of him inside me.

Bracing himself over me, Henry's forehead drops to mine, his body moving so slowly it feels like sweet torture. I run my hands through his hair, kissing him, feeling the flex of his shoulders as he holds up his torso.

"Fuck, Norah, you feel so good." It comes out choppy, overwhelmed, and I'm right there with him.

I rock against him as he thrusts deeper into me, our rhythm becoming more frantic, desperate. His lips roam around my neck, my throat, my breasts, but never straying too long from my mouth. My whole body feels electric, or on fire, my mind unable to discern much of anything besides the mounting pressure inside me.

Henry leans down, wrapping his arms around me, his face buried in my wild hair, driving deeper into me. My fingers dig into his arms, losing myself in the delicious feeling of his body, his weight on top of me, pressed together everywhere we can be. His hand slides under my ass, tilting me up slightly to him, the change in angle making us both ragged. I start to weave my hand down, to just above the spot where we're joined, my clit throbbing with need, but Henry realizes what's happening and grabs my wrist, pulling it above my head. I let out a whimper, first in frustration, but then he rocks against me, hitting exactly where I need him. My back curves up to meet him as he drops featherlight kisses on my jaw, my cheeks, my eyelids, my forehead.

He lets go of my wrist, his fingers lacing between mine, and he rolls us over so I'm now on top of him. I sit up, arching against him, my hips circling in a figure eight, and I know I can't last much longer. His eyes are hungry, messy, and I feel him throbbing inside me.

One hand grinds my hips against him, his other thumb circling the point that will undo me. "Come with me, Norah."

My name on his tongue topples me over the edge. My hands

fall to his chest, pressing into him as my whole body shivers. He groans, and I can tell he's unraveling with me, muscles flexing, breath haggard, eyes never leaving mine as we descend together into bliss. As the waves rocking through us subside, he pulls me down flush against him, our chests rising sharply, breaths that won't steady. His mouth falls to mine, the gentlest brush of his lips.

"Fuck, Norah," he says against my lips with a smile of disbelief, and I can tell he's thinking the same thing I am.

I've had great sex before, but it was nothing compared to that. That felt like more than just sex. It was something else entirely. Emotional, transcendent, *him*.

"I know," I say with a shaky laugh.

"I can't believe we could have been doing *that* all this time. My God."

"Well, it wouldn't have been like that when we were teenagers," I point out.

He runs his fingers along my spine in a way that makes me shiver. "I think we always would've fit like that." He rolls me next to him, planting a kiss on my lips, then gets up to discard the condom.

Henry saunters back toward the bed, naked and confident, and so very *mine*. He sinks back onto the mattress, wrapping himself around me.

"In all the times I imagined you, this, us, and believe me, I've thought about this a *lot*, I have to say," he murmurs into my ear. "It is infinitely better in real life than I ever could have dreamed. I lo—latke," he corrects himself, "you. So much."

"I latke you too. All of you," I reply, letting my eyes wander down his entire body.

He laughs into my hair, running his hands all over me.

"Hen, you better quit while you're ahead or I'm going to need you back inside me pronto, and I don't know if I can go again without eating first."

He dips down to kiss my neck, tongue moving flat against the hollow of my throat, until he reaches my lips, devouring them. My hips start to undulate, but he pulls away.

"Let's get you some food, then." He sits up, knowing he's torturing me.

Chapter 19

I PULL MY leggings back on, the chill of no longer being enmeshed with Henry seeping into my body. His closet is open as he hangs his suit back up, trading the slacks for drawstring pants and a hoodie. My eyes fall over him, looking like the version of Henry I knew before, and my whole body sighs. He glances over at me.

"You're shivering," he says, pulling something off a hanger and walking toward me. He tugs the fabric over one arm, and then the other, zipping me in.

I look down and see the unmistakable Laketon Academy Baseball logo. It's too big for me, but he looks so pleased with himself that I can't help but return his goofy smile. I spent years stealing this sweatshirt every time I came over here. I make a mental note to not return it. It wouldn't fit across his broad shoulders anymore anyway, I reason. It's mine now.

Back downstairs in the kitchen, Henry rummages through the fridge. "Mom had me empty this before we left for the lodge," he says. "We were going to go to the store tomorrow."

I shrug as he pulls out a loaf of bread and two sealed blocks of cheese. "Grilled cheese?"

"I . . . don't have any Lactaid on me," I say, embarrassed, my very Jewish digestive tract betraying me once again.

"Second cabinet on the left," he says, gesturing with his elbow as he starts to cut slices of cheese. "Mom has them for Sara."

"Thanks," I say, reaching up to grab the pills that will allow me to enjoy dairy in peace.

I flip my phone back over and see a few texts from Hannah.

Hannah

Date was a bust

Another, half an hour later.

Hannah

Hey where are you??

"Hannah knows I'm not home," I relay to Henry. "What should I say?"

"Tell her you're fine and that you'll see her in the morning," he says with a wicked glint in his eyes.

"Won't our moms know too if I spend the night over here?" I ask slowly.

"They will."

"And you're okay with that?"

He sets down the knife he's holding and circles the island to wrap his arms around me. "Norah, we got through the proposal. They're living happily ever after. Mission accomplished. Every cliché sentence in the books." His hands dip underneath the hem of the baseball hoodie I've once again claimed as mine, grazing the bare skin of my hip. "Now we can do whatever the hell we want. Plus, I'm pretty sure they know *something* is going on between us."

"There was always something, huh?"

Henry nods. "Always." He drops a kiss to my head before returning to the task at hand.

I hear the clicks of the gas lighting, heating up a pan, and text Hannah back.

Norah

I'm okay. I'll see you in the morning

Her response comes immediately.

Hannah

???!???!?!?! HENRY?!??!?!!!!!

Norah

😉 😚

Hannah

I fucking told you bitch!!!!

I put my phone back down, smiling.

"So, when do I get to see this letter?" I ask as Henry places the buttered bread down on the pan.

"Hmm?"

"Don't play coy," I say, raising a playful eyebrow. "I would bet just about anything, given certain information that has come to light over the last few hours, that you still have it somewhere."

"I can neither confirm nor deny." He turns back to the sizzling pan on the stovetop.

"You're really not going to give me the letter?"

He smirks at me over his shoulder, then flips the sandwiches. "When do you fly back?" he asks instead.

"The day after tomorrow. What about you?"

"Well, now I'm flying back then too."

"Now?"

"Yes, Norah, I want to fly back with you. Is that okay?"

I nod as he turns off the burner, shaking the sandwiches out onto two plates.

"Fine," I reply in a singsong voice, "but if you sit in front of me again and ruin another favorite sweater of mine, I swear—" I don't get to finish the sentence as his lips descend on mine, hot and slow.

"I promise I'll make it up to you," he says into my mouth before he pushes me a plate with a perfectly golden grilled cheese on it.

My stomach roars at the proximity to food, and I rip open the Lactaid pills with enthusiasm that nearly matches Henry and the condom wrapper. He laughs as he slides onto the barstool next to me.

"*Ormagawd,*" I say, mouth full and happy.

Henry smiles. "You're very easy to please."

I whack him gently on the arm, his biceps flexing under my touch, even through his sweatshirt.

"Eat your sandwich."

We chew in comfortable silence until there's nothing but crusts left on his plate. I feel overwhelmed, watching Henry steal glances at me in my periphery. I reach over, grabbing the crusts, just like I used to when we were little.

"Hen?" I say, once I'm done chewing. "I just wanted to say I'm sorry. I was a jerk this week."

"It doesn't matter. I deserved it."

"Not all of it," I say simply. "And everything with the houses—I didn't think I was going to react like that."

Henry nods slowly but doesn't say anything. He just swivels slightly to face me, somehow knowing I have more to say.

"I hated coming home without him there. This is the first time in two years that I've been back, and before that, it was probably another year or so too. It's been nine years, and I keep thinking it's going to get easier, that it'll numb in some way. And when I'm in New York, and no one knows I'm the girl whose dad dropped dead at the Jewel-Osco deli counter, the ache gets quieter.

"I should be thrilled that Mom is selling the house. Really. And she says that Dad always hated it, which I don't fully believe, but I get why it helps her to say that. I should be so happy to be able to move on from this place that feels haunted to me. I couldn't stand being in the house, but knowing it was there, that the memory of him was present, that my room was still how he would have remembered, I don't know, it was comforting."

Henry hooks his foot around the leg of my stool, pulling my seat closer to him. Our knees press together, and he places his hands on my thighs, looking at me softly. "I don't think losing your dad is something you can get closure from. But that's okay. You can keep his memory locked away if you need, but I just want you to know, with me, you don't have to."

I nod, feeling my eyes getting hot. I try to blink away the

tears, but they're already falling fast. Henry's hands move to my face, gently brushing them away with his thumbs.

"I loved him too," he says quietly.

I meet his gaze, noticing that Henry's eyes are glassy. "I know you did."

I stand up, pushing my stool back and lowering his head to mine. I gently kiss all the places the salty tears hit his face, his arms anchoring me, holding me up when I feel like I might just dissolve into him. It's not even sexually charged at this point, just raw emotion, the two of us bound by something so much deeper than I'm ready to admit.

"He would have gotten a real kick out of this," I say finally.

"Yeah, I bet," Henry chuckles. "Would've loved me ravaging his daughter."

I roll my eyes at him. "You know what I mean."

Henry kisses me softly. "I do."

Chapter 20

I WAKE UP the next morning in Henry's bed, his body cocooning mine. I feel sore and exhausted from the two other times we had sex throughout the night, but I can't stop smiling. I shift on the bed, and Henry grunts, pulling me closer, my ass flush against another erection.

"I think we have to go face reality," I say, rolling onto my other side to face him.

He adjusts, eyes still closed, pressing himself against me, arms coming around to circle my hips, my ass, my face. His hand weaves through my messy hair, pulling my lips to his, his tongue dancing against mine until I feel that low pull again.

"We should shower, but . . ." I trail off, running my palm along the length of him.

His eyes finally open, and he looks starved for me, even though we have spent most waking moments of the last twelve hours fucking furiously.

Henry rolls onto his back, throwing a forearm over his face. "I only had those three condoms."

"Okay." I prop my head up with my hand. "I have a few thoughts on this. One, there are plenty of *other* things we can do. Two, we can get more today, which actually leads me to three." I pause. This idea had been racing through my head as I fell asleep. "Three, we can make appointments today at Planned Parenthood and get tested. I'm sure we're both clear, but just to be safe, you know? We'll have results when we're back in New York, and then . . . if you're comfortable, we could ditch the condoms. I have an IUD, and I know we haven't talked about what this all means, or exclusivity, but—"

"Yes," he says quickly, and I can feel his heart racing in his breathy tone alone. "Norah, I'm all in. What do you think me telling you I'm hopelessly in *latke* with you means?"

I smile at him.

"Honestly, though, the thought of being inside you without any barrier, really feeling you . . . Jesus, Norah, touch me once and I'm a goner."

Feeling wild with power, I inch toward him. "Better make it count, then," I say with a wink.

THERE IS NO hiding what's going on between us. We eventually make our way back to my house, me still wearing Henry's baseball zip-up hoodie. If Hannah hasn't filled in the obvious to our moms, it will be clear as soon as we walk through the door. I can see them through the bay window, drinking coffee on the couch.

He takes my hand, circling the base of my thumb with his own. "I've got you."

We enter the house, and my mom's eyebrows practically shoot up off her face.

Kristine, meanwhile, looks completely unfazed and unsurprised. "I told you, Sara," she says, rubbing my mom's outstretched shin.

"If it isn't the fiancées!" Henry exclaims, and Mom's face immediately warms.

"A good night all around, I take it," Mom says, eyes still flitting between Henry and me, and then down to our hands, which I forgot were still joined. My cheeks flush.

Hannah bounds down the stairs, still in pajamas, pointing at the two of us. "I knew it! I knew it!"

"Shut up," I say half-heartedly.

"So this is the real deal?" Mom asks. "Because we're all going to be a family now, and especially with the wedding, I don't want there to be drama or conflict or—"

Henry drops my hand, taking a few steps forward to squat down in front of my mom on the couch. "Sara, I mean this with all the respect in the world, honestly. But I loved your daughter long before you loved my mom. We were just a little stupid in the middle to get to this point. And it's as real as it gets."

My mom gives a slow nod, then leans forward and kisses Henry on the head. "Well, good. It's about time, then."

Hearing Henry speak so clearly to our parents makes my heart flip all over again. His confidence in me, in us, in what we could be, feels contagious.

I head to the kitchen to grab some coffee, certain if I stand there any longer, watching him be so tender yet firm with my mom about our relationship, I'll do something embarrassing like squeal. I grab two mugs, and as I'm pouring, Hannah pinches my side, nearly causing a spill.

"Tell. Me. Everything!" she demands.

"We just . . . we figured it all out." My sister fumes next to me at the lack of details. "What else is there to say?"

"And you're like, *together* together?"

I shrug. "Yeah, I suppose so."

Hannah looks me up and down. "And you're not freaking out?"

I roll my eyes. "Hannah."

"What? I know you. This just seems very serious very quick for someone who *doesn't do relationships*."

"It's Henry," I say simply, and my sister nods.

"Just be careful with him," she warns. "He's so hopeless over you it makes me want to punch a puppy."

"I will be," I tell her. "I—" *Love him, love him, love him.* "He's it, Hanns."

"And you told him that?" she asks.

"In as many words," I reply, and she gives me a heavy look, knowing I've never said *I love you* to a man before.

"I just want you to be happy. And to not screw this up for Mom."

"Why are you suddenly so concerned about my ability to hurt him? He's the one who wrecked this every time before. And you practically shoved me in his direction yesterday. You're supposed to be on my team. Always."

"This is me being on your team, Nor," she tells me, wrapping her tiny body around me in a tight hug. "I hope you can see that."

"Coffee?" a deep voice behind us asks.

I tilt my head toward the mug I poured for him, and Henry grabs it, taking a grateful sip.

"Hey, Hannah," he says.

She lets go of me, giving him a quick side hug before scooting out of the kitchen.

"I made us those appointments for this afternoon," Henry says, his voice low as he raises a suggestive eyebrow at me.

I nod at his efficiency.

"Oh, and can you send me your flight details?"

I open my phone to forward him my confirmation email, and the realization hits me.

"I don't . . . have your info," I say awkwardly.

He laughs, taking my phone. He types his email address in to forward the email. "My number's the same as it's always been."

I feel my fingers tense at my side.

His eyes sweep over my body. "You don't have it anymore?"

"I blocked it after we got back from New York," I admit, feeling my cheeks go red. "Then deleted it once we went off to college."

Something I can't discern flashes across Henry's face, but a moment later it's gone as he puts his info into my phone.

"That's fair," he says. "Yours still the same?"

I nod.

He hands me back my phone, and I look down at the contact card. He's put in his number, email, address, everything. And he's added a red heart next to his name in my contacts.

I give him a dumb smile. "You better have a stupid heart next to my name too."

"Text me and see," he says, putting his phone on the counter.

I quickly type out You're cheesy but I like it.

The message pops up on his screen. Multiple hearts.

"I was trying to play it cool," he explains.

"That was you playing it cool?" I laugh.

He gives me a sheepish smile.

"I latke you," I tell him as he swoops down to kiss me.

* * *

DESPITE IT BEING my idea in the first place, once we're sitting in the Planned Parenthood waiting room, it all starts to feel very real. We fill out our intake docs while sitting on a small bench, thighs pressed together, and it suddenly feels so . . . *domestic.* I'm secretly very pleased with myself for being moderately responsible, since the times I've had unprotected sex in my early twenties all stemmed from me being careless and too horny. I did get tested whenever any questionable situations arose, and nothing had ever happened, but here, I was thinking ahead! Or mostly, anyway. Our mouths had already been less responsible when I proposed this field trip, but I was sure it would all be okay.

I'm called back first, and go through the familiar questions, paper gown, speculum opening my already sore parts. It's the first real moment that we've been apart since we both admitted our feelings and I expect the usual relief, a break from suffocation, but instead, I can't wait to get back to him.

Somehow, even though I went back before him, Henry is already out in the waiting room when I emerge. He stands to leave, and I cannot help but scoop some of the condoms on the check-in desk into my bag. Henry laughs at me, and once we're back in the brisk December air, his warm breath brushes my ear.

"What, you don't think I can afford condoms, Gold?"

I shrug. "They were right there."

Henry unlocks the CR-V and I get back into the passenger seat. "Sara texted the grocery list," he says, holding up his phone. That had been our excuse, our way of slipping out of the house without having to explain that we were going to make sure we could safely have unprotected sex in the near future. We would do the grocery shopping.

He drives us through our town, briefly pausing in the right-turn lane, and then cutting someone off to keep going straight. The car behind us lays on their horn, and I'm about to ask what the fuck that was about, when I look to my right. He had almost taken us to the same store where my dad died. To be fair, it is the closest supermarket to our houses, but he'd realized and stopped himself. We don't talk about it. I'm not sure if he realizes that I noticed. But it's those small, simple acts of being known that keep hitting me right in the chest.

Henry continues on until we reach the Whole Foods, which my family never shopped at, but Kristine always had organic snacks and food without hydrogenated oils when we were kids, so this all tracks.

We scoot around the store, absolutely not sticking to the grocery list. Eventually, Henry points out that we fly back tomorrow, and then we attempt to put back all our off-book choices—mirin and sambal oelek, the base for a pork udon noodle dish that I make him promise to cook for me once we're home; a case of water that I grabbed because it was labeled as "organic" and we couldn't for the life of us figure out what that meant.

After checking out, we load the bags into the trunk, and I get in the car as Henry returns the cart to one of those racks. As he slips into the driver's seat, Henry kisses me on the forehead like this is a normal part of our routine, something we could do every week for the rest of our lives, and then he throws the car into drive, taking us home.

IT'S THE LAST night of Hanukkah, Henry's and my last night home, and one of the last nights I'll ever spend in this house.

There are no special traditions for the eighth night of Hanukkah, but seeing my family's Tree of Life menorah fully illuminated makes my heart feel whole.

I think about that first night, my fuming hatred of Henry Cole, and how many iterations of ourselves he and I have been in these last eight nights. He's setting the table as Mom roasts a whole chicken, and I snake my arms around his body from behind. Henry's eyes dip over his shoulder toward me, heavy-lidded, lovely, and mine.

"Can I tell you a secret?" I ask quietly. The silverware clatters on the table as he places it down, spinning around to face me. "I did switch the wine that first night."

A slow smile spreads across his face. "Knew it. And for what it's worth, I could have easily dried those dishes without touching you."

"You chose chaos!" I exclaim, hands on his firm stomach, feeling the curves of muscle through his Henley.

"I chose to test the waters. Plus, the way it made you so mad was kind of irresistible."

I roll my eyes at him and scoop up the rest of the utensils, finishing his task.

This dinner is our most civil meal yet. Mom and Kristine talk about moving, and wanting to take their time planning the wedding, and I feel much calmer about the whole discussion. Maybe it's because Henry is finding every excuse in the books to touch me in between bites. A hand on my knee under the table. Fingers briefly intertwined. His arm across the back of my chair. He's not subtle, and the magnetic draw to him is impossible to ignore. I can't stop stealing glances at the beautiful man next to me.

As much as I want to put all of the condoms I stole from

Planned Parenthood to use, we decide to spend this final night in our own homes. I stay up way too late with Hannah, snuggled on the couch, debating what to watch. I suggest putting on this new indie film that absolutely blew up last year, but my sister tries to impale me with the remote in response.

"I was in freshman sem with *Brooks Harper*," she says, drawing out the name of the guy who wrote, directed, and starred in the indie darling in disgust. "His real name is Barry Himmelfarb, and he's an absolute tool bag. So no, I will not give him a single cent of mine, understood?"

I bite my tongue regarding that fact that it would actually be Mom's money, and instead pivot to back-to-back Meg Ryan/ Tom Hanks features. This suggestion is met with much less threat of physical violence. Hannah falls asleep partway through *You've Got Mail*, but I keep watching as Joe Fox discovers that his nemesis, Kathleen Kelly, is Shopgirl. This movie held so much hurt for me for so long because it used to be part of Henry's and my New York fantasy when we were kids, and I'd avoided it for years. It's nice to watch it again—it always was one of my favorites. My phone buzzes and I quickly silence it, glancing down at the screen. A text from Henry, with that cheesy red heart. I open the message.

Henry ♥

Are you up?

Norah

Is this really your first text to me?

I hit send with an incredulous smile on my face.

Henry ♥
I saw the lights on in your house. We have an early flight. You should get to bed.

He texts in complete sentences like my fifty-five-year-old mother.

Norah
Oh, so the grammatically correct "u up" had no impure intentions then?

The three dots bubble up, then stop. Then bubble up again, then stop.

Henry ♥
To be honest

The text comes through, and I'm gripping my phone so hard, waiting for the remaining bubbles to release their message.

Henry ♥
My pillow smells like you, all citrus and summer. Every time I roll over, your scent alone makes me hard.

My eyes bug out of my head as I read the words on my screen. Is Henry Cole sexting me after all? I am unable to think too much about him being hard while lying on the couch with my sleeping sister.

Norah
Plenty of opportunities for that when we're back in Eastern Standard Time 😉

Henry 💜
I can't believe this is really happening.

I appreciate that he's taking my lead and shifting the subject.

I smile. I can't believe it either. I try to find the closest emoji to a latke, and opt for a potato and a stack of pancakes, sleep finally starting to set in.

Henry 💜
Sleep well, Gold. 💜 Tomorrow night in my bed.

Tomorrow, we'll be back in New York, and then this can really begin.

Chapter 21

OUR FAMILIES TAKE us to O'Hare, but it's not a tearful goodbye. So many happy, life-changing things have happened on this trip. I hug Kristine just as tightly as my own mom.

"Have a better return flight," Hannah says with a wink, and Henry shoots her a look, like they've got a secret.

"What was that about?" I ask once our families have left and we go to check our bags, but he just smirks at me, dropping a kiss in my hair. "You should know I'm a nightmare to travel with," I tell him. "I love overpriced pre-packaged salads. I love seven-dollar chocolate chip cookies. And I will buy the trashiest magazine I can find."

"Plus you like to start drinking early," he says with a grin.

We step forward to the agent, who checks our IDs and boarding passes as she takes our suitcases. "The lounge is in Terminal 2," she says with a smile, and Henry nods his thanks.

"What is she talking about?" I ask as we head for security.

"Look at your ticket."

I open the boarding pass on my phone, which I hadn't really

glanced at since I changed my return flight a week ago. I am now seated in first class. Not some cramped middle seat between two asshole men. First class.

"Henry, I've never flown first class."

"I know," he says simply.

"How?" I ask, searching for the words.

"I usually fly business. And I wanted you to have a better trip than you did on the way here. Consider it my full apology for that first flight."

His smile looks uncertain, like he's not sure if he did the right thing. I reach down and squeeze his hand.

"Thank you."

We go through the security line, placing our bags and shoes on the conveyor belt, when a thought occurs to me.

"Wait, why were you in a middle seat in economy on the way here?"

Henry flushes. "I missed my flight that morning, so I was on standby. With the holiday, I had to take what I could get."

"How on earth did *you* miss a flight?" I ask as we collect our shoes.

He sighs and squints at me, contemplative, like he's wrestling with whether he should open his mouth. He finishes putting his boots back on and stands before he says, "I knew I was going to be seeing you again, after all this time. And it made me really fucking anxious, because I knew what was coming but you didn't. I was worried you were going to keep hating me, and the more I thought about that, the more my whole chest ached with regret for how everything went down nine years ago. How I never stopped thinking about it. When I can't sleep, and the insomnia demons crawl into my head, sometimes it's something embarrassing I said in a meeting, or something harsh I said to a friend, but most of the time, it was you, that trip and the aftermath, that haunts me.

"I was so in my head that I never fell asleep, period. That's why I crashed so hard on the flight. I was nervous about seeing you. I never thought this would happen, Norah. I never thought we would have this chance."

I stop him in front of a gate that's boarding, not caring how many people are watching. I drop my duffel at our feet and wrap my arms around his neck, pulling his face down to mine and kissing him hard. His hands drop everything, pulling me close until we both stop before it escalates beyond what's suitable for being in public.

"Let's go to the lounge," he says as we collect ourselves. "They have these great breakfast sandwiches."

"Wait, Henry, are you rich?" I ask as it dawns on me.

"I do okay." His shrug reveals he's doing much better than okay.

ONCE WE'RE IN the air and I've fully immersed myself in the spacious seat and my very own armrest, Henry leans over to me, taking my hand and kissing the inside of my wrist.

"Only two hours until we're home," he says.

"Back to real life." It comes out more ominous than I intended. "Or almost. I don't go back to work till after the New Year."

"Me too," he replies.

"Is it going to be awkward at work with the whole Genevieve situation?"

He shrugs. "It was already awkward."

"Henry," I say, a thought that's been swirling around coming to a head. "What would have happened if we didn't both live in New York?"

"Well, we wouldn't have been on the same flight, and you wouldn't have been so angry with me from the start."

"*Hen*." I shake our joined hands at him. "You know what I mean."

His eyes are heavy on mine. "We would have both ended up there at some point. I knew it deep down in my bones. I think I was always searching for you, whether it was intentional or not. We figured it out, and we were granted this beautiful second chance. I don't want to dwell on hypothetical situations that take you away from me again when I finally have you."

"Okay. No more *what ifs*," I agree, letting myself be happy and quieting my mind at thirty thousand feet. I stare out my window at the clouds passing by.

"I would like to take you on a date, Norah. A real one."

"A date," I repeat. My mind wanders to what a date means to Henry Cole. Probably a nice restaurant, where he's made a reservation. A full dinner, appetizers included. My dates usually involve one or two drinks at a dive bar.

"I may or may not have already put some plans in motion, but they can change. Truthfully, all I want is to bring you home with me and not leave my bed for the next seventy-two hours, but I think I owe you a proper date. It's been two decades in the making."

"No pressure," I laugh.

"Is that a yes?" Henry asks, hopeful.

"Yes. But I am also intrigued by this seventy-two-hour sex marathon."

Henry's eyebrows shoot up, as if that statement hadn't originally come from his own mouth, the gold specks in his eyes dancing in a sea of blue.

"Wow, you like, really want me," I tease, but he leans in close to my ear, making the hair stand up on the back of my neck when he whispers, "You have no idea how badly I want you."

I feel the pull of need between my thighs, and I uncross and recross my legs.

Henry leans back in his seat. He seems to enjoy watching me squirm. "Date first. Then bed."

I absolutely hate this plan. I want to flag down the flight attendant and request a blanket just so I can touch him this very second. I want to lock us in his roommate-free apartment as soon as we land in New York and fuck until neither of us can walk.

But he's right. I should go back to my place for the night. If I don't unpack my suitcase tonight, it will sit on my floor until St. Patrick's Day, and soon I won't be able to see the carpet of my bedroom.

"Fine," I say, folding my arms across my chest so he knows this is a reluctant yes.

"It'll be worth it," he promises, "with what I have planned for you." His hand brushes my inner thigh for just a second, but I can feel my nipples pull taut through my sweater. "You should definitely bring an overnight bag."

"You're like an old man," I laugh.

"I'm an adult," he says simply. "You have roommates and I don't. I'm happy to go back to your place after, but I thought we might have more privacy at mine." I nod. "And I want you to be comfortable."

"What if our date is absolutely terrible? Are we being too presumptuous?" I ask, only half joking.

"Not possible."

"If nothing else, I promise not to steal your wallet."

He's quiet for a moment, tucking a curl behind my ear. His hand lingers, fingers grazing the delicate skin. "I can't promise I won't sneak-attack kiss you."

"I mean, you better, or I'll be very upset."

Henry pulls my face toward his, brushing his mouth softly against mine. "We can't have that," he says, the breath of those words dancing on my bottom lip.

LUCKILY, I DO not run into the same trouble of a lost suitcase as I did on the trip to O'Hare. Henry gets us a cab from LaGuardia, saying he'll drop me off first since my Astoria apartment is more or less on the way into Manhattan. A huge part of me wants him to come upstairs with me when we pull up in front of my building. When he realizes I wasn't kidding about the fifth-floor walkup, he asks the driver to keep the meter running and takes my suitcase from me. Not exactly what I had in mind.

We go inside and he carries my fifty-pound suitcase with such ease that I get distracted just watching him and trip up a few of the steep stairs. We reach the door to my apartment and I lean into him. "Come inside," I say, pressing myself against him. His breath catches in his throat, and his hands graze my hips. I let out a whimper when he presses me away from him, taking a step back, even though I can see the muscles in his jaw betraying his desire.

Henry leans down, using his finger to tilt my chin up. "Tomorrow, love," he breathes into my lips before giving me one last, albeit tame, kiss, and I hold on to those two words as I watch him fly down the stairs.

I let myself into the apartment, where Luisa is watching an old episode of *Top Chef*.

"You're back!" Luisa says, leaning over the couch to face me. "It's been too quiet and clean the last ten days."

I make a face at her but can't hold back a smile. "Where's Aya? Michael?"

"Michael's working. He'll be back tonight. Aya went home, but I still couldn't tell you where *home* is."

"We're never going to figure that girl out, huh?"

"Nope. Was there someone outside with you? I thought I heard voices."

I feel my face and ears flush hot, and there's no hiding it. "There was."

Luisa's eyes narrow. "Did Rob pick you up from the airport? I thought we were fading him out."

"The Rob thing is very, very over," I say as Luisa raises an eyebrow. "Hardly even qualified as a *thing*. And that"—I gesture to the door—"is a very, very long story."

Luisa swivels around. "Well, how about you start unpacking, 'cause we both know it's now or never, and I'll sit with you so you can tell me your long, long story?"

I nod, and Luisa follows me into my room to hear, for the very first time, the story of Henry Cole.

Chapter 22

I'M EMBARRASSED TO say that I spend a lot of the next day primping for my date with Henry. Paint my nails. Shave my legs. Let my curls hang free and bouncy. Spend a painstakingly long time selecting two rounds of lingerie—one decent set to wear underneath my black sweetheart knit dress and tights, and another truly sexy set packed into my overnight bag so everything is as fresh as possible. I know Henry couldn't care less about any of this stuff, but it all feels good for me. It's not every day that you finally go on a first date with the person you've been in love with your entire life.

When our buzzer rings, I tell Henry I'll be down in a moment. I grab my bag, charcoal peacoat, and a scarf, and fly down the four flights of stairs. He's standing outside my building, wearing a navy overcoat with a sky blue scarf folded into it. The scarf makes his eyes shine bright, even through the dirty glass door to my building. Or maybe he's just feeling the same way I am, his whole face lighting up when he sees me.

"I would have come up," he says as I throw my arms around

his neck. One hand presses into the small of my back as his face tilts down to kiss me.

When we separate, I notice why his other hand was occupied. He's holding the base of a mason jar.

"I thought flowers were a little cliché, but . . ." He trails off, embarrassed, as he presses the mason jar into my hands.

And that's when I see what's poking out. They're pretzel rods, dipped in colorful chocolate, and topped with chocolate flowers.

"That moment at the inn with those pretzel rods," Henry says, "that was the first time my fingers brushed against yours and you didn't flinch or stew. That was the moment I thought *maybe*. Maybe this isn't one-sided. Maybe there's hope."

I feel the twitch in my nose that always happens when I'm about to cry, and I tamp it down, not wanting to ruin my makeup. "Henry" is all I can get out. I reach up to touch his face, and he leans his cheek into my hand. "Thank you. This is so much better than flowers."

He takes the overnight bag off my shoulder and starts to walk.

"You also may not be surprised to learn that I can't keep plants alive."

He laughs, taking my hand as we walk. "I parked in the lot around the corner. I'll take you back to my place," he says, and my eyebrows shoot up. "So we can drop off my car. We won't need it the rest of the night." He gives me a look. "So eager to get back into my pants, Gold."

"I mean, when you do things like bring me a bouquet of pretzel rods, what else is the appropriate response?"

He rolls his eyes, but the wide grin hasn't left his lips. I like seeing this side of him, the one who gives me his smiles so freely.

We reach his car, a midnight blue BMW. "Ah, the famous city car," I say as he opens the passenger-side door for me.

Henry laughs, shaking his head as he closes the door after me.

When he gets into the driver's seat and starts the engine to warm up the car, he turns to me for a moment. His clear blue eyes dance across every centimeter of my face. "God, you're beautiful." Then he buckles his seat belt and throws the car into drive.

We make our way across the Queensboro Bridge and into Manhattan. Henry finally turns onto Amsterdam, then circles down into a garage underneath a high-rise. A valet greets him by name as Henry hands over the keys.

"We'll just throw this upstairs," he says, gesturing to my bag on his arm, "and then we'll head out."

We ride a glass elevator up to the twenty-eighth floor, and he turns down a hallway, leading me to apartment 28-D. He unlocks the door, pulling me inside with him. The apartment itself is very white, almost sterile, without many personal touches. It looks like it's been staged for a showing, to be honest. But I take one step past the tiny kitchen and into the open living/dining room, and those floor-to-ceiling windows that the exterior promised do not disappoint.

Henry brings my bag through a door that I assume is the bedroom, but I don't follow, transfixed by the view. I can see the entire Upper West Side, lights twinkling from the early December sunset. This is the part that never gets old for me. Seeing the expanse of the city, laid out like it was built for me alone.

I feel Henry's presence behind me, and then his arms wrap around my waist at the window by the round, dark wood of his dining room table. His lips graze my neck, his body flush against my back. I sigh, tilting my face toward my left shoulder to try to meet his lips.

"We have reservations," he says before placing one more kiss at the base of my neck.

I sigh, frustrated, and feel his body tighten behind me at the sound. A low groan from his throat surprises both of us as he spins me around and kisses me fiercely against the window, like a man who's just returned from war. He kisses all the lipstick right off my face, and when we break apart, riled up and breathless, I can't help but laugh.

"We have reservations," he repeats, muttering with disdain as he adjusts himself in his wool pants.

I wipe the color off his swollen lips with my thumb, then go to a mirror to reapply, before we head out into the city.

WE WALK A few blocks from Henry's apartment, then turn down an alley. Halfway down the narrow, trash-laden stretch, Henry opens an unmarked black door grate next to a dumpster and gestures for me to enter.

"This better not be where you murder me," I say, and he laughs, leading me down a dark flight of stairs.

As we head deeper, I see the warm orange glow of light, and then walls of exposed brick. An older man stands and approaches us at the bottom of the stairs.

"Cole, for two," Henry says, and the man nods. I guess we really did have reservations. The man leads us past the half-dozen other tables, with handcrafted wooden chairs and candlelight, and over to the back corner against a wall. The brick forms a wide arch, filled with rows of wine bottles.

"Enjoy," the man says as he hands us each an ivory piece of printed paper.

I finally remove my coat. Henry does the same, hanging them on an empty coat rack in the corner. He strides back over to me, and I finally get a real look at him now that he's sans overcoat. The excruciatingly fitted almost-black button-down tucked into his gray wool pants, one extra button open with no tie. When he starts to roll up his sleeves, exposing his forearms in the warmth of the restaurant, I very nearly pass out.

Henry slides into the chair next to me. "You okay, Gold?"

You're trying to kill me, I think.

"Henry, where are we?" I ask in a hushed whisper.

"We are at Ignoto, the best restaurant in the city that no one will ever know about," he says simply.

"Why did we have to enter the way they would have featured in an episode of *SVU*?"

He gives me a coy smile. "I thought it was more mysterious than going in through the Starbucks at street level."

"We're underneath a Starbucks?"

"Don't worry about it," he says, waving his hand dismissively. "Do you trust me?" I nod.

A dark-haired man in his forties, dressed in a crisp white shirt and thin black tie, approaches. "Henry, hello. I was happy to see you on the reservation list tonight," the man says warmly.

Henry extends his hand and they shake. "Leo! It's good to see you."

"And you brought a lovely date this time," Leo says, eyes gliding over me as a question.

"Leo, this is my girlfriend, Norah."

The words slip out of his mouth in a way that I don't think was intentional. His eyes immediately shoot over to meet mine.

I give a slight shrug of my shoulder, stifling a grin. Leo looks between the two of us.

"Welcome, Norah. Can I get you anything to drink?"

"Do you like Valpolicella?" Henry asks, and I shrug again because I don't have an answer. "Do you still have any bottles of the 2016?" he asks Leo. "I think you'll like it," he says back to me.

Leo nods. "I'll bring that right out."

"So, I'm your girlfriend, huh?" I give him a devilish grin, elbows on the table in a way that probably isn't appropriate for the setting as I rest my chin on my folded hands.

"Guess so," Henry says, cocking an eyebrow at me. "Do you have any objections?"

"I mean, I was going to see how badly we could bomb this first date before making any decisions, but—"

"And how'm I doing so far?"

"Shamefully good."

"Good."

"Can I tell you something embarrassing?" I ask.

"Of course."

"I've never had a boyfriend before." I watch Henry swallow slowly, his Adam's apple bobbing at this new information. "I told you, I don't really do relationships."

Henry reaches across the table until I give him my hand. "Norah, I've been dying to be any first of yours since we were twelve years old. I'm honored to be your first boyfriend." He's looking at me like he wants to be my first, last, and only.

I flush as Leo carries out a tray. He shows Henry the bottle, then carefully opens it and tips the deep purple liquid into a decanter. I watch as he tilts a little into one glass, then a second, coating all the sides, then pouring a small amount for Henry to taste.

Henry inhales slowly into the glass, his eyes fluttering, then takes a sip. He nods at Leo. "Beautiful," he says, and Leo prepares a glass for me, then one for Henry.

"I've never seen that whole process before," I admit. "You look like a pro, though."

"To new experiences," Henry says, raising his glass by the stem. "And new boyfriends."

I roll my eyes at him as I say, "To us," and we clink glasses.

My mom always has good wine at her house, but one sip and I know this is the best wine I've ever tasted.

Henry laughs as I make a near-orgasmic sound. "I told you to trust me."

"Order me whatever you want to eat," I tell him. "You clearly know what you're doing."

"I come here a lot. It's close to home, quiet, and the people are great. And wait till you have the pasta, Norah. Just wait."

I raise an eyebrow at him as I take another sip. "It didn't sound like you bring many girls here."

He shakes his head. "I didn't want to risk introducing someone to this magical place and then losing it in a breakup. There's only six tables. That would be so uncomfortable. I always come here alone."

"Until now."

"Maybe I just found the person worth sharing the secret with."

He holds my gaze long enough for me to feel it in the base of my spine.

Henry orders an obscene amount of food. A salad with oranges and fennel, perfectly crisp calamari, the best bread I've had in my entire life, that somehow remained warm at every stage of the meal. And then there was the pasta, all handmade and fresh. A deceptively simple spaghetti with tomato and basil. Tagliatelle with a beef and pork ragù. A squid ink pasta with clams, shrimp, tomato, and chili.

"This is one of the best meals I've had," I tell him, mouth full of carbs, "but I gotta say, not ideal for pre-sexy-times."

Henry just shakes his head, swirling his fork against the spoon to gather spaghetti. "How naive that you thought this was going to be the only stop on our date."

We finish the bottle of wine but don't come close to finishing the food. I'm so full I barely feel the alcohol. When I come back from the restroom, the bill has already been taken care of, and the table is cleared. He must read the disappointment on my face at the thought of missed leftovers, because Henry says, "We're going to come back for them," before grabbing my coat and escorting me back up the murder-stairs.

HENRY LEADS ME a few blocks farther, the cold air whipping against us. He takes my ungloved hand and folds it into his coat pocket as we walk. I feel like I'm in a dream, on a date planned by the producers of *The Bachelor* or something. This is not my real life. It's not possible.

And he's my *boyfriend*. We nearly breezed right past that part. Henry Cole, the boy next door, is my boyfriend.

He stops walking as we land in front of what appears to be a 1950s-style diner.

"No more food," I plead as we push past the neon lights and shiny silver archway at the entrance. Inside, I see the classic black-and-white checkerboard floor and bright red booths. But then I hear the opening chords of "Jumper," and a balding man starts singing enthusiastically. I grab Henry's arm. "No!" I exclaim with glee.

"You said you love karaoke." He's trying to brush it off, but I can tell he's pleased with himself for eliciting such a reaction from me.

"I'll grab drinks. You go sign us up," I say, pushing him toward the binder. "Bourbon?"

Henry nods and says, "Rocks," before making his way toward the binder.

I head to the bar and order him Maker's on the rocks, mine mixed with ginger ale. We reconvene at a booth whose fabric squawks with every movement, but I don't even care. The booth allows us the intimacy of proximity, our arms and thighs pressed closely together. My body hums at every place we touch, even through multiple layers of clothing, but the core vibrations are centered in my chest. *You love him*, my heart screams over the unfortunate rendition of a Taylor Swift song sung by two members of an absolutely wasted bachelorette party. *You are stupid in love with him.*

It's not long before I'm called up, and I center myself, prepared to go all out for Madonna. I start to sing and begin my interpretive dance, acting out the song with conviction. I make full use of the stage, a black platform raised about eight inches off the ground, arms flailing wildly. I fly through the air, channeling a jeté from my childhood ballet class. I know I look ridiculous, but this is what karaoke is all about. My voice is decent enough to get away with it. I get down on my knees. I take the audience there. I look out at Henry, who has the absolute goofiest smile imaginable on his face. Heaven help me.

The bachelorette party joins in singing from their table, and

I concede the microphone for the end of the song, sliding back into the booth with Henry, who grabs my face and kisses me so hard I nearly forget we're in public.

"You are perfect," he says when we finally break apart to the fading song.

"Not too weird?" I ask cautiously.

"The exact right amount of weird," he replies, tucking a loose, sweaty curl behind my ear. "My dream girl."

"You're next, buddy," I say, detaching myself from him to push him toward the stage.

Henry immediately grabs my hand and pulls me up with him. "It's a duet," he says low to my ear, and I raise an eyebrow at him but he doesn't give me anything.

I hear the unmistakable bop and am immediately transported to a carnival, black leather, teased hair, shimmies. I purse my lips to stifle a laugh as Henry moves his shoulders to the beat, eyes fixed on me. I shake my head at him just in time for him to shriek out, "I got chills, they're multiplying!" His voice is terrible—it can't decide which octave to be in, but at the same time, I know this performance is meant for me and me alone, and this man is committed.

The September we were eight years old, Kristine had the flu, and Henry came to spend a few nights at our house. The most epic sleepover, we thought. Though now, eighteen years later, and heading into another potentially epic "sleepover," I reason that we can probably beat it.

We were desperate for anything new to watch, and found a VHS of *Grease* in the basement. We still had a VCR in the playroom, so Henry and I popped it in. We immediately became obsessed, many, *many* plot points going over our young heads. At dinner, we started singing "You're the One That I Want," the song Henry is currently pouring his whole heart into, and my mom's eyes narrowed.

"How do you know that song?" she asked, immediately growing furious that we'd seen a highly inappropriate movie under her watch. It was only made worse when we informed our parents that we wanted to be Sandy and Danny for Halloween the following month.

I think my mom was picturing the sweater and the long yellow skirt, but I screamed, "No! Tell me about it, *stud*, Sandy!" I wanted the black leather pants, the tight off-the-shoulder top, the leather jacket. Pretty sure I broke my mother's brain that month.

"It's electrifying!" he shouts, and the bachelorette party goes wild as he shakes his hips like John Travolta. I have never seen this side of Henry Cole before, so willing to let loose. *I* know he can move his hips in intoxicating ways, but I wasn't prepared to share that information with the class.

I join in for Sandy's verse, Henry's attention fully locked on me despite the fact that the bachelorette party is excitedly throwing penis paraphernalia in his general direction. I can't blame them. It's hard to believe that a week ago he was telling me he *wasn't much for karaoke*. I no longer trust anything he says. Tone deaf or not, my man is in his element.

He shimmies toward me, and I shimmy back, alternating with him as we sing together. It takes everything within me to not pull another Sandy move from the film, placing my hands on his shoulders and jumping up, wrapping my legs around his waist while he carries me around. *Keep it together*, my brain warns, but my heart is too smitten.

When we finish the song, Henry exacts more PDA than is probably socially acceptable, and the bachelorette party boos as we leave the stage. I push him off me playfully, barely even embarrassed, as the bride-to-be begins Lady Gaga's "Bad Romance."

Without even discussing it, we both silently agree it's time to go. We grab our coats, shoving dollar bills into the tip jar of the guy running the karaoke machine, and burst back out into the cold air.

"So, on a scale of—" Henry starts, but I wrap my arms around his neck, pulling his face down to mine. "Ten, I take it?" he says when we finally come up for air, and I nod, but I don't let go of him. Henry presses his forehead into mine as strangers brush past us, but neither of us cares.

"I latke you," I say, and the corner of his mouth tugs upward. "This is the best date I've ever been on, but please take me home."

"Yes, ma'am," he says, grabbing my hand and leading me north. We walk back mostly the way we came, but this time Henry parks me briefly inside the baffling Starbucks while he dips down to Ignoto to grab our leftovers. I want to turn to everyone in there and scream, *Do you even know what's under your feet??*

But I don't, obviously, because it's a secret.

Henry's secret.

And now, mine.

When he emerges minutes later with a huge white paper bag, Henry extends his arm to me and says, "Home?"

And I reply, "Please."

WE MAKE OUR way back to Henry's building. When he greets his doorman, Henry reaches into the bag and fishes out a small round container and a spoon. "Stay warm," Henry says as the doorman pops open the container.

"Zuppa toscana, my favorite!" the doorman exclaims, and I give Henry a funny look. That wasn't something we ordered. I love that he's the type of person to grab something warm for the man standing out in the freezing December night. I'm not surprised by this, but I'm even more charmed. With other guys, this could be a move, something to impress the girl, but with Henry, I know it isn't that. It's just who he is, the man he's grown into. We ride up the glass elevator to the twenty-eighth floor, and I wonder what other surprises may be in that unmarked paper bag.

Sure enough, we get inside, and Henry unpacks many more containers than should have been included with just our leftovers.

"Henry!" I exclaim as I notice the slice of chocolate cake through the clear plastic cover.

"I can't take credit for the cake. That was all Leo. He said it's Madagascar chocolate."

I gasp and he laughs.

"I'll be right back," I say.

He nods as he continues to unpack the bag.

I slip into Henry's bedroom for the first time, the two walls of floor-to-ceiling windows betraying an even more unreal view of the city than the living room did. The other two walls are still a stark white, with the king bed (and headboard, of course) taking up most of the room. There's a dresser with clean lines, and a small tufted armchair in the corner that looks like it's never been sat in before, where I spot my bag.

I tug the bag over to the bed and sit down, rummaging through for my sexier lingerie, when I realize exactly how comfortable this bed is. I'm sitting on a cloud, floating through the sky. I personally *love* a plush pillow-top bed, but I would have pegged Henry as having a firmer mattress. I lie back, just for a minute, and sigh into the pillow. It smells like him, fresh linen and sandalwood. The mattress at my apartment has nothing on this one. It must have cost thousands of dollars, but I get it 'cause it's a direct line to heaven. My whole body relaxes. I let my eyes briefly flutter closed.

Chapter 23

I WAKE WITH a start, shooting up in bed. The lights are out, but sunlight pours through the edge of the blackout curtain. Under the blanket I'm still fully clothed in my outfit from the evening, down to the tights, minus my shoes, which are lined up in an orderly fashion next to the nightstand on my side. The other side of the bed looks slept in but is currently empty.

Oh God.

I fell asleep.

We had the most perfect date, and then got back and I promptly fell asleep. I glance at the clock, because of course Henry Cole has an actual clock in his room, and realize it's already nine a.m. We didn't even get back that late. God, I slept *so long*.

I'm absolutely mortified.

I grab a hair tie from my bag, throwing my curls up haphazardly on top of my head, and take a quick look in the mirror above his dresser to make sure last night's eye makeup isn't a total disaster. It could certainly be worse. Then I make my way out into the living room.

Henry sits on the couch, in a gray long-sleeve Henley sleep shirt and flannel pajama pants, a mug in his hand. "Good morning," he says with a smirk.

I'm grateful that he looks more amused than annoyed or disappointed, but I still cover my face with my hands.

"I ruined everything," I say, my palms muffling the sound. "I don't know what happened."

He smiles. "You fell asleep."

"I mean, it's really your fault for having such a nice bed. I didn't stand a chance."

Henry places his mug on the coffee table and strides toward me. He lightly touches my wrists, bringing them away from my face to make room for his own hands. He strokes my jaw with his thumbs before descending on my mouth. He tastes bitter and heavenly, the dark roast from his mug laced on his tongue as it dances with mine. I feel like I'm getting caffeinated just by kissing him, and my mouth trails up with his as he breaks away.

"It's okay, Norah. We have plenty of time. Frankly, I'm glad you slept."

"Did you take off my shoes?" I ask, and he nods.

"I didn't want to wake you up, and it felt a little creepy to try to put you into pajamas, but I couldn't have shoes on the bed, even if they belonged to Norah Gold."

He walks over to the kitchen, then brings me back a mug. I feel ridiculous, standing in his living room in a walk-of-shame ensemble that disappointedly didn't even earn its title, but I'm grateful for the coffee.

"Can I shower?" I ask, suddenly feeling beyond gross.

"Of course," he says, walking back toward the couch. "I have nowhere to be. And no expectations," he adds hurriedly, as if he needed to make it clear.

"Maybe you should," I call over my shoulder as I head out of the room. I hear him let out a shaky breath just before I turn the water on.

I OPEN THE glass door of the spacious shower and mentally decide I'm never leaving. The water pressure is delicious, and I'm grateful to have my bag with me after all, pulling out a shower cap to keep my hair dry. I wash my face and get rid of the remnants of black eyeliner and mascara with the only makeup remover that doesn't burn my eyes. I quickly down the coffee, then brush my teeth.

I decide that post-shower, I have a lost night to make up for, so instead of getting dressed in real clothes, I step into the lacy black thong and matching see-through bra I'd packed. My hair is probably unsalvageable, but it looks fine in this messy bun at my crown, so I leave it.

I step out of the bathroom in my lingerie, and I swear Henry nearly drops his coffee mug.

"Fuck, Norah." He takes a sharp breath in through his nose, gives his head one shake, and then stands. He approaches me slowly, as if any sudden movement might scare me away. Or maybe he's just trying to pace himself, the bulge in his pajama pants instantly more prominent.

"I thought we might have some unfinished business from last night," I say once he's in front of me, his eyes unable to stop raking over my body.

Henry's lips pull into a barely-there line, disappearing into his mouth. He cocks an eyebrow at me and pulls the same move I used on him the first time we undressed completely together, raising his index finger in the air and gesturing for me to spin around. I comply, making a slow circle around myself. Henry's hands are by his sides, fingers flexing like he's Mr. fucking Darcy.

"Did you . . ." Henry trails off, his voice shaky in a way that makes me feel incredibly powerful.

"Did I what, Hen? Put this on just for you?"

He shakes his head once, eyes dipping down. "No. I mean yes, that, Christ, Norah, but no. Did you check your email?"

I momentarily drop the whole sexpot act because why on earth is he bringing that up at a time like this? "No, I didn't check my email," I say, frustrated. "I'm trying to seduce you."

Henry's tongue glides over his lips, seemingly having regained the upper hand. "Check your email."

I cross my arms over my chest, and he looks briefly disappointed that I've covered my tits. "I come out like this and *that's* what you want to say to me? What could possibly be so important in my email that it warrants—" I'm ranting as he walks over to the counter and hands me my phone. I roll my eyes, unlocking the screen and clicking on my mail app. The emails load, a slew of end-of-the-year sales spam.

But then I see it.

The email from Planned Parenthood that my results have been uploaded to the patient portal.

I have never been so grateful that an app allows Face ID because fuck if I know what my portal password is at a time like this.

As I click through my results, Henry gives me space. He

doesn't look over my shoulder or crowd me, but I can feel the weight of his eyes on me. I didn't expect anything to come back. I'm pretty careful. But it's always a relief. I look up once I've been through all the results with a smile. "All negative."

"Me too." Henry takes the phone out of my hand and places it on the bookshelf closest to where I'm standing, just an arm's reach away. And then he finally allows himself to touch my bare torso, running his finger featherlight down the curve starting at the base of my bra to the thin line of lace at my hips, and back up. There is no hiding the way my whole body shivers at his touch. "So," he says. "We're both—" He gives a double thumbs-up with a click of his tongue.

I laugh, which I think was his goal with that awkward move, but then it all hangs in the air between us. What our results signify. The whole reason behind it.

"Does that mean—" I start, but then close my mouth. "Do you still want to . . . ?" I should be able to say it like an adult, but I feel lightheaded from need and I really don't want the end of that sentence to fall out of my mouth as *Do you still want to raw-dog?*

But he clearly knows what I'm asking, and that's part of why we're both breathing so shallow, exchanging the same hot air, our heads angled inches apart but no skin touching. "Yes. I mean, if you're comfortable. It's fine if you're not. I bought a value-sized box of condoms when I got home so we'll be good either way."

I shake my head. "Hen, I want to feel you inside me. Just you."

His body shudders at my words, and the next thing I know, I'm being hoisted in the air. My legs wrap around him as he kisses me, hard, his hands roaming against my bare ass. He takes a few steps toward the couch and stumbles, knocking into the coffee table with his shin and cursing into my mouth. I laugh, pressing a kiss into his collarbone so I'm not obscuring his vision. He finds the couch, laying me down gently on my back, and then tears the soft gray Henley off over his head before returning to my mouth.

We lie on the couch, making out like desperate teenagers until I can't take it anymore. I push him up and slide out from underneath him. I kneel down on the shaggy rug in front of him and tug down Henry's flannel pants and boxers together, before moving in between his calves. I have never in my life wanted to go down on a man as much as I want to go down on Henry Cole in this moment. I sit up on my knees, placing kisses on his thighs before taking him in my mouth. His hips buck in surprise, and I feel him grow even harder on my tongue, and then against the back of my throat.

Henry lets out a groan before reaching down and pulling me into his lap. "I don't want to come in your mouth, Norah, and if I let you keep going, that's how this will end. I have much bigger plans for us." He palms the lace of my bra, seemingly mesmerized by my taut nipples visible through the thin fabric. I think his lips form the word *perfect*, but no sounds come out of his mouth. With one hand, he unhooks the bra, tossing it to the side as his mouth descends on my nipple, teeth pulling gently, infuriatingly, like I'm a treat he's trying to savor.

Henry turns us slightly to lay me back down on the opposite side of the couch, before pulling my calves over his shoulders. His face disappears between my legs, one finger pushing the useless black lace to the side to make way for his tongue. When

I start to feel the pressure building from the consistent circles he's making, I tap his head with the heel of my palm, and he pops back up, planting a kiss on the inside of my thigh.

"What's wrong?" he asks, his hair a mess from my fingers.

"I didn't want to come if you didn't let me make you," I answer, breathless.

"Norah. Please let me keep going. Please let me make you come. Your taste is driving me wild. Please." His pupils are completely blown out, overtaking the blue of his eyes with want.

"Okay." I nod, the desire in his eyes alone sending a pulse to my clit.

Henry resumes his position with so much intention, this time adding two fingers inside me as his tongue goes to work, and before long, I'm over the edge, the back of my hand falling over my mouth to stifle the feral sounds I can't help but release. Without breaking his current movements to work me through the wave of my orgasm, Henry reaches up with his other hand to move mine from my mouth.

When I come back up for air, Henry takes my hands and pulls me up to a seated position next to him. He brushes his thumb against my jaw. "I always want to hear you come, Norah. Don't ever smother those sounds. They go straight to my cock."

I flush, eyes flicking down to the hard length of him, and stand up briefly, knees shaky, to finally slip off that drenched thong.

I turn back to face Henry and step one knee onto the couch, then the other, so that they're straddling his hips, and kiss him hard. His fingertips trail along my bare back, and I want desperately to sink into him, but I keep my body hovering over his lap.

When I can't take it any longer, when I feel his hips tipping toward me, I break the kiss, my hands on his shoulders, and pull back. "Henry, please let me feel you."

"Are you sure?"

I nod, and he reaches down to guide himself to my entrance. He looks back up at me, and I've never been more certain that he's in love with me. I take his face in my hands, and we hold each other's eyes as I lower myself onto him, gasping with each inch. The pureness of him is almost too much before we even move. We stay there, completely still, just looking at each other, and it's already transcendent. His cock pulses inside me, and I hum into the feeling of it.

Henry reaches for my hair, piled up on the top of my head. He tenderly pulls one loop of the elastic out, then the second. I wince, certain that my curls are way too messy to be loose at this moment in time, no way that they've still got any discernible pattern. But Henry shakes my hair out, helping the dark curls fall down my back, shoulders. He takes a gentle handful and kisses it. "So beautiful."

Henry's mouth finds my shoulder, my collarbone, the hollow of my throat, before we start to rock against each other. I want to wrap myself around him, bury my face in his neck, but I can't tear my eyes away from his. He shifts his hips slightly and suddenly the angle makes me feel drunk at ten in the morning.

"God," I sigh, my nails digging into his shoulders.

"You feel too good," Henry says, his voice unsteady.

I couldn't agree more. With every tiny movement, I feel certain that our bodies were crafted just for each other.

Henry lets out a slow exhale through his nose. He moves one hand to the small of my back, and the other between us, his thumb drawn to the spot where I'm aching for him. I arch into his hands, all my instincts telling me to shut my eyes, but I keep them open, his gaze still searing through me in a way that unravels me as I writhe into him.

As waves of pleasure subside, Henry's breathing goes ragged. "Where do you want me to come?"

"What?" I ask, dazed.

"Norah, where can I come?" Henry repeats, his voice firm, and I snap back into reality.

"I want you to come inside me," I say with certainty, and the muscle in his jaw twitches.

His movements become more frantic, but he's hitting exactly where I need him, and I start to feel the build again. I gasp as his release pulses inside me, and suddenly, I'm descending with him once more, this time violent, animalistic. Henry presses his forehead against mine as we both ride through the bliss. When it finally subsides, and we're breathless and boneless, I slide off him, kissing him briefly before scooting off to the bathroom.

When I reemerge, Henry is lying down on the length of the couch. He raises his arms for me to come back to him, and I curl up into his sticky-sweet body, our noses pressed together. He grabs a blanket from the back of the couch and pulls it around us.

"I promise I usually have better endurance than that," he laughs shakily.

"It worked for me," I assure him.

"You just wreck me, Norah."

Tell him, tell him, say it, idiot, my brain urges.

"I latke you," I whisper, hating myself every time I can't make the right word come out of my mouth.

"I'm so fucking in love with you," he replies, and then he kisses me so slowly my whole body melts into him again.

When we come back up for air, Henry smiles, victorious. "I have to hand it to my old roommate, Nick. Sex on the couch is infinitely better than I gave him credit for."

I roll my eyes and run my hand up his thigh, coming across the ridges of a scar. I trace the outline. It's high enough that it's in a spot I never could have seen in our childhood, but I know it. "When you biked on the ice?" I ask, and he nods. This feeling of knowing his body on so many levels is almost scary.

"This is good," I say, maybe more for me than for him.

"Really good, Norah." Henry holds my eyes for a moment longer until a chill runs up my spine. "Now what are your feelings on cake for breakfast?"

Chapter 24

WE SPEND THE next full day wrapped up in each other, eating leftovers from Ignoto and playing house in Henry's luxurious apartment. When he asks me to spend a second night in a row, I don't even hesitate.

I've never referred to sex as "making love" because it always felt cheesy, but we alternate between fucking and making love all over that apartment. In the bed, on the counter, up against the windows that overlook the city. The couch, the shower, the couch again. Until neither of us can walk, but somehow still can't get enough of each other.

I only packed one spare outfit, assuming I would return home far sooner than either of us was ready to part, but it doesn't matter because any of the limited times I'm wearing clothes, I just steal his. His boxers, his sweatshirt, his giant wool socks that come up to my midcalf.

On the third consecutive night, Henry swipes around on his phone, and groceries appear at his door in under an hour.

"It's our third date," he tells me as he unpacks a crown of

broccoli, a vibrant green cabbage, a box of shiitake mushrooms. "I'd like to cook you dinner."

"Does it really count as the third date if I never left?" I ask. "Isn't this more like one extended date?

"We make the rules," Henry says simply. "None of this is normal. On a third date I wouldn't usually know all your childhood baggage."

"Don't forget my daddy issues," I joke, glancing at the mirin in his hand. "The pork udon dish you promised me when we were back home?" I eye him, skeptical. "Is this your go-to move?"

Henry laughs, removing the last items from the bag, before folding it up and storing it away in a cabinet. "I do tend to cook on the third date. It gives us an opportunity to talk more. But the pork udon is just for you."

I'm suddenly extremely grateful that we never kept kosher. "How can I help?"

Henry puts me to work tearing the leaves off the head of cabbage as he grates ginger and separates the white and green parts of the scallions. He tells me to chop the cabbage and then immediately takes the knife away when he observes how I hold it. To be fair, I subsist mostly on takeout and Luisa's generosity with groceries I help pay for. Henry and I maneuver around each other in the kitchen like a choreographed dance, like we've always done this, even though I never actually witnessed him cooking before the trip.

After the prep work is finished, he lifts me up and seats me on the counter. He gives me a kiss, then starts to heat a skillet on one burner and boil a pot of water on another.

Henry moves with such an easy confidence in this space. I don't think it's the fact that he's in his home, which still feels somewhat sterile to me even after being here for days. It might be that he's extremely comfortable in the kitchen; I don't want to take too much credit. But there's a part deep inside of me that thinks the answer is me. Us. That something as simple as cooking dinner together could be a perfect moment. That whatever's happening between us is natural enough to feel like forever.

The fact that this doesn't actually scare me terrifies me most of all.

AND THEN SUDDENLY, somehow, it's the last day of the year.

New Year's Eve is a nightmare in New York. There are too many people, the subway is a mess, and you can never get a cab that's not surge-priced to the extreme. The worst thing you can do here on New Year's Eve (besides going anywhere near Times Square) is travel any distance.

Which I suppose is how Henry and I find ourselves in our first fight as a couple. Maybe *fight* is too strong a word. It feels more like a quiet standoff.

My friends and I were going to attend the Sick Hypnotic dance party. Luisa and I often went to their monthly parties, whose locations shifted to different clubs and warehouses throughout the city, but their NYE parties are the best, and Luisa had assembled a whole group to go dance the last year out of our bodies.

Henry had other plans. A dinner party at the home of a friend and former colleague from the brokerage he worked at before Karlin Stein. In *Jersey* of all blasphemous places.

Neither of us wanted to budge, but we didn't discuss anything until that morning, too consumed by our love bubble to think about what comes next. The only explanation that seemed to make sense, Henry suggested, though it looked like it pained him, was that we go our separate ways this evening, but meet back up later to spend the night.

"I've never done New Year's with a guy I actually liked before," I tell him, sitting cross-legged on his bed, body turned to face him but still closed off.

Henry shifts toward me, his head propped up with his hand. "You've never had a New Year's kiss?" he asks with a slight smile, his fingers grazing my knee.

I guffaw at the question. "No, dummy, I've had plenty of those." I take a deep breath. "Just never with someone I cared about. Someone who actually meant something."

Henry sits up, turning fully toward me. He places a hand on each of my knees and looks at me with intention. "I think we can do both. We can go into Jersey for dinner, and then come back to the city after, do the dance party thing, spend midnight here."

"Am I even invited to the dinner party?" I ask tentatively.

"Of course," Henry says without hesitation, and I try to push the lingering thought that maybe he already had a plus-one for Genevieve out of my mind.

WE CAN'T COME up with a solid logistical plan for the ludicrous idea that we're going to Tenafly, New Jersey, and then to Brooklyn tonight, but Henry insists on driving us. It's been days since I've been home, and it's going to be a journey to even figure out an outfit that can double for the events of this evening, so I head home first, knowing that Henry will pick me up later.

When I get to the apartment, Luisa gives me an appraising look. "You can't just disappear for days at a time," she greets me. "You have to text me that you're still alive."

"Sorry, sorry," I say.

"And with some random dude I don't even know." Luisa shakes her head.

"He's not some random dude. He's . . ." I pause, knowing the reaction I'm about to get. "He's my boyfriend."

"The three-day pipeline of first date to boyfriend is a slippery slope," she says. "Seems a little much? Especially for you. No offense, I just . . . I know you, Nor. And I only just heard about him."

"It's not like we met three days ago. I've known him basically my whole life. And I appreciate the concern," I say, not entirely appreciating the concern, "but none of this is normal. So normal rules"—I channel Henry's words from the other night like a crutch—"don't really apply."

Luisa shrugs. "Are you still coming tonight?"

I nod and explain the situation. She raises an eyebrow and disappears into her room. I stand there, in the living room, about to go shower when Luisa reemerges with a sparkly black minidress.

"This will work for both," she says simply. "Just wear a cardigan or something at dinner."

I fling my arms around Luisa, who wraps me up in a hug.

"Thank you," I say into her ear. "And you're going to love him, by the way."

"Yeah, I better," she says, the ever-overprotective friend.

Luisa and I spend a few hours watching old episodes of *SVU*, and then Michael arrives with Thai takeout, which we eat on the floor, until I realize I should have started getting ready an hour ago. I lost track of time, and hear Henry buzz up while I'm in the shower, legs half shaved, moisturizing mask still in my hair.

Shit.

I finish up as quickly as I can, and hear voices in the living room. I pop my head out and see Henry standing, his shoulders braced. He hasn't taken off his overcoat, but he's wearing delicious black slacks and shoes that I know cost more than a month of my rent. Luisa and Michael are standing by the couch with him. It doesn't look like the jovial encounter I would have facilitated myself if I'd been here. Henry looks over at me, a tight smile on his face.

"I'm running a little behind, I'm sorry!" I say, scooting past everyone toward my bedroom, my wet curls bouncing around me.

Henry gives Luisa and Michael a single nod before following me.

"Traffic is already a nightmare out there," he tells me when he closes the door. No hello, no kiss, just that sentence, tension emanating off his tight body.

"I'm really sorry, I'll be quick," I say, knowing I still have my makeup to deal with, and that I probably shouldn't go out in the cold with my hair this wet.

Henry looks around my room, assessing. There are heaps of clothes everywhere even though I swear I unpacked my suitcase in full when I got home the other day. On the floor, on the bed, on the chair, on the bench at the foot of my bed. Henry's eyes glide over the mess, his face stoic. I shove a pile off the bed and onto the bench, and gesture that he can sit there. He doesn't move. But he doesn't say anything either. I immediately feel anxious, so I turn to my dresser and start applying makeup.

"You can wait out in the living room if you'd rather," I say finally as I find my black eyeliner. Frankly, seeing him hovering, silent in the reflection behind me, is unsettling.

"I don't exactly have anything to say to them." He practically spits out that last word.

I swivel around, sure that I look ridiculous with liquid liner only on one upper eyelid, but I don't care. "Don't be an ass to or about my friends, Henry. You didn't even say hello to me. What is going on?"

"I thought you'd be ready to leave," he says. "And . . ." He waves his hands at me, indicating nonsense.

"Is this really how you want to start tonight?" I ask, annoyed. I don't want to drive to fucking Tenafly. I don't want to do any of this. I turn back to the mirror, drawing a surprisingly steady line across my other eyelid. All that subway-makeup-application training has prepared me for this moment as my hands shake.

But when I open both eyes to blink, I watch him approach me in the mirror. His arms snake around my towel-clad body, and he lays a soft kiss on my bare shoulder.

"I'm sorry. I got flustered. Alexander is my mentor, and I don't want to be late. But that doesn't mean I should act like this. Can we start over?"

I nod, reaching for my mascara, but Henry's grip tightens around me. His fingers trace up my thigh, then just underneath where the towel ends.

"If you keep going, we'll be even later," I laugh. I give him a gentle push, and he takes a few steps back, sitting down at the spot I cleared on the bed. Once he's seated, I drop the towel completely. He immediately goes to stand, but I shake my head, turn back around, and apply my mascara. He stays on the bed, and I feel invincible knowing he can't tear his eyes away from me. I step into tiny black panties that make him pant from the other side of the room, and then slip on Luisa's dress. The thin black straps give way to a completely backless number. I have to go braless. I now understand her cardigan comment.

"Holy shit, Norah," Henry says. "I don't know if I can make it out of this room."

I dig through the jewelry case on my dresser. "You have two minutes to get a hold of yourself." I find a pair of long silver earrings, slipping them on, then grab a sweater from my closet. I empty my purse into a clutch, throwing in a lipstick from my makeup stand.

Finally, when I've got my heeled black boots on, I step toward Henry, still seated on the bed. He runs his hands up the backs of my thighs, under my dress, to my ass, his thumbs kneading.

"Ready to go?" I ask, and he nods, but his eyes fall closed, legs refusing to move him anywhere. I tilt his face up and kiss him slowly. His hands travel up to my bare back, causing him to practically hum into my lips.

"You just want to drive me wild, huh, Gold?" he asks when he finally opens his eyes, the evidence of this question straining against his tight slacks.

"We have a dinner party to get to," I say, knowing that I'm teasing him. Henry stands, adjusts himself, and off we go.

Chapter 25

IN THE TIME it takes for me to finish getting ready, the accident Henry saw that was causing delays on the George Washington Bridge has cleared, and we're actually on time. We pull up in front of a huge brick 1930s colonial at the end of a small court of equally breathtaking estates. Large white pillars frame the entryway as Henry knocks, a bottle of Macallan 18 in his hand. I remember to slide on my lipstick just in time for the door to open.

A beautiful blonde woman in her fifties answers the door in a navy one-shoulder long-sleeve knot dress, looking elegant as fuck, and I instantly regret the sparkly dress that's barely skimming my thighs.

"Henry," she says warmly, kissing him on each cheek. She notices the bottle in his hand as he starts to present it. "That can go directly to my husband. And—oh, hello." Her eyes skate over me, eyebrows forming a question.

"This is Norah," Henry adds. I don't miss the fact that he doesn't introduce me as his girlfriend, but I try not to think too much about it. If this woman knew Genevieve, as I now suspect she does, my presence definitely raises some questions. "Norah, this is Agnes."

"Welcome," Agnes says, ushering us inside. The hardwood looks freshly polished throughout the whole main floor, and I spot at least two dining rooms (the formal one set up for tonight's meal) on our way to ditch our coats. Agnes leads us to a sitting room where a dozen other grown-ups are milling around, enjoying cocktails. My entire apartment could fit in this room alone. The furniture looks too pristine to sit on, as evidenced by the woman perched on the arm of a chaise. Henry takes my hand, leading me over to a man, also in his fifties, with more salt than pepper in his hair and thick-rimmed glasses.

Henry extends the bottle of Macallan. "Alexander. Happy New Year."

"Son! Welcome! I am glad you could make it." Alexander straightens his charcoal tweed jacket as he stands up to greet us.

"I'm Norah," I say, holding out my hand, wanting to avoid another opportunity for Henry to not claim me as his.

Those two words are probably the most I say to another person for the entire meal.

It's clear that everyone here is incredibly fond of Henry, and no one cares to get to know a single thing about me. Which would be fine if that was what I knew this was going to be like. But I thought we were going to a friend's house. I thought this would give me some insight into who Henry is outside of our bubble.

And I guess it does, in a sense, but not in the way I imagined.

Several different people whose names I never learn tell me he's brilliant. I nod and smile, and drink their expensive red wine to compensate for Henry's lack of drinking so he can drive, and eat the rib eye that was prepared by a professional chef in the kitchen down the hall. Henry smiles, laughs, tells stories, but makes no move to include me in anything that's going on. I thought my role here tonight was as Henry Cole's girlfriend, not some arm candy who doesn't open her mouth.

I keep checking my phone under the table, watching the estimated travel time increase as dinner drags on. An hour and nineteen minutes to get to Brooklyn. An hour and twenty-seven. An hour and forty. As it gets later, and the dinner doesn't seem to be winding down, even after plates have been cleared, I nudge Henry under the table. He nods curtly at me, raising a finger that says *hold on*, and I think I might hate him a little in this moment. That dismissive nod. I lean over to him, and whisper, "Maybe I should just call a cab and go meet my friends alone," but he says, "No, no, we'll go shortly," and it's another forty minutes before we finally have our coats.

I do the calculations as we get into the car. Traffic seems to have somehow died down slightly since I last checked, and we can probably get there before midnight, but the imbalance of the night and time in his world versus mine is abundantly clear. I'm frustrated, but I don't want to fight. I don't want to ask if they had been expecting Genevieve. I don't want to get into how the last few hours made me feel.

He must be able to tell that I'm stewing a bit because Henry takes my hand as he starts to drive. "Thank you. I know that wasn't the most fun way to spend the evening, but it meant a lot to me. The rest of the night—all about you, sweetheart."

Sweetheart.

I don't know why that word agrees with me the way that it does. I release the tension in my jaw.

"Luisa's gonna kill me if we miss the countdown."

"We won't," he promises.

And I trust him.

Henry explains that Alexander was his first boss in Los Angeles after he graduated from UCLA. His mentor. Alexander split his time between coasts, but when he ultimately came to New York full time, he brought Henry with him. And when his good friend, Joel Karlin, had an opening at his office that was better than what Alexander could offer, he called Joel personally on Henry's behalf.

A lot of pieces fall into place in that moment.

"I'm here because of him," Henry says simply. "I'm in New York because of him. In a way, I have you because of him. So try not to hate him too much. Or me."

And I can't. Because even in those moments where I do kind of hate Henry, I love him so much more.

HENRY NAVIGATES THE agonizing traffic like a true New Yorker and gets us to Sick Hypnotic faster than I expect, with half an hour to spare before midnight. In a miracle, he finds a parking spot up the block. The line outside the unmarked building hosting my favorite dance party is daunting, but I text Luisa and she pokes her head out, screaming something to the bouncer, who ushers us in, groans and drunken slurs shouted at us by the people who were diligently waiting. It seems like the night has finally turned around.

Henry and I dance with my friends in a circle. We move close together, his hands on my hips, mine in his hair, sweaty, happy.

The power surges and cuts out for just a moment. People

around us grumble, stop dancing, shout at the DJ, but Henry just presses closer, pulling me into his chest. That's the moment I feel the word bubble up, ready to break free.

I'm breathing heavy. "Henry, I lo—"

"You've got to be fucking kidding me," I hear to my left, interrupting the moment. A voice that's familiar but I can't place it in this second where I'm finally ready to tell Henry that I love him.

I turn, and there's Rob. His sandy hair is slicked back, arms crossed over a maroon button-down and sparkly vest.

Shit.

It shouldn't surprise me that he's here. I should have realized that this was a possibility. I met him at the Sick Hypnotic Halloween party. That was the first time of many that I went home with him over the course of our two-month fuckbuddyship.

I break away from Henry as the lights flicker back on, telling him, "One sec," and walk over to Rob. "Hey" is all I can muster. I see the hurt all over his face as he looks between me and Henry.

"You're a real asshole, Norah," Rob says when I raise my arms to entertain the idea of a hug.

I drop them, immediately clear that he does not want my touch.

"I know. I'm sorry about how it all . . ." I search for the words that will make this better, but they don't come. "How it all went down."

"Are you really? Sorry? Because two weeks ago you were in my bed. I really thought this was something. I opened up to you."

I rack my brain, trying to think about what he means, but realize it's not the time for *well, actuallys*.

"I ask you to be my girlfriend and you respond days later with a middle of the night *That's not what this was* text. With five exclamation points. *Five.* You know what you are, Norah?"

A bitch? A cunt? I'm ready for whatever word he throws at me because he won't be wrong. I handled his feelings poorly.

"You're cruel, Norah. That's what you are. You used me. For my body. And that sounds ridiculous coming out of my mouth but you did. You really hurt me."

"Rob, I'm so sorry. You're right. About all of it. You're right."

"Yeah," Rob says a little louder. "I am right. Who the fuck are you?"

In my hyperfocus on Rob, I hadn't seen Henry approach, his blue eyes narrow and steely.

"I'm her boyfriend. And you need to walk away."

I touch Henry's arm. "I can handle this," I say quietly. "Please just go back to the group. I'll be there in a minute.

"*Boyfriend?*" Rob exclaims with a warped laugh that feels savage. "That's rich. That is fucking rich. She's not capable, you know. Can't get close to anyone. Can't let them in. It's not in her DNA. Good fucking luck, man. I'm sure you'll see what I mean in about two weeks." Without another look at me, Rob pats Henry on the shoulder firmly and disappears into the sea of people.

"Are you okay?" Henry asks, low to my ear, his breath hot.

I'm not okay. I am definitely not okay. Because I was finally ready to say it. To tell Henry that I love him. To use the real word, not a Band-Aid word. But in that exact moment, Rob appeared as some kind of twisted divine intervention. He was right, though. Everything that Rob said about me was true.

I'm not capable.

I don't want to think of this as a sign, but as soon as the thought enters my mind, it won't leave.

"I can't do this," I say, and the next thing I know, cold wind smacks my chest, my arms, my thighs. I'm gasping for air but my lungs can't take it.

Henry chases me outside, his long legs and practical footwear allowing him to catch up with me almost instantly.

"Norah, come back inside. It's freezing."

"I can't do this," I repeat.

Henry reaches for me. "That's fine. Let's go home."

"No."

Henry's hand drops immediately. He looks at me, his brows tented with concern. I'm shaking. Henry slips off his blazer and holds it up for me. When I don't take it, he quickly drapes it over my shoulders, then steps back to his position a few feet away from me.

"I don't know why I can't tell you I'm in love with you." I stare down at the concrete under my boots. "I don't know why I can't say that word to you. Don't you think that means something?" I finally look up at him.

Henry gazes at me, his blue eyes laser-focused. "No. I don't." He says it with so much conviction I almost believe him.

I slip my arms inside the jacket. It's warm and a little sweaty from all the dancing, but the smell of him instantly makes my brain swirl with questions, confusion.

"I think you're looking for an excuse to push me away," Henry says, filling the silence I've left. "I don't care that you haven't said it. I know how you feel."

"Well, maybe I don't."

"Don't know how you feel?" he asks.

"Don't love you," I answer. The lie burns in my throat, but as soon as I've said it, I immediately feel relief. Because Rob was right about me. Maybe this dutiful-girlfriend shit isn't in my DNA. I was nothing but miserable all night.

"Norah, what is *happening*?" Henry rubs the back of his neck, as he often does when he's trying to make sense of something. "Are you serious right now?"

"We got swept up, Henry. We got distracted by the question of *what if*?" I continue, doubling down. "And now we got that *what if* out of our system."

"You're saying . . ." He trails off, searching for the words. "You're saying you don't even want to try? To see what this could be? I thought we were so good, Norah. I don't understand what's happening."

"This isn't real. This is a fantasy we had when we were kids. You were my first love and we never got to see it through. It was just another *what if* we can check off the bucket list."

"I don't believe that," he retorts quickly. "I don't believe that this isn't the realest thing you've ever felt and that terrifies you, so you're running away."

"How did today feel for you? Because all it showed me is that we don't work in the real world. I'm messy. I'm late for everything. And that is going to drive you crazy. I'm not good at being arm candy when I don't understand what's going on and you make no effort to include me. I don't fit into your world. You don't work in mine."

"You didn't say more than five words to any of those people at dinner, so how could you possibly know that?" Henry spits out.

"They didn't care about me. They were just wondering where Genevieve was. You didn't even call me your girlfriend at dinner. So on some level, what I'm saying is running through your head too."

"It's *not*, Norah, *fuck*." Henry reaches for me again, and this time I let him weave his fingers around my back, pulling me close to him. "I know you. I know how you feel. I am one hundred percent certain that this is just you getting in your own head. Over that fucking guy of all people. I'm not listening to him, so I don't understand why you are."

Because he's right about me, my brain screams. Rob laid all my insecurities, my shortcomings, bare, and he was right about everything.

My face is so close to Henry's right now. I can see our breaths commingling in the cold air. I trace his biceps with my fingertips and he sighs.

"I can't do this," I say quietly. "I'm sorry. I just can't." I place my hands on his chest. I could push him away right now. But my fingertips linger, and he presses into me.

"Stop," Henry says, his voice barely above a whisper. "Stop, Norah. Let me love you. I know I can do a good job. I've been doing it for as long as I can remember. And I know I fucked up once, but that's exactly why I can't let you go again. So just say yes. Please, Norah. I missed you for nine years. I missed you so fucking much. Please don't do this."

If I move my lips half an inch, we'll be kissing. I want to. Badly. He looks desperate for me to close the distance between us. But that would just confuse things. For him and for me. I know what I have to do.

I never could have been Henry Cole's girlfriend. Not really. I don't know why we let ourselves be convinced otherwise.

I gently press my hands against his chest, and he drops his arms instantly, letting me go. His eyes are full. Mine are too. Hot, stinging tears threatening to run free at any second.

"Can I at least drive you home?" Henry asks, his nose twitching.

I shake my head because if I try to speak, I will definitely burst into tears. I slip off his jacket and try to hand it back to him, but he won't take it. I walk around him, placing it on his shoulders the way he'd done for me a few minutes earlier. Henry shivers under my touch even though I'm now the one standing bare. He looks at me with so much love, so much hurt, so much betrayal that if I stand here any longer, it might kill me. I turn away from him, not even sure which direction I'm going.

"You can walk away," Henry says after me. "I'm not going to force you to be here if you don't want to be. But I need you to know. I love you, Norah." My name comes out soft on his tongue in a way that nearly makes me turn around and run back to him. "And I don't believe you for a second."

I take a shaky breath, wrapping my bare arms around myself. My big coat and my cardigan are in his backseat. But if I stay here, if I get in the car, if I let him take me home, I'll give in. I know I will. I can't do that.

So I force one foot in front of the other, down the street, refusing to let myself look back even though I'm certain he'd still be there if I did.

A BLOCK AWAY, I hail a cab and thankfully, one pulls up quickly. It's almost midnight, and once the clock strikes, it will be a mess to find a car. It'll cost a fortune, but I figure that walking any farther without a coat will probably cost me more, and I'm not in a frame of mind to find the nearest subway station. I text Luisa from the cab.

Norah

Went home early. So you're not wondering where I am

Luisa

Sounds good. You OK?

Norah

I'll see you in the morning

Happy New Year

Bless the taxi driver for not trying to engage me in conversation. He just drives silently as I cry, my makeup a disaster streaked across my face. I chew a hole on the inside of my cheek so deep that I taste pennies.

Midnight comes and goes while we're inching along I-278, somewhere in Williamsburg.

Henry texts me while I'm in the car.

Henry ♥

Please just let me know that you got home safe. I'm worried.

When the cab pulls up in front of my building, I pay the exorbitant fee on a credit card that I'm pretty sure won't get declined, and am beyond relieved when the charge goes through. I hurry up to the fingerprint-laden glass door of my building, jiggling the key in the handle until I hear the click, letting me inside.

I climb the four flights of stairs, my legs so heavy I can barely move. Once I'm inside my empty apartment, I collapse on the floor by the radiator, trying desperately to get warm but unable to move any further to get additional clothes or blankets. I look out the window above the radiator and see a car double-parked on my street, lights still on. A midnight blue compact SUV. I open my text thread with Henry and finally respond.

Norah

I'm home

Suddenly, my phone rings. It's Henry. I hit the red button, declining the call.

Norah

I'm sorry

It's all I can text. All I can think to say before putting down my phone. The car outside turns its blinker on, then drives away.

Chapter 26

I DON'T KNOW how, but I fall asleep at some point. I only know this because I wake up, eyes swollen, mouth dry. My jaw feels tight, as if my teeth have decided to shut down for the season. I'm in Henry's Laketon Baseball sweatshirt, the one I stole when we were back home. It just barely smells like him already, and I'm scared if I wear it any longer, I'll lose that forever.

The first days of the new year are a blur. Henry calls me a few more times. He stops by at one point, but Luisa doesn't let him in per my instructions. Mom calls. Hannah calls. Frankie calls. I don't want to talk to anyone. I can't. Because how do I explain this?

I go back to work on Tuesday, when we're all mandated to return after the holidays, but I'm a mess. I can't focus. I'm not living up to the promotion I got before the holidays; I know this. I try to compartmentalize, and that works sometimes in the mornings. I did that when I had to finish out my senior year after Dad died. All your bad feelings go into a drawer in this space, and then only get to come out again once you're out of class. Or work, in this case.

I try to explain this to Luisa at one point when she brings me a stir-fry she and Michael made. She knows I haven't really been eating unless she foists food upon me like she's trying to trick a toddler into eating vegetables.

Luisa looks at me for a moment. "Whatever happened on New Year's Eve," she starts, because I still haven't been able to talk about it, "Henry's right across the East River. If it's making you so miserable, just go see him."

But I don't. I don't explain further. I don't go see him.

One evening, when I get home from work, Luisa has a white paper bag waiting for me. My jacket, my cardigan, a pair of underwear I left at his house. All cleaned and folded nicely. Some hair ties. The orange stuffed turtle, which I didn't even know Henry had grabbed from the lodge when I left with Trevor. And another smaller brown paper bag with a plastic container. A slice of the Madagascar chocolate cake from Ignoto.

When I don't respond after that, Henry stops trying to contact me.

I get a little more focused at work. But when I come home, I break down.

A few more weeks float by, and then one Friday evening there's a small knock at my apartment door. And then another. I know that knock.

I open the door slowly and my sister practically tackles me to the ground.

"Norah Abigail Gold," Hannah says into my shoulder, "don't you ever ghost us again, I swear to God."

I break away long enough to grab her suitcase and shut the door to the hallway.

"What are you doing here?" I ask, half wondering if I'm hallucinating from a lack of food and sleep.

My sister has only been on two flights in her adult life. She hates planes, claims she doesn't trust them. I know it's really because she doesn't like being away from home, from Mom. She doesn't ever want to be too far, in case something terrible happens and she can't get to her. Hannah doesn't believe she's built for that.

But here, on her suitcase, is a bag tag from O'Hare, the edges of the long white slip misaligned and still sticky.

Hannah flew here.

She flew here for me.

"You're not okay," my sister says simply.

"No, I'm not."

Gingerly, she asks, "Can we talk about it?"

I know I have to. I know that. But right now, all I want to do is curl up with her and feel something normal, so I say, "Tomorrow?" and she nods.

With my sister cuddled beside me, emanating way too much heat, as she always does, it's the first time I've slept even moderately peacefully in weeks.

THE NEXT MORNING, Hannah forces me to shower, and then we run downstairs to grab some pastries from next door.

Talha greets me with a wide smile. "It has been too long," he says, and I nod.

Upstairs, we sit cross-legged on the floor of my room, mouths full of pistachio baklava, and Hannah finally looks at me. "It's time, Nor. What happened?"

"You were right," I admit.

She raises her light eyebrows in a question.

"I couldn't do it. I failed you, and Mom. Kristine." I take a long breath. "Him."

"But what *happened*?" Hannah asks again. "I don't understand." Then a little quieter, "He doesn't understand."

The knowledge that Hannah has been in touch with Henry nearly wrecks me. I feel the tears threatening to make an appearance behind my eyes. Hannah senses them too, and puts her hand on my arm.

"He must hate me."

Henry once told me that he couldn't, even when I'd hurt him in the past, but he'd never looked at me then the way he did when I walked away from him.

"He doesn't hate you, Norah," my sister assures me. "He's just confused. Look," she continues, "I'm not here to get answers for him. I hope you know that. I'm on your team. Always. But can I be honest with you? I don't think you can tell me what happened because you don't even know yourself."

My sweet, insightful little sister. Having it put into words like that is a relief. Because no, I don't know why I did what I did. Why I can't just go see him and fix it. Why I can't let myself be the person for him. Which is exactly the reason I don't deserve to.

"I think I'm fucked up."

"You're not," Hannah says simply.

"I mean, I am, though. I can't be with anyone. It freaks me the fuck out. I couldn't even tell Rob I didn't want to be with him—I just disappeared halfway across the country for a week."

Hannah nods slowly, listening intently.

"And now Henry's gone—"

"He's not gone," she interrupts, and it feels like a knife in my side.

"It doesn't matter, Hannah. It won't work. It just won't. We're too different. We got caught up in vacation and sex and pheromones and fantasy, but when it comes down to it, when I really think about it, our worlds are just too different."

Hannah thinks for a moment before opening her mouth. "But you come from the same place."

We do, but she wasn't there on New Year's Eve. She doesn't know. If the whole mess back in high school had never happened, if we'd figured it out when we were kids, then sure. Maybe that would have superseded reality. But our paths to New York, to this moment and place in time, diverged too much. We're not the same.

I'll never be the same.

"The same place. You mean the childhood home we're losing? Mom and Kristine are moving to the city. *Home* will never be home again. I feel like I'm floating in space, like I can't grasp onto a tether to bring me back down to earth."

My sister's dark eyes narrow at me, thoughtful. She places her hands, still sticky from the baklava, on each of my knees. "I can do that."

"Do what?" I ask.

"Be your tether."

HANNAH STAYS THROUGH the weekend. She gets me out of the apartment, and we do cheesy tourist shit. A bus tour. Times Square. A boat to Ellis Island.

At some point, on Sunday afternoon, she disappears for a few hours, returning with takeout from my favorite Indian restaurant. I don't ask if she saw Henry, and she doesn't offer it up, but I know. And I also understand that it's not about me. They formed their own bond. It was selfish to assume I was the only one Hannah was checking up on.

But halfway through my aloo gobi, when Henry's image hasn't left my mind, I ask softly, "How is he?" I don't look at my sister, instead taking interest in the large piece of cauliflower on my fork.

Hannah taps my foot with hers, causing me to glance up. "Would you want me to tell him how you are?"

I shake my head. "No, probably not."

I should drop it. I know that. But the confirmation that she was with him, only hours earlier, turns me desperate for any sliver of information.

"I just need to know that he's okay. Or that he's going to be," I add.

Hannah points accusatorily at me with the chicken on her fork. "See for yourself. Stop being such a coward."

I don't know how. My sister knows it too.

We eat in silence for a while, until Hannah puts down her fork and turns to me. "There is one more thing. Since you won't answer anyone's calls. I don't want you to spin out any further, but the house is in escrow. They close in two weeks. Mom asked if there's any way you could come home again, even just for a day or two, to clear out your room. You don't have to fly back with me tomorrow, but you could."

I consider it for a moment, the idea of getting out of the city immediately comforting. "Let me email my boss."

* * *

AFTER GETTING PERMISSION to work remotely, I book a ticket back on Hannah's flight. I try not to ask any more Henry-related questions, even though I have many tumbling around in my head. *Did Kristine's house sell too? Will he be back home when we're there? Did he ask about me?*

Are you sure he doesn't hate me?

Is it possible he still loves me?

When Hannah and I arrive at our childhood home for the last time, Mom greets us with open arms. Hannah dips out quickly, leaving me with Mom, and I immediately burst into tears.

"Oh, honey" is all she says. No *I told you so.* No *I warned you not to do this.* She sits us down on the couch, petting my hair for what feels like hours, her fingers winding through my disastrous curls.

"I'm so sorry," I tell her at some point, but she just shushes me gently.

I spend the next week at home, waking up early to work on East Coast time, then helping Mom pack up the house. She forces food on me at every opportunity, and I eat more bagels than I ever have in my adult life. Even if New York bagels are scientifically better, there's just something about the ones from the shop I grew up going to that's impossible to beat. Hannah pops back every other day, in between her shifts.

We don't do anything as a soon-to-be family. I see Kristine once, in passing, and she gives me a warm, sad hug. A few days into my stay, I notice Henry is here too. He pulls up in the CR-V with takeout from Pepe's. I watch him carry the bag up the porch and let himself into the house next door, and I feel like I can barely breathe. I wonder how long he's been here. If he's spent any time looking at me out the window. And then I immediately realize how unfair it is for me to even think that.

I see Trevor come and go a few times throughout the week, the bed of his truck filled at various points with boxes, trash bags, and random pieces of old furniture. Even though the thought of it makes my heart hurt, I'm glad Trevor is there for Henry through all of this.

We pack up Mom's Camry three times with clothing donations. I fill some boxes to ship back to New York. Yearbooks, my Meg Cabot collection, rom-com DVDs that I have no way to play but feel like I can't give up. The *Grease* VHS, its paper cover tattered and worn like my heart.

On my last day home, the last day I'll ever spend in this house, I move to the final section in the back of my closet. The one remaining spot to go through before I've cleared out this room that will never be mine again.

It's there that I uncover the sealed memory box I used to keep. A thick, shiny cardboard box I'd taken once when someone sent a Harry & David gift basket to my parents. Movie ticket stubs that dated back to age ten. A letter from my dad the night before I started high school. Old games of MASH and Soulmate, scribbled onto torn notebook paper and napkins. Scorecards from bowling nights where I very nearly always won. Notes passed between me and Frankie in a Spanish class that are almost entirely in code, so much so that I can barely follow it or remember the context. But I would recognize her swirly cursive anywhere, the easy way we've always been able to talk to each other. I snap a photo and text it to her.

I dig deeper into the box, finding a scrap of paper with Henry's unmistakable handwriting—block letters like an architect—ripped from the corner of a math worksheet.

You realize I'm joking when no one else does.

Hannah comes in while I'm still clutching the note from Henry. I don't even clock that I'm crying until my sister sits down on the floor of my closet with me, wiping my face with her sleeve.

"Sorry, sorry," I sniffle. "This is just all bringing up a lot."

"I know," Hannah says. "But I'm your tether, remember? So what's going on?"

"Do you ever feel . . ." I trail off, unsure even what I'm saying, "like it's just too much? To trust anyone to catch you. To let anyone in."

"What would happen if you did?" she asks gently.

"They'd tear apart all the things that mean the most to me."

I look down at the note in my hand.

I may have fucked things up with Henry beyond repair. I may not trust myself to let him in. But it's gone beyond that, affecting all of my relationships. Maybe there's a reason I have a hard time opening up to friends too. Frankie stayed a constant, but I mostly orbit around people I know on a surface level. People I can go out with on the weekends, or grab brunch with, but not many of those I'd divulge my secrets, my heartbreak, my story to. Luisa is one of my best friends, and it took Henry resurfacing for me to even tell her about him in the first place. *Why am I like this?*

My phone buzzes with a reply from Frankie. I shove away the tears with the edge of my hand so I can read the message.

Frankie
Any chance you can make it down to the city today? I know it's your last night, and you better not leave without seeing me

Frankie has always been there. She's another person who will catch me no matter what.

Norah
What time?

AFTER PROVIDING EVIDENCE that I do, in fact, have a valid driver's license, Hannah reluctantly lends me her car so I can drive down to meet Frankie. I've been avoiding my best friend too over the last handful of weeks. I mentioned I was home this week, but skirted around every opportunity to see her, including her offer to come to Laketon. It's forty-five minutes from the city, and the familiar curve of Lake Shore Drive reminds me of school trips into Chicago for museums and bus rides back filled with gossip.

I meet Frankie at her apartment in Lincoln Park. It's too cold to be outside, so she quickly buzzes me in. I haven't been to this apartment before. The last time I visited Frankie in the city, she was living with her sorry excuse of an ex-boyfriend, but this apartment doesn't feel like hers either. It looks like a Pinterest board, all bright, natural light and pink accents. I know she moved in with a coworker after the breakup, but it seems like even in the last two years, she's barely made her mark on this space.

Frankie leads me to a ridiculous-looking biscuit couch that definitely belongs to her roommate, hands me a mug of fresh coffee, and gestures for me to sit. There's a coating of hair from Frankie's orange tabby cat on the cushion between us.

"You've been avoiding me," Frankie says, her dark brows furrowed in contrast with her platinum blonde bob, my best friend's signature style.

I take a sip of coffee, trying to hide my sheepishness.

"You know Hannah and I text, right? You're pulling some real bullshit, Nor."

I'm a little taken aback by my best friend's tone. She's always blunt and to the point, but it's not usually directed at *me*.

"I'm here now?"

Frankie sighs. "On your last day in town, yes, you are technically here." She shakes her head like she's not sure if she wants to get into it. "I can feel you slipping away again, and I have to be honest, this is much harder to do across different time zones."

My lips pull up to one side. "It's just a bad breakup. I'll climb out of it eventually."

"We've been best friends since we were nine. I know you better than that."

"I'm not sure what you mean," I say honestly. I'm feeling a little lost here. Monsieur, Frankie's cat, slowly meanders out of her bedroom to join us. He eyes me on the couch, skeptical. There's no way he remembers me. I lean down to place my hand nearby so he can sniff it. Maybe some kitten cuddles will make me feel better.

He takes one whiff of me, then turns, completely uninterested.

"It's only by sheer force of will that I was able to keep our friendship going senior year," Frankie says finally, and I feel like the wind just got knocked out of me.

"What are you talking about? We've always been friends."

Frankie scoops up her cat with one hand and places him on the couch next to me, as if she knows what I need, and he hesitantly settles in. "When your dad died and everything with Henry imploded, you were like a ghost. I get it, and it was fair at the time, but you just shut down entirely. I put in the work because I knew you needed me, even if you couldn't express that. I wasn't going to allow you to cut me out too. I watched so many terrible rom-coms for you. I hate rom-coms."

"You're trying to be a wedding planner. How can you hate rom-coms?" I gasp.

Frankie rolls her eyes. "I don't have to be a romantic to be a smart businesswoman. The point is that I did it for you. I initiated every text to hang out. I sat at home with you. I dragged you out for bowling so our other friends wouldn't forget you existed whenever you wanted to participate again. It's fine that it never happened. Who cares about high school? But you would have run away from me too, Norah. I just didn't let you."

She takes a sip of coffee and Monsieur shifts so his back is now to me. I'm sure Frankie's recollection is real, but I blocked out most of the rest of senior year. All I remember is locking up all my vulnerabilities and storing them far away so no one could have the power to make me feel that way again. Since I was seventeen, that's been my default. Between my dad's death and Henry's humiliation, it seemed like the only way to protect myself.

"You're doing it again," Frankie continues, "and this time, I don't know how to stop it. I can't make sure you're leaving your apartment from eight hundred miles away. It's infinitely easier for you to disappear under these circumstances, and I really need you not to do that. You know I hate mush, but you're my best friend. You have to let the people who love you . . . love you. I love you. Hannah loves you. A certain someone we're not going to mention also loves you," she adds pointedly. "Monsieur, on the other hand, does not care for you. But he hates almost everyone. He takes after me."

Things get lighter after that. We finish our coffee, and talk nonsense, and her cat continues to ignore me. As I get ready to drive back to Laketon before the traffic gets too bad, my touch-averse best friend pulls me into the tightest hug, and I promise her that I won't run.

Chapter 27

I GET BACK to the house after seeing Frankie and feel drained but lighter. Since my room is finally clear, Mom and I finish packing up the kitchen too, the boxes that will travel to the condo I've chosen not to visit on this trip. I've promised to return to Chicago in February for their engagement party, and by then, I have to assume I'll be feeling more settled.

For my last night, Hannah, Mom, and I stay up late, drinking wine from Mom's celebration collection. We share memories about the house, about Dad, and for the first time in weeks, my tears come from laughing too hard at Hannah's recollection of Dad failing miserably as the Tooth Fairy.

I finally go upstairs to bed, much too late for my eight a.m. flight back to New York, and notice something on my pillow. A stark white envelope, the flap tucked inside the back, not sealed. My name across the front in Henry's block print, unchanged after all these years. I slide the envelope open and carefully remove the folded sheets of paper, finding a classic yellow Post-it over the first crease.

I still mean every word and more.

At the top of each page, there's the swirling logo of the chain hotel we stayed at during that fateful New York trip. I run my finger along the crisp edges as I unfold the thick stack of paper, pressing it flat on my leg. The black ink is still sharp as ever on the page. I take a deep breath and start to read.

Dear Norah,

I messed up. I messed up so badly. If I could rewind the last thirty minutes, I would do everything differently. Maybe the last hour—then I wouldn't have had all that beer, and my head wouldn't be spinning so much as I write this. I just panicked. I was caught off guard.

Because here's the truth.

I've been in love with you since we were twelve. Probably even before that, before I knew what that word, those feelings, what being around you was to me. Meant to me.

Do you remember our first party in middle school at Julia Schmidt's house? Everyone was spinning that empty Cherry Coke bottle around on the floor of the unfinished basement, but I could only look at you. You had this watermelon lip gloss on. I smelled it in the car when your dad drove us over there, and something just hit me. I couldn't stop staring at you. So I got out of the circle, said I wasn't feeling well, but the truth was, something didn't feel right to me. And then Kevin Chen's spin landed on you, and you seemed nervous, but you smiled at him, and you were so cute and hopeful, I couldn't take it. I wanted to push Kevin aside and be the person you looked at like that. I knew neither of us had had our first kiss yet, and it felt so monumentally wrong for it to be with anyone else. But you kissed him, and then you giggled, and you kept touching your lips. A normal guy would have just sat back down in the circle, taken the odds, and evened the score, but I didn't want to do that. That night unlocked something inside me. I only wanted you.

I can't believe Kevin Chen ruined another chance for me to kiss you. I know I'm the one who stopped it, but you have to understand, Norah. I didn't want it to happen like that. When I kiss you, I don't want it to be part of a game. I don't want either of us to have any question about what it means.

You're my favorite person of anyone I've ever known. We've been best friends for as long as I can remember, and I never wanted to mess that up, but God, it's been brutal loving you for so long and never being able to tell you how I feel. Because I never thought it was possible that you felt the same way. But you wouldn't have reacted the way you did if you didn't want to kiss me too, right? I don't think that's just the beer talking. I think you might want this exactly as much as I do.

Last year at homecoming, you tapped on my shoulder during a slow song, and I swear I stopped breathing. I thought this was going to be the moment, our moment, where everything finally fell into place.

But then you asked if I would dance with Ashley Majors.

I thought it was a joke. I actually might have said that. I can't remember because I think I blacked out for a second. It felt surreal. I wanted to touch you. Hold on to you. If you'd ever thought about me the way I always thought about you, you wouldn't have asked me to dance on another girl's behalf. That felt like the final straw of the Friend Zone. And I was okay with that, honestly, because I can't imagine my life without you, and if that was just as friends, I'd be the best friend you'd ever have, Norah. I would do anything for you.

You're witty, you're smart, you're sharp, you're funny. You're so pretty that there are times where I look at you and suddenly I feel like I'm going to burst if I don't tell you, or kiss you, right then and there.

In case you couldn't tell, I'm dying to kiss you. I probably shouldn't tell you this, and maybe you already know, but it will be my first. I've just never been able to see a world where it isn't you. But it's more than that. I want to hold your hand. I want to put my arm around you when we're watching a movie instead of sitting two feet away and staring at you the whole time, inching my arm toward yours in the hopes that maybe our fingers would brush together. Norah, I haven't actually watched one of our movies in so long.

I'm sorry about how I handled tonight. I shouldn't have let you walk out of this room. I shouldn't have let another minute go by without telling you exactly how much you mean to me. I was being dumb, that's all. But tomorrow we're going to interview at NYU and I know we'll both nail it. And then next fall, we'll be together, here, in this place we always dreamed about. We'll figure this out, I promise. I think this could be so good, you and me. You're the person who knows me better than anyone. And now I won't be carrying the deep dark secret of my feelings, so you'll really be able to know all of me, the way I'm dying to know all of you.

I'm going to give you this letter after your interview, when I go in to do mine. And afterward, we're going to walk around campus, where we'll spend the next four years, and I'm going to take your hand, and kiss you. Then, when we get back to Laketon, I'm going to take you on a date (just not bowling—I want to impress you and not get slaughtered). Because I love you, Norah, and I want to be with you.

Nothing is ever going to change that. Nothing could change the way I feel about you. I need you to know that. Just don't push me away. Don't give up on us.

Love,
Henry

I finish the letter and immediately turn it back over and read it again. A tear drops from my cheek, blurring out a few words, and I scamper to dry it off with a tissue, to preserve everything he put on paper so long ago.

I think about his versions of these events—the watermelon lip gloss I'd worn with the very intention of trying to kiss him. The movie nights where I spent just as much time watching how close his knee was to mine, rationing out an accidental bump or a grazing of our hands. Our shared dreams about the future, what being together in New York meant to us both.

To read, so clearly laid out, how Henry saw me feels so disconnected from who I am now. It's the person I am, but the one I've shoved down, hidden away inside myself. The one desperate to come free, to be able to tell him that I love him, that I'm stupid, that I'm sorry.

I fold up the letter to protect its precious contents, carefully place it back in its envelope, and then I let myself cry.

I CAN'T SLEEP that night. I can't do anything but read Henry's words over and over until I have them practically memorized. I feel restless and pent up and desperate to talk to someone.

Which, I guess, is how I find myself wrapped in Mom's fluffy down snow coat, walking in below-freezing temperatures in the dead of night. I know this isn't my best idea, but it's my last chance. Mom and Kristine aren't staying in Laketon, so who knows if I'll even have a reason to come back here. It's not far from the city, but I've managed to avoid this place for years and years, so the added distance probably won't make my visits more likely.

Of course the cemetery is closed. It's the middle of the night. I don't know what I was thinking. The bitter cold pricks my eyes, making them water, and the tears freeze on my face. I shake my head, and with a last-ditch effort, a spark of rebellion, I reach around the metal hinge of the gate and hope for the best. Somehow, the gate creaks open, and I slip inside.

I turn on my phone's flashlight, not exactly sure where I'm going. I've only been here twice—the day we buried my father, and a few months later, for the unveiling of his tombstone. I don't remember anything from that time, if I'm honest with myself. I was numb to it all, and now, almost a decade later, in the middle of the night, I'm so lost. I can't even do this one thing right. An absolute fuckup. That's me. Norah Gold, complete and total fuckup.

Kicking up the remnants of snow from the last storm, I find a small winding path through the side of the browned grass. Something in my gut draws me up the path. It's not familiar, but I'll take any instinct I can at this point. I clearly can't trust my own, but this feels like another source. It's hokey to think it's my dad, but when the path bottoms out and I see his headstone, it's hard to believe anything else.

I run my gloved hand over the top of the stone. *David Isaac Gold.* I try to open my mouth, but it immediately feels wrong to stand here and speak out loud. That's a trope from a movie for maximum emotional gut punch, not something that real, human people in pain do.

Silently, I mouth the Mourner's Kaddish, like I should have been doing every year I didn't visit him. I add the Shehecheyanu too, reveling in the idea that my dad would find it absolutely hilarious that I'm reciting it to mark the first time I finally came to see him.

Eventually, I sit down, not caring that the ground is wet, that the cold is seeping through Mom's coat. I sit down and I let myself think about the person I was when my dad was still alive. The person I was when he knew me. Would she have pushed away everything good that she never thought she could have? She was scared, but she was just a girl. I shouldn't still be that scared. I have to hold myself accountable. I'm messed up, but I did this to myself. I kept myself in this stasis. Dad wouldn't have wanted that. Henry didn't deserve that.

I don't deserve that.

I spent so much time blaming other people and other circumstances for fucking me up. And yeah, sometimes you get dealt a shit hand. But between the conversation with Frankie today and Henry's letter, I start to wonder. Maybe I'm the problem. I've somehow found a way to hurt everyone who means the most to me without even realizing what I was doing or intending that outcome. Maybe it's time for me to take some responsibility for that.

I stay until I feel the cold deep in my bones, then trudge back home for the very last time. In just a few hours I'll go to the airport. And then I have work to do.

Chapter 28

WHEN I GET back to New York, the first thing I do is unpack because, again, if I don't do it right away, my room will become a disaster area. I've never once dealt with my suitcase in full the day I arrived home, and I take it as a sign that I can do this. If I'm the problem, maybe I can fix myself too.

Henry's letter was a call to action. He hasn't given up on me. But I need to get my shit together. I need to prove that I'm ready, and I can't do that until I figure out how to stop running away from my problems. From the people who love me.

It's not for Henry—it's for me. I need to learn to be better for the people in my life. A better daughter and sister, who doesn't only visit once every two or three years. A better, more present friend. And then, maybe, I can worry about the other stuff.

Maybe he'll still be here. Maybe I'll have earned him.

Before Mom woke up to take me to the airport, I'd swiped her keys and white-knuckled the drive to the Jewel-Osco. I hadn't stepped foot inside there since before my father's "episode," but it was the only grocery store open early enough for me to get what I needed. Maybe I felt empowered by the visit to my dad, but for the first time in over nine years, I braved it.

And I was okay.

Unfortunately, they didn't have any pretzel rods in stock, so I had to settle for a bag of the regular kind, but I hoped that leaving the package on his doorstep would let him know that I appreciated his letter. That I'm not a complete coward. That I'm trying.

As the month goes on, I attempt to check in more with Mom and Hannah, but whenever I talk to them, they simultaneously remind me about the looming engagement party while also making it clear that no one believes I'm actually going to attend. Mom says she's *sure I'm very busy.* Hannah doesn't shy away from reminding me that I *can be a selfish bitch*, and even when she couches it in affection, it doesn't sting any less.

I purchase my flights and go so far as to send the airline info to both of them, but that doesn't seem to make a difference. The frustration about my family is almost enough to make me forget that I'm going to see Henry.

Almost.

The day before I'm set to fly out, I text Hannah that I'm not going to bother packing my shampoo and conditioner, since we use the same ones, and that elicits an immediate phone call.

"You're actually coming?" my sister asks, no room for pleasantries.

"I've been telling you this the whole time."

I try not to get frustrated with her. I'm putting forth so much effort to think about more than just myself, to follow through on my promises, but I guess I'm the same person I'll always be to them.

"Oh," Hannah replies after a long pause. "You can't crash with me."

"Why not? The condo's really not—"

"He's staying here," she blurts out. "On the daybed."

Hannah has a small one-bedroom apartment just outside the city. She's still debating if she's going to give it up and move closer to campus when she starts her MFA program at Northwestern in the fall because it's such a steal. Whenever I visit her, we share her bed like we've done since we were little, but she also has a daybed in the living room, where she likes to read.

"Why is Henry staying with *you*?" I don't mean it to come out so accusatory, but between the lack of faith she has in me and this new information, it feels like a betrayal.

"We're friends! We talk all the time. And he's going to be our stepbrother. Not everything is about you."

"He can afford a hotel. Or he can take the guest room at the condo."

"Kristine's aunt is staying at the condo. You really should have made it clearer that you were planning to attend."

I squeeze my eyes shut and count to five. "Yes, I can see how the screenshot with my flight info and the four follow-up texts in the family group chat about how I would be there could be misconstrued."

My sister lets out a rough exhale. "Well, we've seen this before. Thanksgiving, for example."

"I'm really trying here, Hannah," I insist, but it feels like a waste of breath.

Every instinct inside me is screaming that this is a sign. I shouldn't even bother flying to Chicago. No one expects me at the engagement party anyway. That couldn't be more clear. It's hard not to feel a little like no one wants me there either.

It would be so easy to use this as an excuse.

But I don't want to be the person they've come to see me as. I want to be reliable. I want to be included. I want to know I tried my best. If they can't see that, if I'm perpetually stuck as the selfish, flaky girl I've been in the past, at least I'll know I'm trying.

I text Frankie before I've even hung up with my sister, and she says I'm more than welcome to crash with her for the weekend.

With that settled, I stare at my phone. There's one more person I should talk to before the party. Normally I would just ignore it and hope the circumstances were too uncomfortable for it to become a thing, seeing each other in person for the first time.

Henry deserves more than that, though.

Before I can talk myself out of it, I scroll to his name and hit *Call*. The phone rings. It goes for long enough that I assume a voicemail will have to kick in soon, or maybe that's just my anxiety stretching every millisecond. I should have thought this through before I dialed.

"Norah?" Henry sounds like he's hurrying down a flight of stairs, his breath short, steps echoing. "What's wrong? Are you okay?"

Relief rushes through me at the sound of his voice. I take a second to breathe with him, knowing he's at the other end of the line.

"You there?" The background noise changes and I can tell he's now outside. I wonder if he's by his apartment, or maybe he stepped out at work? I hate that I don't know small details like where his office is in the city.

"If this was a pocket dial, I'm going to be—" Henry mutters, and I realize I still haven't said anything.

"No, no. I'm here. Hi. Hi," I say again, slower this time.

"Are you okay?" he repeats, his tone urgent.

"I'm fine, sorry. Didn't mean to scare you." The embarrassment hits me now. He clearly thinks the only way I would ever call him was if something was tragically wrong. "I was hoping we could talk."

Henry goes so quiet that if I didn't hear the sounds of traffic around him, I would think he hung up. "You want to talk. Now," he says, measured.

"Yeah," I reply, feeling stupid. "Do you have a second?"

"Do I have a—" he mutters. "You went radio silent for almost two months."

"I know."

"You got my letter."

It's not a question. It feels more like an indictment.

"I did. I've read it so many times I could probably recite it back to you from memory," I admit.

Henry lets out a snort. "And yet in the five weeks since you first read it, you couldn't be bothered to call."

"I left you the pretzels. I thought—"

He cuts me off with a brusque "What do you want, Norah?"

He's hurting, I remind myself. *Be brave.*

"I wanted to talk before the engagement party. Since we're going to see each other there. I was hoping to . . . clear the air."

"You're actually going?" he asks.

I can't read his tone. It's not the cruel disbelief I encountered from Hannah. There's something thick like honey behind it that I can't entirely place.

"I am. I don't know why everyone's so surprised. I said I would be there. I'm really trying here," I say as gently as I can. "I don't want to be a joke to everyone. I'll be there for the party.

I'll raise a glass to the happy couple. And I hope you and I can be civil."

"Civil." His voice is hollow.

"Civil," I repeat.

"You broke my heart, Norah." My name on his tongue is heavy with emotion.

"I know I did," I whisper, and that lingers between us for a few moments. "I'm sorry."

Henry's back to being quiet. I hear someone lay on their car horn on his end of the line.

Finally, he sighs. "You don't have anything more to say than that?"

"I am sorry," I add quickly. "About everything. I guess—" I look around at my bedroom, which I've managed to keep from being a disaster zone since I returned to New York. "I guess I wasn't ready. I should have said that then. I was acting immaturely."

He lets out an affirmative grunt, and I take that as a sign to keep going.

"I'm so sorry, Henry. You didn't deserve any of that."

I want to tell him how good it is to hear his voice, anger and all. How I watched a nature doc about turtles even though I hate documentaries, just because it made me think of being in that toy store with him. How I want to be right for him, but I can't figure out how to untangle myself from the ways I instinctively self-destruct, even when I try my hardest.

"I really do hope we can still be friends." The words feel sour on my tongue, but it's the most I can give him right now.

"I'm not your friend, Norah."

The line goes dead.

Don't take it personally, I try to tell myself as I finish packing.

It's going to be fine, I repeat as I go through TSA.

I have this inkling that Henry will be on my flight, and that we'll both see the parallel to our December travel, and laugh about it all.

But he's not here.

When I arrive at Frankie's apartment, her cat is slightly less skeptical of me, which I call a win. We take the L to Belmont because my best friend tells me it looks like I need pizza. We split a terrible bottle of wine while we eat, and Frankie, who rarely has more than a glass, tells me she's proud of me for coming. For asking for a place to crash. She offers to help make a game plan for seeing Henry, but it feels useless after our call.

I'm not your friend.

It's the thing I could always count on when he was in my life, and now I don't even have that.

I SHOW UP to Mom's new home, a large, sleek building with tons of amenities, an hour before the party. Hannah gives me a banner to hang in the community room, which they've rented out for the party. She tells me we can't use any adhesive on the walls, so I climb onto a precariously wobbly bar table to try to tie it to the exit sign affixed to the ceiling.

When I knot the string with a little too much gusto and start to fly backward, I feel strong hands grip my hips to settle me onto the ground. I turn to say hello, but Henry's back is to me before I can even right my brain.

Once the party is underway, I can't help but smile at how happy Kristine and Mom look. They introduce me to some new neighbors from the building, and I greet lots of my mom's co-workers and friends I've known since I was in diapers.

Seeing how full my mother's life is now gives me a twinge of guilt for not being around more, but realizing the full picture of the community that she and Kristine have built together makes me feel oddly hopeful.

I want a life that's bigger than the apartment I've hidden myself away in for the last few months. I want to learn how to let people into my world, how to trust them.

How to trust myself.

Mom taps on a plastic champagne flute, which doesn't exactly have the intended effect, so Kristine gives a whistle, and the room falls silent.

My sister, ever the instigator, shouts, "Kiss!" and the fiancées have no choice but to oblige.

When they pull away, my mom swipes her thumb at the corner of Kristine's mouth, catching some rogue lipstick. Kristine grabs her hand, kissing the inside of her wrist with so much tenderness it feels like far too intimate an action for this audience of thirty-five of their closest friends and family members.

They're going to be together for the rest of their lives. I sensed this before, but now it's abundantly clear.

My eyes mist and I glance away from them, unavoidably drawn to Henry, who's standing in the corner of the room by a large plastic monstera plant.

Henry gives a slight nod, as if he just read my thoughts and agrees.

I take the gesture as an invitation, and make my way over to him. If I didn't know Henry so well, I'd think he looked the same as he did when we were standing outside that club in the cold on New Year's Eve. But I can see the violet half-moons that tell me he hasn't been sleeping either. The way his blue eyes have dulled into a lack of emotion.

I know it's my fault.

"Thank you for earlier," I start when Henry doesn't immediately bolt in my presence.

He nods again, eyes closing for just a moment, but he doesn't say anything.

"We ordered way too much food, so please eat!" Kristine's voice rings out and the crowd disperses as people get in line.

Henry and I stay frozen in this spot.

"It was pretty generous of you to save me. I'd even go so far as to say *friendly*."

His eyes turn to ice and I immediately know it took me a single sentence to cross his boundary.

"Stop," he says, venom on his tongue. "It's always about you. What about what I want? You don't get to dictate what we are anymore. Friends, lovers, everything, nothing—it's exhausting, Norah. I'm done."

I open my mouth, but can't think of anything useful to say.

"I wish things were different," he continues. "Someday it won't be so painful to be near you and know what we had, and how easily you gave up on us, but I'm not there yet. It isn't that I don't want to be your friend," Henry says just loud enough for me to hear over the buzz of the room. "I can't. It's too hard. Please respect that."

He looks down at me like he's fighting for his life. As if it took everything within him to get that out. So what else can I do besides say "Okay," and "I'm sorry," and then stay as far away from him as possible for the rest of the party.

Chapter 29

WHEN I ARRIVE back at Frankie's apartment, she takes one look at me and then forces Monsieur into my lap as a designated Emotional Support Cat.

How could everything come out so wrong, both on the phone and in person? How can I find the words to express what I'm actually feeling without torching any more of the relationships in my life?

From Frankie's weird biscuit couch, with her cat resigned to lying on my stomach, I log into my insurance portal and search for therapists.

I always thought I was so self-aware. *I can identify the problem, so what's the point of talking to someone else?* But that's no longer enough.

Back in New York, I start seeing a woman named Reagan once a week on Thursday mornings. At first, I'm skeptical about the fact that we're the same age, and she appears to have been a sorority girl (because I know you're not supposed to do a social media deep dive, but I absolutely had to), but it ends up being a good fit. We talk about my dad, high school, relationships. She cracks me open in ways I never could have done on my own.

I work on letting people in.

I invite my roommate, Aya, to coffee because in the year-plus that we've lived together, we've never hung out one-on-one. I learn she's also a member of the Dead Dad Club, and from there, one coffee turns into a weekly Saturday afternoon ritual. She stops being so mysterious and starts leaving her bedroom door open when she's home, an invitation for me and Luisa to stop in.

I try to be more transparent with Luisa. I let her take care of me when she wants to, and for my part, I attempt to keep our space a little tidier. I even send Rob a genuine apology. Granted, it's over text because I don't want to see him or rekindle anything, but at least it's a step in the right direction, Reagan-approved.

I FaceTime with Mom and Kristine from their condo. I ask about Henry, but I'm always met with sad smiles. I want to scream at them about how hard I'm trying, how brutal therapy is when you actually put in the work, how I'd like to understand why I do what I fucking do too, but at least I'm finally dealing with it all.

And then, somehow, it's spring, and New York is finally lovely. My company moves from Greenpoint to an office on the Upper East Side, and I find myself running more frequently through Central Park, glancing up at Henry's building sometimes.

One day, in April, I walk past a Jewish deli on my warm-up to run in the park. They're offering a "Pre-Chametz Special." *Almost Passover already?* I think. Before Passover, you're supposed to clean the house (or the restaurant, in this case) of chametz, anything that's not kosher for the holiday—so no grains, no yeast, the list goes on. I look in the window and see a man behind the counter carrying out a tray of latkes to put in the display case. This must be part of the special. Potatoes are okay, but not flour, and God knows there is flour in latkes.

I think about my now-ruined flour-coated sweatshirt from that day I went to Henry's house to borrow some oil, and I suddenly get the overwhelming need to see him. I feel it bubbling up in my chest, telling me I'm ready. That there's still a lot of work to do, that I'll continue doing, but I just know. It's time.

I call Henry as fast as my fingers can find his contact info in my phone. It rings once, then goes right to voicemail. I immediately wonder if he blocked my number, like I blocked his all those years ago.

I fly inside the deli, purchase a half dozen latkes, and then, without any real thought about boundaries, and without worrying that maybe Reagan would not approve of this measure, I find my legs taking me right to Henry's building. I recognize the doorman immediately from the night of our first date. His eyes narrow like he's trying to place me.

"Don't I know you?" he asks slowly.

"I'm a . . . friend of Henry Cole's. 28-D."

The doorman nods fondly at the mention of Henry's name. "Of course. Of course. I miss that guy."

"Miss him?" I ask.

"He's been out of town for quite some time." I feel my brow furrow, and the doorman's eyes go wide. "I shouldn't have told you that."

"Secret's safe with me." I give him a warm smile. "Do you like potato pancakes?" I pass him the bag from the deli, just as Henry did that night of our first real date, and start to walk away. I pull my phone back out of my running belt and call Hannah.

"Hello?" she asks slowly. It's clear I woke her up.

I cut right to the point. "Why isn't Henry in New York?"

"Norah," Hannah says, her tone warning me not to go there.

"I think he blocked my number."

Her lack of response on the other end of the line confirms it.

"Well, that's rude. What if something happened and I needed to get in touch with him? Like about Kristine or you or—"

"Norah," Hannah says again, growing more impatient with me.

"I need to talk to him. I think I can finally make this right. But I can't do that if I can't find him. I know you know where he is."

The line goes silent for what feels like forever. I check to make sure the call hasn't dropped completely, but eventually, she sighs. "He's not doing well, Nor."

"I know."

"You don't." Hannah is quiet for a moment, then says, "I can't tell you where he is." Her voice is firm, and even though it's not what I want to hear, I'm proud of her for standing her ground. But then she sighs again, very softly, almost like I wasn't meant to hear it. "But you could try calling Kristine."

I hang up and immediately dial Kristine.

"Sweetie? Is everything okay?" she answers, sounding concerned. Which is fair, since I talk to her often, but always call my mom.

"I know I don't have any right to ask this of you, but is there any way you could tell me where Henry is? I know it took me a while but I needed to make sure I was really ready. I didn't want to promise him something I couldn't give him again. But now"—I feel the tears welling up—"I just need the chance to talk to him. I don't know if he'll listen or if I already blew it completely, but I need to see him. And I can't do that if I don't know where he is."

Kristine sighs on the other end of the line. "Is this for-real for-real this time?"

"Yes," I say as quickly as I can make the word come out of my mouth. "I need to tell him I love him. That I'm in love with him." I feel a rush at how easily those words came. Reagan may not like much of what I'm doing right now, but at least that counts as progress.

"I'll text you the address. But you didn't get it from me, okay?"

"Yes, of course, absolutely. Thank you, Kristine."

"Be gentle with him, sweetie."

After we hang up, Kristine's text pings across my screen. Henry is in Los Angeles.

Things really must be dire if he's willingly ventured to his least favorite city in the world. Which means I have a lot of making up to do.

When I get back to my neighborhood, I grab a few things at the bodega. My mind is already whirring. It's good he wasn't here, that I couldn't just go see him in my running clothes with no plan and a bag of greasy latkes. The word I hid behind, the word I no longer need. After all this time, he deserves a grand gesture, something to show him that I love him. That I mean it.

I book a nonstop flight I can't afford for this afternoon, and an Airbnb just in case. I throw a bunch of nonsense into my suitcase, killing time by preparing one step of my plan with glitter glue I pray dries before I roll up the paper and shove it into my bag, and then I head for JFK.

Chapter 30

I GET INTO LAX just after three p.m., thankful for the time difference that allows my day to grow three hours longer. I take a Lyft to my Airbnb in Santa Monica, trying to get oriented. I freshen up, drop off my bag, and call another Lyft to the address in Hollywood that Kristine sent me. I've never been to Los Angeles before, and I guess I didn't understand how sprawling the city is. By the time I arrive at the building, it's almost six. I thank the driver and survey the area as the car pulls away.

The street is lined with tall palm trees. I can see a hint of the Hollywood sign from my vantage point on the sidewalk. Kristine mentioned that Henry was staying with a friend, Nick, who I think was his old roommate here in LA. I wonder if this is Henry's old apartment. The building I'm about to infiltrate is not a place I would have expected him to ever live. It looks straight out of the 1960s, painted a bizarre salmon color, with a kitschy sign that reads *Guava Towers* over the garage. It feels like someplace designed for Vegas, or Boca maybe, as opposed to what I thought Los Angeles was supposed to look like. The building is three stories tall, with balconies facing the street. I see a surfboard on one, a Pride flag on another. A couple sitting at a table drinking wine.

I approach the wide glass doors and see a buzzer. I start to scroll through to the apartment number I was given, 301, when I notice that the door isn't closed all the way. Probably not the best safety feature, but I pull it gently and slip inside. I walk through the open-air patio, looking up at the sky, until I reach the elevator. I press 3 and ride up, the elevator making sounds so severe that I remind myself to take the stairs down when I leave.

I circle around, fascinated by this donut-shaped building and the feeling of the Los Angeles air (smog?) on my face as I locate the apartment. *Please be home*, I think, because the idea of turning right around and traveling back to Santa Monica without even seeing him feels like it might kill me.

I land in front of the door marked 301, stepping onto a doormat blazed with the interlocking *S* and *D* that I recognize as the San Diego Padres logo.

I knock and hold my breath. After a few moments, the door opens, and a guy about my age with honey-colored hair and a well-groomed beard stands before me. I see a full-sleeve tattoo of grayscale flowers creeping up his muscular biceps, under the edge of his white T-shirt. He looks at me for a moment, and his dark eyes narrow.

"Hi, I'm—" I start, but he cuts me off.

"I know who you are."

He folds his arms across his chest and makes no move to welcome me inside.

"And you're Nick?"

He nods.

"If you know who I am, then you probably know why I'm here."

Another nod.

"Is Henry around?"

Another.

"Can I see him?"

"I don't think you can."

Nick is giving me absolutely nothing to work with. I briefly consider pushing past him, the idea that Henry is on the other side of the door too overwhelming to stay away when I've come so far already today. But this man could definitely tackle me to the ground if he wanted. He could just put his tattooed arm out and block my entry. So I try another approach.

"I came all this way. From New York. And this place is really far from LAX. I had no idea."

That gets a soft chuckle. "Pro-tip: LAX is for suckers. Next time try the Burbank airport."

I nod. "So you're really not going to let me in? Or go get him?"

Nick dips back inside briefly and emerges with a small red cooler. He checks the set of keys on his belt, then steps out, shutting the apartment door behind him. Closing away any glimpse I hoped to get of Henry. "Have you ever seen the Hollywood sign?"

I FOLLOW NICK up a staircase, past a door that reads *Do Not Enter—Alarm Will Sound!*, and out onto the roof. No alarm sounds. Scattered pebbles and satellite dishes aside, the rooftop of this building gives a panoramic view of the city. I see the

Hollywood sign in plain view, and my breath skips. I turn to another side and see skyscrapers that must be downtown.

I follow Nick over to a couple of lawn chairs set up on one side of the roof. "This is incredible."

He places the cooler down next to the chairs and kicks it open. He holds up two bottles of beer, a Stone IPA and a Ballast Point Grapefruit Sculpin. An offering. I never did grow to enjoy beer, perhaps a little traumatized from my first experience with it on the New York trip, but I nod and point to the Sculpin. Nick flips off the cap with an opener on his keys, then hands the cold bottle to me. He gestures for me to sit down on the low, neon green chair as he pops off the other cap, and I fumble to do so. He squats down onto the bright blue one, this motion seeming to be second nature for him.

"Do you know much about me?" Nick asks finally.

I shake my head. "I know you used to have a lot of sex on Henry's couch? That . . . that's about it."

He grimaces, running a hand along his chest, revealing another tattoo of twisting vines just below the V neckline of his shirt.

"Never gonna move past that, is he?" Nick mutters. "Henry and I were roommates freshman year at UCLA. I didn't get him for the longest time. He didn't go out. Didn't drink. A real nerd." Nick laughs softly, and underneath, I can see all the affection he has for Henry. "Meanwhile, I was a complete mess, drunk on the freedom of being independent for the first time and way too many cheap-ass beers. We weren't really buddies yet, but one night, he—" Nick pauses, gripping the neck of his bottle hard. "He helped me out. And that night changed everything.

"I'd just found out my parents were back together. Had a

real on-again/off-again thing. They divorced when I was thirteen, and as soon as I left for college, they were back on. The whole shebang, all over again. When I mentioned this to Henry, his eyes fucking lit up. He had so many questions. How they got back together, all this stuff I didn't know and didn't want to think about. That was when I first learned about you. As soon as I knew that his moping was about a girl, it all made sense."

I didn't particularly remember Henry moping through the rest of high school, but I was also in a complete grief stupor and had made it a point to think about and engage with him as little as possible. So who knows.

Nick takes another sip of beer. "I was the one who had to break him out of this goddamn spell he'd been under. Drag him out with me. Make him make friends. Make him meet girls. He wouldn't take a sip of booze until April of freshman year. *April.* He kept saying that the one time he drank in high school, he ruined everything. That first night I got him drunk, you know what he did? Started reciting calculus. Fucking derivatives. And then he got sad, and we were back to the girl next door who he'd never get over.

"And now here he is again, only this time it's so much worse than when he was my scrawny nerd of a roommate. He's a wreck, Norah. That's why I can't let you see him. I don't trust you with him."

He's trying to protect Henry. From me.

"But your parents. They got back together." I'm grasping at straws. Anything to crack this guy next to me open just a little bit.

Nick snorts, shakes his head. "They got divorced again eighteen months later, and now they hate each other so much they can't stand to be in the same room, even if it's filled with two hundred other people. Not even for my brother's graduation. So forgive me if I have trouble believing it ever works out when it already failed once. Or twice."

Not the response I was hoping for. Man, he really does not want me here. Yet he's still sitting next to me, slowly sipping his IPA. So there must be a chance, however slim.

I pick at the label on the bottle of beer I'm barely drinking. "How long has he been here?"

"A month, maybe?"

"A month?"

"Yeah, he was in Chicago for a while, with your moms, but then he went back to New York for all of three days before he called me. He said being in his apartment was unbearable. That the city was suffocating. He had to get out. I told him he was lucky I never got another roommate when he moved east. Made his room a photo studio I barely ever use, and now it's his again. For as long as he needs."

"He's lucky to have you" is all I can muster.

"There is no better man than Henry Cole," he says. "I would do anything for that guy, and it still wouldn't measure up to everything he's done for me." Nick doesn't elaborate any further, but I feel the weight of his words heavy in my chest.

"No one better," I say softly in agreement.

Nick gives me a tight-lipped half smile, which feels like we're slowly inching toward progress.

"He knows I'm here?"

Nick nods.

"And he really doesn't want to see me?"

The sun is starting to set, painting the Los Angeles sky with swirls of pink and purple. It's the most beautiful sunset I've ever seen but it starts to blur, becoming more like a Monet piece, as the tears build behind my eyes.

"What do you want me to say, Norah?" Nick's tone isn't cruel, but it's firm enough that I know if I leave this roof in resignation, I will never get the chance to tell Henry how I feel.

I sniffle, trying to get it together. *Let him in.* "He held on to a love letter he wrote me for nine years, but when I need a couple of months to try to get my head on straight, that's where he draws the line? What does he think I've been doing these last few months? Prancing around the city like that wasn't the most devastating thing I've ever done? I wasn't okay, Nick. I know you don't know me, not really, but I hadn't been okay for a long time. And I couldn't figure out how to get on track if I was with him. That was something I had to do by myself. For me. Mostly for me. But also for him. So I could be ready for him, for real this time."

Nick stares at me for a while, interrogating me with his dark eyes. He doesn't say anything, but he's not telling me to leave, so I take one final swing.

"I'm going to come back tomorrow," I say slowly, trying to gauge his face.

"I don't think that's a good idea."

"Please, Nick," I continue, not loving the desperation I hear in my voice. "This is my last chance with him. I'm aware of that. I know I need to fight for him. But I'm prepared to do that. Because it would be worth it. I just need a day. I was planning to do this at my Airbnb, but I'm guessing it's pretty unlikely that I can get him to come all the way to Santa Monica with me. Or that you'd let him."

"Wait, you're staying in Santa Monica?"

"Yeah?"

Nick drops his head to his hands. "Henry really didn't tell you anything about LA geography, huh?"

I shake my head, and Nick laughs a little. I feel him softening.

"If you come back tomorrow, I can't promise he'll talk to you. But I won't run interference."

I feel a sudden rush of hope. "Thank you! Thank you, thank you, thank you!"

Nick just nods, and we sit there a little while longer in silence, finishing the beers.

"There's one more thing," I say, fiddling with the label I've completely picked off at this point.

His eyebrows narrow.

"Is there any chance I could get access to this roof again? Before I see him? I kinda have a whole thing planned."

Chapter 31

WHEN I FINALLY get back to Santa Monica, my stomach reminds me that I've barely eaten all day. I don't know if the beer on an empty stomach went right to my head, or if I'm just running on pure adrenaline at this point, but I feel unlike myself in a wonderful way. I get a sandwich to go from some shop that has good Yelp reviews, and walk down along Ocean Avenue until I see an empty bench overlooking the beach below. As I eat, I watch the waves crash gently, blurring the reflection of the moon above. It feels peaceful, somehow, even in this state of total upheaval in my brain.

I know there's little chance of me sleeping tonight, and I pace around the bungalow I'm staying in for hours, thankful that I was able to rent out the entire (albeit tiny) studio. I repeat everything I want to say to him over and over in my head, and maybe sometimes out loud, until I feel like it's right. I read his letter again, even though at this point I practically have it memorized. It feels like a pep talk coming from Henry himself, in lieu of any real contact these last few months. I can hear his voice at seventeen, and I hear his voice now.

I wake up the next morning, rolling over onto the letter beside me in the Aerobed. I stop at a coffee shop, then walk down to the water. I sit in the cold sand, letting the waves lull me into an almost meditative state. And then, once I realize that the Target I'd passed is finally open, I stop in to grab several picnic blankets, a new addition to the plan given the change in location. Then I walk back to my Airbnb, nearly getting hit by several vehicles. I guess people don't jaywalk in LA? It's contradicting every instinct I have developed over the last eight years as a New Yorker.

Back at the Airbnb, I shower, trying not to psych myself out. Because whatever happens today, this won't be the last time I see Henry. Whatever happens, he'll be at the wedding, at holidays. But this might be the last chance I have for him to really *see* me. I have to make it count.

The hard California water confuses my curls, and I spend longer than I wanted to trying to make them bounce playfully. Now is not the time for my curls to go stringy on me. As I carefully wind strands around my fingers, defining individual ringlets, I think about Henry taking my hair down while he was inside me, and a shiver runs across my spine.

I apply a little makeup, just to try to look alive, and swipe a balm over my lips. I debate what to wear for a long time. It's cooler here, by the water, than it is where Henry's staying, but my plan does now hinge on significant outdoor time. I slip into my favorite jeans, sliding them up my hips like a wearable security blanket. I know I can sit in these, and that's very important, both for the long ride and for the plan. I ultimately choose a soft pink V-neck T-shirt, not wanting to look like I'm trying as hard as I actually am.

I shove the rest of my things into my suitcase since I was only able to book this Airbnb for one night. I have no return flight, but if I have to stay longer here, I will find somewhere closer to Henry. Or if this all goes to shit, I'll look into that other airport that Nick mentioned.

I text Nick, who reluctantly gave me his number after agreeing to grant me access to the roof again yesterday, and tell him I'm on my way. He says he'll meet me at the front when I get there.

I fidget the entire drive. I feel too hot, too clammy, too much. The driver is a chatty woman in her forties, and I let her tell me all about her kids since I can't get her to be quiet, but also can't bring myself to engage. Once we pull off the freeway and turn down the palm-tree-lined street that is quickly becoming familiar, I feel instantly relieved.

Nick is sitting on the steps outside the building. He greets me with a head nod when the car pulls up, his eyes narrowing when he sees me go around to the trunk and yank out my purple suitcase.

"I told you, I have a whole thing planned," I say quickly, not wanting him to get the idea that I'm planning to stay, whether the fact that I hadn't yet secured lodging for tonight is true or not.

"Does he know I'm back?" I ask Nick as we ride that death trap of an elevator up to the third floor again.

He shakes his head. "Not yet. But I assume he's expecting it."

I try to convince Nick to bring Henry up here, to me, once I'm finished setting up, but he declines. He seems to think it's too much of a betrayal or something. Nick goes back down to his apartment while I get everything ready, telling me to knock again when I'm done. I'll have to get Henry up here myself.

ABOUT TWENTY MINUTES later, I shove my suitcase behind a satellite dish, out of sight, and take the short staircase back down to the third floor. I knock on apartment 301, and Nick answers. Without a word, he swings the door open, allowing me to slip inside.

The apartment looks much more lived in than Henry's place in New York. The walls of the living room I'm standing in are painted a shade of blue just lighter than navy. There's a huge bookcase covering most of one wall that's filled with a mix of books, DVDs, and records, not organized in any discernible fashion. A large TV against the opposite wall. And a long black leather couch between them, facing the television.

I see his feet before I see any other part of him. Crossed on the arm of the couch closest to me. And then his head slowly rises above the back of the couch, his blue eyes sending shock waves through my whole system, even if they don't look pleased to see me. Henry's legs swivel around, and he places a book down on the coffee table.

"I'll be in my room if you need anything," Nick says, avoiding Henry's gaze as he sweeps across the apartment and disappears.

I close the door behind me and take a few steps inside. Henry stands and moves around the couch. He looks thinner than the last time I saw him. Gaunt, even. He's grown out a dark beard. I've never seen him anything but clean shaven, and it surprises me. There's one spot that's patchy, just under the right side of his lip, and I briefly wonder if that has to do with the scar he got when he fell out of our tree house when we were six. He's wearing a pair of blue athletic shorts and a gray T-shirt, which feels so unlike *my* Henry. The beard does too.

Hannah was right. He does not look okay. I immediately regret how hard I worked on my appearance this morning, masking how shitty I've been feeling this whole time.

"Hey." Everything I spent the night rehearsing has flown right out of my brain. "Look who ran away this time."

I mean it as a joke, but Henry's face is a brick wall.

"What are you doing here, Norah?" he asks, sounding so tired.

"I needed to see you. To talk to you."

I take a few more steps forward, toward him, but Henry raises a hand for me to stop, his face so wounded that I almost want to back out of the front door and leave him alone forever, just so I don't have to cause that look ever again.

"I didn't run away," he says finally. "I escaped. I had to. The apartment was holding me hostage. I thought seeing you in Chicago, telling you I needed space, would help me move on, but as soon as I got back to New York, the finality of it all crashed through me. Reminders of you were painted everywhere in my mind. My apartment still smelled like you somehow. Citrus and summer. I had to get out. It was too painful to be there without you."

"I'm so sorry," I say, feeling the tears already. Feeling like I made a mistake by coming here, by putting him through any of this. Feeling almost like I never should have kissed him in that bed-and-breakfast.

Henry runs a hand through his dark hair, which is longer now, and beginning to curl at the ends. "Yesterday I woke up to a text from your sister telling me she'd held her ground with you, and one from my mother saying she'd caved immediately. Mom told me to hear you out. That's the only reason I'm still standing here. So I'll ask again. What are you doing here?"

I take a deep breath. "I've been seeing a therapist for a minute now. I needed to understand why I do the things I do. To find a way to make better, healthier choices. For me, and for the people I care about. Reagan, that's her name, she told me I need to stop running. That instead, I need to walk with intention through the matter at hand. I'm sorry it took me a while to get here. It was a long trek. But I was always walking toward you."

Henry's eyes sweep around me, like he's searching a desert, desperate for water. It takes a while for his gaze to glide up to meet mine, and when it does, I can see every ounce of pain I've caused all over his face. "I can't do this. I think you should go."

I fold my lips into my mouth, trying to keep it together. "Okay. I will. But there's one more leg of the walk. One more thing I have to show you, and then I promise I'll leave."

Henry shakes his head, his hand gripping the back of his neck. "I don't want to go anywhere with you." The words feel like knives in my heart.

"It's only like, ninety steps," I plead. "Probably fewer for you. It's just upstairs." I point to the ceiling. "I have so much more to say. I just have to do it up there. And then I really will leave." I'm losing him. I can see it. "Please," I beg, a last-ditch effort before all the tears building behind my eyes break free.

"Fine," he says so softly that I would have believed I'd imagined it if I didn't see him grab a key ring from the counter and raise his hand, a gesture for me to go.

I turn the knob of Nick's front door, checking behind me to make sure Henry is following. He slides on a pair of flip-flops (flip-flops!) by the door, then keeps several paces behind me. I lead him up the stairwell, past the alarm that I know won't sound, and out onto the roof. I take a long, slow breath through my nose, and let my eyes fall to Henry. He's looking around, taking in the space, his eyebrows tented more with confusion than anger.

"I know I can't take back things I've said or done," I start, and Henry's head turns quickly toward my voice. "And I know we had a lot of almost moments."

I walk over to the first picnic blanket, filled with New Year's hats and glasses. I'd begged the guy working at my bodega to see if they still had anything in the back and he grumbled the entire walk into the stockroom but reemerged with the sparkly gold paraphernalia I'd been hoping for. There's a bottle of champagne I bought alongside the picnic blankets this morning, and two small plastic cups I stole from the coffee shop.

"Our New Year's kiss. The first one that would have meant anything to me. Don't worry," I add quickly, "I'm not going to kiss you if you don't want me to. I know I haven't earned that yet. I didn't think it was going to be that easy."

Henry looks relieved as I walk him over to the next blanket. The *Laketon Academy Homecoming* banner I made with art supplies I borrowed from Aya, in our school colors of scarlet and gray. I take out my phone briefly so I can press play. "Drops of Jupiter" starts blaring through the portable speaker that's holding down one corner of the polyester fabric. I step onto the blanket.

"I should have tapped you on the shoulder that night and asked you to dance myself. It was all I ever wanted. *You* were all I ever wanted, Henry."

He doesn't say anything, but he gingerly steps onto the

blanket with me. This is the closest we've been yet, and I almost lose focus.

"So, Hen, will you dance with me?"

I see the indecision in his eyes, but the next thing I know, his hands are on my waist. Not wrapped around me. Maintaining a healthy amount of distance between us. I place my hands on his shoulders, too scared to try to wrap them around his neck to bring us closer. I feel like we're back in that photo from my bat mitzvah. His thumbs gently stroke my waist for just a moment before stilling, almost like he hadn't meant to do it, but through the thin cotton of my shirt, I feel everything.

We sway with the music, my eyes on his face the entire time. He looks down at his feet, never meeting my gaze. *But he's still here. He's still dancing with you*, I tell myself, trying to hold on to a small shred of hope. But as soon as the song fades out, he drops his hands back down to his sides. I can't help but let out a sigh. I guess I should have expected this. He still hasn't said a word since we got up to the roof. I step off the blanket and lead him to the third one. The final one. My last-ditch effort. I reach into my jeans, pulling out a thin tube, warm from my pocket. I slide the gold wand across my lips, coating them in a shiny gloss.

We reach the final blanket, adorned only with an empty bottle of Cherry Coke, another acquisition from the bodega. When I got home, I started drinking it while making the homecoming banner, but then quickly realized it was barely ten a.m., and the looming sugar crash was not sustainable given the day I had ahead of me. I opted to pour the rest down the kitchen sink.

"Will you sit down?" I ask.

He hesitates, but sits, and it's only once he's cross-legged on the picnic blanket that he seems to notice the bottle. I see it register across his face, but I can't read beyond that. I sit down across from him, legs folded. I watch as his eyes glide over my lips.

"In therapy, I've been talking a lot about Dad, obviously. And it's brought up a lot of memories. Like how sometimes Dad would call you my bashert. It's Yiddish. I never knew what it meant, but it came back to me all the same. *Bashert* is destiny. Or soulmate. I don't know if I believe in that kind of stuff, but I believe in you, Hen. In us. Because there's always been an us."

I take a deep breath, knowing that this is the part I have to get right. "Henry Cole, I love you. I've been in love with you my whole life. I'm sorry it took me so long to say it. I'm sorry I pushed you away. You were right about everything. I have issues with trust, with abandonment, but I'm working on it. I want to be better. I want to make this work. I want to try."

Henry's face is stoic. I can see him taking in what I'm saying, but he's giving me absolutely no hint as to what he's thinking. So I keep going.

"Because if I tear away all the parts of me that are scared, that are stupid, that are broken, and I'm really honest with myself, this is it for me. You're it for me, Henry. You always have been."

I lean forward, placing my hands on that empty bottle of Cherry Coke between us.

"That night, at Julia Schmidt's party, I had a plan to kiss you. I had been practicing in my room for days. Not the kissing part. But how much force to spin the bottle so I could make it land exactly where I wanted. I thought it was the perfect ploy to find out if you felt the same way I did. If you didn't, it was just part of the game. But if you did, I was certain I'd be able to tell. But then you opted not to play. The watermelon lip gloss was for you, Henry. It should have been *you*. Everything should have been you. So that's what I came here to say. What I needed you to know. Falling in love with you made me want to be better. And I'm so fucking in love with you, Hen. So." I fiddle with the bottle in my hands, laying it on its side.

He stretches out his legs on the blanket, leaning back on his arms behind him. I swear he looks almost smug as he raises an eyebrow in challenge.

This is what I prepared for. I'd been practicing again, just like I did when we were kids. For this moment. My grand romantic gesture. My declaration. But that was on the floor of my Airbnb, and the wind on this rooftop is threatening to ruin all of my prep work. I can tell my hands are shaking. Everything comes down to this, huh? Which is ridiculous because we're fucking adults. Would he really let this bottle decide the fate of our relationship? Is this some kind of sick joke? Is he trying to hurt me the way I so clearly hurt him?

As soon as I twist the bottle, I grimace, afraid to look. But before it even passes him twice, before it starts to slow, Henry leans forward, reaching out with one hand, snatching the bottle up.

I hold his eyes, oceanic and opaque, for a moment too long. I've lost him. I just know it. I stand up, blinking back tears. "You can tell Nick I'll be back to clean all this up later, I . . . I have to go." I head for the stairs, feeling like I can't get enough air in my lungs on this rooftop.

But that's when I hear his voice, so low I almost miss it. "I don't want to play Spin the Bottle."

"Yeah, I got that," I say, my back still to him. I can't bring myself to face him like this, my eyes burning hot with the tears I'm desperately trying to keep in.

"I want to play Truth or Dare."

"What?" I ask, slowly turning around, not believing that those words just left Henry's mouth.

"I want to play Truth or Dare," he repeats.

I make my way back to the picnic blanket and slowly sit down. Henry has placed the bottle off to the side, his face still giving me nothing.

"Pick," he orders once I'm seated.

I've just laid out every truth I have for him. There's nothing left inside me in this moment.

"Fine." It comes out weary, my voice shaking. "Dare."

Something soft breaks in Henry's eyes. "I dare you to kiss me." It's a challenge, an opening, a lifeline. "Seems like that was an almost moment you were missing here. So kiss me, Norah. Please." A slow smile spreads across his face.

I burst into tears immediately at the sight of it. "That was mean, Hen," I laugh, wiping my face with the heel of my hand.

"What? I've been miserable the last few months. I can't have a moment of fun? I knew if you came here and you actually told me you loved me, I was a goner. If you finally said it, there was no way I was letting you leave here as anything other than mine."

Getting a grip on my tears, I lean forward on the blanket, crawling toward him. Henry scoops me up, drawing me into his lap. I let myself sink into his touch, the feeling of his hands on my thighs electric.

"Say it again."

"I love you," I tell him, this time close to his face, and I feel his body relax.

"I love you," Henry echoes, one arm moving to hold me in his lap, the other snaking through my hair. He tilts my head toward his, pulling me close to him. I feel his beard against my chin, and my hands reach up to touch his furry face. His eyes flicker closed for just a moment, and then his lips are on mine. Henry kisses me like we're making up for lost time, and I suppose we are. Not just these last few months, or the nine years we didn't talk, but everything from that moment in Julia Schmidt's basement on. His teeth skim my bottom lip, drawing a low moan out of me, and I feel him immediately harden underneath me.

"I'm so sorry," I tell him again as we catch our breath. "I never want to hurt you like this again."

He twists a curl of mine lightly around his finger. "I know."

"Do you forgive me enough to try one more time?"

"Of course. You're it for me too, Norah. Always have been. Always will be. I just have one more question."

I lean back to look at him, one eyebrow raised. "Yeah?"

"This isn't actually the same lip gloss from middle school, right?" The corner of his lip quirks up on one side as my nose crinkles up in disgust.

"Gross, Hen, I bought it this morning."

"Oh thank God," he heaves in mock-relief.

I smile so wide I'm afraid I'll break my face, so I kiss him again. To preserve my face. And because I love him.

UNABLE TO STOP ourselves, we make love on the roof, and I don't even feel weird anymore about using those words to describe it. Henry later jokes that we should have had sex on the couch instead, to make up for all the times he'd walked in on Nick, but ultimately he decided his friend had done too much good at this point to deserve that.

Afterward, he helps me clean up the roof, and we go downstairs. He plops me in the room he reclaimed as his while he has a long talk with Nick. When he returns, he tells me it's time to go home, and we book flights for the following morning. Then he packs up the room, gives Nick a long hug, and takes me to the Roosevelt for the night. He says the walls in the apartment are super thin anyway, and he does not intend to be quiet just for Nick's sake. And it's not just the sex. We talk all night. The most brutally honest and vulnerable we've ever been.

The next morning, we fly out of a small airport in the Valley, walking right through security. When we land in New York, we go to our own apartments. Because we're two separate people and are working on boundaries.

Henry returns to work in person after what he described to me as a "sabbatical," and we both start thriving professionally. We see each other a few nights a week. We eat dinner at Ignoto, or the tiny Jewish deli around the corner, or get takeout from the Indian place I love. I watch him like a hungry animal when he cooks for me because he's so sexy when he feeds me. He wins over my roommates the first time he makes everyone what he refers to as "our special pork udon dish," and forms a particular kinship with Michael whenever Luisa and I start talking too fast for the guys to track. I go to his work dinners and smile and rub his back while he talks his face off. He goes out with me on the weekend and dances or sings his heart out, no longer hiding behind the statement that he's not much for karaoke. He's terrible every time in the most perfect way. Our moms are in no rush and take their time planning the perfect wedding. We find ways, both big and small, to blend our worlds into one that works for the two of us. We keep communicating. We keep choosing each other. We are always, always trying.

Epilogue

Twenty months later . . .

HENRY

I SIT IN the center of the camel-colored sofa flanked by the Gold sisters as we watch Sally Albright tell Harry Burns that "Auld Lang Syne" is about old friends, and I feel an overwhelming sense of gratitude.

For the girl I grew up with, the complicated history that led us to this point, the time I've had with Norah since she flew to Los Angeles and finally said what I've known deep down since we were kids—that she loves me too.

To be here, in our moms' condo in Chicago, watching a movie that meant so much to us in another lifetime, feels surreal. But so much of the last nearly two years has been that way, as I built a life with the only woman I've ever loved.

Norah stretches her legs, placing her feet in my lap, and I instinctively start to knead her arches.

"Don't be gross," Hannah says, scrunching up her nose. "I cannot be smothered by all this affection right now."

Hannah is currently in an off-again phase with her grad school boyfriend. Norah is certain it won't stick, as much as we all despise Cal. I must say that this Hanukkah is already off to a better start without him.

This holiday last year was the first time we met Cal. While I try to be impartial, knowing how stubborn and overprotective the love of my life can be, he really was the epitome of an insufferable film school bro. He was judgmental about the movies the girls (and I) wanted to watch, clearly had no interest in getting to know Hannah's family, and never shut up about himself.

I'm sorry that Hannah is hurting right now, but as my mother would say, good riddance.

"Don't give me that," Hannah continues, throwing a pointed look at her sister. "You know how they are."

"Oh, we know." Norah raises her eyebrows suggestively. "You didn't share a wall with them."

Our moms' wedding last month was filled with heartfelt vows and the Jewish traditions I always love learning more about. I file away what seems meaningful to Norah, what caused her eyes to mist up during the ceremony, what we could make our own one day.

Afterward, Mom and Sara headed to Paris for an extended honeymoon, making sure to return in time for Hanukkah, which is much earlier than Christmas this year. This evening, we'll light the menorah for the first night, which is why Norah and I flew back in from New York. We decided to stay in the condo this time, since Sara has handed over the reins, and I'm now on latke duty in perpetuity, but regretted the decision after discovering that three weeks in France did not dull their newlywed . . . enthusiasm.

Regardless, it's been special to witness how important Sara is to my mom, and vice versa. And I love the way our family has evolved. The five of us have created new traditions together, and we're all better for it.

My mother still insists on making pajamas for everyone, though now Sara keeps her on track to finish them early so we can take our photos in time to send cards out before the holidays. It's a welcome relief not to be the only Type A person in the family. Last year, we did the photos at Thanksgiving, but they were still in France this time, so we're planning to do them tonight instead.

We'll all get changed into the maroon pajamas that Mom chose because "the color suits Sara so well," and sit in front of the tree that I picked out and decorated with Norah and Hannah when we got into town two days ago, a surprise for our moms. Tonight, when we light the menorah, I hope my future wife is no longer surprised that I learned the prayers. I'm desperate for that crinkle-eyed smile when she eats the latkes I make for our family. We'll raise a glass of wine (the good stuff, of course) to David, because his memory is the greatest blessing.

And when we go to take our family photo, we'll set up the little LED menorah that Norah and I found at that toy store two years ago in the background. Sara claims it's because it photographs better than real flames, and I would never argue because that day with Norah made me all the more certain that we would get to this point.

Before we go back to New York, I'll head out on an errand

with my mom. Norah, I'm sure, won't think twice about it. But I'll return in possession of my grandmother's engagement ring.

When Mom went to the safe-deposit box to get out some jewelry for the wedding, Norah took one look at my grandmother's ring, a simple platinum solitaire with Art Deco etchings around the band, and said, "When you propose to me, I want something like that."

It was the first time Norah had mentioned marriage in any capacity, even though we were already living together. I wanted to let her take her time. We'd get there when she was ready. I would've married her any day of the goddamn week. In the year since Norah moved into my apartment, she made it our home, and I swear my heart grew a size larger just from her everyday presence. The space is now full of personality, life, joy. Just like her. Just like everything she touches.

Over the last month, I've been trying to suss out if she's ready. If she'd meant it, or if that was just a passing comment. But one day, when we were sitting on the couch, her legs draped over my lap, and I thought I was being subtle, she turned her whole body to me, her big brown eyes fluttering as if she finally got the hint. "Hen," she said, placing her foot flat on the top of my thigh, "when Mom admitted that she was going to propose to Kristine, she told me, *Before you say it's too fast, remember that I've known her for over twenty years. And when it's right, it's right.*"

Tentatively, I asked, "Is it too fast?"

Norah shook her head so hard that several curls sprang loose. "It's just right."

With the memory of that day and the knowledge of what's to come at the top of my mind, I pull Norah toward me by her calves. I never take for granted that I get to touch her this way. Like she's an extension of my own body. A physical manifestation of the other half of my soul. My bashert.

Hannah rolls her eyes as if she can read my thoughts exactly and propels herself off the couch.

"I love you," Norah whispers against my mouth, and I don't think I'll ever get over being the one she gives those words so freely to either.

I gather her in my arms and kiss her like this is forever. Because it will be. It always was.

Acknowledgments

I thought this book was dead so many times. After countless rejections, I'd grieved it and started moving on, so it's wild to me that you're holding it in your hands right now. If you're a writer in the querying or submission trenches, please know that it doesn't happen overnight for everyone. Keep going.

To my brilliant editors, Kerry Donovan and Genni Eccles: It's a literal dream come true to get to work with the two of you. Your vision for this book, and thoughtful, heartfelt guidance has made it something I'm so proud to put out into the world. Thank you for seeing Norah so clearly, and for taking a chance on me.

To Sam Palencia for the most gorgeous cover I could have hoped for. To Alaina Christensen, Anna Venckus, Anika Bates, Sarah Oberrender, Daniel Brount, Jennifer Wong, Shana Jones, Megha Jain, and the entire team at Berkley for all their incredible hard work making this book a reality.

Thank you to Nicole Payne for loving Norah and Henry (and Trevor) as much as I do, and for getting their story out there. To Elizabeth Copps, for your help with the contract.

Lauren Spieller and Hannah Teachout, I am so excited to enter the next stage of my publishing journey with you.

Thank you to the people who read early, terrible versions of this book, and then helped make it better or promised me it wasn't as bad as I thought: Anna, Rekha, Caitlin, Lindsay, Jackie, Jordan, and Kiran. Thank you to Isabel for reviewing my query package and offering such fantastic advice.

To Jason Katims and the *Dear Edward* writers—working with and learning from you made a huge impact on me both personally and professionally. I wouldn't have been able to write about grief in the same way without the years we spent finding the heartache and joy in it all.

To Meg Cabot, for showing me at age ten that my voice was valid.

To Michelle, my writing soulmate, for retitling this book, and for the infinite voice notes, cheers, screams, and real talk. To Haley, for our conversations about motherhood and being sensitive little babies and trash day. You are both such talented writers, and I can't thank you enough for lending me your brains. Heather, I am so grateful to be on this Berkley debut journey with you. To my fellow 2026 Debuts and the Group Chat, for sustaining me through all the ups and downs of this weird industry. To the Berkletes and so many other authors who I spent years looking up to and devouring all your books, thank you for your guidance and support. It feels truly bananas to call you peers.

To the friends who put up with me rambling about fictional characters for decades. Michelle, for surviving the mess of our twenties together and encouraging me to get out of my comfort zone and go on adventures. Brittany, who gave notes on the books I wrote when we were in high school. Sophie, for all the lyrics we composed on Mr. Eric's bus. Anna, you're in here again because I think you've read everything I've written over the last decade, and you've always been so generous with your feedback and friendship. Josephine, for two-hour phone calls about nothing and everything, and for always sending me photos of my place on the bookstore shelf. To my LA community, the Augtember mamas, and anyone who hurt my feelings enough to give me something to write about.

To my family, by both blood and marriage, thank you for being so enthusiastic and excited about my writing. Let's please never discuss the spice.

To my parents, for being endlessly supportive of my unrealistic dreams. I always felt like things were achievable because you made me believe it was true.

To Emilia, who didn't even exist when I started this process. I'm so lucky to be your mom, and I can't believe you'll grow up knowing I'm an author, even though it'll be decades before you're allowed to read this. I hope I can show you that all your dreams are possible.

Anthony, we always joke that the men in my books are nothing like you, but the feelings you inspire in me are in every word I write about falling and staying in love. Thank you for being the first person who read this book, and for always talking out story with me and giving thoughtful notes. Thank you for telling everyone we meet that your wife is a romance author. Thank you for everything you do for our daughter and for me. You're my biggest cheerleader and my best friend. I love you and I like you.

And to you, dear reader, for picking up this book and taking the time to read about these lil disaster babes I made up. I will simply never get over it. Thank you, thank you, thank you.

Keep reading for an excerpt from

Picture Me with You

Rachel Pologe's next novel.

NICK

"ARE YOU THE perv who's been stealing women's underwear from the dryer?"

The words launch their assault the second I push open the heavy door, frankly, scaring the shit out of me. I grab my chest, trying to catch my breath in the hot, damp air of my apartment building's laundry room. There's no actual circulation down here in this cramped space off the building's garage with little to no ventilation, and my lungs feel heavy. I focus on the low buzz of the fluorescent lighting overhead, and the occasional hiss and whir of the water heater in contrast with the consistent banging of the dryer.

"Well?"

My eyes settle on the person making such bold accusations. She's seated on a highlighter-yellow lawn chair that's never moved in the entire six years I've lived in this building. She must be a new tenant, or she would know better than to go anywhere near the mysterious furniture that finds its way into the public spaces of Guava Towers. Her long dark waves are pulled into a thick, messy braid over her shoulder. I follow the trail of her hair down to where it ends, my eyes dipping to her chest.

Do not look at her tits, man, come on. *You're better than that*, I have to remind myself, like I'm some thirteen-year-old kid who's never seen breasts before.

I catch a glimpse of lilac lace where the thin strap of her tank has slipped off her shoulder, and suddenly I know that's all I'll think about for the rest of the day. She puts down the book she's holding and steps toward me. She's petite, probably not even five three. Huge hazel eyes, all their focused fury directed at me.

"You don't have any laundry with you, and you're lurking in here, staring at me, so I'll ask again. Are you the one stealing my underwear?"

With her standing so close, I have no choice but to get it together and remember what I'm doing down here.

"Sadly, in all of my many, many spirals into debauchery, panty theft has never come into play."

Her eyebrows shoot up somewhere between the words *debauchery* and *panty*, an instantaneous flush spreading down her pale face, neck, and chest. I'm not sure which word caused this reaction, but I can't help the smirk that spreads across my lips at her surprise. I hold up the forest-green and black plaid fabric I've been clutching in a death grip ever since I heard her voice. "I'm just trying to clean this flannel."

"A whole wash cycle for one article of clothing seems pretty wasteful to me." Her eyebrows narrow as she continues to hold my gaze.

"Yeah, well, this girl I was seeing was holding it hostage. I think she sprayed it to death with some floral shit from Bath & Body Works, trying to make sure I'd think about her when I wore it and call her again," I explain. "But honestly, I'm mostly pissed that she may have ruined my favorite shirt."

She steps a bit closer, crinkling her nose when the oppressive fragrance hits. She shakes her head in disgust, her braid dipping off her shoulder and down her back. And then she eases up. Retreats a few steps, clearly trying to reclaim some air that hasn't been affected by the damage done to my flannel.

"So," I say, heading over to the small locker with my apartment number on it. I grab the bottle of detergent. "You're camping out down here to make sure you don't lose any more panties?"

She flushes again. So it was *panties* after all.

"That's exactly what I'm doing. You can't be too careful." She sits back down in the lawn chair and picks up her book but doesn't open it.

I go over to the unoccupied washing machine, taking my time placing the six necessary quarters in the tray. What is the deal with this woman?

We're both quiet as her dryer slows to a stop. She stands again, opening the door and then letting out a frustrated sigh. "Do these machines even work?"

I turn to her, not realizing the question wasn't rhetorical until I see her expectant eyebrow raise.

"They're pretty old. The forty-minute dry cycle doesn't do too much. Pro-tip: If you add an extra quarter when you first start the machine and hit the start button a second time, it'll give you an extra twenty minutes. Easier than having to wait for it to finish to start it again. For next time."

She nods, her face softening a little as she puts another set of quarters in.

"I'm Nick, by the way," I say. "301."

"Becca," she replies, turning briefly to me, gold flecks in her eyes glinting, before directing her attention back to the dryer. "Sorry, I don't give my apartment number out to potential pervs, no matter how charming they might be."

I drum my fingers against my beard. "You think I'm charming?"

She cocks her brow at me, but her eyes dance playfully. "I was trying to put a polite spin on accusing you of being a perv. Plus, you've got women dousing your clothes in their scent. So."

I fold my lips between my teeth, suppressing a smile. I'm getting to her, and we both know it. But she holds my gaze. She doesn't look away. She is masterful at unwavering eye contact.

"Sure, Becca," I say finally. "See you around."

I push the door to the laundry room open with both hands, letting it clang behind me as it hits the frame.

BECCA

Nick propels through the door and I immediately sink back into that awful fluorescent-yellow lawn chair, cursing myself for how awkward I made that whole interaction. Granted, it's the first conversation I've had with an actual human in six days, so maybe I'm out of practice with how to be functional around others. Especially torturously hot men. Who knew that tattoos would have such an effect on me? I grew up with my Jewish mother constantly in my ear, reminding me that if I even glanced too long at a tattoo on Instagram, I would not be allowed to be buried in our family's cemetery plot. Yet five minutes alone with Nick, and I had to pick my book back up just so I wouldn't reach out and touch his arm, the full sleeve of black and gray shaded flowers woven around other symbols I tried not to stare at.

I did notice the road sign for the Pacific Coast Highway about halfway down, right where the sleeve of his white T-shirt strained against his toned bicep. After the amount of time I spent in the car over the last few weeks, getting my shitty ten-year-old Corolla across the country, it was almost like I was magnetically drawn to it. The guitar-pick shape with a *1* in the center, *CALIFORNIA* arched in small block letters at the top.

In the ten days since I arrived in Los Angeles from my tiny hometown of Wynston, Pennsylvania, I've had underwear stolen out of the dryer twice. I can't take any chances today and risk having to purchase more. With my bank account dwindling from the cross-country move, even a five-for-twenty-dollar deal would be pushing it if I don't absolutely have to.

There is a lot to like about my new apartment at Guava Towers. The location in Franklin Village, close to the 101 freeway, with a hint of the Hollywood sign visible from the street. Lots of shops and restaurants nearby that I've been too frozen with fear to explore yet. The palm trees that line the street like something out of a stock photo of California. The somehow-affordable one-bedroom *with* a covered parking spot included, which is apparently quite the LA luxury. I know I lucked out. This is truly the unicorn of my housing search. When I received the call that I'd gotten the apartment, on the afternoon of my twenty-sixth birthday, I was so relieved. This was my only shot to move here. And it felt like fate. I don't know a single person in this city, the state of California, or the Pacific Standard time zone, yet here I am.

But as I was quickly learning, there were also a lot of . . . *quirks* that came with this building. The three-story complex was constructed in 1962, a kitschy Vegas-inspired building with open air corridors that are painted a nauseating coral color. The building hasn't had many updates since it was first constructed. That is abundantly clear. I googled *1962 thermostat* when my air conditioner crapped out two days after I moved in, making the July heat unbearable, and an exact image of the one on my wall came up. The plumbing and the kitchen appliances are original too, I'm sure of it. The elevator is claustrophobic if anyone rides it with you, and it makes horrible screeching noises as if you're slowly meandering toward imminent death. And, of course, the underwear thief.

Los Angeles isn't what I expected. Not that I've done much exploring because, again, all-consuming fear after having turned my entire life upside down without any plan whatsoever. But it's more than that. I've never been particularly insecure about my body before, but now, here, everyone is tanned, toned, and flawless. Look at Nick. Prime example. His caramel hair falling just above his chocolate eyes like he's a dessert I can lick. Devastating long eyelashes. A well-groomed beard. Clean, short fingernails. By all measures back home, he is possibly one of the most attractive men I've seen in real life. And he's just some guy who lives in my building!

Meanwhile, my stomach is too soft, thighs too wide. My breasts are liars—I know they look great in a bra, but my insecurities about gravity once they're free have already set in due to the sheer size of them. My skin is too pale, the little color I've gotten from the California sun so far making the tops of my shoulders sun-slapped instead of sun-kissed. Not freckled or bronzed, just magenta and peeling. Everything about me is too short for this place—my body, my legs, my list of life experiences. I already feel like I made a mistake. Like maybe this isn't the place for me after all. A whim brought me here, and I was stupid enough to sign a one-year lease with the first two and last two months already paid, and penalties if I break it early.

With no job to pay said rent beyond the quickly waning savings account I built up working as an office administrator for a dental practice, I'm stuck. So, for better or worse, I'm here. One year in Los Angeles. One year.

TWO WEEKS INTO my time as a resident of Los Angeles, I force myself into a routine of sorts. I start taking walks around the neighborhood, trying to orient myself. I go to Gelson's and spend way too much money on groceries and toilet paper, but the occasional glimpse of Bob Odenkirk checking out in the express line somehow makes it worth it. I attempt to counteract my exorbitant grocery bill with a cheap Groupon for a yoga studio nearby. At least it gets me out of the apartment. I've never lived alone before, and without a job, it's far too easy to become a hermit.

Over FaceTime, my mother tells me I'm "nesting well" in the new apartment, which translates to getting the most baseline furniture possible, and having a white-walled space completely devoid of any personality. I'm sure it'll get there, but if I really am only here for one year, if I fail and move right back to Wynston, what was even the point of buying framed art? Do you know how expensive it is to frame things? How does anyone afford to do this?

The one thing I've been busying myself with is cooking. More accurately, baking, but at least I'm putting my overpriced groceries to good use. I place a homemade pizza in the oven, set the timer, and then head to my car to grab the toilet paper I couldn't carry on the first trip.

I take one long deep breath as I ride down to the garage—my standard ritual over the last couple weeks upon entering this death trap—retrieve the package from my trunk, and then use my key to call the elevator back down. The doors creak open and, while balancing the toilet paper package in my arms, I hear the clanking of metal at my feet and watch as my keys fall down the elevator shaft, into the gap between the base and the ground.

Well, shit.

I place the toilet paper down on the floor of the elevator and reach for my phone to text my landlord, Mrs. Rosie. She usually sends her husband, whose name I have yet to learn, to fix things, like the toilet that wouldn't stop running when I first moved in (turns out you have to jiggle the handle for ninety seconds after each flush), but last time he took days to respond. I feel my back pocket and start to panic when I realize that my phone is locked inside my apartment, right on the kitchen counter.

There are eleven, maybe ten minutes before my timer goes off. Probably another ten before the pizza starts to burn and smoke out the apartment, with no way to get back into my place. And I can't stay down here and let those elevator doors close or I'll be trapped with no way to call the elevator back. I feel around in my braid. I could try to pick the lock with a bobby pin, but with my luck, these locks are also from the 1960s, and it seems too risky.

I pull the emergency hold button on the elevator and crouch

down. I can see the keys glinting right underneath me. If I had something long and thin, I could probably pull them up. I sigh.

There is one more option. I suppose. If I must.

Reluctantly, I get back into the elevator and hit 3. When the doors squeal open, I pause for a moment. My apartment is on the second level, and it feels a bit like I'm in another dimension to be one floor up. Everything looks basically the same, but it still feels slightly off, like a Spot the Difference puzzle in a magazine. The black plastic mat when I step off the elevator doesn't have a hole bitten off the top left corner. There's a slight dip in the walkway as I head toward apartment 301.

Please be home, I think as I turn, but I immediately see his kitchen light on. I step onto his doormat, recognizing the interlocked *S* and *D* for the San Diego Padres, and knock lightly.

After a moment, the door swings open, and I'm greeted with a mischievous smile as he leans his forearm on the frame. "Well, hello, Becca the Panty-Thief-Hunter."

"Do you have a wire hanger?" I ask, no time for bullshit.

"Sorry, what?" Nick's confusion is written all over his face.

"I dropped my keys down the elevator shaft, and it's a little time sensitive. I've got something in the oven."

Nick nods, pursing his lips. He holds up a finger to tell me he'll be right back.

I take the moment to peek my head inside Nick's apartment. It's much larger than mine. Must be one of the two-bedroom units. I wonder if he has a roommate. The living room is painted a color halfway between navy and midnight blue, and the dark walls suit him. There's a long black leather couch in the middle of the living room, facing a television. I watch everything on my laptop, and the idea of watching a movie on a larger screen is something I didn't realize I missed. The other wall is nearly completely covered by a tall bookshelf with DVDs, records, and books all positioned haphazardly. I don't see a record player, but maybe he's a collector? I have a lot of questions about this man.

Nick returns with a hanger, a flashlight, and some magnets. He checks a set of keys clipped to his belt, and then cocks his head, indicating that I should follow him.

"Can't have you burning the building down now, can we? I've been here six years and it's rent-controlled, so I'd like to keep this residence as long as possible."

I nod as we step into the elevator, our arms practically brushing against each other. My cheeks flush, and I turn my head, hoping he didn't notice.

We reach the garage and Nick pulls the emergency hold. He tears the paper reading *Bob's Cleaners* off and then gets to work unwinding the hanger he grabbed with a set of pliers.

"I can do it," I say, but Nick ignores me.

When he finishes, he sticks the pliers in his back pocket and crouches down on the ground.

"Seriously, I can do it," I repeat.

He lays flat on his stomach and looks up at me. "You can hold the flashlight. That would be helpful."

I see it in his back pocket and go to reach for it when he gives me a funny look, intercepting me and handing the flashlight over himself. Of course he wasn't asking me to grab it. I don't know why on earth that was my initial instinct.

Nick works the wire down the shaft, hook first. After two tries, I hear the clanging, and he quietly pumps his free fist. He pulls my key ring up and then sits back on his heels. His white T-shirt has a streak of grease on it, and I immediately feel guilty.

"Thank you! I can, uh, buy you a new shirt?" I say, but he shakes his head.

"It's all good."

We step back into the elevator. I hit 2, and he hits 3.

"Do you want some pizza?" I ask as we ride up, slow as ever. "If it's not burned beyond belief. As a thank-you?"

My eyes glide over his lean torso. He certainly doesn't look like a man who enjoys pizza, but . . .

NICK

"That'd be rad," I hear myself say, and Becca gives one short nod, like she wasn't really prepared to follow through on this offer. I haven't thought about dinner yet anyway, and it is kind of entertaining to push her buttons.

We get off the elevator on the second floor and walk to 206. I point up at the brass numbers on her front door. "See, it's not so hard to be neighborly." She rolls her eyes at me, clearly anxious to get inside and assess the damage. The timer is already beeping from the other side of the door. One twist of the keys, and she goes flying inside, over to the oven, flapping a kitchen towel she grabs off the counter at the rising smoke.

I look around the apartment, much smaller than my own. Her furniture is generic, probably IKEA or Target, and she doesn't even have a TV. Mr. Rosie (Mrs. Rosie's husband who, in all the time I've lived here, has refused to ever tell me his name) probably did a fresh coat of paint before she moved in. The walls are pristine, nothing adorning them, as if she barely even lives here, except for one large black scrape along the doorframe to the bedroom.

"It survived!" Becca exclaims with what I can only describe as glee.

I glance over at the counter. Despite the smell of smoke in the room, the pizza has remained relatively unscathed.

"The cheese is maybe a little browner than I would have liked, but all in all, we're okay!"

"Nothing is better than burnt bits of cheese on the crust," I say. "Nothing." She smiles, appreciative.

Becca slides the pizza from the metal pan onto a large wooden cutting board. She opens two, three drawers, eventually finding a small round pizza wheel. She cuts several slices, transferring them to slate blue plates, and brings them over to a small dining table that only has two wooden chairs.

"Hope it doesn't suck!" she says, raising her slice in cheers.

I take a bite and let out an audible groan. The crust is pillowy, the caramelized onions rich, the roasted garlic sweet and nutty.

"Holy shit, this might be the best pizza I've ever had," I mutter between bites, and I mean it. "Where did you get this crust?"

Becca looks pleased despite herself. "Oh, I . . ." She gives me a once-over, like she's trying to suss out if I'm serious, so I nod my head, encouraging her answer because when I leave this apartment, I am going straight to the store to buy more of these. "I made it," she says finally.

I have to put down the slice, which I really don't want to do, but I need both hands for emphasis. "You made this?" I ask, pressing my palms to the table. She nods, looking a little sheepish. "From scratch?"

She nods again. "I . . . don't have much else going on right now. I'm just trying to pass the time. Watching the dough rise. Literally."

I shake my head in disbelief, devouring the rest of my slice. "Can I?" I gesture toward the cutting board with the rest of the pizza.

"Oh my god, of course," she says, covering her full mouth with one hand, waving me over with the other.

As I grab another two slices, I notice the boxes piled up in one corner of the room and a stack of broken-down cardboard next to it.

I cock my head toward the boxes. "So you're brand new to the building, huh?"

Becca nods. "Brand new to LA, actually."

"Fresh blood. Welcome."

She doesn't say anything to that. Just looks down at her pizza. She picks it up, takes another slow bite.

As the silence stretches on, I offer up a question in hopes that I can draw this out long enough to finish the pizza. "You here chasing the dream?"

It takes Becca a while to look at me. So long, in fact, that I'm almost finished inhaling the two extra slices by the time she meets my gaze with a quiet, "Something like that."

Her plate is empty now too. I should go. I feel like she wants me to leave. She's giving me a very weird look, her eyes drifting down the length of my arm, over my tattoos, when she thinks I won't notice.

Finally, I wipe my hands across the already ruined T-shirt and push back in my chair, standing. "Come with me?"

"Where are we going?" She doesn't budge.

"My favorite place in the building. But hold on tight to those keys this time," I say, raising an eyebrow.

Her face blanches, and I instantly feel like an asshole.

"Come on," I say, softening. "I'll make sure you don't drop

'em." I extend a hand to her. She looks between my face and outstretched palm, then stands, decidedly not taking my hand. That's fine. I lead her out of the apartment and watch her grip her keys with so much fervor that I can't help but laugh. Her nails are painted the color of the sky on a clear day. We go up the stairs to the third floor, and then a few steps down the hall to another shorter staircase. I reach for the door with the sign that reads *Do Not Enter—Alarm Will Sound!* but I feel a tug on my arm, blue-tipped fingers wrapped partway around my wrist.

"Wait," she says, pulling me back. I turn to her, looking into her eyes, which are glinting emerald green in a sea of brown. She drops her hand as soon as I look at her.

"Relax," I tell her with ease. "The alarm's never worked." I push the door open, gesturing for Becca to go first. She doesn't hesitate this time, stepping onto the gravel of the roof. The day has cooled down only slightly now that the sun is setting. The clouds are wild pink wisps above us. But I can't look at the cotton candy clouds or the skyline of the city. My eyes are trained on Becca, her whole face lighting up when she spots the reason I brought her up here. She looks overwhelmed, hopeful, happy. I think it's the first time I see a real smile from her. It's a moment with herself that I almost feel like I'm intruding on.

The roof of Guava Towers has a perfect, unobscured view of the Hollywood sign.

"Watching people see it for the first time never gets old," I say, and suddenly the full force of that smile is directed at me. Why does that send a shiver through me in this heavy July air?

"It's amazing," she says quietly.

"Okay, this was worth ruining my shirt over," I reply, and she glances sidelong at me.

"Is this whole thing . . . is this, like, a move?" she asks, her whole face changing into something I can't read, and damn, this is a moment I need to be able to read this woman.

Truthfully, it's not *not* a move, but the look she gives me makes me hold back. I think about downstairs, when she was so pleased with herself as she bit into that masterpiece of a pizza she'd so skillfully made. The way she seems so determined, yet a little sad underneath. I want to know why. Normally, I would say yes immediately. But something tells me to take a slightly lighter approach.

"What would you think if it was? Hypothetically speaking, of course," I add quickly. I give her an easy smile, trying to communicate *No pressure*.

Her nose scrunches up like she's nervous, then she takes a huge breath. "I just moved to this new city and found the one good apartment I can afford. I can't hook up with you and then have it become awkward when I see you around the building. Because it *will* be awkward. I'm no good at casual hookups. Oh god, it would be terrible. I'd have to move. I'd have to break my lease, and there's no way I can afford that. It would be such a mess. And to be honest, I'm way too fucked up to even think about a guy right now. In case my rambling didn't clue you in to that. So I'll shut up now."

This is the most she's spoken since she knocked aggressively on my door earlier this evening, and I find myself hungry for more of the way her brain works, so I let the mild rejection roll off my back. It's not a big deal. And Becca isn't wrong. When Liv and I ended things, I lost my favorite sushi restaurant because she works next door. It would be even worse in the building. What was I thinking?

"For what it's worth, that really was just a hypothetical. So don't worry." Her shoulders relax. "No awkwardness. Promise." But there's something about this girl. I want her to be comfortable. The little glimpses I've seen of her letting her guard down are rad. I want more of that. "Friends?"

"Friends," Becca repeats. "I can do that. It'd be nice to have a friend here."

I can't help but smirk. "So what you're saying is that I'm your best friend in Los Angeles?"

I mean it as a joke, but the way she looks away from me, back at the Hollywood sign, which is now disappearing into darkness, and says, "I guess so," makes something stir in me. I don't have a ton of female friends other than my coworkers and the ones dating my buddies. But this girl could clearly use a friend in this city. It's hard enough to be here, even when it's your home. It's isolating. It's brutal. You lose people when they move three miles across town. I could use a friend who's one quick elevator ride away. Who maybe sometimes makes pizza from scratch.

Friends.

Photo courtesy of the author

RACHEL POLOGE writes swoony, character-driven contemporary romance novels about messy but relatable people you can't help but root for. Rachel has spent her career working in television writers' rooms, but books were her first passion. In sixth grade, a popular boy said something nice and unprompted about her creative writing assignment, and she's been riding that high ever since. Originally from Baltimore, Rachel now lives in Los Angeles with her husband and daughter. *Now That We Don't Talk* is Rachel's debut novel.

VISIT RACHEL POLOGE ONLINE

RachelPologeWrites.com
RachelPologeWrites